# ❧ SHINING WINDOWS ☙

# SHINING WINDOWS

BY
KATHLEEN NORRIS

*PALO ALTO EDITION*

*New York*
P. F. COLLIER & SON CORPORATION
BY SPECIAL ARRANGEMENT WITH
DOUBLEDAY, DORAN & COMPANY, INC.
NEW YORK

MANUFACTURED IN THE U. S. A.

## For Margaret Ann Thompson

Margaret, pearl of pearls, daisy of daisies,
Until that day comes when yourself shall weave
Your own bright web of printed words and phrases,
An older traveller begs that you receive
One book the more: possibly to remind you
Through hours before success and fortune find you,
Her love and confidence are close behind you.

# SHINING WINDOWS

## CHAPTER I

THE END of a warm October day was closing down in a drift of chill mist. At noon it had been actually hot, and women shopping downtown in San Francisco and going in and out of the smart clubs on Sutter and Post streets had loosened their furs and gasped as they discussed the eternally variable weather. But at five o'clock the light was fading into cool dusk; fog in a heavy creamy bank was moving in from the ocean; the lights of steamers shone oddly in the strange half-luminance on the bay.

Far across on the eastern shore the homes of Berkeley and Oakland showed in a long line of twinkles like a chain of diamonds; toward the northwest the majestic flowing lines of Tamalpais were veiled in white—showing for a moment in the driving vapors, were gone again.

The city, on its seven times seven hills, was teeming with life in the last business hours of the day. Down Market Street poured the river of the commuters, all turning toward the long Ferry Building whose clock kept half the watches and clocks of the town accurate. Men and women swung into step on the long blocks of the Gore; motorcars were parked in trim lines at all the curbs; every vacant lot was a parking station; every streetcar was loaded with home-going office workers.

The times were prosperous. Half the windows of the shops wore signs asking for workers; Chinatown's bazaars were thronged with tourists twelve months a year; cafeterias and beauty shops and movies sprang up everywhere. The westernest city had known some queer ups and downs in her crowded eighty years of life; she had known earthquake and fire, pestilences and civil war; this was one of her serene times, when everyone was rich, everyone was busy, everyone was making money. Always a gala city, San Francisco rose at such periods as these to a sort of Bagdad splendor. Down the Peninsula beautiful homes multiplied by the hundred, and a motorcar twinkled beside every one. The summer valleys glowed with fruit—scarlet, yellow, orange, purple. Grapes and figs, apricots and peaches and plums and the famous prunes poured into the harvest vans. To the feet of an unseeing and unthinking people flowed a very river of milk and honey, and gray-headed men who had toiled all their lives, and little hospital nurses, and timid widows left in the world with a few thousands, and butchers and bakers and candlestick makers all saw ahead of them the glittering word "Millionaire!"

In the somewhat dingy quiet office of an inventing engineer far down on Beale Street, a man in the early fifties sat thinking about it, while the October fog wrapped the city in white and darkness silently crept out of the corners and engulfed him. He was all alone. There had been no business in the office today, nor for many days; his few clerks had gone home.

He spoke aloud in the silence:

"I don't know why we all want to be so rich. Sally and I were just as happy—happier maybe—when we hadn't so much. Why, when I was a boy they used to talk about the ten millionaires in America! America was a great place because she had ten millionaires. Nowadays you don't meet anyone who isn't talking in terms of hundreds of thousands!"

Silence. Silence. After a while he spoke again:

"I sort of hoped Joycie would come in and walk home with me. Well, I guess she's forgotten it. I may as well get started!"

He got his hat and coat, locked the door, went down to join the home-going crowds in the street.

Joyce Ballard had indeed forgotten a sort of half-engagement to stop in at the office late in the afternoon. A thousand things more important to her had put it out of her mind. She had felt brisk and businesslike and well satisfied with life as she walked home under the thinning trees, but quite suddenly as she entered the house everything seemed to go flat, and she was depressed and jaded. It was dusk now, the early dusk of October, and she felt that she had wasted the whole day, and the day before it, and that she would waste tomorrow. What had it all been but time-killing— Margaret's luncheon, and walking to the Library afterward with Eileen, and then quite gayly, while having a sundae at Marchard's, deciding to walk all the way home? What of it? Why and about what had she felt so gay and confident today? Nothing had happened.

She hated the big handsome hall of her father's house in this grim dusk. Fanny the housemaid, having let her in, was proceeding to the orderly lighting of lights. Drawing-room lights; hall lights; library lights. Joyce went upstairs in a flood of light, Fanny demurely following, to snap up more lights on the bedroom floor.

Felicity was home; the sound of scales being fleetly, accurately practised came from behind her closed door. Dora was home; she was calling, "Edna, Edna!" in a plaintive tone. In fact she was in sight; wrapped in a kimono, she stood in her half-open doorway shaking her curled head in gentle impatience as she waited.

"Is Edna there?" she demanded, as Joyce came upstairs.

"Fanny was a minute ago," Joyce said. Dora jerked her head.

"I can't find my brown coat!" she said pathetically.

"I'll bet you a nickel it went to the cleaner's, Do," Joyce suggested. Dora looked stricken.

"Oh, dear, I'll bet it did!" she muttered. "Joyce, is your white one clean?"

"You couldn't wear a white coat this weather," the younger sister said. "It's getting awfully cold. Where are you going, anyway?"

"Oh, nowhere! I wish somebody could do *something* in this house without having the whole family in on it," Dora said, in a fluttered voice. "Dev Patterson has to go out to the country club to get some golf clubs or something, and he asked me to go with him. I'll be back in half an hour. But I've a run in my stocking, and now my coat's at the cleaner's——"

"Listen, do you both have to yell at the top of your lungs out here in the hall?" Felicity said, composedly, at her door. "I'm trying an extremely difficult thing, and it's very hard to work over your two voices!"

"Lissy, lend Dodo your sport coat," Joyce said.

"I haven't worn it myself yet. I'm not even sure I'm going to keep it."

"Well, then I'll just telephone Dev that I can't go!" Dora said in instant despair.

"Dev who?" Felicity said, wrinkling her brow surprisedly.

"Patterson."

"Is he home?"

"He got home last week."

"Oh, for pity's sake——" Lissy sounded pleased, as Joyce had felt herself pleased at this bit of news. Devereaux Patterson was a name with which to conjure. "Meet him?" she asked.

"He was down to see Sunny off. He said he had to go out to the golf club for something, and he'd get his car and stop for me."

"Here, take it, let's see how it looks on you!" Lissy, perfectly willing to be generous now that there was some purpose in it, had produced the coat; Dora was buttoned into it in three seconds and had run downstairs. Joyce dawdled into her sister's room. "It's terribly nice, her meeting Dev," Felicity said.

"Luck."

"He's about—let's see, he's about twenty-five," Lissy observed.

"Well, that's all right," Joyce said, and both girls laughed.

"Wouldn't it be swell if Dev Patterson actually did fall in love with Dora!" Joyce presently resumed more seriously. "Why shouldn't he? She's pretty."

"Yes, she's pretty," Lissy agreed thoughtfully. "But just the same——" she added, and paused. "I don't believe she's the type that would appeal to a man like Dev," she added. "I know him, you know; I was in High with him. Dodo's so *mild*. Yes, I know Dev."

Joyce was aware of this. Lissy had had wonderful breaks in her school days, Joyce and Dora thought. All sorts of interesting boys had been in school with her. Joyce and Dora had gone to a private school: Miss Percival's. All the exclusive girls in town had been going there when their high-school days had come along. But in Lissy's day nice girls and boys went to Lowell High, and consequently Lissy knew most of the eligible men of the moment.

"Dora," Felicity said, reluctantly, "has no *appeal*."

"Boys like her," Joyce said feebly. This kind of talk made her feel depressed. With Lissy twenty-four, and Dora not attractive to men, the family stock seemed at a standstill.

"What boys?" Felicity asked. "No," she went on, as Joyce was silent, "Dora's pretty, and goodness knows she's as sweet as she can be, I wish I had her disposition—but she simply lacks *something*——"

"Well, I'll tell you," she went on brightly, as Joyce still did not speak. "She tries too hard—she tries too hard to get men to like her; that's it. You can't do that. Whatever you do, you can't do that. That drives them wild!"

As Felicity had an authentic if unexciting admirer in the person of one Archie Ross, Joyce was respectfully receptive of whatever she said of men. Lissy had had another man friend, too. Terman Parko. Terman had not been thrilling, either, but the undoubted seriousness of the two men had made its impression, and Joyce, who was nineteen, felt that Lissy was a woman of considerable experience. Lissy often said that she would not marry either Terman or Archie if he were the last man in the world; Joyce admired her independence. She felt that she herself would marry the first man who asked her, let him be whom he would.

After a while she left Lissy's room and wandered idly to that of her mother. Mrs. Ballard had just come in from a club meeting; it had been hostess day, with tea and sandwiches and cake, and she immediately confessed to having eaten injudiciously.

"You and I ought to go on the chops-and-pineapple diet, Joycie, and take off ten pounds apiece."

"I ought to take off forty," Joyce said with a yawn. She had taken a chair and was idly watching her mother change from street to house wear.

"Nonsense, darling. But like myself and Aunt Rose you have to think of it. Lissy and Dora are so lucky! But you've stopped eating in the afternoons, haven't you?"

"Eileen and I said we would. And then today after Margaret's luncheon, which was one solid feast of calories,"

Joyce said with a guilty little-girl grin, "we walked down to Marchard's and had marshmallow-chocolate sundae. So then as a penance I walked home. It was lovely with all the leaf fires burning!"

"Oh, it's lovely now." Mrs. Ballard was not so tall as Joyce; she was plump and soft and easily made breathless. "I wish," she said, dropping a hand straight to her heel as she sat changing her shoes, "I wish we could get Daddy to walk home. It isn't more than a mile and a half; it would do him a world of good! I never would have come to St. Francis Wood if I'd thought he was going to give up his nice morning and afternoon walks. When we lived on Baker Street he always—— Where's Dora? Is Lissy home?"

Joyce, and indeed everyone who knew her, was accustomed to Sarah Ballard's easy flight from one topic to another. The daughter gave her a bit of news.

"She ran into Devereaux Patterson at the station today—they were both seeing Sunny Urner off. And he took her out to the golf club."

A great light came into Mrs. Ballard's still pretty eyes.

"For dinner?"

"No; just to get some golf clubs."

"Oh, that's nice, Joyce."

"She was all agog," Joyce said.

"He's a delightful fellow; I used to know his mother well," Sarah Ballard said thoughtfully. "Dora and Devereaux Patterson, eh? How nice. Daddy," she said gayly to the gray-headed man who at this instant entered the room, "what do you think of your second daughter going out with Dev Patterson?"

"Who," said William Ballard, sitting down heavily in a chair, his hands hanging, his shoulders fallen forward wearily, his tired eyes on his wife, "who is Dev Patterson?"

"One of the Hastings Pattersons, Will."

"Oo-oo-oo," the man murmured, pursing his lips to the soft little whistle. "How'd she meet him?"

"At the station."

"That's funny," William Ballard said. "I went to see Judson Patterson at the bank today."

He got up, moving as if his limbs were stiff, and went to his dressing room. Joyce's mother began to talk to the yellow cat who lay watchful but relaxed on the couch. Joyce herself went to her own room, moving in a dream in which the Patterson-Ballard nuptials were solemnized, the bride's younger sister acting as maid of honor and wearing apricot silk organdy with a frilled saucer hat. Well, but then what would Lissy do? Lissy was so horribly sensitive, she would be deeply hurt to have Joyce maid of honor.

What fun a big wedding would be! Joyce laughed aloud, splashing her round face with cold water, dragging a wet comb through the thick mat of her chestnut hair. The hair had reddish lights in it, and the round brown eyes that looked back at Joyce from the mirror had red lights in them, too. All the Ballards had round brown eyes, but the other girls and Ben had black hair. Joyce was pleased that her coloring was different; she was like Grandma Fellows, who had been a beauty and a toast. Grandma had left Joyce some silver spoons and a Chinese shawl because of this likeness; this room had once been Grandma's room; some of her things still were here. On Joyce's bedroom wall was a picture of the old Fellows mansion in Virginia; a faded pale brown photograph taken the year that Grandma was born and Lincoln assassinated. Sometimes in imagination Joyce, hoop-skirted, with roses looping her chestnut curls, floated up the steps of this mansion and was met at the top by an elegant young man in a stock and long striped trousers and an embroidered vest. He and she, against a background of magnolias, moonlight, softly harmonized songs from the Quarters, nightingales, then entered upon love scenes that never staled. Almost every night Joyce went off to sleep living and reliving them. The man's name was Tom Cumberland; Joyce had given him the name because she liked the sound of it. Cumberland was not a family name, but in the waking dreams she always called him "Cousin Tawm."

Of late, she thought with a little shame, she had fallen into a silly habit of talking to her friends, Margaret and Eileen, about her Cousin Tom; Margaret and Eileen really believed in him. Joyce wondered why she did silly things like that. When she was with the girls she seemed to have no sense. She and Margaret and Eileen were so constantly together, now that school was over and none of them had anything to do, that they talked and giggled and gossiped too much—there was no doubt about it—and often they did decidedly foolish things, too. One egged the other on to escapades that were really undignified and that would make Dad and Mother frantic if they ever heard of them.

For instance, asking the man at the soda counter in Marchard's to give them a second chocolate malted milk free! They had done this on Saturday. Of course they were there nearly every day, and he knew they were good customers, and it wouldn't come out of his pocket anyway. But his look at Joyce as he winked and filled their glasses had remained with her as something distinctly unpleasant, and alas entirely deserved!

Then there had been that affair in the cemetery ten days ago. She and Margaret and Eileen had picked out three graves one day when they had been quite small girls; they had been picnicking in the cemetery when Joyce, always the ringleader in absurdities, had chosen a handsome tomb with the name "Augustus P. Lombard" on it, and had draped herself over the headstone with a tearful allusion to the dead. Then Margaret and Eileen, who always followed her example, had found other graves, those of unknown men, Francis Jay Francis and Fulton Baker, and since then the three girls had frequently spoken of their "darlings" and at long intervals had revisited their resting places, always in gales of mirth. Ten days ago, on an afternoon walk, they had been there, and making a good deal of noise and laughing themselves helpless, too, Joyce remembered, her cheeks reddening suddenly. There had been some bluejackets in the graveyard, watching them and doing a little byplay of laughter and talk on their own account. No real harm in it, of course, but Margaret had suddenly grown serious, even stern, and the girls had walked quickly out to the street and down toward the city, but the bluejackets had come along close behind them. It had all been horrid; Joyce wished she had set an example of dignity to Margaret and Eileen— they would probably tell their mothers! It did not matter, only it had been so silly. They had not spoken to the boys, but they had heard the boys' allusions to someone who was hoarding gold—that was Eileen's hair, of course—and one hoarse young male voice had said, "I like the fatty!"

When Joyce remembered this she wished that she had turned around and shot him. Impudence! She hoped the other girls had not heard the hateful word; she determined to forget that she had. Perhaps she had been mistaken.

She was just ready when the dinner bell rang in its old-fashioned way. Dad insisted on that. He said that Fanny had enough to do without going all over the house telling perfectly healthy persons who were lying on their beds listening to radios, or taking baths, or gossiping at the telephone, that a meal was ready. Joyce's mother was always patient and bright under these unreasonable attacks from Dad; the children must respect their father in his vagaries. But if a family *had* servants, Mother would sometimes say afterward very mildly, it might be just as well not to spoil them for the next job they might have to take!

Tonight Lissy and Joyce and their father and mother descended the stairs together and took their places at the well-set dinner table. On the white cloth there were old blue glass candlesticks that had been Grandma Fellows's, and blue candles and a low bowl of late blue bachelor's buttons. The old silver salt cellars had inner bowls of blue glass; Lissy happened to be wearing blue, and Joyce thought her dark hair and clear skin becomingly set off by the color. While the soup was being served Dora came racing in, apologetic for not having changed her clothes, but breathless over her adventure.

"What'd you do, Dodo?"

"Oh, nothing, only it was lots of fun!"

"Is he nice?"

"Oh, terribly nice. No soup, Fanny, thanks. He's an idiot," Dora said, seizing a roll, buttering it, beginning to eat. "He's an absolute idiot, but he's terribly nice!"

"Make a date?" Lissy asked practically.

"He's going to telephone." Dora smiled fondly at some pleasant thought; her mother's eyes were bright with interest and satisfaction. Fanny passed the olives, the celery, the little square brown crackers.

"How'd your little speech go over, Mother?"

"Oh, well enough," Mrs. Ballard said, satisfied reminiscence in her eyes.

"Which means you were a knockout," Lissy said indulgently. "What fun you girls have throwing bouquets at each other!"

"Throwing bouquets nothing!" the mother said with spirit. "We're in a really serious campaign now, we're in a nation-wide movement. Twenty of us pledge a hundred dollars; either give it or earn it some way—Mrs. McCoy instantly said she'd have a luncheon-bridge . . . "

The conversation ambled on pleasantly, half-heartedly. Joyce was principally concerned with a feeling of impatient self-blame. Why did she always start a meal with a large slice of bread and butter and jam? It was so *weak*. It was **so** *senseless*.

"I'll go to a movie with you, Dodo," she presently said, as the talk wandered to evening plans.

"I think Archie's coming," Lissy observed. "We'll probably do something. He has an idea of late that he wants to learn to play bridge. We may go over to Georgia's."

"Marching to Georgia," Joyce said.

Fanny went steadily about the table with French dressing, cream cheese, gooseberry conserve, more crackers, these last white and thin. Dad hated this way of serving salad; he sat in grim endurance waiting to get started on his lettuce.

"Now, Daddy—Daddy . . . " Mrs. Ballard soothed him sympathetically. Joyce was conscious of a sudden savage wish that Dad would either make up his mind to have things done Mother's way or talk her into doing them his way. After all, what *difference* did it make!

Lissy always took an unconscionable time in helping herself anyway. It was one of her small elegancies. Everyone else waited while Lissy looked thoughtfully at the turkey or the asparagus or the gelatine, as one roused from deep musings and hardly aware of the mundane necessity of eating.

The candles burned on sedately in the handsome old-fashioned room. Mrs. Ballard said that it would soon be time for fires.

"I ordered the coal today, Daddy."

William Ballard's answer was only a glance from heavy-lidded eyes, and a quiet shrug. Joyce and Dora asked Fanny for the morning paper; what shows were at the picture houses? They rustled the sheets of it. They had seen this; they had seen that; they had heard that the other was a flop.

"Mother, want to go to a picture?"

"I think I'll stay home with Daddy tonight."

"How about money, Dad?" Dora asked. "I haven't a red

cent. I got my hat yesterday, it was cheap as dirt, but it took my last cent."

"Here you are." The man tossed five dollars across the table; Dora accepted it with an exclamation of gratitude.

"I'll divide what's left with Joyce," she promised.

"I had to pledge a hundred dollars to that peace thing today," Mrs. Ballard lamented. "Of course there's no hurry about it. We have until January first. It's a national thing. We're going to have Jane Addams and I don't know who-all else in a series of lectures——"

"Pay 'em?" the man of the house asked, looking up.

"Oh, no. But there are expenses. We have to send someone to Washington to the Conference."

"Would they send you, Mother?"

"Well, they spoke of it. But I don't know who'd run things here." Mrs. Ballard's mouth curved in an excited smile she tried to control.

"They asked you! What fun!" Joyce said. "Take me, Mother. Take me along as secretary. I've studied the touch system; I can keep books."

"Nonsense!" the mother said happily "I've no idea whom they'll choose. I did say to Mrs. Beaton that I knew Washington on account of your father and I being there years ago, but I have no idea how they'll decide."

"Joyce," said her father unexpectedly, "how d'you mean you can typewrite and keep books?"

"I had it the last year at Miss Percival's, Dad," the girl said, surprised at his interest.

"But you couldn't go into an office and take a job?"

"Well, no, I suppose not. I wouldn't want to, anyway. Joan Cate did on account of her father committing suicide," Joyce said, pouring cream on huckleberry pie. "But she hates it. She looks terribly ugly, and she says she gets awfully tired."

"She went right from school into a job?"

"No; she took a three months' course at Mays'."

"I see." William Ballard relapsed into indifference again. "He's thinking of business," his wife thought anxiously. "I wish men wouldn't be so silly! I don't know what gets into them. William made eighty thousand dollars—or was it eight hundred thousand dollars?—in one week, once. I don't see why he shouldn't invent something else. A control on a petroleum refiner. What could be simpler than that? It certainly didn't *look* like anything. And yet they paid eighty—I'm sure it was eighty thousand dollars for the patent."

Benjamin was not dining with his parents tonight; he came downstairs just as dinner was finishing, looking extremely handsome in evening dress. He drew a chair up beside his mother and stayed for a few minutes, nibbling at grapes, teasing his sisters, the very model of a handsome affectionate twenty-year-old son.

"Where is it tonight, Benny?" the mother asked. She or his father asked Ben this on about three hundred evenings a year.

"I don't honestly know, Mom," Ben said, his dark face one friendly open smile. He always answered with this phrase; it was the easiest way. If he said, "Shindig in San Rafael," his mother would worry about the long drive; if he said, "Gordy's bachelor blowout," both parents would apprehensively expect him to make a drunken return. "I don't know" was honest inasmuch as none of the gang's plans were ever very definite, and it kept Mom and Dad from fussing. "By the way, I've got to use something for money tonight, Dad," he went on lightly. "If you'll advance me a ten I'll drag it out until the first."

"You'll have to drag it out like a heretic on the rack, then," Joyce said. "This is only the twenty-third."

"What do you know about heretics on the rack?" Lissy asked amusedly.

"Don't forget I had three years of medieval history, and how I loathed it!" Joyce said fervently. "Oh, to think I need never study again; oh, to pass that old ber-*rick* school and shake the dust from my little boots upon it!"

"You seem to be in rather a—platformy mood tonight," Ben said, folding a ten-dollar bill small and putting it away in his pocket.

"I think I'll have to be a beggar, too," Mrs. Ballard said. "That is, if you have twenty dollars with you, Dad. Joyce and Dora started that German course—Fräulein called this morning. It's thirteen eighty-five, I believe—there were some exercise books or something."

"Make it fifteen, Mom," Joyce suggested. "The poor thing looks hungry!"

"You can't do that, Joycie, and they wouldn't like it if you did."

"I haven't any more money with me," William Ballard said. "I can write her a check."

"Do that, then. I'm overdrawn, I believe. If you do go to the Star, girls, take a taxi. I don't like your walking those three dark blocks."

"Oh, Mother," Dora said patiently. "Together?"

"I know. But I don't like your walking those dark blocks. I don't like it. Fanny, will you telephone Pacific three-three-three and ask them to send a yellow? Now, Ben," Sarah Ballard said, crushing her son's face against her own with a hand on his jaw, as he stooped to kiss her good-bye, "if you drive anywhere drive carefully, and don't be too late. Keith told me the other day that the first term of the third year was the most important of all. *Do* be a good boy!"

"I'm always a good boy!" Ben assured her cheerfully, departing.

"Don't he ever take his sisters out in the evening?" William Ballard demanded, when he was gone.

"Certainly he does sometimes, Daddy. But a boy at his age

finds life so fascinating; he's absorbed in his own affairs!"
Mrs. Ballard led the way from the table. "I believe it would
be more comfortable upstairs tonight, it's quite chilly," she
said. "I've got some telephoning to do."

"Don't miss Kitty Macrae and Mike Lucas, Daddy!"
Joyce reminded him, flying downstairs with her coat over
her arm.

"Oh, no, I'll not miss them," the man said. In the taxi
Dora observed that Dad looked tired and blue tonight.
"You'll have to wait," she said to the driver, "I've got to
change five dollars."

She and Joyce in loge seats sat absorbed for two hours
and eleven minutes. It was not a particularly good movie; it
had good spots. When they came out into the sharp night
air at quarter to eleven they were both drowsy and partly
stupefied.

"I hate to go to a middle-class movie, seems such a waste
of time," Joyce said, on a yawn. "Let's walk."

They talked of Devereaux Patterson.

# ❧ CHAPTER II ❧

Meanwhile Mrs. Ballard had done her telephoning to various club women, talking to some for fifteen or twenty minutes at a time; had recalled Mrs. Porter, telephoned again to Marian Jenks. For more than an hour she was busy in her bedroom, while her husband in the adjoining upstairs sitting room turned the radio low and listened to Kitty and Mike, who had bought a fish store tonight and were making side-splitting mistakes in the handling of the stock. Lissy's young man had come, and they had gone out. "We don't know where; we may go to a movie; he has his father's car," Lissy had said, upon leaving. "Perhaps we'll dance somewhere."

The kitchen regions were very quiet now; the big house was still, except for the rustle of William Ballard's newspaper, the scratch of his wife's pen, and the little radio voices.

"I must make notes of all this while it is fresh in my mind," said Mrs. Ballard.

"Sally," said her husband after a while, "I saw Judson Patterson at the bank today. He says that they won't do anything about the note. Says they can't."

"Oh, that's good!" Mrs. Ballard said, turning herself about to look at him over the back of her chair. "Or is that bad, Will?" she asked, with a change of expression.

He looked at her heavily.

"It means losing the plant," he said simply.

"Will Ballard!" She was not alarmed; she was only admonitory and soothing.

"I mean it, Sally. I saw Edmonds after I talked to Patterson."

Sally Ballard came across the room to take a chair opposite him at the hearth; the man stretched an arm to turn off the radio. His wife sighed; she hated business talks; it was obvious that they were in for one.

"Now, darling, don't take things too seriously!" she said. "Remember the night we knew Dora was coming, and we had no money, and I was sick and you were a clerk on eighteen hundred a year and afraid of losing your job at that! You *worry* too much, Will. I want you to know that I've got a very smart husband, who has only to invent something to make everything all right again!"

"Ha, that time is over!" William Ballard said with a brief rueful laugh. "This——" He rumpled his graying hair. "I'll be darned if I know what to do about this!"

"You and Dan Edmonds will talk it over tomorrow after a good night's rest, and it'll all seem much brighter."

"You see," the man began slowly, hardly listening to her, "it's a pretty heavy load. Three girls with their German lessons and their dresses——"

"German lessons, Will! Five dollars a week!"

"I know, but it all counts up. Ben's expenses in college, his car——"

"Will, he couldn't take the train every day to Stanford. That would mean taxis both ends, it really would cost more in the long run, *really* it would!"

"Three servants," William Ballard went on, with a sigh. "Well, I suppose there's no cutting down anywhere, until the girls marry, at least!"

"There isn't for this reason," Mrs. Ballard said sensibly

and readily. She had defended this position before. "You simply cannot get a cook to *come* into a house this size unless you have a second girl downstairs. Edna is *invaluable* upstairs, on account of the girls' mending, and the cleaner, and things like that. She really takes a personal interest, packs their bags and puts their laundry away. Three isn't many in a house this size, Will; lots of places all around here have four. If I let Edna go, then I'll lose Fanny, they always work together, and they took ten dollars off their regular rate to be together."

"They eat," the man offered mildly.

"Of course they eat, poor souls, but there's very little waste. Lotty is really economical, she isn't as economical as Olga was," Mrs. Ballard went on in a musing undertone. "Olga used to scrape the butter plates . . ."

After a while she came out of her monologue to find her husband staring at the fire in a mood apparently unaffected by her optimism.

"We could sell this house," he said, as if to himself.

"Will, that would be crazy! Just as the girls are at the age to need a home, a place to bring their friends!"

"I don't see their friends here very much. Their friends apparently only come here to take 'em off somewhere. There's not one of them that ever spends an evening at home as far as I can see."

Mrs. Ballard said nothing to this for a while. After a silence she said gently:

"You're tired tonight, Will."

"I'm awfully tired!" he conceded, in a broken tone that suddenly demanded sympathy.

"But why do you *do* it, dear?" the woman pursued. "Why do you let yourself get so tired? Why do men slave and struggle and throw away the best years of their lives making money, without ever stopping to enjoy it? It's a fault of American men, Will. In Europe they have a leisure class—

men who have time for walks, gardens, hobbies, reading. American men . . . "

She was not conscious of his presence for some moments, after which she saw that he was not listening; he was staring into the fire with a most unwonted frown on his face.

"I wish you never had gone to Patterson for the old loan!" she interrupted herself to say, trying to meet his thoughts.

"I had to go to someone."

"Why not borrow the money from someone else, Will, and get through with Patterson once and for all?"

"Not so easy, Sally. Money's beginning to be terribly tight."

"What I wish," Mrs. Ballard recommended brightly, after a compassionate glance at his weariness, his bowed shoulders and rumpled gray hair, "what I wish, and what I think we must do, is go ahead now until Lissy and Dodo, at least, are married. Ben will be in with some good law firm then and taking care of himself. Then we'll either place Joyce in college, or take her with us, and enjoy a long leisurely trip around the world. Once the children are settled, you and I can really take a holiday, a little leisure. We might easily rent this house; I hate to rent a house because of what those *vandals* in Pasadena did to Molly's house: sheets used on ironing boards and nails driven right into the paneling! But if we could get the right tenant—a nice quiet doctor or a judge, something like that——"

"You wonder sometimes why you have 'em!" William Ballard muttered, out of thought. His wife stopped short.

"Have what?"

"Children," he said with a sigh. Mrs. Ballard laughed on a scandalized note.

"Will, *dear*, what blue glasses you've got on tonight! Come now, cheer up. Why not turn in early, and have a long night's rest? *La nuit porte conseil,* you know."

"I don't speak French, Sally."

"Well, that's a very innocent little bit of French! As for the children," Sally Ballard went on cheerfully, "never in this world was there a father crazier about his children than you. Felicity and then Dodo—why, you couldn't wait to take them out walking on Sundays so that everyone on Bryant Street could see the little Ballard girls! And finally, when Ben came, you came in and knelt down, and his little finger curled around yours and you whispered to me: 'My son, Sally-girl! My boy!'"

She took out her handkerchief and wiped her eyes. William Ballard did not change his position; he still sat staring darkly at the fire. But there were tears on his cheeks.

"That was a cute little house we had in Palo Alto," he said. "Twenty-two-fifty a month was what we paid for that house. You had chickens."

"Well, just the few the washwoman gave me instead of the money she owed me."

"I remember little girls chasing chickens on lazy Sunday mornings while I was burning up the rubbish out by the garage."

"I remember," the woman said gayly, "your coming home with Yeats—remember what a big man we thought Yeats was then?—and his saying, 'I think this man of yours has struck oil, Mrs. Ballard!' My dear, and that was only the soda-percentage thing, and the refiner-control thing didn't come along for years after that. What is a refiner control, Will? Is it a sort of faucet?"

She had asked him this before; he had answered before as he did now:

"No, it's chemical. Maybe it was a mistake coming to the city, Sally," he added, pondering.

"Now don't begin *that,* Will. You've got your own plant, the girls have been sent to fine schools, we own this beautiful home in St. Francis Wood. All we have to do is sit tight for another few years and they'll all be married, and then I'll feel my responsibilities over. Here's Lissy out with a young man now, and Dodo has evidently made quite an impression on young Patterson. It's all going to work out, Will," his wife said confidently. "If you *only* won't worry!"

"What do we get out of the children, Sally?" William Ballard said suddenly. "No, I mean it seriously; what do we get out of them? When they were little, yes; they paid their way then. But now? When are they ever home? When do they ever want to do anything we do? Every week-end they're all gone, one place or another, or the girls have a girl or two here, and boys come and take them out. Don't girls cook and sew and sit around and talk to their families any more? Don't a father . . . "

"I wish he wouldn't use 'don't' that way!" Mrs. Ballard thought anxiously. She lost the thread of what he was saying, but she knew it all; she had heard it before.

"The boy asks me for money," William Ballard was continuing when she picked up the conversation again. "Well, that's all right. Gas for the car, tires, syllabus fees, slacks, tennis rackets; he has his camera films developed and I foot the bill; he sends someone a wedding present, I foot the bill —well, that's all right. But what do I *get?* If your children are done with you when they reach the twenties, why don't they get out, and let you live the way you want to live, and pay your bills?"

"You're *not* talking very sensibly, dear," Sally Ballard said in faint affectionate displeasure.

"You and I'd have been rich; we could have traveled everywhere, if we'd not had children," the man said. "China —I saw a movie of China the other day. I'd like to see China before I die."

Mrs. Ballard did not answer. She was thinking.

"I must get the girls to be a little more affectionate with Dad," her thoughts ran. "I'll ask them to make a little fuss about him. Of course they're young and they don't think . . . You and I'll go to China, Will," she said aloud, "when the girls are married. I don't know whether Lissy really likes Archie or not; I was glad when she sent Terman packing. But whether it's Archie or someone else it won't be long now, and here's Devereaux Patterson beginning to like Dodo. As for my Joycie, she'll have them all buzzing about her, never fear! She's like my mother—tremendous magnetism!"

"She ought to take off some weight," her father said gloomily.

"She's going to. She and I both."

"Here's the situation, Sally," the man began presently. "The plant has been in the red for seven months; we can't go on that way for three more months. I scraped together what I could and put it into Yellowgold Olio Incorporated, and that went flat. Then I got all the plant would carry from Patterson to go on with, and plastered this house. Now he says he can't renew——"

"Will, do look at that cat!" Sally Ballard interrupted him in a low tone of intense enjoyment. "He's been looking right at the bird for ten minutes without moving a hair. Suddenly he saw me watching him and he began to roll about and lick his paws as much as to say, 'What am I doing, Missus? I wouldn't eat your bird if you gave it to me!' Oh, Toodles, Toodles," she went on, dragging the great yellow creature toward her to scratch his head knowingly, "what an ole bluffer—what an ole bluffer—yes, he is, he is a fat ole bluffer——"

"I believe I'll turn in," William Ballard said. His wife did not look up from the cat's magnificently frilled tiger face as she said absently: "Good boy. I believe I'll wait for the girls."

# ✵ CHAPTER III ✵

THE ENGAGEMENT of Felicity Fellows Ballard, oldest daughter of Mr. and Mrs. William Anderson Ballard, to Archer Joseph Ross, was announced a few weeks later, and Lissy had engagement cups and kitchen showers and callers and all sorts of excitements to acknowledge. She seemed less thrilled about it than Joyce was; to Joyce it was a source of deepest satisfaction.

Not that Archie was particularly interesting. But it would mean a wedding, and bridesmaids' dresses, and that Lissy lived somewhere else, and that Joyce could have Lissy's room. And then it meant that one of the three Ballard girls was settled; that would be pleasant. "My sister, Mrs. Ross." Joyce liked the sound.

At nineteen, tall, with red lights in her brown hair and brown eyes, playing a little tennis, riding sometimes, talking a great deal, and secretly determined to be a great actress, Joyce had found her chief emotion one of fear that life would somehow pass her by. As a small girl in lower school she had looked up to the high-school girls as tremendously superior, and the senior-class girls as goddesses. But somehow graduation had not been as sensational as it had always seemed in prospect; Eighteen had flashed by and become Nineteen; Twenty was close ahead, and even now she had never had the feeling of really living, of really doing the dashing and self-expressing and free and important things of which her whole life had been one long dream.

Why, walking home with Margaret and Eileen, at thirteen and fourteen and fifteen, a small roly-poly girl in a white blouse and pleated skirt, how she had talked, a few years ago!

"My husband is going to be . . . My little boys will always . . . If I marry a navy man and go to Manila . . . When I have a house . . ."

Hours, hours, hours of this sort of thing; walking home, sitting on each other's beds eating crackers, picnicking up in the green fields back of Stanford in the spring; spending nights together and hearing the solemn clocks in silent houses strike eleven and one and three, how the talk of husbands, homes, babies, professions, trips, triumphs had gone on!

"And now here we all are, nineteen, and the magic hasn't begun yet, and Lissy is twenty-four, and nothing wonderful has happened to her yet; and Dodo is twenty-two and she's still idling at home," Joyce had reflected uneasily more than once of late.

So that Lissy's engagement had its cheering side; things would now happen to Lissy. She was being kissed and flattered by Archie. Joyce knew it because Lissy began to put on superior and important airs, and there would be parties, clothes, presents, a new house, Lissy's new cards, everything stirring! Archie might ask some stunning young New York attorney to come out and be his best man, too—a Yale man; no, a Princeton; no, a Yale—and he might see Joyce for the first time in apricot organdy ruffles with a frilled saucer hat and bangs! She would have taken off at least ten pounds at that time . . .

The original plan was for a quiet wedding, with "just the members of the immediate families and a few old and intimate friends for guests," as the newspapers glibly put it. It was Lissy's mother who stood out for white.

"Just a plain white frock, darling, that you can wear afterward. I want my first bride to be a white bride!"

"Well, if it were June, Mother, it could be sports. But in March you can't wear summer things!"

"No, dear, but the *plainest* little satin?"

The plain little satin soon had a train and a veil. And since the sisters were to be there, anyway, and would want new frocks for the great occasion anyway, why not have them alike, as attendants?

"If you're going to put a hundred dollars into a dress for me, I'd rather have a street outfit," Dodo pleaded. "We'll never wear those orange organdies again!"

"Now, now, now, now, wait until you see them," Mrs. Ballard murmured soothingly. It was she who talked to Suzon, the red-headed excitable little modiste in the big old shadowy house on Van Ness Avenue.

"I will have zem luss-ci-yeuse!" promised Suzon.

Luscious indeed they promised to be, but Dora and Joyce fretted somewhat as to their practicability. However, they would photograph well in the wedding pictures. Various professional photographers came out to talk about the pictures, and look at the conservatory as a background, and the stairs. A bride always looked very pretty on a stairway.

They made lightly penciled calculations, with very sharp points. Each print, this style, twenty-two dollars. One hundred dollars the half-dozen. Sally Ballard kept these and the engraver's estimates on her desk. Three hundred announcements, on this stock, with these double envelopes, one hundred and seventeen dollars. There must be a detective; there must be insurance. She met the oncoming waves gallantly; she told William only what she wanted him to hear. Let the flood rise, once Lissy was Mrs. Ross!

About three weeks before the wedding Joyce's father said to her one night:

"Funny thing happened today. I don't know whether to tell your mother or not."

Joyce looked up abstractedly. Paul von Schwerin had called on her this afternoon, and she was almost out of her senses with excitement. It was the first time—there was no use fooling herself, no matter how she fooled Margaret and Eileen about her admirers!—it was the first time any man had called on her. She had met him at the house of Margaret's cousin Marie Louise Towers, at a casual tea. It had been a girls' tea, no men; Margaret's set had not reached the age when men friends drop in for tea. But Paul had come in, and he and Joyce, just introduced, had fallen at once into a delightful, an absorbed conversation that seemed to her more completely unreal every time she thought of it, and she had thought of it almost without interruption ever since.

That had been Sunday. This was Wednesday, and he had come to call this afternoon! Big and lean and brown and infinitely attractive, he had been here by the fire for an hour, not wanting any tea; no, nor anything else, just wanting to jabber in his delightful idiotic way, and ask her if her people came up to the Lake in summer, and where she had been all his life, and things like that. Oh, it was too thrilling!

She had called him "Mr. von Schwerin," of course, but he wouldn't have that. "Oh, help, call me Paul!" he had said in simple surprise. And quite without permission, in the friendliest way imaginable he had called her Joyce.

Joyce's breath was taken away. This was the way things happened, was it? You met a boy at a tea, a delightful, rich boy just home from college—oh, this was better than all

her wildest dreams, and Paul was simply adorable! Joyce
could hardly wait for dinner to be over and the evening
somehow to get itself spent, so that she could be alone in
her room, to dawdle over her undressing, thinking about
him, thinking about him, and finally to jump into bed and
go on thinking about him in the dark.

Because of all this she could not pay much attention to
what her father was saying. It was not important, anyway.
It was merely that Archie's father had come to see him in
the office; Archie's whole family, married sister and all, had
come out to have dinner with the Ballards a few nights
earlier; a mere office call had no especial significance. Joyce
was conscious that her father said something, and said something else, and was still, rustling the pages of his paper;
she contentedly lapsed back into her own thoughts.

Later, when she was undressing, her mother came into
her room. Joyce was accustomed to evening visits from her
mother. Miss Larke, during her last year at school, had
told her to study all by herself, but Joyce loved to talk to
her mother about her homework and have her help on
themes. If she had a speech to make she always had rehearsed it for her mother. She welcomed her tonight with
a bare soft young arm laid about her mother's shoulders
and a soft cheek against her mother's cheek.

"Sit down, darling," Joyce said, jerking an old silk night-
gown of pink satin over her head, dropping to the floor
such scanty clothing as she wore beneath it. She stood still,
checking. "Teeth—hair—cold cream," she said, springing
into bed, jerking the covers up, settling herself for a chat.
"Dad go out?"

"No; he's still reading the paper," Mrs. Ballard said. "He
was telling me—— I don't suppose it means a thing!"

"Mother, did you see Paul von Schwerin? Isn't he cute?"

"He seems a very nice boy. His mother used to be a great
friend of Bertha Edmonds."

"I met him at Margaret's cousin's. I had no idea he was coming up. Mother," Joyce said earnestly, "is there any chance of our going up to Tahoe this year?"

"Oh, darling, I don't think so. Not with Lissy's wedding and all. Daddy says we'll have to economize dreadfully for months and months! Why? Do the Von Schwerins go to the Lake?"

"His father and his stepmother have a big place up there, and a launch and everything."

"You might visit——" Sarah Ballard said dubiously.

"But I don't know them, Mother!" Joyce said, almost crying. "I wish," she added fretfully, "I *wish* we knew all the people you used to know, Mother. Why didn't we keep up with some of them, like the Von Schwerins and the Pattersons?"

"I married a poor man, Joycie," her mother said, absently. "Archie's father called on Dad in the office today," she added. "Joyce——"

"What about?" Joyce asked.

"I don't know that I ought to tell you this," her mother said hesitatingly. "It's just that it seems—so queer. Joyce, a man couldn't break his engagement at this point, could he? I mean a man like Archie?"

Joyce stared at her mother, red-brown eyes wide in astonishment.

"Good heavens, no!"

"Well, of course he couldn't!" Mrs. Ballard said hastily.

"You don't mean he went in to break the engagement! Why, the invitations are going to be out next week!"

"No, no, it wasn't that. He didn't—— Well, it was funny," Mrs. Ballard said. "He wanted your father to put some money into his business—wholesale tea and coffee. He suggested that Dad invest about—I don't know how much— I think it was twenty-five thousand for Lissy."

"Ha!" Joyce ejaculated noncommittally, a little premonitory chill at her heart. "And is Dad going to do it?"

"He says he can't."

"I think old Ross has a nerve!" Joyce said, after thought.

"It isn't that, exactly. It's the European idea. They're Scotch, you know."

"I never heard the Scotch did it! Wedding portion, hey?" Joyce mused. "Does Lissy know?"

"Oh, goodness, no! And she mustn't. No-o-o," Mrs. Ballard said musingly. "It really doesn't mean a *thing*. But he suggested that Dad invest this money for Lissy; 'Felicity,' he called her, Dad said, and of course it was a little awkward saying that it wasn't convenient just now. He said that he had had no suspicion that his son was all ready to marry a rich American girl, that Archie had been expected to marry his brother's daughter in Edinburgh—something like that. Evidently there was some sort of family understanding or something. Dad said that Lissy wasn't rich—I don't know, I imagine it was all rather embarrassing and—and funny. At the end he said that he hoped there wouldn't be any need for Archie to go to Scotland right away——"

"Oh, fun for Lissy!"

"No, he meant before they're married."

It was out. Mother and daughter faced each other; Joyce's cheeks grew red.

"He couldn't!" she said, with a glance in the direction of Lissy's room. "It's February now. They're going to be married in four weeks."

"I don't see how he could. But Dad said he spoke as if some business arrangement had to be made with the family at home; he said his brother had money to invest . . ."

A silence. Joyce presently said:

"How does Dad feel about it?"

"Well, he doesn't like it, of course. I don't know that

he doesn't like it—I mean I don't know exactly *what* he thinks about it, or what I do!" Sarah Ballard confessed with a rueful little laugh.

"It would seem to me," Joyce said cautiously, although she knew that Lissy and Archie were at the Palmers' dinner, and could not possibly overhear her, "it would seem to me that the best thing for Dad to do would be to *get* the money somewhere and invest it for Lissy! I mean, it's nervy of him to force us into it, and it would make Lissy boil—she'd ber-*reak* the engagement if she ever found out! But at the same time, now that things have gone this far——"

She stopped, and there was a troubled silence.

"That's just it," the older woman presently said. *"Would* Lissy break her engagement?"

Joyce hesitated.

"I don't know," she said thoughtfully. And then impatiently, "What a pest! Why did this have to happen?"

"Well, don't you bother your precious head about it to-night," Mrs. Ballard exclaimed suddenly. "It'll all come out right, and Lissy'll be married next month." She stood up. "Devereaux Patterson's going around the world," she said.

It was another shock. Joyce looked at her mother with bright stricken eyes and said nothing.

"He told Dodo so today."

"Dodo feel badly?"

"I imagine she does. He's to be gone a year. His uncle is giving him the trip, and he's to do letters for the *Times*. It's too bad," Sarah Ballard said simply.

"Yep," Joyce agreed briefly. "It's too bad."

"Of course there never was anything *serious* between him and Dodo," Mrs. Ballard offered half-heartedly. "I don't know that she felt—expected—I don't *know* that she did. I know that his mother asked her over for Christmas tea—but that was weeks ago." Joyce did not speak; she repeated vaguely: "It's too bad," and there was a silence.

After a while Joyce, her hands locked about her knees that were drawn up under the bedclothes, said seriously:

"I don't know what girls—do."

"Do?" her mother echoed.

"Yes. To—to get started. To meet men. We have a lovely home, we—we're good-looking enough. Or if not to meet men," Joyce amended it, a little ashamed of the flatness of the original idea, "to do something. To begin."

Usually Sarah Ballard had something definitely heartening to say at this point in her talks with her daughters. "Just be patient, my dear, and have a happy time and don't worry!" was her ordinary formula. "When the right man comes along it doesn't take long!"

But tonight she was tired and puzzled and a little anxious. She merely stood looking at Joyce for a few minutes thoughtfully without seeing her, and then shrugged her shoulders and sighed.

"Well, I suppose troubles are good for us in this life," she said piously. "It seems odd. I look at other women, women like Archie's mother, for example, and the Gracie girls' mother, life seems to go on with them smoothly enough. With us—well, I don't know. I think if Daddy would be a little more philosophical about it I might be. But I suppose things are quiet downtown now, and those men all sit about at the club talking depression . . ."

There was more of this before she gave Joyce a troubled kiss and went away. She had barely left the room before Joyce, with her heart bounding for joy, had snapped off the light, snuggled down in the soft covers, and returned to dreams of Paul.

## ❦ CHAPTER IV ❦

BUT that was not the end of the Ross matter. A day or two later Joyce tore herself from her own happy musings to discuss Felicity's affair with her brother.

The one son of the family had to make eight-o'clock lectures in college five days a week; he spent that time in the jumble and noise of fraternity house life. On Saturdays and Sundays he was therefore allowed to sleep as late as he liked in his own comfortable room at home. Joyce intercepted Edna in the upper hallway, took the tray from her, and entered Ben's room just as the clocks were striking eleven.

"Wake up, Benjamin my beloved. Chester telephoned, and he's stopping for you at noon. Where're you going?"

Ben rolled over; rumpled dark hair; yawned luxuriously.

"Don't burst in on me with bad news like that!" he said, affectionately returning the sisterly kisses that Joyce, having set down her tray, was bestowing upon him. She knelt beside him and tousled his hair with her lips. He smelled of sunburned young boyish flesh and barber's tonic and linen pajamas faintly scorched by irons. "Here, wait a minute, kid!" he exclaimed.

He leaped from bed, disappeared into the bathroom, returned after a moment with his wet hair combed and his cheeks cold and fresh from icy water. Joyce had straightened his bed, set his tray conveniently; reëstablished, with his back against the pillows, he first took a skimming look at the headlines of the sporting green, flung the paper aside with a satisfied ejaculation, fell upon his strawberries, and beamed at his sister.

"Strawberries in February, hey?"

"They've got no taste."

"They're better than the garbage we get at the fraternity house."

"Is fraternity house food awful, Ben?"

"Rotten. But we eat at Shove's. Shove has a swell joint. Well, kid, how's everything?"

"Everything's fine. But we think Lissy's wedding's off."

Ben's round brown eyes came up suddenly from his tray.

"The hell," he said mildly.

"Yep. Liss has been crying all morning. Mother says she hopes to talk Dad into sending her to Paris for a year."

"What happened?"

"Oh, everything. You weren't home until late last night or you would have heard some of it."

"You're right, *ma petite*, my little," Ben said, with a glance at the clock. "I—was—not—home—until—late—last—night. Proceed."

"Well, Archie has to go to Scotland."

"Scotland! Not Scotland, Scotland?"

Joyce laughed; they laughed together.

"Yes, really."

"What for? Liss going?"

"No, that's just *it*. His father came to see Dad this week in the office, you know, and he wanted Dad—or at least he suggested that Dad—anyway, Dad was to put up some money for his business. Alexander Ross's Sons, you know. The ger-*rand*father started it. It's spices and tea and all that. Well, anyway——

"Anyway, Dad said he couldn't. He's sort of hard up just now, Mother says. So Mr. Ross seemed sort of worried, and he said that then Archie might have to go to Scotland for the money; he has a brother there who has nine daughters."

"Help!" Ben interpolated. "I thought the Scotch were so canny!"

"And he said, Mr. Ross said, that there had always been a sort of understanding," Joyce was proceeding. She stopped to laugh in a scandalized fashion at her brother's last remark. "Ben!" she said reproachfully. "He said there was a sort of understanding that Archie and one of his cousins—I think it's only his step-uncle or half-uncle or something—would marry, so now he's going!" Joyce finished in some confusion.

But Ben understood. His handsome cheerful young face darkened.

"Going over to marry her?"

"Well, he doesn't *say* so. But our wedding will have to be put off."

"He said so?"

"I'll tell you. He came in to see Dad, that was Tuesday. That was the beginning. Then he came into the office again yesterday—yes, yesterday—and he and Dad came out here and talked to Mother. Mother was going over to play ber-*ridge* with Mrs. Termany, but she telephoned. Mr. Ross said that if his son was to get this advance from his uncle it would be better to have him go alone; that is, not to take Lissy along, and that they had better say to the papers that because of family matters in Scotland the wedding had been postponed."

"What'd Mother say?"

"What *could* she say?"

Ben reflected.

"Ha!" he said in dissatisfaction. "It might be a good idea to go punch his face," he suggested. "Then he'd reach the bonny banks of Loch Lomond with a black eye!"

"I'd like to strangle him," Joyce said simply.

"Who told Lissy?"

"Dad had her come downstairs. She just happened to be here; she'd come in from some lunch and was going down to Georgia's. Dad said he thought she ought to hear it. Mother nearly had a fit; she didn't want Lissy to know anything about it. They said Lissy was wonderful, that she talked right back to old Ross and said that certainly the wedding could be postponed. I hope," Joyce finished viciously, "I hope that while he's away she meets someone ten times as good and turns right round and gets married!"

"What a break!" Ben observed, thinking.

"But afterward," Joyce resumed her narrative, "poor Liss just went crazy. Oh, we had a nice time here last night! Dad said he couldn't stand it, and he went out for a walk, and Liss just sker-*reamed*. Dodo wasn't here, but Mother and I quieted Liss down the best we could. She said that our family was hoodooed, and that she never could hold her head up again. She went over to meet Annette Overman at the Library, and they're going to Mill Valley, and Liss says she's going to stay there! It worries Mother; she says she doesn't know anything about Annette's family, but Liss was perfectly wild and would go. I'm glad you're home! We had an awful time."

"Well, that's the catch; I'm not really home," Ben said reluctantly. "A lot of us are going down to Santa Barbara tonight—that is, if I can catch the old man and get a little ready cash. I'm overdrawn, darn it! I bumped my car and it cost me eleven dollars, and I stopped on the Bayshore and had to pay another five. Rotten luck! Dad home?"

"No. He was here about an hour ago; he and Mother

were talking in the dining room. Dodo's with the Pitmans in Piedmont. She didn't want to go much; she said nothing would happen. But Elinor kept telephoning."

"I'll get dressed and go see Mother; darn it, I wish I hadn't made the date!" Ben said. Joyce left the tray at his bedside and wandered to her mother's room. The big house seemed dreary this Saturday morning; there was a heavy fog rolling in from the near-by ocean; on the boulevard cars were honking bewilderedly, and the shriek of brakes told of frequent accidents narrowly avoided. Horrible dull foggy world! Nothing to do at noon on a Saturday in February. Nothing ever to do in all the sixty or seventy years that stretched ahead!

Mrs. Ballard was capably telephoning the market.

"Three split broilers, please, and the soup meat. How is the asparagus? Two for a quarter? Better send me six pounds."

She presently set back the instrument and smiled at Joyce. Sally, as soon as she recognized the need for heroism, could be heroic.

"Running a big place without ever knowing who's going to be here for meals and who isn't is not as easy as it sounds!" she said cheerfully. "Well, how's my baby this morning? Did you get some brekky?"

"About half-past ten. Edna was sour as green apples because the dining room was waiting. However, she was all right when she was bringing Ben's breakfast up."

"See Ben?"

"Yes, I was telling him."

"Lissy's gone over to Mill Valley with Annette."

"I know. It's a good thing, too. They're quiet, religious people, you know, not smart, Mother, but they have lots of books and walks and talks about character and lectures— that sort of thing. I don't know how Lissy stands it usually, but it'll probably quiet her down now."

"It's a dreadful thing, and I declare that in the night—I couldn't sleep, I lay awake practically all night listening to Dad snoring, and worrying!—in the night it seemed to me almost like a *death*," Mrs. Ballard said. "But I think now—I was just telling Lissy—that the only thing to do is to meet it sensibly and go right straight ahead. Archie'll be back in June, and we'll have a lovely little June wedding; your dresses will be even more appropriate, and maybe we could borrow the Simons' lawn or something, and it'll all come out beautifully! It's unfortunate—no question of that—but it's just one of those *things*."

"Liss didn't actually ber-*reak* her engagement, then?"

"No. You knew Archie was here for about ten minutes this morning? Well, they agreed that they must wait until he comes back, and then go ahead quietly, without any publicity——"

"I thought Liss said it was all over?"

"Well, she did; she gave him back his ring and said that she never wanted to see him again, but she said it quietly—not angrily, you know. And Archie said—and I must say he behaved with great dignity—that when he came back he would come and see her right away and that he regretted it as much as she did."

"Well, then, *is* she engaged or *isn't* she, Mother?"

"Why, certainly," Mrs. Ballard began brightly and stopped. "I don't think she is, really," she said, doubtfully. "But I think they're in love with each other, and that it's just one of those *things*."

"What does Dad think?"

"Well, your father was walking part of the night, and then he slept; he says he slept badly. I didn't notice it. He was late this morning for the first time since I can *remember*, and had breakfast at—it must have been ten. He said he didn't know his own children, much less other men's children," Mrs. Ballard recalled with a mirthless, anxious little

laugh. "He said he didn't know what it was all about!
I made one practical suggestion: it just came to me that
the wise thing to do would be for Dad to find some man
who *would* put twenty-five thousand into the Ross business,
and go right through with the wedding on the original plan.
It isn't ideal, but after all Archie isn't his tight-fisted old
Scotch father! Lissy's marrying Archie, not his father, and
we have to be sensible in this world. I know Dad's worried about money, but these bad times come and then they're
better again. We could catch Archie at Vancouver——"

"Oh, has he started?"

"Yes. Some cousin or someone has an interest in the
Canadian railway, and they get rates, something like that.
He started this morning; he's on his way now."

"Nice mess!" Joyce commented.

"It's terrible. I'm going to tell people that Archie's
grandfather is very ill and he had to rush over to see him.
I mean, you have to tell people *something*. And if we can
possibly manage it, if he comes back in late May or June
and they don't settle it, I'm going to try to send Lissy to
Paris for a year. She could keep up her music and get her
French perfectly; I've always hoped to do it. I'd send Dodo,
too, if I could. Is Ben here for lunch?"

"No; he's going to Santa Barbara. Nelson's calling for
him at twelve."

"I wish you'd take his car and go out to the hospital with
some books for me. I'm chairman of that committee and
I've not——"

"His car's in the garage being fixed."

"Bump?"

"No; carburetor and magnetos, or whatever they are!"

"I'll go in and have a little talk with him before he goes.
Then I may go to see Cousin Laura. She loves to have
someone come in and sit with her."

"Is she awfully rich, Mother?"

"Well, she has a good deal. But from what she says it's in annuities, and all tied up. I might *broach* Lissy's affair, but you know how cranky she is," Mrs. Ballard said dubiously.

"Tell her you had a dream that she didn't help you and that two black cats scratched her eyes out; she believes in dreams," Joyce said. "She'll have Susie Waite interpret it for her, and they'll nearly go out of their skins."

"Cousin Laura's never done anything for anyone," Mrs. Ballard said with a sigh. "It makes her terribly nervous to have you even suggest it. She's always had so much, and now she has less. However, I may sound her."

At one o'clock Joyce and her mother sat down to a delicious little luncheon of bouillon, sweetbreads, artichokes, a delicate pudding composed of gelatine and lady-fingers, sherry and custard. The toasted crackers were passed; the mayonnaise was embellished with a touch of paprika; two crisp nasturtiums were on each plate of asparagus. It cost nothing, Sally Ballard sometimes said, to have things *nice*.

"I wish Daddy had come home to this nice lunch!" she lamented. "But he had such a late breakfast. What's the plan for this afternoon, dear?"

"Movie. I'm going to telephone Margaret; we might walk downtown if her heel's better."

"I want to stop and see if I can get some Parmesan cheese. We're having onion soup tonight."

"Oh, dear, I love it," Joyce yawned. "More weight! If you'll give me the taxi fare, Mother, I'll take your books out to the hospital."

"I had only some change and a ten, dear, and Ben took it. He missed Daddy, and I didn't want him to go off for the week-end absolutely without money. He says he may not even break it. But I'll tell you: Young's Drug Store will cash a check."

"I think I'll read for a while." In the dull soft foggy day

Joyce felt sleepy and stupid. She had still not exhausted her thoughts of Paul; those sweet swimming thoughts that blended and elided and surged and receded and began all over again whenever she was alone. After the shock of Lissy's affair she was jaded; one got over those wretched scenes in which everyone cried and shouted, but they were shocking just the same. She thought she would lie down for an hour anyway.

Roused, and dressed, and starting out briskly in sensible shoes for a good foggy walk with Margaret at three, she noted that her father had come home and was reading in the library. Not reading—working over papers. He looked very busy and absorbed, and Joyce did not interrupt him.

Much later she telephoned home: would Edna please tell her mother she was staying with Miss O'Shea? It was not particularly thrilling, Margaret's house, but her brother almost always took them to a picture, and afterward took Joyce home. She did not like Leo O'Shea; he was a thin tall pimpled boy with a big Adam's apple and a convulsive hoarse laugh, but any plan was better than no plan at all. When Leo left her at her own door at midnight on this particular night everything was dark. Dodo and poor Lissy and Ben were away, and her mother and father had gone to bed.

Joyce was tired and sleepy; she felt somehow depressed, creeping upstairs, snapping off lights. Paul had not telephoned; this was Saturday night, and he had said on Tuesday, "See you soon. I'll give you a ring!" He was probably having a wonderful time somewhere, over the week-end.

And now that she was alone in the dark and had time to think it over, it seemed simply incredible that Lissy had been jilted. That was what it amounted to. Lissy and Archie were not going to be married next month, the money spent on apricot bridesmaids' dresses might just as well have been invested in sports or street wear; the saucer hats would not be made at all!

## CHAPTER V

IT WAS three days later that all six Ballards gathered in the library. Sally Ballard, fluttering about, pale and anxious, had made a special point of getting them together; it was an incredibly hard thing to do. A telegram had brought Ben from Stanford, surprised and puzzled; some little feeling had had to be displayed to hold Dodo, who had had plans for going downtown.

"Nothing important, just some shopping," she had said to her mother. "But I'm sure it's more interesting than Dad's business talk; you *know* I don't understand business, Mother!"

Joyce had been reluctant to get up. The last sub-deb cotillion of the season had taken place the night before, and she had been asked by Margaret's loathsome brother Leo. She had gone because Paul might be there, but he had not been there, and the whole evening had been a failure. Margaret, archly aware of Joyce's state of mind and heart, had said she would ask Paul to a little supper at her house afterward. Paul had not come there, either, and that had been deathly dull, too. Joyce, plunging into bed at three o'clock, her lips still scarlet with lipstick, had pinned a notice on her door: "No breakfast; don't wake me until noon!!!"

It was therefore disconcerting to find her mother gently shaking her at nine, and to hear her mother say that Daddy wanted to see them all in the library at ten. It was business; even Ben was coming up from college for it.

"What sort of business, Mother? Why am I in it?"

"He wants to talk things over with us all, darling," Sarah Ballard had answered tremulously. "It's about possibly selling the plant——"

"Selling the Pacific Laboratories?"

"I don't know, dear. I know he expects to make some change. And Joyce," her mother had added, "don't worry if he sounds a little—a little extreme. I mean, whatever we have to do I'm sure we can do it—nicely, without letting people know. He says he wants you all to understand just how things are."

When all the others, in various moods of politely concealed boredom, impatience, curiosity, were ready and waiting, it was hard to get Felicity to come downstairs. Almost without movement, since her return from Mill Valley, Lissy had lain on her bed, staring blankly at the wall. She had not wanted to eat or to dress; above all she had not wanted anyone to talk to her. Joyce had to go upstairs to tell her that Dad had said that he simply would not begin until she came down.

"Oh, I'll *come*. It doesn't make any difference, anyway!" Lissy said finally, in weary concession. "I don't know what's the *matter* with Dad! I don't know anything about business; why should I be dragged down for a business talk! He knows I don't care anything about it!"

White-faced, uninterested, she languidly joined the family group. The Ballards were all seated in the library, a handsome dark room back of the small drawing room, with sets of books lining it, and a bronze bust of Homer standing beneath their mother's portrait on the mantel. The morning was chilly, but the fire was not lighted; radiators were clanking dubiously; the room would soon be too warm. Sally, the three girls, and Ben all stared in faintly apprehensive expectation at the man of the house, who was sunk in a leather chair, his elbows spread, his fingertips meeting on his chest.

"Well," William Ballard said, looking about the circle through his glasses, "here we all are. I don't know when we've all been together before."

"We're often together for Saturday breakfasts, Will," his wife said quietly. "And we were all here at New Year's."

"Oh, no, we weren't! Ben went to Honolulu for the holidays."

"Well, anyway, we're together now," Sally said patiently.

"The whole point is this, girls and Ben," William said, in an unnaturally cheerful tone. "Things have been going badly for me. The game is up—there's nothing more I can do. I'm broke. Everything's gone!"

"It's like a play!" Joyce said, in the silence. The Ballards glanced at each other. Ben cleared his throat.

"How d'you mean everything's gone, Dad?" he asked.

"Just that," his father answered in a light, careless voice. Joyce's heart suddenly stood still with pity for her father. He was never flippant and defiant like this. He must be forcing himself horribly. "I've lost the plant," he said. "I've worked hard all my life; I've failed. That's all there is to it. I've got three daughters and a son; they're complete strangers to me. I've got to tell complete strangers that I can't support them any more—I'm done."

"Dad!" Joyce said, nervously, dragging the word out in affectionate fluttered reproach. "How can you talk so silly!"

She went over to his chair and sat on the arm of it and put her arm about him.

"It's true," he said. "Your father is a complete failure.

I don't deny it. I've done my best. But whatever I've done I've been wrong. At your ages I was supporting myself, but not one of you can support yourselves! It'll be years before any one of you can. I suppose that's my fault, too. There's something all wrong about it. But the main point is clear."

"Darling, I wouldn't take that truculent, angry tone," Mrs. Ballard murmured. "Whatever it is, it isn't as bad as you make it sound! We'll pick up the pieces and begin all over again. I'm sure we needn't have worried the children; Mother and Dad are still able to keep them from worrying before their days come to worry——"

"That's just it," Joyce's father said, still in the cheerful unsympathetic tone that came so oddly from him. "I think it *is* their time to worry. I'm done worrying! I'm done supporting people. Let them try their hands at it!"

"Will, we will get nowhere if you persist in this criticizing tone!" Mrs. Ballard said patiently.

"Well, let's get down to cases!" He had been pacing the floor, nervously handling the fire tongs, opening and shutting a book as he talked. Now he sat down again, and without meeting any of the eyes that were fixed upon him in expectation and a sort of reproachful curiosity, he said rapidly:

"The business has been in the red for a year and a half. I've done all I could to float it; there's no money anywhere. Last June I put a second mortgage on this house—that's final there. I talked to my cousin Laura on Saturday; she won't do anything.

"Well. Yesterday, Monday, we had a meeting. The bank takes over this house and the plant, and some odds and ends of property your mother and I have—the Dumbarton lots, the Capp Street houses. They run the whole thing and pay me an allowance."

There was a profound silence. Again, bewildered and slightly affronted, the Ballards looked at each other.

"Well, I don't see why that isn't a very comfortable arrangement, Daddy," Mrs. Ballard said presently, in a cheerful tone. "It means that you have less worry and responsibility——"

"I have no worry or responsibility at all!" he said unencouragingly, as her voice wavered in some puzzlement.

"Good for you!" Dodo said, timidly. "But why—— I mean, what do we do, Dad? Are they going to let us live in the house? Do we move?"

"They think they can rent this place for three hundred a month. Your mother's kept it up beautifully; it has six bedrooms; it's well furnished."

"Three hundred a month is something," Sally Ballard said, resolutely optimistic.

"We don't get it."

"We don't get it?"

"No; the bank gets it."

"But they pay it to us?"

"Oh, no, they don't!" William Ballard said, almost in triumph.

"Don't pay us the rent of our own house, Will?" Sarah was being reasonable, but it was something of a strain.

"No. They pay me a given sum. Everything over goes to the liquidation of the estate."

Mrs. Ballard was still gentle and patient.

"Isn't that the same thing, dear?"

"They pay me twelve hundred," the man said briefly.

Another silence.

"A month," Ben said.

"A year," his father snapped, with a quick glance.

"Twelve—— My gosh, Dad," the boy argued youthfully. "That won't go far."

"It's all we'll have!" William Ballard said, and it was almost as if he enjoyed saying it.

"All we have from *them*," Sally Ballard put it pacifically. "What else will we have, Will?"

"Nothing. I put everything into their hands yesterday. House, plant, properties, insurance policies, everything. It was that or bankruptcy. This way my creditors will get something. It may take 'em years to clear it up, but they'll get *something*."

"Will, we'll have to borrow money," his wife said quickly, resourcefully. "I mean—twelve hundred a year! That's how much a week?"

"About twenty-five dollars."

"But, darling, Ben's college costs more than that. I know because I write the checks."

"Ben's out of college."

A faint exclamation that was like a cry escaped Mrs. Ballard. Joyce, looking quickly toward her brother, saw his face redden suddenly and his jaw tighten, but he laughed stoically.

"O. K.," he said gallantly.

"You mean Ben has to go to work, Will?" the mother asked fearfully, dazedly.

William Ballard had sunk back in his leather chair and stretched out his arms, clamping his fingers comfortably on the arms of the chair. Joyce had slipped to a hassock at his knee.

"He can if he wants to," he said, almost on the tone of a yawn.

"Can if he *wants* to! What of his law work?"

"Why, he can go on with that if he wants to," the man said indifferently.

"Will, how could he possibly—— Why, it costs thousands, he's not even in law school yet!"

"He could do it the way other men do, work his way through."

"But you'd rather he'd get a job?"

"I? No," William Ballard said, unruffled, and not raising his eyes from an apparent study of the fire. "I don't care. It's *his* life."

The looks the girls and their mother exchanged at this moment were beginning to be definitely alarmed.

"No, Dad," Mrs. Ballard presently said stoutly, "Ben's your son, he's our boy, we're all in this together, and we must agree. The question is whether it wouldn't be wiser in the long run to manage somehow to get Ben into law school, since he's gotten so far, and then, when he's able to help us——?"

She stopped on an up note, and the girls nodded her their approval.

"Ben's got four years to go," the father said. "Then where is he? Clerk in some law firm, getting sixty a month. However, if Ben wants to do it——"

He shrugged. His wife took another tack.

"We'll adjust ourselves to all this by degrees, Dad. It's come very suddenly. I can't help feeling that with Ben's college work to finish, and Lissy very probably going to be married in June——"

"Oh, leave me out of it!" Lissy put into the pause in a vaultlike voice hoarse from tears and lowered to keep it steady.

"You can all do exactly as you like," the man assured them. "It's your responsibility from now on. While I had money, I gave it to you. I paid servants and garage bills and college bills; I was glad to. As a result I never saw my children except when they wanted money; I don't know them, or what they want to do and how they'll manage! I suppose you've all got clothes enough; I've got enough clothes to last me until the end of my life."

"Will, you're not yourself at all," Sally Ballard's voice said tenderly, reproachfully. "You know we all love you! You know the children are just living the normal lives of

young people today. You want them to be like the others,
don't you?"

"Certainly!" he interrupted harshly. "I'm telling them
they can go right on, for all me! They don't need me, and I
don't need them! I've not been asleep, these last five years.
I've known it all; I've heard it all. 'Just slip in and say
good-by to Daddy, darling—telephone to Daddy and ask
him, at least, it flatters him. Don't forget to wire Daddy
for his birthday Sunday. I bought a book for you to give
Daddy, do try to find time to write in it!' I've known it
all."

In the stricken pause Joyce began unobtrusively to cry.
Her father put his hand down and patted her head.

"Don't cry, Joyce. There's nothing sad about being young.
Let me finish telling you about this while I'm at it. Talking
this over at the bank yesterday, they told me that they have
a lot of ranches all over the state, more than they can handle.
There's one—well, they spoke of several—but there's one,
down in the Santa Clara Valley, that's deserted. It was part
of an estate; there's been nobody on it for three years, except a caretaker, and he's gone now, or going. It sounds—
pretty bad; the people who were there were Japs, and they
don't live as we do. But it's twelve hundred acres, some
prunes, some apricots, walnuts—there are a few cows,
chickens. They're turning that over to me. If I can make
anything of it, it'll help clear up my affairs; if I can't,
there's no harm done. They take over this house, furniture,
cars, silver, everything, as soon as they can get an inventory
made out. You girls and Mother can take whatever'll go
into a trunk. They think they've got a prospective buyer
here already."

"Take whatever will go into a trunk and go where?" Mrs.
Ballard, startled out of her calm, asked sharply.

"Down to the ranch. 'La Perdita,' it's called—it's at
Merriwell, down Gilroy way."

"Meaning 'The Total Loss,' " Ben said.

"Does it? I don't know. I never went to college and I don't speak Spanish. I've not seen it. You go to Gilroy and turn west—I've got the directions."

"Is it furnished, Will?"

"There's some furniture there. The Japs locked it all in the upstairs rooms, I believe. They only used the downstairs."

"Well, I don't think we'll have to become quite such gypsies as *that!*" Mrs. Ballard said bravely, after an appalled silence. "Here's our big boy who can certainly get a job, and our girls who are quite smart enough to earn money some way or other. If I let Lotty and Fanny go and keep only Edna—— But you say we'll have to move? Maybe it would be better to let all three go, and see if I could find some place—there are lovely apartments——"

"This is Tuesday," her husband said, as she paused. "We have to be out of this house by next Tuesday. You girls and Ben make any arrangements you like, or else plan to come with me down to the Merriwell place. I'm keeping the old car; Ben's and the big car go in with the estate. It's sudden, but it's been coming on a long time, and we have to move fast because this buyer is an Eastern man who rented the Packers' place next door to us last summer; he went over the place one day, and he wants it. Next Tuesday morning, about eleven, I'm going to put my bag in the car and get out. Anyone who wants to go with me can go; anyone who can make a better arrangement is welcome to it! I've closed your accounts at the bank; whatever you girls have is yours. Ben's overdrawn, I know. That's all right— that's all right!" he said, raising a deprecating hand, warding off Ben's apology cheerfully. "It's all straightened out. If you girls or Mother want any advice or suggestions, I'll be up in my room!"

He went out of the library, and the remaining members of the family looked at each other.

"Do you believe it?" Dodo asked, in a whisper.

"We couldn't—we couldn't go live in a place Japs have moved out of, down there on a ful-*lat* ranch!" Joyce stammered.

"No, it won't be anything like that," Mrs. Ballard said instantly. "We'll just be patient, and work it out somehow so that it won't be one bit bad! We'll find some picturesque little place, and Ben'll get something interesting to do, and perhaps one of the girls go into a tea shop or something—Lily Trevitt's daughter worked in Ransagoff's last winter, didn't she, Lissy?"

"I don't remember—yes, I believe she did," Lissy said dully, thinking. "I know I'm not going down to bake and get drowned in the mud of a fruit ranch!"

"I won't," said Ben. "There are thousands of things I can do!"

"Mother," Joyce said, "Dad wouldn't kill himself, would he?"

"I don't think your father is very well," Mrs. Ballard answered gravely. "I never heard him talk the way he did today in all the twenty-six years we've been married. It was almost as if he was glad—*glad* to distress us all so dreadfully! No, I don't think he'd ever think of anything like suicide. Well, we mustn't worry about things before they happen. Are we all going to be home for lunch? I'll tell Edna. And then I'll run up and talk this over quietly with Daddy. He's beside himself with anxiety, of course, and I think he's ashamed, too—ashamed that he can't do for you what other fathers do. Don't think of it any more. Cousin Laura would lend us any amount!"

Fifteen minutes later she noiselessly went up to her own bedroom. Everything was very silent there; usually there was a noise where Will was; rustling of newspaper sheets, low whistling or humming, the radio, the victrola, the snap of a fire. Now there was no sound.

Sudden fright possessed Sally Ballard. She felt her knees weaken and her mouth water. Where was Will?

Then she saw him. He was lying peacefully asleep on the big couch by the fire; his even breathing was that of a weary and happy child. On his face was an expression of complete calm. It had been years since his wife had seen that expression on William Ballard's face.

## CHAPTER VI

THE only reason Joyce Ballard lived through the next dark week at all, she herself was convinced, was because Paul von Schwerin came to see her every day. Miraculously, swiftly, just as Mother always had said it would happen, the right man had appeared, and almost immediately he became like a son in the house—very much more like a son than Ben was, in fact.

Paul was tall and lean and fair and irresponsible and giddy; he was deeply interested in the Ballards' predicament, and although he never made a sensible suggestion or seemed able to grasp the full seriousness of the situation, he was so gay, so silly, so eager to push pianos and tables about and say ridiculous things to the men who were making the inventory that the girls laughed and laughed at him, and his very presence helped to carry them through trying and humiliating hours.

"Don't overlook this little number, mister," Paul would say, kneeling back on the kitchen floor to exhibit a rusty old can opener just discovered under the stove. His hearty "Yip-hay!" when dragging or hauling was in order made even the men laugh; when the piano, checked and ticketed, had been pushed into the oriel bay, Paul went out on the porch and played a jazz chorus through the open window.

Everyone liked him. The girls in a few days' time came to know him more intimately than they had ever known any boy except Ben before. "Paul, did you bring some rolls? Have you got the car there? Will you take Dodo downtown to get some chalk?" they called to him cheerily from their various tasks of segregating and classifying.

Mrs. Ballard had immediately assumed a half-affectionate and half-scandalized manner toward him. What was that ridiculous child doing now? "Paul, you are a hopeless goose!" she would say to him fondly. And when Joyce and Paul draped portières about themselves and sang operatic staves she would stop what she was doing and regard them indulgently. "You are the most idiotic young things!" she would tell them happily.

Everyone in the family of course knew why Paul von Schwerin was abandoning his father's magnificent apartment in the Mark Hopkins Hotel and giving all his old friends the cold shoulder. Joyce knew it, too, and her nineteen-year-old heart almost burst for joy. The collapse of the Ballard fortunes, the strained cold atmosphere of the house as one treasured possession after the other was turned over to the representatives of the creditors, the scrambled uncomfortable meals in the kitchen, were only a background to the old miracle. She and Paul von Schwerin were in love with each other.

She had not been able to believe it, at first. Partly because no other boy had ever seemed in earnest, and partly because Paul was so much more than merely eligible, Joyce had schooled herself sternly to believe that nothing was going to come of it. But before she had thoroughly established this policy in her heart and mind, his actions had belied it. He liked her very much indeed. His own home was formal; he felt ill at ease there; he hated the Peninsula crowd; he

loved the Ballards. Their affection for him seemed to be
something for which Paul had long hungered. He told
Joyce about his flunking out of school, his hating the fellows there, his loathing for the military camp where most
of his boyhood's summers had been spent. His mother had
remarried and was living in Paris; he loathed Paris. His
stepmother was "keen," but she was only thirty, and she
and the old man were always on the move. He loved home
life, kitchens, fires. Everything the Ballards did seemed to
him amusing and unusual, and his manner left her in no
doubt that he thought Joyce especially the most witty and
daring and amusing and companionable girl he had ever
seen.

Without Paul the situation would have been insufferable.
Even with him these were strange days. Strange to have
the maids and old Lotty depart, untouched by the family's
misfortune, solicitous only of references for next jobs.
Strange to have shadows and dust gathering in the house,
and the dining room deserted, with one shriveled apple and
two sunken oranges forever fixed in the blue fruit plate;
strange to hear Lissy crying desolately so often, to hear the
new hard note in their mother's voice, to note their mother's
frozen silences.

For Sarah Ballard in her characteristically optimistic,
assured little fashion could not forgive her husband. It was
so unnecessary, she said, for Will to have sprung this on
them in that harsh, unsympathetic way! Weren't they all
in this together? Couldn't they have thought up some plan,
some moderate way of meeting the situation? Why, if she
and the girls had known how things were going last year,
or even a few months ago . . .

She said she was not angry, she was only hurt and surprised. She would not speak unnecessarily to her husband
at meals, or indeed at any time; he had moved into the spare
room, and the children's general sense of everything being

all wrong was accentuated by the stiff unfriendliness of their parents. William Ballard did little to lessen the strain.

He had adopted a casually indifferent air: everything was all right; he had always wanted to live in the country, and now he was going to live in the country. If any of them did not want to do it, why, by no means were they to even think of it!

"Make any arrangements you like," he told them genially. "Farm country's a stupid place for young people. Places like Pebble Beach, Santa Barbara, they're different. They're country, but they have golf clubs, yachting, dances. The real country's not like that. It's a question of grubbing to get enough to eat and tumbling into bed at nine o'clock too tired to care whether you've washed your face or not. We'll have to be up early on the ranch, but I don't know that it matters. We'll never see anyone!"

Lissy would look at him with narrowed eyes and compressed lips when he talked this way; Dodo's big eyes would fill with tears; Ben usually met it by beginning a counter-conversation relative to his finding a good job.

"Good," his father would say heartily, "I hope you do!"

But even at this moment somehow her father never fooled Joyce. She knew how he felt; she knew it was all bravado. She had moments of feeling terribly sorry for him.

One night he brought home new rubber hip boots; he had bought them at a sale. He said that he would need them in winter.

His wife and older daughters looked at the boots coldly, without comment, and after a while he carried his purchase upstairs. Joyce, unable to think of the right thing to say, sat silent, her heart aching for them all.

"Dodo thinks maybe Dad's just fooling, and the last minute he'll tell us we're not really going down to that ghastly place to live," Joyce told Paul on the very last day.

"She's a great pipe dreamer, Dodo!" Paul said with a chuckle. He and Joyce were walking downtown; it was four o'clock on a cold foggy spring afternoon. He had come out to the house for canned beans and spongy fresh bread and tea at noon; had helped box the last of the books. Afterward Joyce had somehow gotten her hands clean and her face creamed, and had made herself look her nicest to go down to the St. Francis with Paul for tea. It was a long walk; they took the Market Street gore at a steady pace, swinging along from block to block, with the setting sun smoldering away in a sea of gray clouds behind them, and the long cold streamers of the fog pouring in over the western hills and through the Gate.

They had known each other only a few weeks, but from the first moment of meeting there had been a special bond between them. Today their feeling for each other had passed some other milestone; both had been conscious of it all through the thrilling hours before this hour. Paul had been not less funny, not less giddy, but today he had had moments of seriousness, too, moments almost of bewilderment. Joyce had felt them as he had. She had heard him call her "dear" more than once as if inadvertently; only it had not been inadvertent. Tomorrow they were parting, for a while anyway, and he was not going to let today go by without some special word.

Carrying herself splendidly, freely, high color stung into her cheeks, her tendrils of red-brown hair blown up against her hat, she looked obliquely at him now and then, smiling. Sometimes he asked her if she was tired, and she always answered, "Not a bit!" and laughed a little laugh of sheer exultation.

They went into the big hotel and found a table. Joyce had not done this often, never with a man before. She loved the atmosphere of warmth and quiet and fragrance;

it was good to sit down and get her breath after the long fast walk, and order orange pekoe and buttered toast, and sit back luxuriously watching other men and women moving about, meeting and talking over teacups and parting.

"Oh, this is thrilling, this is the way life ought to be!" Joyce thought, tomorrow and yesterday alike forgotten in the glory of this hour. She saw Dodo's friend, the Hill girl who wanted to be a nun, having tea with two other girls, and thought it was thrilling to have them see her here with Paul von Schwerin.

"You know everyone, don't you?" she said, when Paul bowed a second time.

"I don't know anyone, really. I was with my mother in Cleveland until I went to college, then I went over to her in Paris two summers. I was only out here with my father two summers. And then he was just married, and didn't want anyone else around. I had a talk with my father last night," Paul said, adding the last phrase with an abruptness that made it significant. Joyce could only look at him expectantly; she could not speak. Stars and rockets were wheeling about her; some woman near was wearing delicate lilac perfume; the orchestra was softly playing "Auf Wiedersehen."

"I told him about us," Paul said. Joyce's eyes were fixed on his; her senses swam. "I said we liked each other," the boy went on. "He was swell."

Joyce saw his eyes mist; she felt her own eyes prick; although she was smiling.

"Oh, I said there wasn't anything settled about it," Paul began again, almost roughly. "I said you had to go away with your people, and darn it!" he broke off to interpolate youthfully, "I flunked my law course at Christmas! You knew that? It made my father awfully mad. I told him that everything was different, now that I knew you, and I said I'd do anything he liked if he'd only——" Paul's young voice had grown hoarse. "You will wait for me, won't you?" he stammered. "I mean—we can wait, can't we? We'll wait, won't we?"

The room was moving about her in slow enchanted circles; the music was the music of Paradise. Joyce could not speak. Her smooth young hand crept over his.

"You knew I felt that way, didn't you, Joyce?"

He had moved his brown hard hand to grip hers; the contact went through her whole being like an electric current.

"I feel that way," she said, swallowing.

"I mean—we're only kids—I'm twenty-four," Paul went on, rapidly, urgently. He seemed to Joyce the incarnation of everything that was dear and honest and handsome, squared about to face her as they sat on the deep velvet seat, his hand over her hand. "I told him we'd hardly talked about it. I didn't tell him about night before last," he added, with an awkward little shred of laughter. Joyce's color rose in a flood, and she laughed in embarrassment, too. "But that was the first time I ever kissed a girl, Joyce, and meant it," Paul ended.

"I guess it was the first time with me, too," Joyce said.

"He wants me—my father wants me to finish up with my last year," the boy burst out anxiously. "And then he says we can go ahead!"

Joyce looked at him, awed. He hadn't really told his father that they loved each other! It couldn't be that matters were moving as fast as this, a whole long month before her twentieth birthday? Fresh love for him welled up into the heart that was filled already with a girl's wild first trembling love. So helpful, and in his fantastic way practical, too, in these troubled days at home, so simple and honest and eager in making his plans! She visualized him as talking to some grim-browed father. "We've only known each other six weeks, Dad, but we love each other!" And to

Joyce all the world was only herself and this fair-headed, brown-skinned boy.

"You see, here's what Dad said," he was going on earnestly. "Dad said it wouldn't be any good my trying for a job; I couldn't get anywhere. I might get into some real estate agency or insurance firm, but it'd take years even to be able to rent a bungalow out at Ingleside; we'd never get into the clear. But Dad says that if I go back and coach this summer—Tanner, who runs a coaching camp up at Lake George, was talking to me about it before I came away—Dad says that if I get in again in October and finish up—I'd finish a year from Christmas—that then I could go right into the firm with him, and we can be married right away."

A year from Christmas! It sounded like centuries. But under the centuries the miracle of their loving each other, waiting for each other, belonging to each other would run. The last phrase, the magic word "married," lighted deep fires in her red-brown eyes as she said simply:

"He's awfully kind. He doesn't know me."

"The old man is swell," Paul said, his own eyes brightening at her reasonableness. "We talked about two hours," he added. "I told him I'd changed. I said, 'You've been telling me I had to wake up all these years; I've waked up!' I told him we weren't just mushing and dancing and all that, but that you were the—the most wonderful companion I'd ever known, that we just seemed to belong to each other from the very beginning."

He fumbled in a side pocket, took out a wisp of tissue paper and unrolled it carefully.

"Listen," he said, "I couldn't buy you a ring. I'm going to cost my father a hell of a lot of money if I go back, and he's kind of hard up as it is. I thought he was going to pack me off to a ranch somewhere and just let me slide and find my own job. But look, this was my grandmother's; it isn't worth much, I guess. It's only an amethyst; it's pretty, isn't it? I want you to have it, and look, there's my frat pin, too. And listen, we'll write each other all the time. I write rotten letters, but you won't care!"

She held the pin and the ring in the palm of her hand; looked up to smile at him through a dazzle of tears.

"They're beautiful, Paul. Do you want me to wear them?"

"Well, sure I do," he said. "I guess everything I have is going to be yours."

They looked radiantly into each other's eyes.

"We're engaged," he said.

"Oh, Paul——" Joyce said faintly. She had always thought it would make a person feel quite old and responsible to be engaged. Oddly enough the first effect on her was to make her only a little girl again. Her mother's youngest, her father's giggling companion at circuses and movies only a few years ago—engaged!

"I never thought of myself as marrying very young," she said.

"Why not?" he asked, amused. Paul seemed to have grown up suddenly.

"Well, I don't know."

"But you like it?" he teased her, triumphant and happy and proud.

"Oh, well, *Paul*——" she murmured.

"We'll get a lot of presents," he said youthfully. "We'll have a swell little place somewhere."

Joyce was thoughtful.

"A year from Christmas," she said with a sigh. "And this is March."

"But I'll be out here next summer!"

Joyce had become responsible and thoughtful in her turn.

"You may have to coach again next summer," she offered.

"I won't! I'm going to work harder than I ever worked

in my life before. I told him so! You see, Joy," Paul went
on earnestly, "I think it's up to us both to make good. I
mean my father kind of relies on me to go into the firm,
and they all depend on you out at the house. Lissy's all
shot to pieces over What's-his-name, Dodo's half asleep all
the time, Ben's no good at all! You're the greatest comfort
your father and mother have, because you're just naturally
wonderful, see? You just naturally are so darned——"
Tears came into his eyes. "So darned *good,*" he finished,
grinning ashamedly.

Joyce's color swept up.

"Oh, no, I'm not!" she said a little thickly.

"Well, you are. You're the *only* one that stands by the
old man," Paul went on in a rush of enthusiasm. "And—
here's what it is, see? You and I both have got to just buckle
down to—well, to what we've got to do! We've got to
develop our characters, see? I mean, it'll be good for us all
our lives. We're young, and we've always had it easy, and
now we've just got to show 'em that we've *got* something!"

The girl was looking at him seriously, topaz lights well-
ing in her brown eyes. They were squared about to face each
other on the velvet seat, their faces only a few inches apart,
her left hand locked in his right one. The soft sound of the
music ebbed and flowed against the tinkle of teacups and the
subdued distant murmur of the city. A Geary Street cable
car jangled on its way; a boy came through calling, "Mr.
Wallingford! Mr. Wallingford!"

"I'm not good, Paul," Joyce said, very low.

"You!" he said, and laughed.

"No, I'm not. I don't know," Joyce said, the fine line of
her brows drawn together thoughtfully, "I don't know that
I ever thought about being—*good,* really," she went on,
with simplicity. "Meeting you, Paul, having this happen,
has made me—sort of wonder about it. It's made me want
to be kind to everyone—different.

"I think we're all being—rather mean to Dad," she recommenced, in a silence. "He—it isn't his fault. He bought himself some big boots, and he was so pul-*leased* with them." Tears welled in her eyes. "If anything ever happens to my father," she said, "I think I'll always remember his opening up those boots in the kitchen yesterday, and nobody saying a word about them!"

"Don't you worry; you're the angel of *that* family!" Paul reassured her, laughing joyously and squeezing the hand that lay in his. "And that's what counts, you know," he added with tremendous gravity. "I mean, here we've found each other, you and I, and we're going to have everything our own way, and it's up to us to—to show 'em! I've always been an awful bum——"

"Oh, Paul, you have not!"

"I say I have. I've had to have coaching pretty nearly every term, and twice I've flunked. But by George, I'm going to do it all differently now, Joyce! You watch me! Now listen," the boy went on, in a suddenly businesslike voice, "we've got to plan. Monday—this is Monday, isn't it? My father wants me to go to Portland with him on Thursday; I've got an aunt there. But you'll hardly be fixed down at Merriwell anyway by then. The place is in pretty bad shape, isn't it?"

"We think so. We've none of us seen it; even Dad hasn't seen it. There's a ranch house, and barns, and water—they all talk a lot about the water rights. But Japs lived there last, so you can imagine! There's a caretaker on the place now, but he won't stay. The bank's been paying him a hundred a month, and they won't go on doing it. But Mother thinks we'll only be there this summer, sort of camping, and that then something is sure to turn up."

"Even Ben going, hey?"

"His filter job didn't turn up. Yes; Ben's driving the girls and me down, and Dad's driving Mother in the big car.

The man who has bought the car lives in Hollister, and he's coming over for it some time next week. The ter-*runks* go tonight."

She was speaking seriously, lifelessly.

"You may be crazy about it!" Paul said hearteningly.

"I don't exactly see us cur-*razy* about it," Joyce answered, hesitatingly. "We haven't any friends there; we'll be six miles from the village, even if it wasn't a very uninteresting village. And we'll be fer-*right*fully short of money. I suppose we can eat, but until something breaks we can't do much more. Mother says we used to spend every month more than we'll have every year now, and of course that—" Joyce's round eyes met his honestly, "that can't go on," she ended.

"It doesn't have to go on. Ross'll probably come back for Lissy, you and I'll be married—why, shucks, a year and a half is no time at all!"

"I'm going to try to be terribly good," Joyce told him, her whole soul fired with the new resolution. "I won't mind how hard it is, as long as I know I'm going to get out of it soon. It isn't going to matter to me whether there are any nice people there or not, and it won't much matter to Dodo, because she really hates dancing and going around. You heard her say she was going to read Shakespeare this summer. Oh, we'll all get through it, Paul, and Ben'll get a job, and everything'll straighten out. But only it's so queer—to have all the old silver pieces gone, and the rugs, and everything we've ever had!"

"You don't know anything about the place, after all. It may be all right."

"No. It's just one of those places you drive through on the highway, with hot dogs and a post office and a bank. Population, I should say," Joyce calculated, "about four hundred."

"It sounds pretty bad!" But he was only sobered for a

moment. "Never mind!" he said encouragingly. "It's only for a little while, and you've got to meet things like that in life, you know. You've got to! We'll get the best of 'em yet!"

Joyce was studying his brown handsome young face with adoring eyes.

"You're *good,* Paul," she said, almost involuntarily. It was the boy's turn to flush and laugh uneasily.

"Sure I am," he said. "Come on, let's go. I said I'd have you back by six, and I'm taking my stepmother to dinner at eight."

## CHAPTER VII

When Joyce got home, her mother, flushed and inexpert, was in the last throes of dishing dinner in the kitchen; Dodo hindering her as she went to and fro. The silver was gone now, and they had to use kitchen cutlery; the beautiful old Minton and the white Spode sets had been taken out of the china closets and stood about in newspaper wrappings on the dining-room floor.

"But, Mother, I can't seem to *find* a big knife!" Dodo's plaintive voice reiterated drearily. Joyce came to the rescue briskly: here, all the knives were in this drawer—no, they weren't, either—they'd all been taken away. Here they were, in the box.

"Does this box go down to the ranch, Mother?"

"I can't hear what you're saying, Joyce, because these eggs make such a frightful sizzling!" Mrs. Ballard's fine soft face was flushed; she was working in a cloud of heat and smoke. "The eggs are done," she said in discouragement, "and those potatoes are hard as rocks! Take a towel, Joyce, and pinch one, and see if it's soft at all!"

Oven heat rushed into Joyce's face; she felt but a languid interest in dinner; her soul was singing in the clouds. Tea and music and violets and Paul; life was a dreamy sea of bliss and hope and love. And this new "being good," this first awakening in her soul of something that was some day going to make Joyce Ballard a fine woman, a gentle, helpful, unselfish woman, adored by everyone, was not the least of the magic! It made life a thrilling game to have a man love you and believe in you, and since hard fortune was inevitable it would be lightened by that simple rule of being good.

"How are the boots, Dad?" she asked him, meeting him as he came into the kitchen with an unwonted kiss.

"The—the boots, eh?" he repeated, bewildered. But she saw how his face brightened. "Well, they seem all right, Joycie, they seem all right," he said gratefully, as they all sat down to overdone fried eggs and underdone baked potatoes. "Last night here, eh, Mommy?"

"It would seem so," Mrs. Ballard agreed, closing her lips with the air of a person who never will voluntarily open them again.

"If you wouldn't be so *cheerful* about it, Dad!" Dodo said in a sort of wail. "We've always loved this place so, and it's our home, after all."

"Oh, well, home is where the family is, home is where the family is!" the man of the house said, buttering a second roll. "Any coffee there, Mommy? Yes, yes, yes," William Ballard went on musingly, stirring his cup, "I guess it'll be some time before I hear Kitty and Mike again; big radio sold with everything else, eh? We accumulate things in this life, and then we lose 'em! I think maybe I'll step over to Mayland's tonight and listen in on Kitty and Mike."

Mrs. Ballard, sitting at the head of the kitchen table, was not sympathetic. She made quick nervous gestures with her hands, pushing in a hairpin, scratching a caked spot from her blouse, leaning over to set the salt in a better position.

"This is simply going native," she murmured. Joyce noticed that she was not eating.

"No dinner, Mother?"

"When you have to cook a dinner you don't want to eat it," Sarah Ballard said with a readiness that showed that she was waiting for the question.

"Mother and I had some hot chocolate at about five," Dodo said, innocently. "It was so cold, and the men were gone, and everything was so horrid, and our hands were all sore from packing! So we made a fire upstairs and had toast and chocolate, didn't we, Mother?"

"The transition is probably the worst of all this," Joyce said unexpectedly. "Once we really get settled at—what is it, La Perdita?—we may love it! Lots of people move down to that part of the country for summer, and it's March now. Probably by autumn something will have changed; maybe Cousin Laura will die——"

"You'd think it would occur to the old girl," Ben said, taking a second potato. The potatoes cut hard; their baked skins were thin and soft, their pulp hard and shining where the knife had touched them. "She can't win!" Ben said, and Joyce laughed so heartily that he presently gave her a gratified glance.

"How old is she, Dad?" Joyce was resolutely keeping alive the languishing conversation.

"Let me see . . ." Her father was almost pathetically eager to get into a family talk; he had been excluded from everything but necessary queries of late. "She's my father's mother's cousin," he said. "My father would be—Cousin Laura's about eighty-two."

"She's extraordinarily bright, Will," Mrs. Ballard said, taken unawares. She had not meant to add the name, or turn to him as she did. She had not shown him so much friendliness for a week. Before she could withdraw it Joyce and Ben were carrying on the conversation briskly.

"She's not bright enough to see her obvious duty and do it," Joyce said. And as Ben laughed appreciatively she sent him a grin. It was unexpectedly exciting, this affair of being the household angel.

Presently she was busily, if incapably, washing dishes. The Ballard girls knew little of kitchen work; they burned their fingertips, streaked their smooth round arms with soot, dipped glasses in lukewarm greasy suds and wiped them hopelessly upon wet greasy towels.

"We'll have breakfast whenever we get downstairs to-morrow," Mrs. Ballard planned, standing in the doorway of the big kitchen closet, with various small tins of spice in her hands. "I'll pack these now; we'll not need them. Then we'll leave things as they are here; they're bringing in a Japanese boy to clean the place, anyway, and we'll finish up our suitcases and get started. Dad said the paper tonight says occasional showers tomorrow; if it rains it'll be simply terrible! Well, we can't help it, we'll just have to take what comes."

"Mother, why are we taking cinnamon and curry powder and vanilla?" Dora asked. "We can't cook anything with them in."

"We may soon find a nice neighbor's girl who'll come over and help us," Mrs. Ballard said lifelessly. "No use throwing them away. Ben, did Dad give you some money?"

"Yep. Only a ten, though."

"That's for gas and for the girls' lunches tomorrow, and you'd better get some bread and butter and oranges and whatever you like for dinner; I'll bring coffee and meat," Sally said, resignedly practical. "If you girls get there early, open windows and air the place, and we'll get it warm later. Dad suggested you take your hot-water bottles, and I think you might as well; it may get cold at night. Dad and I ought to be along early in the afternoon. We'll have to turn this place over to Holmes and finish up things generally. The man didn't say what the coal was worth——"

"Mother, you're wonderful! You think of everything!"

Joyce said enthusiastically. Mrs. Ballard clung to the younger, stronger figure for a moment.

"I'm so tired," she said, "that I feel as if I would drop on my feet!" But there was an appreciative gentler note in her mournful voice, and Joyce knew that she liked the praise.

Her father had gone to a neighbor's to listen to the alluring Kitty and Mike; Ben had disappeared; Dodo was in one of her interminable telephone conversations with Helen Hill. Mother and daughter were alone in the kitchen.

"I marvel at your high spirits, Joy," Sarah Ballard said, wearily. "I really do. Just at your age, and with this nice little friendship with Paul starting, it's too hard on you— on all you girls! I do feel, and I shall always feel, that if Daddy had taken me into his confidence . . ."

The monologue went on as they mounted the stairs. Early in the evening Margaret and Eileen came over, wind-blown and spattered and rosy, to pay Joyce a good-bye visit. Presently the girl called in to her mother, who was creaming her face and soaping her hands thoroughly.

"We're going to a movie, Mother!"

"Eileen got the car?"

"Yep, and Kane's driving."

"That's all right, then. Have a nice time!"

Joyce sat between her friends in the dark loge seats. She would not tell them about Paul; innocent Eileen and Margaret who had had only brief flirtations in their nineteen years apiece! But the thought of Paul made the evening mysteriously radiant; the girl on the screen was really Joyce, and her love affair Joyce's love affair. Do what she would, Joyce could not feel sad tonight!

At midnight she was sound asleep in her dismantled room, with no handsome quilted taffeta spread upon her bed for the first time in her recollection, the once-dainty dresser bare, the windows stripped. When the family met in the kitchen for a demoralized last breakfast at nine o'clock the next morning, she gathered that she was the only person in the household who had slept well. Perhaps her father had had a good night's rest; he had breakfasted alone at eight and gone downtown; all the others said they had not slept at all.

Ben had been out nearly all night; his eyes were bloodshot, and his young face looked pouched and haggard. Dodo said that she had been cold, and had "kept thinking." Lissy began the day with a burst of tears.

"It really doesn't make the slightest difference to me where I go or how I live!" she said proudly, tremblingly wiping them away, thrusting her chin forward, looking into space. "Annette is probably going to Paris next October; she has a friend who's making a fortune painting posters there, and she says she'll give me the trip if I'll go! Of course," Lissy went on, as her mother and sisters listened in impressed silence, "of course I won't let her *do* it. But I said I'd manage somehow, and I will. I loathe this entire state; I loathe America and the cheap and shoddy way we do things! Europeans aren't always going bankrupt and getting themselves into frightful positions!"

"Tie a can to it, sweetheart!" Ben said lightly. Lissy gave him one sulphurous glance from heavy eyes set in dark shadows and was silent.

Mrs. Ballard made coffee; Joyce busied herself with toast. Not knowing how to make it on the electric stove, she had lighted the little electric toaster that in happier days had added a domestic note to the family breakfast table. Presently the odor of burned crust was in the room.

"Nothing but black coffee," Ben said hoarsely. His mother regarded him with fond maternal concern.

"Where were you last night, bad boy?"

He shook back dark hair; looked up with bleared eyes.

"I wasn't anywhere! We didn't do anything," he said,

with an air of surprise. "We were just having a bull session at Ridders'. I was home; I wasn't so late!"

"It was after three," his mother said gently.

"Oh, no, it wasn't, Mother; oh, no, it wasn't!" he said lazily, opening the pages of a wet newspaper. The day was dark, and at intervals rain showers fell steadily. "Sweet weather for driving!" Ben said.

"Sweet weather to get settled anywhere." Lissy pushed back her cup, sighed. "It's all like a bad dream," she said. "If it was any big city—Chicago, Philadelphia—" she went on, "we'd feel that there were opportunities, chances! But to be shut up on a ranch on a California mountain! It's—well, you don't know what it might be! We'll probably murder each other."

"Cheer up," Ben said, in his raw, deep voice. "We'll take a good look at it, and if we can't stand it we'll do something else. Oliver Owen's making a thousand a week in the movies —just a college kid. He's only twenty-two, and he's making a thousand a week!"

"We'll go in as a ter-*roupe*," Joyce, luxuriating in hot coffee and toast, suggested. "Exactly," she added, with a reflective air, "exactly how we'll manage the move from Merriwell to Hollywood we can arrange later, but manage it we will, on a hundred a month! From what I hear of Beverly Hills there are Spanish villas for rent——"

"None of you know what managing on practically no money means," her mother said, as she fell into a dream. They were all silent for a while, lost in their own thoughts, busy with breakfast. Ben lighted a cigarette. Lissy reached across for one for herself. After a while it was time to go upstairs. Breakfast was over, everything was over. They had really had their last meal at "Ninety-nine"; they had always been so proud of their handsome big home, and now it was theirs no longer!

"I keep feeling as if we were coming back," Dodo said forlornly.

"Yes, so do I," Joyce said.

At about eleven Ben brought the car around from the garage, with the rain curtains buttoned. It seemed strange to be going anywhere except in the big car; they started down the wet steps rather silently and stowed their suitcases snugly with the staring help of the Japanese boy. The mother and father watched them from the shelter of the big hood over the door.

"See you at La Perdita!" Joyce called out in farewell. She saw her mother's face wrinkle with tears. Her household possessions had been dear to Sarah Ballard; the handsome lamps, the rugs, the big leather chairs and silver photograph frames seemed to her like part of herself.

"Wonderful thing to have three daughters and a son, Mommy," Will Ballard said hopefully, as the young persons settled themselves in the car.

"Yes, I know," his wife said lifelessly, turning back into the bare, cold, dismal hallway. "But when you can't do anything *for* them——" she murmured. She went to a rain-spotted drawing-room window to watch the car turn into Santa Monica Avenue and go on its way.

Ben drove out past the big City and County Hospital and down to the Bayshore Highway. It was all straight ahead then; the long road went in a direct line southward past the towns: San Mateo, Redwood, Palo Alto, San José. The rain continued to fall steadily; water swished up from under the wheels of flying laundry and bakery trucks; traffic officers swept by like birds with spread wings, water shining on their rubber coats.

"By George, I believe the old bus will make it!" Ben said, when they had had coffee and sandwiches at Morgan Hill, and were nearing the end of their road. Joyce's brown eyes had been busy, had been entertained all the way; Dodo, in the back seat, had dozed, with her head against Lissy's shoulder and the yellow cat in her lap asleep; Lissy had sat stiffly erect, not interested, hopeless, weary.

"Gilroy three miles, Ben. And it's only quarter to two."

"Lord, in any kind of a wagon you could do it in two hours flat," Ben observed. He and Joyce had been chattering and laughing from the beginning of the trip; Ben could be adorable when he wanted to be, the girl thought. But now they both grew a little quieter. Joyce was conscious of being tired of the seat and tired of the rain and a little chilly. Ben yawned, shook his head as a dog might, drove on.

Gilroy. Merriwell at last! A man at the gas station called to another man to direct them to La Perdita.

"Wait a minute; that feller over there lives here. Joe! Know any place round here called 'Perdita'?"

Joe approached, wiping wet hands on a rag black with grease.

"There used to be a Perdita Ranch up at the top of the hill," he said, after thought. He spat, glanced up at Joyce. "Swede's place and Cooley's place and Russilow's used all to be called 'Perdita Ranch,'" he explained.

"I think my father used the name 'Roussilards'!" Joyce supplied eagerly.

"Sure, that's it. Up above Nye's, Charlie," Joe said. He walked across the road to put them on their way. "You take this road, see? Fenton Road, until you pass Gates' Garage; that's just about two blocks up. Then you turn right, and foller along Spanish Road. You'll pass a packing plant, Nye's, and get up to where the road forks. Then you want to go left—south, see?—and through a gate. Then you keep right on up about two miles to another fork, and turn—let's see, left again, and that's Russilow's road."

"Left both times?" Joyce said brightly. Her hopes rose in spite of herself. Oh, suppose it was a lovely old rambling place, with roses and oaks and porches . . .

They took the wet road toward the west, passed the landmarks without trouble; passed the garage, the packing plant. On the right, as the winding highway went up into the hills, was a faded sign: "Cooley's Sulphur Well. Picnics." It looked forlorn and forgotten in the rain.

"Left, Ben, left!" Joyce reminded him. "Don't you remember he said 'south'?"

She was getting very much excited now. They went in at an open farm gate and past a clump of redwoods. Off toward the west the hill rose steeply. The descending slopes were set with prune trees whose young foliage was heavy and beaten by rain. Now and then the thick leafy tent of a great walnut showed above the levels of the apricots and prunes. None of the Ballards knew one tree from another. Joyce thought that she must learn the names of the trees.

Presently a shabby rabble of collapsing barns and fences came into view with some sparse willows and one great oak beside them. Toward the north, on a bare rise of ground, the farmhouse stood, stark, square, dingy, hideous.

It looked what it was, the cheapest structure unskilled labor could devise from planks and paint. The paint had been a cold gray; it was streaked with yellow now and chipping from the walls. There were steep front steps, a forbidding front door. The lower floor was raised some four feet above the level of the packed hard wet earth outside; the house looked as if it were balanced crazily on stilts.

"Dorincourt! Welcome, Fauntleroy," Joyce said, in the appalled silence that held the entire group as Ben brought the car to a stop. Rain was dripping from everything; a coffee-colored gutter ran briskly across the yard.

"Do we get out?" Lissy presently asked fearfully.

"We'll have to get out, I suppose," Ben said, not very sure about it.

"We can't," Lissy said, opening the back door, but making no move to descend, "we simply cannot stay here."

## CHAPTER VIII

I<small>N</small> <small>THE</small> gray rainy light of mid-afternoon the yard presented a desolate picture. It was littered with rusting cans, corn shucks, fruit boxes, rags, chains, ropes. Dust and dirt and rubbish had accumulated upon them and between them and around them; water spattered dismally over the whole. A great gust of wind came down from the hills and moved across the scene like a moving wall.

"We'll go in and start a fire," Ben said suddenly. "No use getting lobar pneumonia! Come on."

Dodo, stiff with cold and fatigue, had just painfully awakened from restless sleep. "Oh, where are we? Oh, is this it?" she stammered, tottering on her feet. The yellow cat was down and away like a flash.

Ben looked at his keys.

"Side door," he read. "Unlocked, of course! I knew it would be. Holy Nelly, what a lair!"

The side door was indeed unlocked and even hanging open. They all went into a small square entry and opened a door that gave upon the kitchen. Joyce suspected that all their hearts failed them, as hers did her, when they saw it. They were tired, stiff from the long run, cold. The drip and chuckle of the rain was like an underscoring of the unearthly silence and remoteness of the place.

The kitchen was a large room, with a narrow wooden stairway angling up from one corner to the floor above. The floor was plain pine, splintery, black, oily; there were a dark old sink, a stove, rusted and cold, a large table. Otherwise, except for a woodbox into which rubbish indescribable had been thrown, the place was unfurnished. In a gaunt great pantry that smelled of mice and rotted wood there were a few plates, a few blackened pots and pans.

On the way down, the travelers had stopped for milk, bread, butter, honey. They set these things in their wet paper bags on the table. Lissy shuddered in the stale smells and vaultlike chill of the kitchen. Joyce said:

"Ben, could we build a fire?"

"Yep," he said, roused from a sort of stupor of bewilderment and disappointment. "The old man couldn't mean that we're to stay here?" he asked, in a troubled undertone.

"I don't know," Joyce answered, doubtfully.

Their wet suitcases were in the kitchen; rain was forming puddles on the uneven floor.

"I wish Dad had come with us," Dodo said falteringly.

"They may be here any moment." This was Joyce. "We'll have to do something; we'll have to get this place warmed a little. See if you can find something to make a fire with, Ben."

They took off their spattered coats and hats; looked into an adjoining room to find it completely unfurnished except for some small square platforms and the trunks and boxes that had come down from the city, and shudderingly shut the door on its dank uninvitingness.

Ben returned from the investigation of an outhouse with an armful of wood. On the kitchen closet shelves were folded and discolored newspapers. The stove lids, hanging with fringes of soot, were opened by Ben's inexpert hands, the fuel crammed inside. Blue smoke poured into the kitchen in clouds; doors and windows had to be flung open to carry away its choking thickness.

Presently there was a crackle of wood and a half-hearted spurt of flame. Smoke still seeped out in circles around the lids, but there was some warmth. The Ballards gathered about it, holding out their cold hands, and Joyce put some milk on to heat in a battered saucepan cleaned with her handkerchief. There was chocolate somewhere in the boxes of groceries that had arrived from the old house; everyone would be happier for a cup of hot chocolate.

They investigated the crates that were in the dining room. It was hard to find what was wanted among all the newspaper-wrapped items. Clothespins and soda, the ice-cream freezer and a cocktail shaker came to light; walnuts, canned corn, marshmallow sauce. Dodo and Lissy set them about here and there; they could not find any chocolate.

The milk on the stove continued to look cold, unaffected; a fine film of soot gathered on it, making it gray. Joyce and Ben went upstairs and unlocked a closed room; here were chairs, piled up on each other, tables, beds.

"Where are blankets, Joyce? It's going to be colder than Greenland here tonight; you can feel it already."

"They're in one of those big rolls downstairs, blankets and pillows and sheets. Oh, and mattresses, too. Ben, will we have to go into town to a hotel tonight?"

"Dad'll decide, I suppose. I can't think," Ben said scowling, "that he'd have let us in for this if he'd known."

They went downstairs again. The milk was surprisingly hot, and a brief but intensive second search discovered the chocolate. Ben had brought down two chairs; he sat on the woodbox and Joyce on the table, and the four drank the hot and heartening food with deep gasps of appreciation.

"Now, what had we better do?" asked Ben, feeling better.

"There's an old broom there. I think," Joyce said, as neither Dodo nor Lissy seemed able to make any helpful suggestion, "I think we ought to clean out this room and that next room, and get out the mattresses and sheets, and sort of get things started. I mean there's probably no hotel nearer than San José, and we can't go back that far! And by the time we get some beds made, Mother and Dad'll be here."

Lissy and Dodo looked actually frightened. Nervously and quietly they followed her suggestion, moving about like girls in a bad dream. Ben found a knife and began to slash the burlap and cords that held the mattress rolls. Rubbish and dust began to move across the splintery floor ahead of Dodo's unaccustomed broom; Lissy carried tins and boxes into the closet; Joyce and Ben labored with the bedding.

"We'll fix mattresses for Mother and us here in this other little room off the kitchen, and you and Dad can sleep on the floor in the kitchen. I mean it's all that we can do," Joyce decided. "Fortunately we have no house guests at the moment!"

Tired, cramped, chilled as they were, they went into incessant gales of laughter. Even Lissy laughed, partly from nervousness and exhaustion, but violently, almost helplessly, nevertheless. They were dirty, weary, their hands were grimed; there was no soap, hot water, or towels with which to clean them. Joyce dared not think of tomorrow—of all the days ahead. She dared not think of the dirt, the cold, the darkness so near them tonight. The kitchen floor was filthy; they could not clean it. The stove, always smoking, was choked with ashes. The ashes must stay there tonight. No baths, no pleasant reading lamps, no books; the books had been tumbled out of the packer's boxes to the floor of the icy parlor.

In the train of her uneasy thoughts came the discovery that there were no lights at all in the farmhouse. No electricity, no gas, no lamps. Dusk was falling over the rainy world like a cloud at five o'clock; there was no way of lighting the kitchen.

By this time, with a housewifeliness of which the three Ballard girls had never suspected themselves, sheets had been laid smoothly on the floor of the small room that flanked the kitchen opposite the dining room, mattresses laid on the sheets, and some attempt made to lay blankets and pillows in place. But by this time also everyone was tired almost to tears, and Dodo so anxious about her father and mother that her small dirty face was quite colorless. A knock at the kitchen door late in the afternoon brought them all to face it breathlessly, with a general gasp of relief. "Mother!" Dodo said.

But instead of the senior Ballards it was a muddy, booted, blond giant of a farmer in a mackinaw coat. This was Knud Paarsen, whose place was next to theirs down the hill; he had brought them a telegram.

Dora's face whitened again when she saw it, but it was harmless enough.

"Dearest children," it said. "Cousin Laura dying we come tomorrow." It was signed "Mother." There was but brief comment on this news. Cousin Laura was always dying at inconvenient moments. The Ballards returned to the problems of food and bed.

Joyce had found among the boxes and packages some scores of tiny red and green birthday candles. By the light of these the Ballards made their supper of bread and stewed tomatoes and more chocolate; at eight o'clock they were all stretched wearily on their mattresses.

Embers glowed and ticked in the stove. Outside the rain fell heavily, without pause, pattering on the porch roof, chuckling along the eaves, dripping in great washes like the sound of waves when the wind touched the high trees in the dark. Dirty, stiff, lame. buried in blankets, yet the four slept as soundly as if they had never known any other sort of bed, and the cold and the damp and the mountain silence reached them no longer.

Joyce wakened to the monotonous drip of rain in the morning. Lamely, stiffly, shuddering with cold, she went to the kitchen door and looked in to see Ben still sound asleep in a rolled cocoon of blankets, gray water running down the window panes, cold ashes sifted from the cold stove.

It was a terrible morning. The strangeness, the inconvenience of the ugly uncomfortable house hampered them in every direction. The stove smoked again; a cow, penned somewhere near by, lowed dismally at intervals of two or three minutes, was silent, and lowed again.

Ben, Lissy, and Dodo were disheveled, tired, despairing. Even Joyce's new philosophy was put to an acid test. There seemed no hope of coping with the needs of this horrible place. The rooms, the halls were caked in dirt and littered with rubbish; the yard was inches deep in accumulated refuse; the bleak decay and disorder everywhere accentuated by the original ugliness and stark plainness of the square high rooms, the obvious poverty and ignorance that had reigned here.

Awkwardly, disgustedly, they again attacked the familiar bread and butter and coffee. Someone had found some tins of milk. The fresh milk was gone, but Lissy dug a small hole in the top of a tin and shook the fluid out reluctant drop by drop. They had merely opened their suitcases on the night before; the surface contents were scattered about. Bedding dragged on the floor that was tracked with rainwater and mud.

"This is simply incredible!" Lissy muttered, clanking a soot-fringed stove plate into place, jerking the kettle forward with a suddenness that spattered water on the hot iron. Steam arose in clouds.

"We'll have to wait for Dad and Mother!" Dodo said, at the sink. "We oughtn't go away until they come. But we can't stay here; they'll see that. Even if we had all the money in the world to fix it up we couldn't stay here!"

Joyce was in a heroic mood of resolute goodness.

"If we could once get the stove to working, and the place cleaned up," she said. "Of course it's got a wonderful view of the whole valley, and there are those little canyons of redwoods back of the barns. It has—possibilities."

"It has possibilities of arson," Ben said. He looked tired and dirty in the cold morning light, and had not shaved. There was no bathroom in the house; there were no mirrors, no plumbing. But in a sort of shed back of the woodshed that opened off the kitchen there was a plain old pine table upon which a nicked basin and a tin pitcher stood as witness to the fact that ablutions had once been customary there. None of the Ballards had as yet made the effort to re-establish the custom. The girls' hair looked fuzzy and disordered; cramped and chilly, they crouched on the chairs at the kitchen table or gathered about the reluctantly smoking stove.

"Can you imagine human beings ever having lived like this?"

"Probably if the sun came out we'd feel better, Liss."

"Feel better!" Ben echoed scornfully. "All the sun would do is show up a lot more filth."

"I can't believe we've actually spent a night here. You *do*," Dodo said pathetically, "because things just—don't stop. I mean you eat and sleep, just because you don't die. But if anyone had ever said we'd come up to this frightful place, without any servants——"

"It's just bad management," Lissy said coldly, in the pause. Joyce said nothing; she felt herself flush. She hated any reflection on her father.

She buttoned on her coat at about ten o'clock and went

for a gingerly inspection of the ranch. Cold rain was blowing about on the wild airs, and the great trees that filled two little angled canyons up back of the barns were tossing and creaking restlessly. She saw chickens picking their way about disconsolately, emitting low caws of disapproval; the cow somewhere went on lowing, lowing. The violence of the late spring storm had scattered fresh clusters of fruit foliage over the rough earth of the orchards.

Suddenly she was back in the stale, languid, still chilly air of the kitchen.

"They're on their way up!"

"Who?" Lissy, huddled beside the stove in a coat, asked lifelessly.

"Mother and Dad! I recognize the car. Now we'll get it all straightened out!" Joyce ran out to meet them, as the car came into the yard; was beside it to open the door.

Mrs. Ballard looked pale and tired; her manner was strained. She descended stiffly, pressed a cold cheek to Joyce's, surrendered her small handbag.

"Cousin Laura died at three o'clock this morning," she said in a subdued voice, moving weary eyes to meet the glances of all her children in turn. She looked at her husband, who had also gotten out of the car, questioned him apathetically. "Is this the place, Will?"

"I guess it is, Sally! Well, how are you all, and how'd you make out without us?"

"It's the most frightful place you ever saw!" Lissy said with feeling. Dodo, clinging to her mother, was quietly crying; Ben and his father had taken possession of the bags.

"It really is unspeakable, Mother," Dodo said, somewhat superfluously. For they were all in the kitchen now, and its naked horrors were displayed in the gray rainy light. The rusty stove, the ashes, the grease-blackened floor, the spread disorderly bedding and open suitcases, the melted fragments of red and green wax, the odds and ends of food were all in full view. Mrs. Ballard clung to Dodo's arm, her face growing paler.

William Ballard put down two heavy bags, went straight to the stove, stooped to shove, to pull, to shove again at some mysterious plunger hidden at the side. Instantly the smoke stopped issuing in gray wreaths about the plates, and the fire started up with the first heartening roar it had made since it had been kindled on the previous afternoon.

"What do you know!" Ben said simply.

"You shut your damper off too soon, son!" the father said.

"Shut what off too what?" Ben asked, perplexed. "We never did anything like that," he said.

"I wonder you got the thing to burn at all, then," the man observed. "Well, this looks pretty sick, doesn't it? But we can't tell much about it until we've cleaned it up," he went on. "How about getting your mother a cup of tea, girls? We had an early breakfast at poor Laura's; we got started at eight."

"If you'll tell me how to do it, Mother," Dodo said tremulously. "We found the tea. Toodles is all right, he's here somewhere."

"Get the kettle boiling," Mrs. Ballard said. In her handsome rain-spattered coat and small black hat she was seated at the table; she had rested an elbow on the dirty torn oilcloth and was propping a cheek on her wet-gloved hand. "One of you slept in here last night? That's one of the best sheets you've got under that mattress," she added apathetically.

"What's the matter with that cow?" William Ballard demanded suddenly, hearing for the first time the desolate moan that had been going on at intervals all day and night.

"I don't know, Dad!" Ben said, injured and on the defensive.

"Is that one of our cows?"

"I don't know, sir."

"He's in our barn. I was just going in there when you came," Joyce observed.

"Come along with me, Joyce; we'll take a look round out there," her father suggested. Joyce was already coated and hatted; she left the dreary group in the kitchen with alacrity.

"Want your hat, Dad?"

"No," her father said cheerfully, almost jovially, "I don't think I'll wear a hat. I like the rain in my face. It's a light rain!"

Joyce, not daring to look back to see what expressions were registered at this moment on the faces of her mother and sisters, guided him through the woodshed, through some outlying sheds and fences, up toward the barns. The rain had stopped for a moment, but a great sighing wind came down over the hill and spattered cold drops from the trees into their faces.

"Well!" William Ballard said, striding along with his gray head bared. "This is great, isn't it? Great!"

Joyce sent him an unobserved sidewise glance. Was this all bravado? Apparently not. He appeared to be genuinely enjoying himself.

"The house is a perfect pig pen," she said mildly.

"Yes, I suppose so; I suppose so. Well, we'll get that cleared up. It looks like most farmhouses—built by men without any money, just nailing planks together to get the women and the children under shelter. It seems sound."

"It looks as if a heavy wind would bring it down in a heap."

"No, no, no; that's because he put a cellar under it. Probably some fellow from the East—expected snows, you see, and thought he had to get his vegetables and fruit into storage. Chickens, eh?" William Ballard said, as a draggled fowl addressed him on an interrogative note.

"There seem to be quite a few here."

"What'd you feed 'em?"

"We didn't feed them!" Joyce said, startled. "I never thought of it."

"Probably whoever's milking the cows did it. You must always feed chickens grain in winter, Joyce, or you'll not get any eggs. They've got to get hot food, too. Who brought the milk in?"

"Who—what, Dad? We got four quarts on the way here yesterday, but we used it all up for chocolate, and this morning we had to use canned milk. Who——?"

Her father paused with his hand on the broad wooden latch of the barn door. The trees in the canyon bowed in a sudden sweep of wet wind; branches creaked in the orchard.

"Didn't anyone milk this morning?"

"I don't know," the girl said, feeling stupid.

"There was a man here, wasn't there?"

"Well, there was, some time or other. But he must have left just before we got here. The man at the gas station said he and his brother had gone through about ten minutes before."

They were in the big dim barn; the sweet smell of hay and of the milky breath of cows made it an infinitely pleasanter place than the house. Joyce wondered why they had not all brought their blankets out here.

With the opening of the door the lowing of the cows increased; there were four of them, spotted black and white, standing with their lowered heads together, watching the newcomers suspiciously.

"Holsteins," Joyce's father said. "They've not been milked. Whoever he was, that feller ought to be strung up for leaving them! Here, boss, boss, boss . . ."

His hands were on their heads; he scraped knowingly at the little hollow between their horns; dust and hair fluffed up under his fingers, and the cows shoved their great heads against him affectionately and breathed stertorously through flat freckled wet nozzles.

"Here!" he said. "Wait a minute!" He crossed the open space of the barn and looked into the doors that stood in a row on the far wall. Presently he disappeared, to come back almost immediately with a stool and an old pail. "We'll fix you up, Daisy!" he said. Joyce looked on in respectful awe as he set the pail and the stool in place, seated himself with his forehead almost touching the nearest cow's mud-plastered flank. Milk began to stream into the bucket, hitting its dry tin with a sharp tinkle that changed almost immediately into a sort of bubbling hiss.

"Two of 'em are running dry, luckily; it's a dangerous thing to let 'em go over a milking!" Will Ballard said, looking up with perspiration standing on his forehead. "It's a good many years since I've milked, but you don't forget it. I used to milk seven of my grandfather's cows every day for years. Yes, sir," he added, transferring himself and his pail to another cow's big side, "we won't get much from this one or that big one until they come in. This one doesn't look to be much more than a heifer; she may have a calf round here somewhere."

Joyce forgot herself, forgot the problems that the house, that cleaning and cooking and sleeping presented, in the sheer fascination of this morning hour with her father in the barn. With unerring instinct, out back of the big building, toward the hill, he found a little shed obviously used as a dairy. Joyce rinsed big pans under his direction and watched him strain the warm dirty milk through a rusty old strainer; it flowed white and clean into the pans. There were already pans of milk here, with the risen cream on them as thick and heavy as leather. There was a pleasant faint smell of souring milk and tin and wet wood. As she and her father worked, they could hear another fresh soft fall of rain on the roof.

"Now they'll get out and get something to eat!" the man said, as the cows filed out into the rain and took the muddy path their feet had already churned through the black deep mire of the cow yard. "Fine grass all through here. They look like good cows, too! We're going to have a couple of calves here, Joycie. It certainly takes me back to be round cows again!"

Still dressed in the handsome gray suit he had worn to so many tense office conferences and throughout so many anxious business hours, he straightened up the back that was cramped by the unwonted exercise, and wiped his forehead with a fine monogrammed handkerchief.

"Well," he said, "that felt good! Now about those chickens, Joyce. Let's nose around here a little and see if we can find them some food. Shame, shame," he added, under his breath, "to let a place run down this way! Well, we'll get at things as soon as the sun comes out!"

They opened grain bins, peeped into sheds. Everywhere was the same dirt, disorder, traces of mice, decay. Finally a sack half filled with wheat coated with green mold was discovered, and Joyce filled a wooden measure with it under her father's direction and was presently out in the yard, in a light soft rain that felt warm against her face, laughing as the chickens gathered eagerly about it and squawked and pecked ravenously at the grain.

"We'll leave the barn door open," William Ballard said. "They like a barn a day like this. Come in here."

Joyce followed him into a dirty little chicken house against one of whose walls fruit boxes partly filled with straw had been nailed, top out. In these, with two glass eggs, were, astonishingly enough, some seven or eight fresh eggs; eggs with feathers still clinging to them; one of them even warm.

"Dad!" she said.

"Didn't you ever find an egg before?"

"Oh, *no!*" Her eyes were wide with wonder. "Eggs," she said musingly, with a little abrupt laugh. "Then these are our chickens and our eggs, Dad," she summarized it. "And our cows and our milk. How—how funny!"

"And our fruit and our vegetables," he added. Joyce's eyes were bright with an entirely new emotion as they went back to the kitchen. For the first time in her life she felt a liking, a real sympathy for her father as a human being.

## CHAPTER IX

HER mother had removed her heavy coat, for the revived fire had made the kitchen actually warm now, but she was still sitting at the table with her hat on and looked dazed and miserable. A teapot was at her elbow, but in answer to her husband's question she presently said apathetically that she thought that the tea had been made before the kettle boiled; it wasn't very hot. No; Joyce was not to make fresh, it didn't matter; it was getting round to lunchtime anyway.

"And Cousin Laura died, Mother?"

"Yes. Your father's told you all about it, I suppose. You've been gone an hour—I don't know what doing. Yes; she passed away at three this morning. We were there."

"And I suppose Susie Waite was there, too?"

"Susie? Oh, yes. Didn't Dad tell you?"

"Well, not much," Joyce said, suppressing a guilty tendency toward laughter. She and her father had forgotten Cousin Laura. "We were milking the cows and feeding the chickens."

"It sounds like a hick film!" Ben, opening a box of provisions, commented casually. "Milking? Can the old man milk?"

"Are the beds upstairs, Joyce?"

"Yes, but not put together. Just tops and bottoms and sper-*rings*," Joyce explained.

"Mother says Aunt Laura's death may make a great difference," Lissy said cautiously from the stove when Ben and his father had gone upstairs.

"She'd *have* to leave Dad something; he's her only relative, after all," Dodo added. She was in a chair crowded close to her mother; she kept hold of her mother's hand.

"We know she has left him something, and it may be—quite something," Mrs. Ballard said. "Dear Cousin Laura, she loved us all!"

"Was Susie obnoxious, Mother?"

"Well, I was telling them, Joyce, neither Dad nor I like her, and of course this was her chance to put on a great deal of authority. She'll inherit a good fat sum, of course, and she knows it. But Treadwell—poor dear Cousin Laura's lawyer—came in this morning just before we left, and he indicated to Dad—I don't know how much right he had to say anything—but he did say that Laura had made a new will a few weeks ago. Dad didn't know anything about it. Treadwell said something like—I can't remember his exact words—but he said, 'She certainly remembered you most generously, Mr. Ballard!' Of course," Sally said, trying not to be too hopeful, "that might mean only a thousand dollars and it might mean only ten. But he indicated that Laura was richer than we thought."

"A thousand dollars isn't much, is it, Mother?" Dodo asked.

"In the position we are now, it's nothing. Ten thousand isn't much, as Dad's affairs stand now. But when Daddy talked to Laura a few weeks ago he told her frankly what his difficulties were, and he thinks—he was saying so as we drove down—that she may have decided right then to get him out."

"Wouldn't it be pretty late now, Mom?"

Mrs. Ballard laughed with a little acid twist to her mouth. "It's never too late for money help, Joyce." Sally sighed, rose to her feet. "We must get at this kitchen, rich or poor!" she said wearily.

The thought of Cousin Laura's positive legacy, large or small, put heart into them all for the rest of the day. Ben, followed by his father in the little car, drove the big car into town and left it there for its new owner. He and his father came back with boxes of necessities: milk pans, frying pans, soap, ammonia, cleansers.

The parlor was aired, and some hundreds of apples that had been rotting on the floor were carried out to the first tentative nucleus of a bonfire. Temporarily two beds were set up in its gloomy depths, the windows of the narrow room were shadowed by overgrown rank shrubs just outside the windows. Sally Ballard herself made up the beds with fine linen sheets upon which the letters "S.F.B." were embroidered; Ben carried in the suitcases; their contents were laid in rows on a dark carved table of the President Cleveland era, with a stained marble top. It was all cold, uncomfortable, wretched enough, but it did become a little less cold, uncomfortable, and wretched as the hours went by, and Cousin Laura's will formed a bright light to guide them all through the strange beginnings of the new life.

Some old glass lamps had been found in the cellar; again it was William Ballard who knew how to cut their wicks, fill them with kerosene, light them. In the room off the kitchen the girls' beds were set up: a double bed, a single bed. Joyce found white counterpanes and spread them; their clothes were hung on pegs in a sort of passage that ran from the bedroom across to the front entry.

Luncheon was meat cakes and beans and bakery buns, with a jar of jam opened for luxury. They were all ravenous; the food disappeared like magic. Some twenty out of a thousand apples had been saved. Joyce's father told her that if she would follow his directions he would tell her how to make applesauce, and hot applesauce was the finishing course at dinner. Three more eggs were added to the eight in the yellow bowl. Joyce and Ben went out at four o'clock and returned with a great brimming pitcher of rich milk and a smaller pitcher of cream.

"Lord, how these hicks have to struggle just to keep things going!" Ben said, stoking the kitchen stove as well as a round-bellied iron stove that stood on three claws in the parlor, carrying out ashes, bringing in wood, breaking open crates. "No wonder they go to bed early! I'm so tired that every time I sit down I practically go to sleep, and all I think of is food."

At five o'clock there was an announcement that anyone who wanted it could have hot water for washing; in turn they retired into the freezing washroom off the woodshed and made such gingerly concessions as they dared to cleanliness. The hot water and scented soap suds felt delicious on Joyce's face; she brushed her hair back wetly and pushed it into neat curls; she had found a plain old tennis frock of dark blue linen somewhere among the half-unpacked trunks; she buttoned a blue sweater trimly about her hips.

"I don't wonder that when real countrywomen get the house cleaned up, and dinner started, and themselves clean, they put on a fresh apron and come and sit on the porch and look triumphant!" she said at dinner.

"They cook for hands, too," her father reminded her, carving steaks with good appetite at the head of the forlorn kitchen table. "And they bear children, and they put up hundreds of jars of preserves. My grandmother never had less than a thousand jars of fruit and black currant pickles and chow-chow and whatever-it-was."

"I've forgotten the very names of them!" Mrs. Ballard

said with a shudder. "Those women used to lead the lives of animals. I don't see how they got through at all!"

"I didn't know your grandfather had a ranch, Dad," Dodo's soft little voice said.

"Oh, yes, a fine farm, outside Philadelphia, but over on the Jersey side of the river. Yes, I lived there all through my boyhood; put myself through two years of Princeton, and finished up at Stanford, after your mother and I were married. Yes; we had a nice old place there at Morristown—not as big as this, maybe, but farms aren't as big there."

"If the rain would hold up I'd see if I could get a woman in to clean this whole place thoroughly," Sally Ballard said, when the hot food had begun to have its inevitably pacifying effect. "That's the first thing we must do, if we're to stay here at all. A man to clean the yard, and a good woman—two women—in here to wash everything from top to bottom!"

"I suppose it depends on Cousin Laura whether we stay here or not," Lissy observed. Joyce saw a shadow come over her father's face; it was there only an instant, but she had seen it. She did not understand it then; a few days later it was to be explained to her.

"In a way it does depend on Cousin Laura," her mother said. "In the first place we don't own this ranch; we have no claim on it. We're just being allowed to stay here—I don't like that. It shows that the place is worthless, and that civilized people can't make a living on it. I don't believe it's healthy; I saw a sign coming up that said 'Sulphur Well.' You can't tell me that if there's one of those nauseous smelling things on the next place there isn't a miasma or something here!"

"Sulphur's one of the healthiest things in the world, Mommy," William Ballard said. "They must have used it to dry fruit—there are sacks of it up here."

"Exactly what I thought, Will!" his wife said with an air

of triumph. Everyone laughed, and presently she laughed a little reluctantly, too. "No," she went on after a moment, "I never would want a place like 'Ninety-nine' again, a place that demands three servants and a chauffeur. I'd find some nice apartment up on the California Street hill, get *one* good Chinaman . . ."

"We thought we were having a hard enough time at 'Ninety-nine' without servants," Lissy said, with a little mirthless laugh when her mother's voice paused on the question of Tahoe or Carmel for summer outings. "It never occurred to any of us—it never would have occurred to me in the longest day of my life!—that anything could be as dreadful as this."

"Marvelous cream! I never tasted such ker-*ream!*" Joyce said.

"You oughtn't to touch it," her mother said in an aside.

"I know, but I'm just toying with it!"

"I don't know why we should hunt up some woman to clean up this place," William Ballard said reflectively.

"William, look at it! And it may be weeks before we get your legacy. They said a month at least."

"Well, but here we are, Sally, six able-bodied men and women. Why should we send out for another able-bodied man and woman? I don't mean you, I don't mean you. But I believe we others could make a pretty good stab at getting this kitchen into shape tomorrow. Tomorrow's Thursday— the funeral isn't until Friday. We could go at it in the morning; I'll get some hot lye and burn this grease out. There won't be anything complicated about it, just straight-ahead cleaning." This remark met with a general silence.

There was another example of strong self-control on the part of the other Ballards when the next morning, after breakfast, the man of the house said briskly, "Well, come on, now, everyone, and let's see what we can do with this kitchen. If we manage to clean it we'll try the other rooms, one by one. There's no secret to cleaning—anyone can do it. Cleaning women are the least intellectually burdened class of workers in the world."

"I somehow don't seem to see myself in the rôle of a cleaning woman," Ben said. He said it good-naturedly enough in tone, but there was a little edge of insolence, of boredom, of contempt in his manner.

"What do you propose to do, go upstairs while your sisters and I work?" William Ballard asked, his own tone harmless, but some menace in the air somewhere of which Joyce was instantly conscious.

"I thought I'd take a book out to the barn," Ben said, sticking his ground, but turning red under his browned boyish skin.

"Well, help us with the start," William said, after a second. The crisis faded. "While the girls are making their beds, you get some wood into your mother's room, and we need some in the kitchen, too. Then we'll move the chairs and the table out, and sweep the floor carefully. By that time the water'll be hot, and we can get right at it."

Joyce looked fearfully at Ben, but Ben was mastered for the moment. He nodded obediently, with a sort of shrug, and set about bringing in the wood, while she and Dodo went into the icy kitchen chamber to make up beds and hang up nightwear, and Mrs. Ballard philosophically attacked the breakfast dishes. Lissy assisted her languidly. When the other girls came back to the kitchen everything was in order, and Ben was sweeping.

Joyce presently had a great clean cloth and was washing the inside of the windows; Dodo, with another cloth, crawled about the baseboard, wiping from it the grime of years. Their father worked busily at the sink; whatever the cleaner he used, it had a miraculous effect, and the old zinc emerged from it shining like silver.

Then came the floor: the tipped inundations of some

strong lye, the swashing of an old broom, the second rinsing with clean water. Then soap suds were pushed into half-moons here and there on the floor by the circular motions of Joyce's and her father's arms, and finally the whole family had backed itself out of the room, and the first sunshine that the Ballards had seen at La Perdita was shining bright and hot on all the drying cleanliness.

"Sunshine! Mother, come out! But don't step on our floor!" Joyce called, in the brilliance and warmth of it under the oaks. The yard was a hopeless disorder of rubbish and pools, but the meadows rising beyond the barn were a sea of bright green; roofs sparkled and shone with rain-drops, and larks, pouring out their heart-breaking notes, went whirling upward against a blue sky.

Armadas of puffed white cloud sailed slowly toward the south; wet leaves twinkled; birds hopping about among the low bushes sent showers of diamonds to the grass. The mountains rising just behind the ranch toward the west were deep ultramarine, but all the eastern world was bathed in light, and the village, in its smother of rounded oaks and tall eucalyptus, looked like a newly varnished toy.

"Oh, this is really lovely," Mrs. Ballard had to concede. "Somehow I felt that we never were going to be done with the rain. Oh, this is nice!"

"I've reached the point when I'm grateful for anything," Joyce said, studying the lines of dirty water that were dry-ing on her round brown arms. "I will never be clean again, I know that now; I will smell like a cow yard for the rest of my life. Namporty, the kitchen floor is simply glorious! Did you look in at it, Mother? It looks like a different place!"

"I wish we didn't have to go to that funeral tomorrow," William Ballard said thoughtfully. "Then we could tackle this yard."

"I always thought farmers lived simple uneventful lives,"

Ben said. "My glory! Getting eggs, milking, feeding stock, washing things, washing the things you wash the things with, carrying out ashes, carrying in wood, filling lamps, cooking, mopping dishes! It's a swell life!"

"You get the flavor of it," his father, still panting from his exertions in the kitchen, seated on an old chopping block in the streams of the warming sun, said hearteningly.

"You certainly do! And it is the rare aroma of manure and garbage!" Ben ejaculated. His father laughed.

"You get a flavor from decent living, too, Daddy," Mrs. Ballard said mildly. "Certainly our beautiful home in St. Francis Wood, with Edna and Fanny and Lotty, had an atmosphere all its own. We're going through a little time of makeshift now, and it's all right, and none of us are complaining, but that isn't to say that there isn't a finer way. Just to struggle for food and warmth and shelter is to be not much better than the beasts."

"I don't know," Joyce began dreamily, rubbing a wet spot on her arm to and fro. "There's something—ter-*remendous* about getting milk and eggs still warm. What it'll be to pick apples and dig potatoes, I can't imagine! But it does make you feel—triumphant!"

"It oughtn't make you feel any better than to be able to pay people for things—pay nice maids who want the jobs," Lissy argued. "Quiet lovely rooms and books and lights and clean beds—I frankly confess that if I ever have them again I'll feel more than triumphant!"

"It seems like a dream that we ever had them," Dodo contributed. "It seems like a dream that whenever there was anything left at the table one of us didn't have to put it into a bowl and carry it down to the cold closet!"

"I never thought what they did with food we didn't eat," Joyce said.

"What did they do with it? Throw it out, Mother?" Dodo asked.

"No, of course not, darling; they ate it in the kitchen," Mrs. Ballard, disliking the turn the conversation had taken, said quickly. "Joycie, you must get clean!" she added.

"I know. But I can't go across my beautiful floor to get the kettle of hot water. There's a little stove in the washroom, and I think I'll build a fire there and do the thing up thoroughly. Oh, that isn't twelve striking in the kitchen!" Joyce said.

"Just twelve," her father said ruefully.

"Isn't it the strangest thing that you no sooner do anything," the girl said, "but what it's a meal time, and you have to get out the bread and cut butter! Come on, Lissy! Let's get started."

The kitchen was dry; it looked an entirely different place. The stove had been cleaned of ashes, brushed of soot, blackened. The floor showed something of the boards' original pine white. Through the sparkling window panes the sunshine flooded brilliantly.

"I love the sun!" Dodo said. Joyce performed superficial ablutions at the sink; she ached all over and felt sleepy. Bacon and beans for lunch, bread to cut, cheap bakery cookies to put on the table.

"Your mother and I will have to drive into San Francisco at about five," William Ballard said. "We'll stay at some hotel, and be down as soon as we can. The funeral's at nine tomorrow. Laura had it all arranged."

"Lucky you don't have to go in the rain."

"No; I think the rain's over. They say it was bad for the cherry crop."

"You sound like a real farmer, Dad!"

"I feel like a real farmer."

"Some day, no matter what Cousin Laura left us, we'll buy you a little place like this, Dad, and let you play with it!" Sally told him generously. She was nervous; Joyce knew she was thinking of the legacy.

"This place, except for the house perhaps, is all right," he said. "We could get a living off it even without the prune crop."

"But all you'd get is just a living," Ben objected, helping himself generously to beans.

"Well, that's something, my son. There are a good many men and women in this state who'd be glad of that."

"Why didn't they stay on the farms, then, Dad?"

"Perhaps," William Ballard said, "their children weren't happy on the farms."

"But this," Sally said quickly, "this isn't living!"

"Food and warmth and shelter, Mommy."

"Oh, well," the wife said patiently. And again her eyes narrowed and she looked into space. What had Cousin Laura left them? What was the will going to say tomorrow?

The girls helped her dress for the city. There was a pitcher of hot water; her dress was brushed. The sun was gone when she and their father climbed into the shabby little car for the eighty-mile run.

"We'll come back with news," Sally Ballard said in an undertone to her oldest daughter, as they started.

The brother, the three sisters, stood watching them out of sight. Back of the line of western hills a cold sunset colored the sky with dull red and lead-colored streaks. Twilight was windless and clear over the ranch; the chickens had gone to bed; the cows had filed into the barn. A wide sense of loneliness and desertion touched Dodo, and she said fearfully: "I'm sort of scared here!"

"Nothing to be scared about," Lissy said. "Nobody who could possibly go anywhere else would ever come here!"

"Don't be scared," Joyce said. "Let's go into the kitchen and get warm, and begin supper. Let's have milk toast and jam and crackers. We've no more meat, but Dad said he was going to bring down a pot roast tomorrow; he said it would last a week. I'm going to read it up in the book."

"Am I supping on milk toast and jam?" Ben asked, alarmed.

"You don't have to. You can have the rest of the beans, and there are eggs."

They all went in together. The night outside was closing in black and chilly, but the kitchen was warm and clean, and still faintly, pleasantly scented with ammonia and wet wood.

"Now I can't wait to get at the closet and the other rooms!" Joyce said. Lissy sighed.

"I don't know where you get your inexhaustible energy!" she remarked. "I don't see what pleasure you get in killing yourself to clean a place that wouldn't be fit to live in if Sloane took it over!"

"The thing I miss," Dodo said, when they were at supper, "is having someone like Edna go in and out of your room and put things away and fix the flowers and the fire and all that. If I drop a sock on the floor now, there it lies until I pick it up. It seems so funny!"

"I miss reading at night," Joyce said. "I suppose I could have a lamp, but I haven't gotten round to it; there's no table for it, anyway. But I think I've read myself to sleep every night of my life since I was on the Oz books!"

Lissy refrained from the long catalog of her own wants. Ben merely observed that he didn't mind it so much, but it wasn't worth the work and worry, and he was going after a job early in the week.

"The old man gets a great kick out of milking and cleaning and all the rest of it; he's been through the mill since the business went on the rocks," Ben said. "All right; that's his lookout. But I'd go straight out of my mind if I stayed here long! I couldn't do it."

"It seems such hard work for so little," Dodo offered plaintively. "It makes me wonder what went on in our kitchen when we had big dinners. We never get through at all here, and yet they always kept 'Ninety-nine' looking so lovely, dusted, and clean!"

Two lamps were burning gallantly in the kitchen now, but after the dishes were finished and the place was in order, the girls wearily decided against a rubber of bridge, against any effort whatsoever, and carried one lamp into their bedroom for an early finish to the long day. It seemed to Joyce that they had been on the ranch for weeks, for months, yet this was only their third night there. Tired, dirty, yet she was beginning to feel at home, to feel somewhat equal to the demands of eating, sleeping, cooking, that had so overwhelmed them all yesterday.

## ❧ CHAPTER X ❧

A SECOND morning dawned through a thick fog; it was ten o'clock before the sun burst out. During breakfast they talked of Cousin Laura and the will; after breakfast someone suggested that they walk up past the barns to the canyons that forked into the hill to the north and southwest, and get a more comprehensive view of their domain. Joyce got herself into riding breeches, belted on an old leather coat, stepped out into the kitchen yard to see a car parked by the oak, and a tall boy beaming at her. *Paul!*

She whispered his name; was instantly in his arms; was jumbled up against his shoulder laughing and crying with joy. They had only a moment together before the others came out.

"I thought you were going to Portland with your father!"

"He's not going until Saturday. I set my alarm for six and came straight down! Joy, how are you, darling, and did you miss me?"

"Miss you?" she said. Tall, lovely, laughing, in her boyish clothes, with an old felt hat pulled down over her redbrown hair, and her red-brown eyes dancing, she stood holding to his arms with both firm young hands. "You darling, to come and find us!" she said. And she poured out to him the desperate, funny story of the week: the rain, the cold, the dirtiness and discomfort.

"Lord, I wish I'd been here for it!" Paul said jealously. "Your father milking the cows and you going for eggs!"

"It's the strangest thing in the world, getting eggs by twos and threes out of the hay or the chicken house, instead of in dozens," she told him, "and having milk in odd lots—not by quarts!"

"And your mother, how does she stand it?"

"Mother doesn't like it, but of course she's awfully decent," Joyce said, somewhat hesitatingly. "I think the more Dad likes it, the less she does," she added ingenuously. "She and Lissy act as if it was only for a few days, much less weeks, but Dad is talking about getting tomato plants and putting late corn in."

Paul surveyed the forlorn high boxlike house, the shabby disorderly yard, and shook his head.

"You couldn't stay here. It's—well, it's all right, but even after you got it all into shape and the tomatoes were growing and all that, what would you have? Nothing! Listen, let's clear the yard before your father gets back! I have to get in on this!"

"You will not!" said Ben, issuing from the kitchen to shake hands with Paul, and overhearing the last remark. "Nix. We're going to walk up the canyon."

"Nix, we're going to clean this yard!" Paul insisted. "Come on, I'm dying to! Come on, it'll be lots more sport than just walking!"

"Oh, let's not clean anything else," Lissy said languidly, as she joined them. "Hello, Paul, it was cute of you to find us! Let's stop cleaning things for a while!"

But Paul, with eager brown hands, had commenced work. He had seized upon a protruding wet corner of some black rough material embedded deep in packed earth that might have been oilcloth or linoleum or canvas. As he tugged it free, the accumulated rubbish on top of it rolled and slid in every direction.

"My Lord, whoever was here last simply went native!" he said. "Where can we have a bonfire, Ben?"

"I wonder we didn't think of doing this to surprise Dad," Dodo said.

"Oh, well, if you're so crazy to turn reformer!" Ben yawned. "Come on, and I'll show you the tools we've got."

Sunshine had driven away the fog now, but the ground was still wet from yesterday's rains; every leaf on the fruit trees and every blade of grass bore its burden of bright drops. Joyce fairly danced along beside the two men as they went toward the tool shed; they were all laughing as they came back to the yard, laden with rakes and shovels.

Dodo helped in an ineffectual sort of way; Lissy huddled herself into a big sweater and sat on a barrel with the sun pouring over her shoulders. The other three worked vigorously, with much shouting and laughter; the yard began to come into order as the kitchen had done.

Joyce was in wild spirits, and as the work and the warmth of the bonfire flushed her face and curled her hair she looked her loveliest: a brown-eyed gypsy in an old white sweater with the trimmest of riding breeches on the slimmest of legs. Paul's presence made all the difference between stagnation and full pulsing glorious life; Paul's laughter, Paul's nonsense, Paul's adoring asides warmed her like champagne.

They raked, they dragged loads of unspeakable débris to the fire; fumes rose into the air like gray plumes, the sunshiny day was sweet with the odor of burning leaves, burning brush. Dodo swept the wet dirt from the kitchen porch, the kitchen steps; Ben sawed away a great broken branch of the oak.

"What do you do with tin cans, Paul?"

"We'll have to dig a trench for them. You'll have to have a regular pit for them. That's what we did at camp." Paul and Joyce wandered away to find the right spot for the trench; when they came back Joyce's eyes were very bright, and her color had all the delicate fluctuating bloom of an apricot. Life was thrilling and pulsating and exquisite for Joyce today; to be young, laughing, busy, to have so close to her this ardent man who loved her and whom she loved had filled her cup to the brim. He had come all the eighty miles from the city to see her; he was putting an open and avowed seal on his devotion; they belonged to each other.

Characteristically, he had brought a great bag of food with him. Sausages, cake, oranges, cheese. This was Paul, Joyce thought; he never forgot anything!

"I didn't know how you were fixed up here," he apologized, as the girls exclaimed appreciatively over the augmented larder. "I knew it was the last jumping-off place."

Lunch was what Joyce described as a bacchanalian orgy. It was late, for they must all make some pretense of getting clean after their work; they carried their plates and chairs to the immaculate yard, and feasted in a sort of circle with the steps for a table.

The freshly turned earth was raked neatly now; there was not a rusted can or an old rope or plank or bit of broken machinery in sight. The fire smoldered sleepily; the sun had already turned to a lighter brown the neat ridges made by the rake. The Ballards could not sufficiently admire the work of their hands.

"It looks like another *place!*" they said over and over again. "We must be strangely dumb," Joyce presently observed, sitting on the steps with a buttered bun and a sausage in her hands. "There was nothing to cleaning this yard but work, and we've been talking ever since we got here about who we could get to clean the yard for us! I suppose we could paint the house or put in a bathroom if we made up our minds to it."

"Somehow you always think of getting someone," Dodo said, in her shy little voice. "I still can't think of not getting —well, *regular* eggs, at a grocery. The ones the chickens lay don't seem like eggs; they just seem like—extra things, somehow. I think I'd always have boxes of apples from Mc-Lean's, even if our trees were covered with them."

"You have to sort of gear yourself to a ranch," Joyce contributed. "What puzzles me is what you do when everything's in order—kitchen clean and dish towels hung out and tomatoes put up and yard swept—then what?"

"Then nothing!" Lissy said with feeling. Ben laughed.

"The first thing I'm going to ask the old man to do with Cousin Laura's money," he said, "is stake me to six months in New York. After that I'll look out for myself. I'll go round on a Panama boat—it doesn't cost any more, and it's lots of fun—work into some line there, newspaper or magazine—and then after a few years I'll be able to help. Here I'm not any good at all. I don't get the kick I should out of sweeping porches and feeding chickens!"

"There's that poor black cat; he's evidently frightened to death!" Joyce exclaimed suddenly. "He lives back of the barn—I fed him, but he won't come near me. Come on, pussy, pussy, pussy!"

"If Annette goes to Paris I'm going to go with her," Lissy said. "It's cheaper than living at home, if you go by one of the Danish boats. I love Paris. We girls were there three weeks with Miss Nuttall, and even with a school teacher for chaperon we had a wonderful time. I've always wanted to go back."

"Some of us will have to stay with Dad and Mother," Dodo offered hesitantly.

"You and I will," Joyce said.

"You will until I come back for you next year," Paul

amended it, when he and she were alone in the kitchen an hour later. The girls and Ben had helped with cleaning up, but had then tactfully vanished. Where they were, Joyce could not imagine, but at all events they were gone, and she and Paul could talk at last. Tired, happy, they sat in the orderly kitchen.

"Does it seem funny to you that it's actually hit us?" the boy asked, his hand warm over hers. "I mean that in a little more than a year we'll be married? You my wife. You and I house-hunting, and having our friends in for meals!"

"It's the one thing that has carried me ther-*rough,* Paul," she told him seriously. "It makes it all so easy. When they praise me I feel so ashamed," Joyce went on, with her cheeks reddening, and her honest eyes fixed on his, "because it's all due to *you*. I'm only playing a part here; it's nothing for me to be—well, *good,*" she added, laughing at the childish word, "because I keep thinking of you, and of what a wonderful wife I want to be to you! I want every man who knows you to envy you!"

"They'll envy me all right," Paul said, his own eyelashes misted as were hers.

"And I've taken off four and a half pounds!" she told him joyfully. "There's an old scale up at the barn in the ger-*rain* room, and Ben's weight was right on it, so it must be all right. Four and a half pounds!"

"I like you the way you are," Paul said. "My father— everyone sees how changed I am since I met you!"

"Ah, but you'll never know," she said, "what *you've* done for me!"

"I love you," he said simply. "I've liked girls before; I've had cases. But you're my mother and my sister and my pal and my sweetheart all in one. I've never liked anyone in the world the way I like you!"

They fell into reminiscence, remembering their meeting at the tea party of Margaret's cousin, their instant recognition of each other. They talked of the future, and Joyce felt that she would not change places with any girl in the world.

"You see, when I'm twenty-five, Joy, I come into some money."

"Like a book," Joyce said in satisfaction. "Much?"

"Quite a pile. My grandfather died when I was seven, and it's been accumulating. We'll go to Europe on our honeymoon."

"No; I can't grasp that!"

"Ben was talking of Panama today. We'll go by Panama. How'll you like to go on one of the big liners with me and look up our cabin?"

"Oh, don't, Paul!"

"We'll do as we like when we get over there, see? Maybe we'll buy a little car somewhere, and cruise around by ourselves. No kings and queens in ours, huh?"

"No kings and queens in ours!" the girl said on a delicious broken laugh.

"We'll stay three months or so, and then we'll come back and get settled. Let's never do things the way other people do, Joy. Let's be freaks, and do freaky things, and not care what they think!"

"You'll always be a freak, and do freaky things, and make life wonderful, Paul," she said.

After a while Lissy and Dodo came back from a walk, their shoes caked with mud and their cheeks glowing. It was late afternoon now, for they had not lunched until three, and Paul had to go. Joy walked out to the car with him, and stood in the windy twilight, lingering for a last word.

"Listen, Joy, I forgot! My stepmother wants you to come up and visit us before I go. I'll come down for you. We're moving into the Keavey place in Hillsborough, and she told me last night that she hoped my girl would come up for a week-end," Paul said. And after he was gone Joyce remembered that as the most wonderful thing that had happened all day. His father and his stepmother were going to recognize the seriousness of her relationship to Paul; it would be a tacit acknowledgment of their engagement, this visit! Her heart was singing as she went back into the kitchen to consider once again the bread, the meat, the vegetable problem for supper.

Dark had scarcely fallen when the elder Ballards arrived, the girls' mother so weary that she could hardly walk into the house. It had been a terrific day, their father reported. The roads had been heavy, the bumpy little car a tiresome vehicle in which to travel, the funeral and cremation had been ghastly. Immediately after the obsequies Treadwell, the lawyer, had asked them to remain for the reading of the will. The Bannister cousins were there from Seattle, and they had to take a boat late that afternoon.

Sally Ballard sat at the kitchen table, looking tired, white, bright-eyed. Her husband satisfied his children only with a brief remark to the effect that it was good to get home and that he thought he would get his milking done.

"You ought to be dead on your feet, Will!" the wife said, in affectionate concern, and Joyce knew from her tone that the news was good.

"What's the verdict?" Ben said, when his father had taken a new milk can and, escorted by Joyce and the lantern, had left the kitchen.

"It's—tremendous!" the mother said, shaking her head.

"Good?" Lissy asked eagerly.

"Cousin Laura died worth more than a quarter of a million," Sally answered simply. "She left several legacies, she left ridiculous provision for her cats, and of course she left precious Susie a fortune. A woman like that, that Laura paid twenty dollars a month when she hired her! Makes you so mad! And then there's the inheritance tax, it seems it's outrageous if you're not a direct heir——"

"Sure, sure," Ben said, listening, as they all were, intently. "Go on!"

"It's so good to get here into this warm kitchen," his mother said irrelevantly, "and dinner smells so good! The rest is ours."

She added the last phrase simply. Her daughters and son looked at her.

"Whee!" Ben said in a whisper.

"After what we've been through," his mother said, her eyes watering, "it seems like an answer to prayer! We've certainly had a fiery trial, and you've all met it like—well, I was saying to Dad today, like aristocrats. It doesn't mean 'Ninety-nine' again; that's sold, and I've learned my lesson, anyway. But it does mean a comfortable little place on California Street hill, and that Dodo and Joyce can lead the life of normal girls in society. If Lissy still wants to go to Europe after——"

"After Archie Ross returns from Scotland," they knew she was going to add. She substituted, "after June," and went on, "I believe your father would consider letting you go, Lissy; I spoke of it coming down, and he said he would think about it. It would be a wonderful change, and meanwhile the other girls would be with me."

"Did Dad seem excited, Mother?"

"About the legacy? Well, yes and no. He's been very quiet. The Bannisters got ten thousand apiece; they seemed more excited than Dad was. Susie got fifty."

"Fifty grand!" Ben ejaculated rather than asked.

"Fifty thousand. It seems ridiculous, for Laura had given her silver and presents—the Piedmont house, loads of things. Five thousand would have been ample. However, he read all that—Treadwell, I mean—and then he said that everything else was Dad's."

"What'd Dad say?"

"As I say, he was very quiet. His eyes filled with tears,

and he said once or twice, 'Very generous! Very generous!'
I think he was stunned," Mrs. Ballard said with a little emotion. "I know I was. It was very impressive."

"That's a lot of money, isn't it, Mother?"

"Oh, it's a fortune, darling! Why, when Daddy sold his
patent he didn't get that for it, and yet we were regarded as
rich people."

"We're lucky!" Ben said seriously. "Gosh, what an escape! I thought we might be stuck here for a couple of
years. He'd like me to go back to school, I suppose. But
I'd rather strike out for myself, now that we've made the
break."

"If it had come two months ago, Mother, we never would
have moved at all, would we?"

"No, we'd still be at 'Ninety-nine.' Well, we've had a
sharp lesson, and I don't believe it's hurt any one of us one
bit!" Sally Ballard said cheerfully.

Somehow the trend of the conversation changed as Joyce
and her father came in, their faces stung to rosy freshness
by the cool early evening air. The kitchen was bright and
warm. Mrs. Ballard explained that she had stopped in San
José for broilers; no need to scrimp now! Dodo and Joyce
began to cook them under her direction.

"New potatoes!" William Ballard said, taking his place
at the table. He looked tired; his manner was unusually
quiet.

"Our own!" Joyce said. "We haven't told you half our
adventures. Paul came, and we cleaned the yard, and we
discovered a whole row of darling little new potatoes hardly
any bigger than cherries!"

They were all talking at once; gay for the first time in
the stiff ugly kitchen. The frying chickens sent a delicious
odor into the air. In the milk pitcher clots of cream showed
like gold against the glass. Nothing was said of the legacy
during dinner; they were waiting for their father to mention

it. But he seemed tired, subdued, and spoke hardly at all. The meal went on cheerfully to the point of Joyce's first rice pudding.

"I want to talk to all of you," William Ballard said suddenly when that was eaten. "I may as well say it now. I've been thinking of this since Laura died—not debating it, I have no choice, but wondering how I'd put it to you."

They all looked at him, surprised and a little uneasy. His manner was grave. Joyce, leaning against the sink, stood arrested, a tea-towel in her hand. Lissy, who had been clearing the table, sat down again. Dodo pushed her chair a little so that she might lean her head against her mother's shoulder. Ben lighted a cigarette.

"Plans, Daddy?" Sally Ballard said.

"Plans. Your mother will have told you—I told Joyce up in the barn—that Cousin Laura left me a lot of money. Not more than I've spent several times over in the past twenty years, but more than I've ever had in my hand before at one time.

"A few years ago," he went on, after a brief pause, "my business began to go on the rocks. It had been a good business—a few inventions of mine that I had patented in the beginning gave it a good start, I suppose; probably it has been running down ever since without my knowing it. I don't know. I'm not a business man.

"I had stockholders, quite a few of them. They were not rich men; most of them the draftsmen and chemists I'd employed. Fifteen, eighteen years ago I gave some of them a chance to buy in. They were like a family to me in a way.

"Three years ago we began to slide, profits went down, salaries were cut. These fellows took it all standing; they owned a part of the business; they understood. But when it came to going into a receiver's hands, turning the whole thing over to the bank, it hit them hard.

"They were all decent about it—Cutler and Roberts and

Larsen and McDonald. They knew how I felt, I suppose. But it meant that they lost their homes, they had to give up their cars, they went to look for work again when they were no longer young."

There was a complete silence in the kitchen as he paused. The clock ticked, ashes fell in the stove grate, and outside in the dark a long sigh of wind went over the house.

"That's been a common story of late, Will," Sally Ballard said defensively.

"Yes, I know it has. But it meant that I've lost hundreds of hours of sleep, Sally. It's meant that I humiliated myself asking favors of luckier men who very quietly didn't grant them; it means I've worried, explained, apologized myself sick. It's years now since my mind has been easy. Every hour in the office has been an hour in hell. It's years since I've had the whole thing balanced and honest, and have been able to sleep at night!"

"You're too conscientious, Dad," Joyce suggested.

"I said all this happened a month ago," he went on, not hearing her. "It's been gathering, of course, for years; I've known it must come. I had a big home, a son in college, three house servants; I belonged to clubs—but I knew I was ruined. We've not lived within our income—within any sort of income—for years. I'm not blaming you, Sally; we're all in this together! It was private schools for the girls, college expenses for Ben, fraternity expenses—Ben's meals were paid for in three places up to day before yesterday. Not your fault, son; everyone else is doing the same thing. Someone was being married; a forty-dollar present. One of the cars crashed; we got off cheap for ninety dollars. Everyone needed a coat, shoes, a new winter outfit. That was all right —I kept feeling that I'd hit it lucky again somehow, pay up the bills, and start fresh without even letting any one of you know how thin the ice had been. Sometimes at night I'd try to warn your mother, ask her if we could cut down

But it was always the wrong time, wasn't it Sally? Lissy was having a little dinner dance; she wanted your mother and me and her sisters to get out of the house—just didn't want us there; we had to spend ten dollars somewhere else for dinner. Ben was sick and went to the Stanford Hospital—didn't come home. Dodo promised some fund a hundred, in school, and your mother told me not to ask her about it. 'She doesn't want anyone at home to know anything about it!' All she wanted, all any of you wanted from us was money.

"When Ben needed a couple of hundred to settle an accident claim," Will Ballard went on, in a silence, "he tried to borrow it from a couple of old friends of mine before he came to me. Jim Butters telephoned me. 'What's your boy want money for?' I had to laugh it off; went up and lunched with Jim, and talked kids. Then Lissy got in with young Ross—that was all right. I spoke to her about it and she said, 'For heaven's sake don't ask me any questions!' and ran upstairs. The engagement was announced without any reference to me. Later on, when things went wrong, I saw her crying one day and I asked her, 'Anything your Dad can do, Lissy?' and she said, 'Just keep out of my affairs, *please!*'

"Meanwhile the business was going on the rocks, and the bills were piling up. Lissy wanted to go to Europe, Joyce was talking Tahoe, Mommy was going as a club delegate to Washington. I asked myself——"

The speaker interrupted himself to send an innocent, troubled look about the circle.

"I asked myself what the deuce it all was, anyway! I wondered who these people were that we'd brought into the world. I realized that, whatever motives had influenced me all these years since you girls and Ben were born, they'd worked out wrong.

"And I told myself then," William Ballard went on

simply—"I told myself then that when I had had money I had been a fool not to make my life and your mother's life secure. I said to myself then, 'If ever I have it again, if ever my bills are paid and my bread and butter safe, I'll not make the same mistake again! Whatever we've done for them,' I said to myself, 'hasn't made these children happy, or sensible, self-supporting citizens. We've sacrificed everything— we've worried—we've ruined ourselves, and all we have to show for it is a few things like pianos and motorcars. The children can't wait to get out of our lives. The bills get bigger and bigger. Roberts' money, Larsen's money, MacDonald's money has all been sunk into this business that is paying for maids and beauty parlors, speeding fines and cover charges. And who's happier?' "

"And you might have added, Daddy," Mrs. Ballard's voice said lovingly and lightly—but Joyce saw how pale she was, and how she was trembling, "that that's what Daddies and Mommies have been doing for their children since time began, and they wouldn't be happy doing anything else!"

He looked at her meditatively; sighed. Presently he began to speak again.

"I can buy this place for twelve hundred dollars," he said. "I like it. The house isn't much, but there are redwoods, and there's water, and there's view—they all count. I like cows and chickens, planting a few vegetables, going into town for oil cakes and sugar. I was raised on a farm. With my creditors settled, dollar for dollar—and God bless Laura for giving me the chance!" he said under his breath, "I'll have a thousand—twelve hundred a year. That's enough for me; that's all I want. If they clear up any more than that, I'm going to settle it on your mother. She can have a trip East now and then, visit in San Francisco if she wants to.

"A week after I get poor Laura's money I'll have just about what I have from the bank now; something between twelve hundred and eighteen hundred a year. But I'll own this place, and I'll have settled up every last bill I owe in the world: dentist, doctor, creditors, stockholders. I'll sleep at night for the rest of my life, and that's something to say, at fifty-three!

"This is home for all of you as long as you want to make it home, you know that. You'll scatter, marry, but whenever you want to come back you'll be welcome here. Until you make plans I know you'll make the best of it, help your mother and me as you would complete strangers who were giving you a home and food. Perhaps that's the answer," Will Ballard finished, "perhaps parents and children are complete strangers, if they only knew it. Anyway, I'm my own master now, for the first time in twelve—fifteen years. I know where I stand! I've got what I want!"

In a dead silence he rose, picked up a lamp.

"You'll want to know about money," he said. "I'm going to give each one of you a check for one hundred and fifty dollars. If you girls owe bills at the 'City of Paris,' or if Ben has school bills, those'll all be cleared up separately, of course. You can do what you like with your money; after that, whatever you get you'll earn. I can't give you any more because I won't have it without touching the little capital that means your mother and I will never be dependent on our children. There'll be pay jobs here when the fruit is ripe.

"I don't know that everyone who's made a botch of things is given a second chance," he said. "I've been given a second chance. I hope Cousin Laura knows what it means to me!"

And then, from the doorway, he added:

"I believe I'll turn in, Mommy. I've had a long day. Goodnight, everyone!"

The Ballards looked at each other. There was a long silence.

## CHAPTER XI

AFTER a long pause Ben said cautiously, in an awed voice, "What's eating the old man?"

"He talks," Lissy said, in a bursting voice that trembled with tears, "as if he didn't love us any more!"

"Of course he loves you!" Sally Ballard said, her own voice shaken with impatience, annoyance, excitement. "It's just—it's just Dad blowing off steam," she said. "He doesn't mean any of that. It would be preposterous to take Cousin Laura's money and throw it away on a lot of people who've quite given up any hope of ever getting it back! They invested it, as he did, and they lost it the way everyone's losing it. I've seriously," she added, lowering her tone, "been wondering if Daddy's mind is—is quite what it used to be. I don't mean insanity——"

"Oh, Mother," Dodo gasped, turning white. "It couldn't be that!"

"No, I don't think it is that. Nothing serious, anyway. But I sometimes have suspected that worry and not sleeping—he was eating very badly—I really wonder sometimes if Dad is quite *right!* I think he will be—I'm *sure* he will be," Mrs. Ballard went on eagerly. "The relief from money worry and the good rest I'm going to insist on his having will take care of that! Meanwhile I think we'll all have to be very gentle with him, and bide our time."

"Meanwhile he may give all that money away, Mom!" This was Ben. "It's a hell of a note!" he muttered.

"Oh, no, he won't. He won't get it for several weeks, not until June, Treadwell said. And by that time—you know *Dad;* he'll be his reasonable generous sensible self again! He's tired tonight; he's in a mood for extremes."

"Then we have to stay here until June!" Lissy said, dismayed.

"That's only two months." Dodo had quite a resolute and philosophical tone for her, as she began to gather the dinner dishes together with an expertness that would have astonished them all, and herself not least, a few weeks ago. Ben obligingly moved salt cellar, sugar bowl, outlying knives and forks toward his sisters.

"We're to be as polite as we would be to strangers; that means more cleaning buckets and lye!" he muttered. "All right, Pop, all right. But I wouldn't do it for any stranger!"

"You might if the stranger was giving you food and a room," Joyce said neatly from the sink, where she stood with a fresh tea towel in her hand, waiting for the first hot wet glass from her mother's fingers.

"Where'd you get that bright thought?" Ben asked, looking up, displeased.

"It seems to me a perfectly obvious thought," Joyce returned. She walked to the pantry to put the hot clean glasses away. "If this is to be the dear old ancestral home," she said, "I wish Cousin Laura's legacy had run to a bathroom. My hands are getting to be something unspeakable!"

"Now, we won't talk nonsense about living here," the mother's voice said soothingly. "We won't lose our heads just because Daddy got a little excited. Tell me about Paul. Did things look too dreadful when he came? What a dear loyal boy he is!"

For the rest of the short country evening there was a conspiracy to ignore the painful subject of the disposal of Cousin Laura's legacy.

Joyce walked up to the barns in a flood of deliciously warming sunshine. April nights were bitterly cold on the hill, and she was beginning to be accustomed to wakening with the tip of her nose as cold as ice. Dressing and descending to a kitchen barely warmed by the crackling wood fire were separate ordeals, but there was blessedly warming coffee to follow, and the brisk routine of bed-making and dish-washing to get one's blood started for the day.

Then perhaps would come an hour like this one, when she had had time to brush teeth and hair, tie her shoes properly, put on a fresh cotton frock, and come out into the strengthening sunshine. Joyce was sometimes amazed to find herself ready to dance with sheer high spirits in the exhilaration of being a part of the spring world, as dew rose from the orchard grass, ice melted in the black hoof ruts of the cow yard, and the wet rank lilacs in the side garden gave forth waves of scent. There might still be frost, like delicate thread lace, on the shady sides of barns and sheds; still damp shadows lying beside the tall redwoods at the mouth of the canyon; but the sun was shining, and the year at April, and Joyce, going up with her basket for eggs, would find life amazingly sweet.

On this particular morning, in a rambling open-faced shed that was attached to the tool house, she found her father tinkering with a scrap of leather and an awl.

"Dad, what a divine morning! Everything just seems to be singing!"

He got off the little barrel upon which he had been seated, and they looked off toward the east together. The untidy paddocks and sheds of the ranch descended to a slope of prune trees; beyond rose the elms and poplars of the Paarsen homestead; then the red roofs of Nye's packing plant down near the village, and the village itself; specks of white, specks of red, plumy tops of oaks and eucalyptus threaded on the valley floor like one more bead on the long chain of little towns that stretched from Sacramento to Hollywood on the connecting ribbon of the King's Highway, "El Camino Real del Santa Cruz." The Franciscan missionaries had so named it long ago for the road of the Cross that they and all pilgrims must follow. Their patient dusty mules had first threaded the winding dirt road between sheep ranches and great stretches of flowery meadow. Now motorcars shot to and fro upon it like bees, north and south, and radiating lines of orchards and vineyards swept away from it toward the rising shoulders of the Coast Range on the east and the lower hills of the western Santa Cruz mountains upon which the ranch sprawled in the morning sunlight.

"It's pretty," William Ballard said.

"On a morning like this," Joyce conceded.

"But you think it would be pretty dismal in winter?"

The girl laughed.

"I *know* it would be pretty dismal in winter!"

"But interesting, Joycie, interesting!" he urged.

She hesitated a moment, spoke slowly when she did speak, as if finding the right words:

"I think Mother feels it would be terrible—always."

Her father looked at her sharply, pursed his lips as if for a whistle, began slowly to nod his head.

"Yep. I guess she does!"

"I mean—she really was a good sport about it, when she thought we *had* to do it, Dad!" the girl argued.

"For this last week, you mean?" he asked, with a touch of dryness.

"Well, she would have been as long as she had to be—as long as we were poor!" Joyce answered loyally.

"But now she feels differently, is that it?"

"You know Mother much better than I do," the girl said simply. "You know just how it would affect her. She feels now that we have all this money that it would be silly— it would be an affectation to live in a place like this. Nothing—nothing goes on here!"

"Funny," her father said musingly, with a certain stubborn set to his jaw that seemed to Joyce quite new in her knowledge of him; "it seems to me everything is going on here! I was thinking this morning of asking someone in the village who'd be a good man to put a fireplace in for us, and where'd be a good place for it, and for a bathroom. Then there are the chickens and the cows, and clearing things up, and the calves coming along, and the question of getting a good vegetable garden going——"

"But, Dad," the girl said affectionately, and not without a smile, "you're a gentleman; you can't plod around here like a farmhand! It really would be different if we were ber*roke,* as we thought we were. But Mother says—she and Ben were working it out—that with four or five hundred a month we can live in some place like Piedmont or Burlingame, have one good maid, see the people we like. . . .

"Not," she went on eagerly, hoping she was making an impression as he regarded her seriously and thoughtfully, the hand that was whittling a stick arrested, his gray eyes narrowed, "not that we ever would put on any airs, or get into debt again; Mother's *definite* about that! But honestly she loathes this, Dad, and Lissy and Ben—well, just naturally, there's nothing for them to *do* here! When you don't have the telephone or the radio or electric light or an electric icebox and a gas stove, there's so much work every day that by night all you've done is just get through."

He was smiling at her appreciatively.

"Did they send you out here to get around the old man?"

"No," Joyce said, laughing and flushing, "they didn't. But we've—they've been talking for several days, of course.

Mother and you are going to town tomorrow, and I suppose she thinks you may say something—decide something."

"I haven't deceived your mother about it," William Ballard said in a troubled tone, in the silence. "She knows exactly what I mean to do."

"You mean to give all that money away, Dad?" Joyce asked.

"It isn't giving it away, dear."

"Well——" She stopped, on a stubborn note. "But isn't the bank adjusting all that, Dad? I mean, don't your kerreditors expect that arrangement to go through? Won't they get it all in time?"

"They may and they may not. But, now look," he said. "Suppose we do it your mother's way. We all go up to town, look about for a place. With what we brought here and the things your mother stored with Aunt Rose we furnish that place. Good! Then the whole thing begins again. Ben costs money, Lissy wants to go abroad, you and Dodo have your expenses, your mother begins to charge again: frocks, dentist, florist, everything."

"As far as that goes, Mother says that she never would owe a bill again! She says it's a perfect slavery."

"Joyce," her father said, not looking at her, looking rather at the stick his knife was peeling away in clean shavings, "running bills isn't a matter of choice; it's a matter of character. You either do or you don't. Your mother might as well say that she wouldn't have brown eyes any more. Money means nothing to her; she's built that way; she was trained that way. She never could have a checkbook; she'd write 'em fast enough, but she kept no track of them, and she used to go into the bank and argue with the tellers when her checks came back stamped 'No funds.' In six months—in six months?" William Ballard interrupted himself to correct it, with a rueful laugh, "in six weeks she'd be started again!"

"No, Dad, not this time!" Joyce said confidently.

"Yes," he said, "this time and every time. She's the best wife in the world and the best mother, but she's made that way. No, Joyce, I was in the trap once, and I'm not going to get back into it again! If any one of you had been happy at home it would have been different, but your lives had all run away from ours, and they didn't satisfy you even then. We had no hold on you. I was ashamed, tired, restless, dissatisfied. Now I'm happy! You—you talk 'em into liking this place, little girl!" he ended persuasively.

Joyce laughed despairingly.

"They never will, Dad!" she predicted.

"Well, we'll see," William Ballard said, refusing to take alarm. "I'll go up with you for the eggs, Joycie. I want to see if I left my file up there in the harness room."

They walked toward the barns. Nothing more was said of Cousin Laura's money. The sun was high now and the grass dry. Jays were squawking in the orchard, looping the fresh green of leaves with flashes of blue.

"The country for old folks!" the man said amiably, as he drank in the richness and sweetness of the morning hour. "And young folks out in the world making their way. That's the history of the world!"

"It doesn't seem fair to Ben," Joyce persisted, in sudden daring. "Not to finish his college courses——"

He was hardly listening.

"I love the smell of a big hay barn, Joyce," he said, as if half to himself. He stood looking up at the high rafters across which chinks of sunlight filtered in long streams like haloes; a cow slumped by on her way to the meadow; a hen looked in at the wide doorway, made an undertoned discontented comment, and flew suddenly squawking up toward a haymow as if pursued by furies. Other chickens, fluffing in the deep straw of the floor, muttered sympathetically.

"Next week I'll get at this place," William Ballard said,

drinking in the homely peace of it, throwing back his graying head and breathing deep.

Joyce felt a little baffled. She said nothing more for the
moment. She felt that she hardly knew her father in this
odd, unsympathetic mood.

They were at the kitchen door now. Joyce's mother, string-
ing beans, looked up quickly and hopefully as they came
in. The girl could only await an opportunity to shrug and
faintly shake her head; she had not made much headway.

There was rather a tense silence at luncheon. During the
rest of the day, as the women of the family discussed meals,
brooms, the groceries Dodo and Ben must bring back from
the village, and the other immediate problems of their
strange new responsibility, their thoughts were only upon
the great question of whether they were to be made rich
or poor by the stroke of a pen within the next few days.

But Joyce's thoughts were destined to an abrupt change.
When Dodo and Ben came back they brought the mail, and
among the letters was a long one from Paul. She carried
its scrawled pages up to the gnarled low-spread branches
of an oak back of the barns where a short board had been
wedged in as a seat. Sitting there, her back resting comfortably against the great trunk of the old tree, the afternoon
sun shining, the grass scenting all the world with green
sweetness, cows idling home through the lowered bars,
Joyce plunged into her first love letter. Its phrases danced
like champagne in her blood; it was so smart, so witty, so
affectionate, so much more a thousand times than she
could have hoped it might be! She laughed aloud in ecstasy
as she finished it—the ridiculous printed "Pall" under a
terrible picture of a little draped coffin!—and started it over
again, and over again after that. The sense of it, the emo-
tions it gave her, stayed with her all that evening, were
with her when she dropped smiling off to sleep, and when
she awakened to the soft fogs of the morning.

## CHAPTER XII

AT ONE o'clock on the following day, when her father and mother had left for the momentous town visit, and when the simple lunch had been cleared away, Joyce found her beautiful writing paper, with its monogram and its fine blue border, and sat down in the kitchen to answer Paul's letter. She spent two hours on the fascinating job, nor did she grudge one moment of it; the afternoon was foggy, cool, and quiet; the voices of the chickens sounded oddly significant, even ominous, in the surrounding stillness of the hills. Lissy had gone into town with her parents. Dodo and Ben had been taken as far as the village, and were to be driven back by Swede Paarsen, the neighbor on the southeast, who had turned out to be friendly and helpful in a limited peasant sort of fashion. Joyce and the kitten and the sleepy superior yellow cat Toodles had the farmhouse to themselves.

"I wonder if you'd give this little fellow something to eat?"

The unexpected voice, striking across the kitchen silence, brought her heart into her throat. She looked up. A thin shabby young man was standing in the kitchen doorway, with a shivering puppy in his arms.

"I've not got anything he'll eat," he said, in a pleasant apologetic tone. "I think he needs meat, or milk, or something. He's only a month old, and he'll not touch cereals or vegetables."

Joyce was on her feet, had met dog and man halfway across the kitchen floor and had the puppy in her arms.

"Oh, poor little fellow! Are you hungry, puppy? I'll give you something to eat—there are soup bones here, and milk—shall I put some cream in it?"

"I think perhaps some hot water—he's hardly more than a baby, don't you know?"

Joyce tipped the singing kettle, set a bowl before the trembling little dog, watched his small body quiver with eagerness as he noisily nosed into the warm rich milk. When she glanced up, the man was watching her rather than the dog, a smile on his thin brown face. His shirt, his old jeans, were shabby to the point of extreme poverty, but his rather fair hair was brushed neatly back, and the expression on his face and the tones of his voice were gentle and intelligent.

"I usually go down with Swede when I need meat," he explained, as he and Joyce sat down at the kitchen table to wait for the puppy to finish his meal. "But like a fool I twisted my foot, raking, the other day, and it's made me lazy. Twice I started to walk down to ask you if you'd any milk or butter to spare, but I gave it up. And poor old Bingo paid for it!"

"Shouldn't a doctor see your foot, perhaps? My brother, playing football once——"

"Oh, no, it's quite all right now. But I've run out of provisions meanwhile."

Joyce glanced at the cupboard.

"Did you have some lunch? There's some cold pork here, and biscuits; they're not very good. My sister and I made them and they sort of sper-*read*," Joyce offered in shy eagerness.

"I'd love it," the caller said simply. Excited and pleased, Joyce brought forth the cold food and the plates; added a tall glass of cream-blotted milk; produced a small bowl containing a dubious-looking brown mixture.

"That's supposed to be chocolate custard—we made it off the gelatin box. It tastes all right, my father said, but it looks sort of der-*roopy*," she explained.

"It'll be marvelous! Real food tastes good," the man said, eating hungrily. "I've been living on cereals and vegetables."

"Have you come far?"

Joyce sat down opposite him at the table; he showed no embarrassment. Still breathing somewhat rapidly from his hasty meal, stroking the dog's head with a thin brown hand, he looked across at his hostess with hazel eyes burned almost colorless in his burned face.

"No, about two miles," he said.

"About two miles from where?"

"Shack," he said, with a jerk of his head backward toward the western hills.

"What shack?"

"There's an old shack 'way up at the top of your woodlot," he explained. "Haven't you been up there?"

"We walked up one of the canyons one night, but we didn't get very far."

"This is up close to the crest."

"But on our place?" the girl demanded, surprised.

"I imagine so. It was a lumber shack years ago."

"But do you live there?"

"Oh; kind of."

"Doing what?"

"Well—waiting for the fruit-picking to start," he said, in a pleasant, fine voice, after a moment's hesitation. "Strawberries are about ready, then cherries, and so on. They go on right to prunes and grapes."

"Is that what you do?"

"That's what I have been doing. I mean I did it last year, when Chuck Chickering was on this place. He went south when you came, and I moved up to the cabin."

"And haven't you a car?"

"A car?" He laughed. "I'm doing it on what I can make," he explained. "I walk down, about once a week, and come back with Swede."

"Swede seems to be the general delivery."

"I get on all right, except when I run out of groceries. This time I hurt my foot and couldn't get down," the man said. "You're one of the Bullards, aren't you?"

"Ballard. And what's your name?" Joyce asked, flatly.

Mike Tallant. His name was Mike Tallant. He was about thirty, Joyce thought, about Archie Ross's age. He had a nice thin face all one tawny color, skin and eyes and hair and eyebrows all brown together. He wore an old brown sweater and worn cords and heavy old brown shoes, but he was nice, just the same. Evidently, alone and temporarily lamed, he had been living on oatmeal and carrots and brown sugar, up on the ridge. Meals, he told her, were no good without grease of some sort—butter or fat or oil. Every race in the world used grease.

Joyce brought a bowl of cold gray soft bacon fat from the pantry.

"That's grease, isn't it?" she asked ingenuously. "I know it is because it stops up the sink drain. But can you use this in any way? We throw it out."

"Use it!" the newcomer said fervently. "It's quite priceless! You can fry things in it, you know, and put it into biscuits."

"We haven't really gotten started," the girl said apologetically. She had already drawn several conclusions about him; he was English and he was a Socialist; also he read Shakespeare. He would make amusing material for a letter to Paul.

Finishing his meal, he told her that he had come to America with a doctor who wanted to make vivisection experiments, forbidden in England. And then he hadn't gone home because there was nothing much to take him home. He had worked in a factory in Lawrence, but it had gotten hot and sticky and there had been too many radios and victrolas, so he had drifted west. He had meant to write a book about labor conditions, but the world was so thoroughly rotten and people everywhere either morons or corrupt, and he had given it up.

"Which daughter are you—Swede's told me about you all," he ended his story, with an abrupt and deliberate change of subject.

"Joyce."

"That's a good English name. I'd a cousin Joyce, once. We called her 'Cousin Joyce,' although she was about eighty when we were babies. And where do you come in?"

"I'm the youngest. I was named Joyce for joy, and my sister Lissy Felicity for happiness, and Dodo is 'Gift of God.' There was another sister, too, Gladys. Mother liked happy names for us."

"That's an idea." He sent her an oblique amused glance over the pipe he was lighting.

"Had you—back in England—sisters and ber-*rothers?*" the girl asked in turn.

Michael Tallant got to his feet, put his pipe in his pocket unlighted. He answered in a gentle steady tone.

"I had two brothers much older. And a sister Gill. Ronny and George didn't come back, in '15. Gill died the day her husband was killed. There was to have been a baby, and she had 'flu anyway. That was that." He was going; they were in the doorway. "If you'll let us have some milk now and then we'll be eternally grateful," he said.

"'Us?' You haven't got a wife up there in the cabin?" Joyce demanded, diverted.

"Nope." His pleasant grin—it was an expression only a gentleman could wear—flashed again in his brown face. "Never married," he said. He raised the bowl of grease like an altar censer. "Many thanks!" he said.

"And don't forget that really and truly we'd love you to use as much milk as you like. Until we get pigs, anyway!" Joyce was laughing as she went back into the house to her unfinished letter. "You do have adventures in the country," she thought. "Or at least, everything's so dull that you feel as if they were adventures. Somehow the littlest things— that nice girl in the bank yesterday, and Mrs. Paarsen bringing us duck eggs—it must be the air that makes everything seem to matter so, and time go so fast! I must write this to Paul!"

Her thoughts fluttered back happily to Paul, like doves to one cote: Paul—Paul—Paul. The shabby lean philosopher of the bowl of grease was completely forgotten before his worn tennis shoes had even reached the dairy.

When the family arrived home two days later, at sunset, it was immediately apparent that the news was bad. Sally Ballard's face was very white; Lissy came into the kitchen on a burst of nervous tears, and William Ballard, although he spoke cheerfully enough to the son and daughters assembled there, was plainly nervous.

Joyce and her father almost immediately went up to the barn for milk; she knew what had happened before he told her.

"It's all straightened out. I think your mother'll see it was wise some day, if she doesn't now."

"Oh, Dad," Joyce said, actually paling before the expected and yet freshly shocking fact, "did you give it all away?"

"I paid back all I owed!" he said cheerfully, stopping under the soft sunset sky to breathe deep, to look up at the hills and the redwoods, and the pink sky off toward the west. "Yes, Joyce, I'm free tonight—free as not one man in a hundred is free in this world. I've been in the trap, and I'm free again!"

She walked along beside him. The day had been warm, and was dying in languid beauty of scent and sound and color; birds were going to bed, faint chirps and rustlings came from the roosted chickens inside the open hen-house door. Long shadows lay across the orchard and the trampled mud of the cow yard; in a last spear of light millions of tiny gnats were spinning giddily. Joyce's cat, complaining, followed daintily to the barn.

"Then we stay here?" she asked, with an odd sinking at her heart. Oh, they were all lovely, the hills and the trees and the orchards, and it was oddly thrilling to eat eggs fresh-laid, to drink milk that had never known a bottle, but it was frightening, just the same. There was nothing to *do!*

"This is home now, Joyce. I get my deeds in a day or two. I can't wait to get the old place into shape."

"What does Mother say?"

"Oh, your mother'll come into line—your mother'll come into line," William Ballard said comfortably, taking down the milking stool. "In time she'll see that we did a wise thing. We're dodging just what makes old age sad, Joyce. When she sees that—steady, boss, steady! Swede come up and look out for 'em?" he asked, of the cows.

"Oh, yes, and always brought something. You'd think we were doing him a favor, not he doing us one. His wife sent up hot delicious fresh Swedish bread and cheese cake. Dad, shouldn't we pay him for helping, and how do you know how much?" Joyce asked, diverted for a moment from the thought of their own fortunes.

"I couldn't pay him a thing; I couldn't offer it!" her

father said quickly. "People don't do it that way, here in these country places, Joyce. We'll have to wait until her baby comes, then you girls can go down and help; something like that."

"I—see," she said slowly, her eyes absent. And later, walking back to the house, she repeated it: "I see. Things are different here. I can begin to see why older people like it, Dad. Only, for young people there isn't much to *do*, is there?"

"Oh, Lord, there's everything to do!" William Ballard sang rather than said. "There's everything to do!"

At dinner he told them the details. Sally Ballard listened with a face of sorely tried endurance. Ben's face said nothing, but Lissy frowned slightly and curled her lip.

"It seems to me that perhaps your own children have as many rights as the McDonald children or the Cutlers, Dad," she said patiently after a while.

"You have to do those things as they appear to you, Lissy," her father said. "You'll have decisions to make in your own life, some day; you'll have to make them! Nobody can help you. I could see this only one way, and I had to do it that way." He stretched out a hand. "Who made the cornbread?" he asked with interest.

"I did. Out of a book," Joyce boasted. There was a lamp in a high bracket with a reflector in the kitchen; its light was gracious on the table. Ben sat next to his mother; Lissy on her other side; William Ballard was flanked by his two younger daughters. Joyce's face was flushed and lovely in the soft glow; Dodo's brown eyes looked thoughtful and dark.

"So we don't have to house-hunt in Piedmont?" she said, dreamily. "It'll be funny, living here always. What'll we —what'll we *do?* There aren't any people we know, no movies and no riding club."

"For one thing, I think we ought to have dinner in the

dining room," Joyce said with animation. "Just because we're doing our own work is no reason why we should go native."

"There's no way of warming that icebox now," Lissy said with a shudder.

"When I think of people like McDonald and Roberts and Harry Cutler calmly walking off with those checks," Sally Ballard burst out suddenly, with a nervous trembling of the lips, "it makes me almost ill! I cannot understand you, Will —I'll never be able to! Your own children—your own flesh and blood———"

She stopped short, under strong pressure. There was a silence.

"Having dinner in the dining room doesn't seem to me a life work," Ben said then, on a drawl, and everyone laughed.

"Frightful amount of work," Lissy contributed. "Carrying stuff in and out, and brushing up crumbs."

"All that can wait until we get some sort of a maid," Mrs. Ballard, who never could hold resentment or indeed any one idea on any subject long, said impatiently. "We shall just have to camp here like savages until Daddy knows exactly what we have!"

"I think I'm joining Nelson and driving down to Hollywood; he's going to get into things there," Ben observed. His father raised interested eyebrows.

"Is that so?" he asked. "Nelson got anything definite?"

"Kind of. I know it seems crazy to you, but we'll get away with it," Ben said.

"It doesn't seem crazy at all," his father answered cordially.

"Boys can do that sort of thing, go to the 'Brown Derby,' and meet everyone," Lissy said, enviously.

"Oh, Mother, I had an adventure the day you left!" This was Joyce. "A man—he looked more like a wolf—is living in the shed 'way up back of the canyon. Remember we saw a sort of ber-*rown* shed on the hills there, Dad?" Joyce broke off to ask interestedly, bringing both parents by this simple device into the conversation. "He's an Englishman, and he lives up there; he came down to borrow some food for his dog, and he was starving himself, so I gave him some lunch here in the kitchen—pork chops and cake and milk—and he was ravenous!"

"How d'ye mean he's living up there?" William Ballard split open a cube of yellow cornbread, passed his cup for more tea. "What's he doing, squatting?"

"A tramp! Where was Ben?" Sally Ballard ejaculated. "He might have murdered you!"

"Oh, no, he's not that sort. He looks like a gentleman fruit picker."

"Oh, I know who he is," her father said. "Swede spoke to me about him. He said this feller—big tall man, isn't he? —Swede gestured up over my head, anyway—he said he'd help with the cherries next week. He'll probably come down and talk to me about it."

"But what's he doing in one of our cabins?" Sally demanded. "I call that pretty cool!"

"I don't believe that cabin's on our place, Mommy. It's a good way south, on the ridge. I'll walk up there in a day or two and see him."

"Well, whoever's place he's on he's not paying any rent!"

"That may be county property, you know. I doubt if it's on the map. It's all pretty wild back there."

"Where'd you see a map, Dad?"

"Buying this place. I paid the whole thing down yesterday, but there are taxes to catch up. Four or five hundred dollars."

"So we own it? What'd you have to pay for it, Dad?"

"Thirteen hundred for the four hundred acres."

"Gosh, less than you'd pay for a car!" Ben said.

"Less than I ever paid for any car."

"We seem always to be talking about what things cost," Dodo murmured. "We never used to!"

"No, and I don't like it," Sally said decisively. "It's an American fault—materialism. As a people we're completely mercenary; everyone knows it!"

This rush of comment was respectfully received; Sally Ballard had spent a year abroad as a girl, and her firm conviction that all Europeans of any culture whatsoever despised all Americans as money-grubbing and mercenary was never disputed in the family circle.

"Funny to own a ranch and chickens and cows," Joyce mused. "It gives you a funny feeling under your feet. Firmness."

"We owned 'Ninety-nine,' " her mother reminded her sharply.

"I never thought of cherries as coming so *thick*," Dodo said. "You can go out there and stand under the tree and just *stuff*, and yet you see masses of them 'way up above you, like the cherries on Lissy's French hat—shiny and red —and you can't even tell where you've been picking!"

"What do people do when they have too many, Dad? I mean, Swede's got cherries, and over at Cooleys' they have ter-*remendous* lots of cherries."

"Sell 'em! What did you think farmers did?" William Ballard said with a nervous chuckle and a placating glance at his wife. "I'm going to pay six dollars a year to belong to the Farmers' Institute. They send a truck to the gate every morning, and whatever I've got—cream or eggs or fruit— they pick up. At the end of the month I get my check."

"They getting a pretty swell rake-off," Ben observed.

"Two per cent."

"Why, Dad, I never knew that!" Joyce said. "Why don't we give them our extra milk? Mike—this man I was talking about—says it's gold!"

"I'm just joining the Institute, Joycie. We've not—why, we've not begun to tap the possibilities of this place yet!" her father said. "A ranch like this might easily be self-supporting."

"Yes; but, Dad, what happens when everyone has too much milk, and they can't sell it?"

"Ah—well, there," he said, "you touch upon the great economic problem."

"Don't tell me, I had two years of it in coll.!" Ben scoffed. "You can study it for years and not get anywhere!"

"It seems to me we've gotten somewhere just with this talk," Joyce said with spirit.

"Good girl, Joycie!" her father said approvingly. Sally said nothing. She compressed her lips, shrugged; her breast rose and fell on a long sigh.

Later she said to her youngest daughter, in a somewhat grudging tone: "You're taking all this beautifully, Joyce, and your father and I appreciate it. But nothing will ever make me feel that it's the right solution for Ben or for Dodo. Dodo ought to be coming out this winter, poor child!"

"Ben seems happy enough now," Joyce observed. "And maybe if he goes south with Nelson he'll get work in the movies."

And for a brief interval there was domestic peace on the ranch.

## CHAPTER XIII

THE Ballards were getting settled and, while that activity lasted, found time flying too fast for introspection or blues. Every inch of the house had to be washed, every room aired, every bit of paint renewed; fresh curtains had to go up; a load of handsome furniture came down from storage in the city. Bits of fine china embellished the rather bare hopeless dining room; a blue-flame kerosene stove was placed in the kitchen.

The days grew hot; the sun rose at five, and by breakfast time the world was dazzling with dry shadows. Joyce's cat produced a litter of coal-black kittens; two calves were born and sold to the butcher; cherries were gone, and blackberries and apricots in full glory.

In the dooryard a rubbish fire fumed and blazed and died down to ashes. Joyce, Dodo, Ben would emerge from the house with arms filled, dump the papers, the old carpets, the rags on the fire, stand panting for a moment's breath, their faces scarlet, their hair plastered to their fine brown skins, their hands filthy. Feeding the cat, feeding the kittens, feeding the stock, gathering lettuce and early tomatoes, digging new potatoes, getting meals in the kitchen, they were working hard from morning until night, and for a while they all rather enjoyed it in spite of themselves.

A plumber came up from the village and installed a bath in the room off the kitchen where the girls had spent their first night on the ranch. Sally studied the rusty dirty tub that lay waiting in the yard.

"Will, that's a frightful-looking tub."

"I only paid seven dollars for it," her husband said.

"Seven——! It's not second-hand!"

"Why not?" he said. "Volkmann, the plumber, had it for sale."

"Will, you're not letting them put in a second-hand tub! Imagine who may have used it! Don't think for one instant I'll ever step into a tub like that!" Sally exclaimed, outraged.

"I'm going to give it two coats of enamel, Sally; you won't know it! Why, listen," Will Ballard argued good-naturedly, "you've used second-hand tubs before—yes, and second-hand blankets, too. Every time you go to a hotel you use blankets and towels someone else has used; every time you eat in a restaurant——"

"I shall think of some dreadful family using it every time I do," Sally said. But she could not but rejoice with the others when the bathroom was complete, and the hot water running clear and swift into the snowy white tub. The room would never look like a real bathroom; it was too big, and it was not the right shape, but it was an undeniable comfort to all the women to get in there, with fresh towels and scented soap, and wash away all the smells of dust and ashes and wood fires and grease and sour milk and peeled onions that so hung about them in these days.

"I shall get off of this place the first second I can," Sally told her daughters. "Daddy knows that. In the meanwhile I suppose we had all better make the best of it!"

In this spirit she directed them all. They had to respect

Mother's knowledge of all sorts of strange things: that cornstarch thickened, and soda lye took off smoke stains from pots, and a little ammonia in the water worked magic with the dish towels. After all, in her early married life she had known all this. It came back to her by degrees, and made her children feel that she was amazingly wise.

"Mix cornbread dry," she told Joyce, for whom baking experiments had great charm. "Put your popovers into a hot oven, and don't look at them for half an hour. Pinch those baking potatoes ten minutes before they're done, Lissy; roll them round gently on that towel, and they'll be white and mealy. Don't worry about the fat on that, Dodo, it'll all form a crust at the bottom of the aspic and you can scrape it off."

Joyce helped her father in the yards and barn. They were in great sympathy that her mother made easier by saying generously: "The others all feel terribly hurt at Daddy, dear, so you be nice to him!"

They raked down hay, hunted eggs, whitewashed the chicken-yard inside and out, spread apricots on wooden trays to dry. With this last job Ben helped Joyce and her father and Mike Tallant, the young Ballards growing quite hysterical with excitement over the hot odorous fruit. Mike was pretty regularly employed on the ranch now, and Joyce had heard him at the farmer's telephone ordering feed from the village, and identifying himself as "Ballards' hired man."

On the day they split and spread the apricots Joyce was in wild spirits and would have laughed at anything. Paul was going to stay overnight, which meant games and fun at the table, and a thrilling walk in the moonlight afterward, and the next day she was to drive to Burlingame with him for a Friday-to-Monday visit with his father and stepmother. It was too much bliss!

When Paul was there she was in a mood of gayety and excitement that infected all the others, too. Everyone felt the contagion of her happiness; everyone was only too willing to feel it. It *was* gratifying to have the big handsome boy with his chatter of Burlingame and of Princeton, his leisurely wider outlook on pleasure and travel and plays and sports, busying himself vigorously in their kitchen, pounding crumbs or peeling potatoes, talking all the time.

Even in the old days that seemed already so far in the past, the unthinking idle days in "Ninety-nine," Mrs. Ballard would have been extremely well pleased with this new friendship of Joyce's. Paul's social connections were very important. Archie Ross had had undoubted social position, too, but he had been no such charming person as Paul. There had always been just a hint of conservatism, of the niggard, in Archie; Paul was the most amusingly reckless spendthrift, the most generous-hearted of eager boys!

Paul was to sleep on his first night at the farmhouse in the boxlike upstairs bedroom that had recently been equipped for Lissy, and Lissy was to have a cot in her sisters' room. Lissy preferred any sort of room of her own to sharing with her sisters. Of the four bedrooms that were squarely set on the upper floor, without imagination or variation, this was perhaps the least desirable, but it had been cleaned, and the curtains were fresh, and the bed comfortable. The other rooms were the front and largest chamber, where the senior Ballards slept, the room back of it for the two younger girls, and the fourth corner room, just a shade larger than Lissy's, where Ben was established. All four rooms opened upon a small square hall from which the steep slant of the straight stairway descended to the narrow lower hall. It was all hopelessly uninteresting and ugly.

However, all this only made fun for Paul, and he rioted over it with his usual wild bursts of laughter and in his usual high spirits.

"One bathroom! We'll all be meeting on the stairs in our pajamas and having piles of fun!" Paul predicted. "I'll tell you what: I'll sing all the time I'm in the bathroom except when I'm brushing my teeth; I can't sing very well with my mouth full of suds!"

"You can't sing very well anyway, Paul," Joyce told him, and they both laughed.

Dinner was in the dining room tonight, and the four women changed their clothes for the event for the first time since they had moved to La Perdita. Lissy looked lovely in the lamplight, in her blue frock; Dodo lovely in white. Joyce had enhanced her rich young beauty with a yellow frock. She had to save her smartest and freshest things for the Burlingame visit, but this old gown had always been becoming, and was becoming still. Four green candlesticks, purchased at what Thelma Volkmann, down in the village, called simply the "Dime," were set on the table, with four green candles burning in them. A certain beauty and grace that the kitchen meals had somehow lacked made pleasant this meal, to which father, mother, guest, son, and three daughters sat down.

The biscuits Paul had so carelessly tossed together from a cook-book recipe had come out splendidly. The broilers Ben and Mike had killed and plucked and cleaned a few days before were melting with rich tenderness. There was an apricot shortcake upon which the brown cream fell in thick clots from the blue pitcher. Everyone was hungry and happy; Sally was loyal mother and wife enough to suit her mood to the others' moods; her mind was on wedding plans for her youngest. Rose Meredith would lend the Pine Street house for the occasion—it had big parlors; or possibly they might get the Trevor place on the Stanford campus; that would be exquisite for an autumn wedding. . . .

After supper and a riot of dish-washing, everyone took turns at the bathroom washstand; the door was left open, the towels passed from hand to hand. Joyce quite frankly ran a wet comb through her hair while carrying on a general conversation. Presently everyone else had seemed to melt away from the scene, and she and Paul could walk through an orderly kitchen and step out into the white world of the risen moon.

The night was chilly. The family had gathered about the air-tight stove in the parlor. "Let's not be so consummately affected as ever to call this box with the horsehair furniture anything but the parlor!" Sally Ballard had exclaimed some days before with a sort of exasperated humor. "If ever a room was a parlor, this is!"

But Joyce had Paul's big soft coat belted about her, and she was not cold. They walked across the transfigured yard. Every leaf was tipped with silver; the barns and sheds and fences were made magical in white light and velvet black shadows.

"It's everywhere!" Joyce said, in a hushed voice. "There's so much of it! Down there on the oaks, and on the village, and on the fields. How wonderful fields are in moonlight!"

"Where'd Mike disappear to?" Paul asked, one hand bracing her elbow in the way women love, as he guided her across the yard.

"Oh, he never dines with us! He lives up there on the ridge, and he always goes home to dinner. Sometimes he takes cake, or a slice of ham, but he always goes home."

"Is he in love with my girl?"

"In love with me!" She laughed. "Girls don't seem to mean anything to him," she said. "But if he were, you wouldn't be jealous of a hired man?"

She used the phrase as Mike himself had used it at the telephone a few days earlier. But instantly she regretted it: it didn't seem fair to Mike.

"He's not like most of 'em; at least I imagine he's not," Paul said. "But I'd be jealous of anyone who liked you! That's the worst of your living down here—Lissy and

Dodo'll marry hicks, you'll see! Listen, there's something I want to tell you——"

They were at the bars, looking down at the moon-washed world of the valley, the furry tops of the oaks, the solemn shafts of the tall redwoods. Nearer, close to the fence on the other side, Joyce saw something stir: a man's shadow down on the dry grass; a man with a pipe got to his feet, was facing them. Mike!

Instantly her senses were in complete confusion. He had been right there, within a few inches of them while they talked; he had heard everything they said.

"Hello, Mike, didn't see you!" Paul said. And she knew from his tone that he was as completely embarrassed as she was.

"I'm sorry," said the pleasant crisp British accents. "I was hoping you'd move along and not see me! I often hang around here a bit, and see that the cows are fed, and to-night I told your father that I'd go up to the dairy with him after supper. I'm really sorry——"

"Nothing to be sorry about!" Joyce interrupted the somewhat halting sentences gallantly. "Only you've not had any supper."

"Oh, that!" he said carelessly. "I shall have something to eat when I get home."

They were all walking back toward the kitchen door now; before they reached it William Ballard's substantial figure suddenly blocked it, and he called, "Mike!"

"Here you are, sir!" Mike answered, joining him. Paul and Joyce walked away into the moonlight again. Joyce was in a state of youthful agitation not unmixed with rueful laughter.

"Oh, wasn't that awful! Oh, Paul, what did we say? What did he hear? I said—he wasn't ther-*ree* feet away, he couldn't miss it! What on earth did I say? That I wouldn't marry—no, that you oughtn't to be jealous of a hired man!

I did say 'hired man,' Paul. Oh, I could die! He's so *nice*. He's so terribly kind. How'll I ever look him in the face again!"

"What of it?" Paul asked. Back at the fence again now, he had his arm about her, and her head was on his shoulder. "It was all true enough, and if a man takes a job like this he ought to be sensible about it," Paul argued.

"Yes, you're quite right, except that it sounded so *cheap!*"

"Oh, well, you should worry about him!" Paul said. "No one knows anything about him. He's probably been married three times!" They began to talk of themselves.

## ❧ CHAPTER XIV ❧

SHE stepped down from the train at Gilroy late in the languid hot June afternoon a week later, her linen suit crumpled, her face flushed and dirty from the heated cars, her dark hair pressed in damp rings on her forehead.

"Oh, Ben, you were a darling to meet me!" she exclaimed joyfully, scrambling to the seat beside her brother, who had drawn the car up to the station platform. "Oh, how lovely it is to get back, and how lovely everything looks! Ben, has it been boiling? It was foggy in the city, but it's been getting hotter and hotter, and San José was simply fer-*rying*—everyone looked wilted!"

"Have a good time?" Ben said, not unappreciative of the charms of this eager sister in her tumbled white, with her brown eyes glowing in a rather pale face.

"Oh, good time!" Words failed Joyce. "You'll hear about it until you're sick of it," she recommenced. "There never was such a good time in the world!"

The day had been burning hot; it was six o'clock now. Already the sun had gone down behind the western hills, and in the clear shadowless light the burned world was cooling. The village might swelter all night, and the village boys and girls spin away to the mountains and the beaches, but as the shabby Ballard car took the hill road the air was already freshened; there was a good sharp smell of heavy dew on dried grass and tarweed and yarrow, and a promise of evening chill.

"Figs ripe," Ben said.

"*Our* figs?"

"Yep, Swede says they're early. And the peach tree you propped up is just loaded!"

Sweet restful airs fanned her hot face; the infinite peace of the hills enveloped the nerves that had been tensed and jangled by too much noise, too much amusement, too much happiness.

"Dad gave Mike the kicking heifer."

"He didn't!"

"Oh, yes, he did. He was going to pay Mike for June, and Mike asked him what he intended to do with the kicking heifer. Dad said he was going to try to sell her for a milker; he didn't want five cows on the place; there's no market for milk this time of year, everyone's cows are in, and Mike said he'd like her! He's going to lead her up to his place to-night."

"He's crazy!" Joyce said, with an affectionate laugh.

"And if I don't sound like the prize hick," Ben drawled. His sister's joyous laugh broke out again.

She burst into the supper-time kitchen like a breeze, kissing, embracing everyone in turn, noting rather tardily that Mike Tallant was dining with them.

"Oh, Mother, it's baking here! We ought to have supper out in the yard a night like this. Dad, darling, am I glad to get back! Hello, Mike, I didn't see you. Dodo, darling, if you knew what a good time I've had!"

It bubbled from her all through the meal. It had been the happiest six days any girl of twenty had ever known. Everyone, everyone had been simply marvelous, and the *fun,* and the way they had laughed.

"And then, Mother, I was all packed up to go, and this Alice Goldthwaite who was staying there—we roomed together, and she is just a darling!—Alice had gone down to tell Paul I was ready, and then his mother—his stepmother, you know, but she's simply adorable, and crazy about his father. He says his father and mother got on each other's nerves terribly, so why stick together if you're completely wretched?—his stepmother came in and said, 'Joyce, this is Monday and Paul's going Thursday, why don't you stay and see him off with the rest of us? I'll wire your father.' Oh, she was simply wonderful! So I knew you wouldn't mind . . .''

It was all jumbled together; she couldn't keep the pattern straight, but it all had been bright. "So we all got into the car—it was nearly eleven, but nobody paid any attention to time—no, that was the night we had theatricals, and we simply laughed ourselves sick—I mean we were lying on the floor ker-*rying,* we were laughing so hard, and every time poor Alice would start to speak, she'd sort of whine, and then somebody else would say, 'As the sailor said to the girl,' and we'd be off again!

"The first time we all went into town Alice Goldthwaite and I changed outfits, and mine was so becoming to her she asked to keep it, and, Mother, hers is from Blainstyne, designed for her by Odna, and dated and ev-verything, wait until you see it——

"And in the mornings we'd all loiter over to the club and watch the golf, or else sit on the porch. We rode before breakfast nearly every morning——

"Oh, and it's so good to get home, and be telling you all about it," every section of the narrative ended. "I mean— nothing went wrong. They thought I was funny—I mean Alice laughed at ev-verything I said—oh, and I won the pool at the club, twenty-five dollars! I sent Mrs. von Schwerin some roses, Mother; was that right?"

Dodo's eyes glowed with joy as she listened; Lissy gave the narrative but grudging attention.

"After all, Mrs. von Schwerin was his secretary," Lissy said, as her only comment. "It's amazing to me that they'll accept her at all. I know they didn't for *months.*"

But even this could not damp Joyce's excitement, and Lissy softened when she had had a talk alone with her sister. Lissy and her parents and Mike Tallant played bridge after dinner. This it seemed was almost a nightly custom now. The two younger girls, with Ben's somewhat erratic help, finished the kitchen. It was when they were all going to bed that Joyce had her first opportunity to tell Lissy an important bit of news.

She went into Lissy's room, sat on the foot of the bed at Lissy's feet. The older sister was comfortably established against her pillows; a lamp on the bedside table shone on the white quilt and the blue comforter. Lissy liked things nice.

"Liss, I saw Archie Ross," Joyce began. Her sister's eyes came to hers instantly and were riveted there.

"Home again?" Lissy asked, trying for a natural tone. She had colored deeply, painfully, but she was not being proud, Joyce noticed with relief, she was not repelling confidences. Instead there was an odd look in her eyes, a look not quite hungry, not quite wistful, not quite broken, but somehow suggesting all these; a look that made Joyce's heart ache with sudden fierce loyalty and pity. How helpless a fine, proud, lonely girl was, when a man chose to be cruel to her!

"Let me tell you about it, Liss. It was at the country club on Sunday," Joyce began her narrative briskly. She talked for twenty minutes with no interruption from her sister. Archie, she reported, had been placating and friendly and simple; "he seemed sorry," Joyce said. He had remembered Dodo's impacted tooth and Mother's twisted ankle; he had asked—getting as red as a beet—for Felicity.

"He wants—the next time you go into town—to have you telephone him, Liss," Joyce finished.

"I'll see him," Lissy said suddenly. "I've wanted to have one talk with him for my own self-respect. And perhaps—perhaps I'll tell him what I think of him!"

"He's handsome," Joyce contributed, irrelevantly. "He looked awfully slim and well in white flannels, with a dark blue coat. Paul," she added instantly, "is simply stunning in dinner clothes. He wore a white mess jacket with ber-*lack* ter-*rousers*,—simply stunning!"

Another silence. Both girls' thoughts were far away. After a while Lissy said: "I'm glad you told me this. I'll never like Archie again—not that it matters!—but I'm glad he has the decency to feel that he has to see me himself, not write me."

But somehow Joyce suspected that Lissy felt a little happier about it than she would admit. She fancied that in the next day or two she noticed a real change for the better in Lissy's mood.

The days went by, cloudless summer days burning hot and dry over the valley and the mountain ranches, days that ripened peaches, pears, apples, prunes. The world began to smell deliciously of ripening fruit. Trucks laden with fragrant globes of color went up and down the road; Nye's packing plant was working overtime now; the village smelled of sweet tomatoes. On the Ballard place the grapes were no longer hard green buttons, but were putting on tint and shape, size and transparency: black Isabellas, long finger grapes, firm fleshy red-pink Malagas, seedless Tomsoms, yellow-brown enormous muscats with the finest flavor of all, and with soft little raisins hidden in every cluster.

A day or two after her return from the memorable Burlingame visit, Joyce had seized an opportunity to speak

to Mike Tallant in an aside. It was when he had asked her
to go up with him to one of the unused sheds to "see something."

Walking beside him, through the still hot glowing morning, up past the chicken yard, where panting fowls had been
fluffing in the dust and the water trough dripped under the
windmill, Joyce had found the something to be a long narrow table, half buried in broken farm machinery, old ladders, ropes, and all the other rubbish that had accumulated
here as everywhere else on the place.

"You were saying the other night it would be nice to eat
in the yard?" Mike suggested.

"Oh, Michael! It's *perfect!*" the girl exclaimed. Her eyes
danced with one of those inspirations that any new line of
thought seemed to bring to her. "Oh, I'll tell you," she
rushed on eagerly. "Let's wait until tomorrow, when Mother
and Dad have to go up and sign those last things, and then
move it down, and put the candles on it, and have supper
outside! And we can have lunch outside, too, and keep the
kitchen cool——"

And then quite suddenly, with lowered eyelashes and in
a little confusion she added, "Listen, Michael. There was
something I wanted to say to you; it's been on my mind
since the night before Paul and I went away. I feel terribly
about that—that dumb thing I said—out by the fence, you
know—that night?"

His hazel eyes in his brown face had been looking at her
honestly.

"I suppose I ought to say that I didn't hear you," he said.
"But as a matter of fact, I did. The first thing I heard let
me into it so," he confessed, coloring and laughing, "that I
thought—if I thought at all—that I'd much better sit still
and let you wander away. But you didn't wander away,
damn it!"

They laughed together, and Joyce colored in her turn.

"I don't mind your hearing the stupid thing I said," she began bravely. "But it was my calling you the—calling you —I mean I never think of you as———"

" 'The hired man'?" he supplied with a grin, as she floundered.

"But you see, this was ter-*ruly* it," Joyce hastened to say, her cheeks red. "You'd called yourself that at the telephone the day before. You were ordering feed, and you called yourself that, and I stupidly—*dumbly*———"

"Why, it was nothing!" he said. "My only embarrassment was that I'd been listening."

They walked toward the house. It was almost noon; the sun was directly overhead, and the shadows shriveled. Heat waves, far across the valley floor, rose from wheat fields in dazzling lines of light.

"You were in great spirits that night," the man commented dryly.

"I'm terribly happy," Joyce told him simply.

"So I gather. Why, Joyce," Michael Tallant said, "you oughtn't worry about what I think, or anyone thinks. You're nineteen and you're in love. What else is there?"

"Michael," she said suddenly. Since the bridge-playing had become an almost nightly custom and the lodestar of Mrs. Ballard's dull days, they had all come to calling him "Michael." "You've been married?" Joyce asked.

"What makes you think so?" he asked, with an amused side glance.

"We were wondering."

"No, I've never been married," he said, with a laugh. "I've had very bad luck with the girls. Or maybe it's good luck."

"It's bad luck," Joyce decreed.

"Well, we'll let you have the say on that, at least! No," he added, ruminatingly, "I don't know quite how it's all come about. I should have married, of course. My people died when I was quite a kid, my grandmother brought me up, and picked a wife out for me, too. But somehow, as you said of the butter the other day, it didn't 'take.' I think the girl was a gypsy, that's my honest impression—wild sort of girl!"

Joyce's joyful laughter broke forth.

"A gypsy! But your grandmother wouldn't want you to marry a gypsy!"

"I give you my word she looked like one."

Her mirthful eyes moved to his sidewise; she was not quite sure he was serious.

"I don't believe it, but I don't see why you should make it up," she said, doubtfully.

"I don't think your grandmother should ever pick out your husband or wife," he pursued it. "But at the same time aren't you rather young to be picking out for yourself? You'll be the first married, won't you?"

His direct look and question almost took her breath away. She hadn't thought quite that far.

"Lissy was engaged, but everything went wer-*rong*," Joyce told him. "The man was one of the Rosses; they're Scotch descent. He's really very nice, and clever, too, in a narrow sort of way. But, I don't know, he had to go to Scotland, and the marriage was postponed. They say it's unlucky."

"So you'll be the first."

"Well, we have no *definite* plans. Paul has to finish law college—then he'll go in with his father's firm—he has to wait until he's ther-*rew*," the girl said, happily fluttered.

"I so much like the way you split those words of yours!"

"I do? How do you mean sper-*lit* words?"

"And yet nineteen's awfully young," Michael Tallant said.

"Twenty."

"Twenty, then."

"I feel ter-*remen*dously old," Joyce assured him with a grave look. "It seems years ago that I used to fool around with Margaret O'Shea and Eileen Pierce—those were my friends. We used to talk and go to movies, and sometimes we'd make a resolution to walk or to give up candy; we just wasted our time. And then Paul came along," she added simply, for somehow it was easy to talk to Michael, or easy to talk to him today, at any rate, "and *that* made me feel older—ever so much older, and then Lissy's engagement, and breaking her engagement came—we'd ordered our bridesmaids' dresses, too, and the wedding dress and everything, and that was like ger-*row*ing up ten years overnight. And then the bad times changed everything, and Dad was worried, and we came down here, and since *then*," Joyce finished, with pleasant childish emphasis, "you can't think how old I feel! I really feel like a woman, cooking, and deciding things, and hearing Mother and Dad talk——"

"And holding them all together," Michael added pleasantly, as she paused. "I don't know what they'll do without you!"

His praise warmed her heart; she loved to be praised, even if it was only by Mike. Joyce, going her way to the kitchen, tying on an apron, plunging whole-heartedly into the problem of lunch, wondered with a pleasant little thrill in her soul if she was really becoming a lovely person, one of those wise, good, self-sacrificing women whose whole circle adored them. If so, the way was extremely simple; one only had to do graciously and perfectly the things that had to be done anyway.

"Cold ham," Mrs. Ballard said, coming into the room. "I'm so tired of it. I wonder if we will ever finish that ham!"

"Mother, would you let me poach you an egg? Honestly, it wouldn't take me a minute," Joyce said. Her mother put an arm about her.

"You are getting to be the greatest comfort to me, Joycie," her mother said. It was all beginning to be like a game to Joyce.

"Where's my girl!" her father would call, as he started off on some farm round that promised to be interesting. Joyce felt her soul expanding; she grew all the busier, the more obliging and sunshiny and capable, under their praise. It was like playing a part, this impersonation of the youngest daughter of the transplanted bewildered city family, laughing over all the strange new duties and discoveries, equal to everything, making a joke of everything.

## ❧ CHAPTER XV ❧

LETTERS, telegrams, little presents from Paul arrived almost daily; he wrote as he talked, joyously, irrelevantly, cleverly. Joyce could not but believe that he was thinking of her all the time, referring everything that happened to her, missing her as much as she missed him. Missing her more, he assured her. "Because gosh, you have all the others!" he wrote.

It was hot in Connecticut, with a wet sticky heat that wilted him. He did not like the man with whom he was coaching; no matter, it would be all right as soon as school opened. Only it was deadly dull now, and he could not help thinking of the fun they could have had down on the ranch. He would have liked to be with her and her father the day they cleaned out the sheds. He would like to see the table out in the yard where they were having almost all their meals in these hot midsummer days.

Joyce wrote him regularly. She loved to find herself, in the early afternoon, tubbed and dressed in a fresh cotton frock, when luncheon was out of the way and dinner still in the distance, and she had blessedly, miraculously, nothing to do. The sense of earned leisure was exquisite after the hot hurried morning hours; three times a week she employed it to write to Paul. Evenings were no good for letters. She was always tired then; they all were, and when the mountain cold shut down and her bedroom was chilly, she usually contented herself with a dreamy half-hour of huddling by the parlor stove, watching the bridge game, or playing a few games of solitaire before hurrying through cold halls upstairs to bed, snuggling down in the warm blankets after only one look at the starlit, moon-washed night that spread away across the valley beneath her window.

Ben had gone away now to try his luck in Hollywood. Joyce's father was up at five every morning, and off for a round of the barns, and to milk the cows. She set her alarm for half-past six, and was the first of the four women to go noiselessly downstairs and start the long day by building the kitchen fire. It was a simple enough process once one understood the old stove: first a vigorous shaking of the ash sifter, then crumpled paper cautiously put in through the open top that was always ready to smooth her arm with fine wood ashes, then kindling and split short logs, and a dash of kerosene. In six minutes the kettle would be boiling madly, and the center plates a clear glowing red.

The kitchen lay northwest and was cold in the early mornings, but before the milk was skimmed, the table set, the long loaf of French bread cut, it would be warm, and Joyce warm, too, as she stepped out into the yard to face the full glory of the rising sun, far off across the transparent opal silhouette of the Coast Range.

Dew everywhere still, but rising fast; the cows trailing up to the redwoods again, larks crying, chickens eyeing the kitchen door hopefully, and long rays of sunlight blasting through the wet oak leaves. Apples were ripe now, incredibly picturesque in red and yellow among the dusty thick leaves, and prunes were beginning to fall in rich purple sweetness to the earth. Joyce had never known until this year that prunes were never picked from trees; now she felt that she always had known that, and when she saw the purple carpet down in the valley—two full weeks ahead of the mountain prunes—already her one thought was: "No market for prunes this year! Isn't it a shame! So many of the farmers counting on the crop!"

Breakfast was always a pleasant meal, for everyone was rested and everyone hungry. The country-cured bacon that Swede sold them was better than any they had ever known at "Ninety-nine"; the eggs were milky fresh. Joyce's experiments in breakfast breads were supplemented by the sour crisp delicious French bread that Madame Covillaud made down in the village, and that whoever shopped for the Ballards picked up three times a week.

Usually Dodo and Joyce went down to market at about ten; sometimes their father went with them, occasionally their mother. They took penciled lists that often began hopefully with "Sweetbreads? Tongue? Brains?" But sweetbreads, tongue, and brains had no value in the local market, and even by driving to Morgan Hill they were not sure of them. They could always get beef and mutton, pork chops and sausage meat. Mrs. Ballard, planning the meals, rang the changes on these over and over again.

The girls stopped at Frenchy's for the bread, loitered into the always-fascinating "Dime" to get pencils or paper napkins, blue candles or a new can opener, chatted with pretty Thelma Volkmann in the bank or Marie-Thérèse Sallock in the post office. The handsome big Labaree boy, who was so delighted with his own charms, might come out of the real estate office to talk to Dodo and Joyce before they started their car; the Bowdish boy once asked Dodo to a high-school dance, but Dodo had been on her way to San Francisco to visit Helen Hill, and providentially could excuse herself.

Throwing all their purchases into the back seat, the girls would start up the hill again. It would be almost twelve o'clock now, and very hot. In the back seat there was always a fifty-pound block of ice, wrapped loosely in a "gunnysack." When they finally drove past the little pool of shade under the big redwoods at the turn, and came up under the home-stead oaks, Michael usually came forward and took charge of it. It went down into the springhouse cellar, which was the coolest place on the ranch anyway, and lay on the floor there, with pans of milk and jars of meat set about it. In ordinary weather the dairy was cool enough for the milk, and the meat was placed in the "safe," a wire-gauze box swung on ropes from a tree in the shade where the best breeze was, but for a few burning midsummer months there must be ice.

When they got home from marketing and carried their packages into the house, Joyce and Dodo were usually breathless, exhausted, and in a condition of heat almost in-sufferable. Their foreheads would be wet, their hair plastered against their temples, their faces scarlet. But that did not mean that lunch could be slighted. Again the bowls of cold cauliflower and stewed blackberries must come out of the pantry, and while Dodo chipped ice for the coffee, Joyce began the business of ash-shaking and of putting paper, kindling, short madrone and oak logs into the stove again. Meat cakes, fried potatoes lyonnaise, tomatoes and lettuce, fresh bread, coffee, blackberry shortcake—that would be plenty!

Sometimes Lissy set the outdoor table; usually Dodo did. Joyce would make her lunch of crackers and creamy milk, or iced tea slowly sipped and accompanied by a plate of salad. But the men were always hungry; Mike and her father could always eat, heat or no heat.

When the last plate was put away, and the hot orderly kitchen darkened, with lettuce in a pan of ice water chilling for supper, the woodbox filled, the scraps put into the covered chicken pail, then it was luxury to take a warm soapy bath, to make oneself fresh and clean, to select a book and wander off toward the canyons to find a shady spot under the redwoods and dream and rest and gossip for an idle hour—two hours. Dodo and Joyce never tired of their leisure. They could pity the men, still toiling in the hot dry orchard. They could look far down at the hot village and pity everyone who had to stay in the valley.

Whole families moved up into the orchards to pick the Ballards' and the Paarsens' and the Cooleys' prunes. Brown lean ungroomed families who perfectly illustrated Nature's rule of protective coloring, Joyce called them. Screw-faced little colorless children were rapping prunes into tin pails all day long; haggard women in dirty calicoes cooked at smoking little outdoor fires. All day long they wiped grimy brows on grimy sleeves as they worked, but in the cold fresh nights victrolas and banjos sounded under the trees, and there was singing.

On the afternoon of a smoking hot September day one of the women had a baby, and Joyce came flying down to the house, ashen-faced, to telephone for a doctor. Afterward she and her mother washed the tiny mottled thing in the big bathroom off the kitchen; the mother of the sixth Lukins baby did not make half as much fuss about the matter as the Ballards did. She lay in her tent for a few days, and then was to be seen languidly wandering through the hot orchards again.

Joyce and Dodo and Ben walked up with their father to Michael's house one Sunday, and the girls cooked lunch in his tidy little shabby domain and laughed at his bachelor arrangements. That day, when they came home late and dusty and happily weary, they were met by Sally, mysterious and solemn, who announced that the smart car parked in the yard belonged to Archie Ross, and that he and Lissy were walking, up by the spring.

"How things *happen!*" Joyce said in enormous satisfaction. The kitchen was warm and bright and friendly; Dodo began tea preparations; Ben lighted the dining-room stove, and the girls spread a fine Italian linen square and set out blue cups that had come from the "Dime" in Merrivale. There must be some hospitable recognition of Archie's return to the fold.

When Archie and Lissy came in, Dodo was rolling golden butter balls, and Joyce, flushed and lovely in her dark blue linen gown, was vigorously hacking a great orange pumpkin into cubes, and scraping away its feathery yellow heart to prepare it for baking. Both girls welcomed the deserter with friendly dignity; Archie was nervous, but admiring and interested, and Lissy looked lovely; she was evidently deeply pleased to see the tea preparations, although she said little, and even after Archie left was rather silent. Late that evening, when Archie was long gone, and supper was over, and the last hot plate put away, Lissy and her father and mother talked long and seriously in the warm dining room, while the younger members of the family, with Michael, who was a great lover of games, played at all sorts of nonsense in the kitchen. Ben had gotten home only this afternoon. He had been away for a long time, trying his luck in filmland; he had little that was cheering to say of the chances that awaited an unknown and inexperienced beginner in the big movie market, and seemed glad to get home.

"As long as they'll talk in there, we oughtn't disturb them," Dodo said.

"Are they friends again?"

This was Ben. Dodo shook her head, her eyes round and serious.

"Oh, heavens, no! He just came down to explain; I think he thinks it makes him interesting."

"Discovering a way to communicate with Mars wouldn't make him interesting, the Scotch—thistle!" Joyce said.

"You mean he's going on with the marriage to his cousin?" Ben demanded, outraged.

"Oh, yes! He goes back for her in December or January."

"Maybe she won't love him in December as she did in May," Joyce suggested, and they all laughed.

"But I thought he wrote Liss all that before he came back?"

"He did, and he wrote Dad long, typewritten letters. No, this is just a—a luxury of renunciation," Joyce explained. "You should have heard him telling Mother that he was entirely to blame; he felt it deeply. I would have liked to touch him up with the cul-*lea*ver from behind!"

"He explains just why he threw her down, and then stays to tea," Ben marveled.

"Oh, well, he's Scotch," Joyce reminded them, and they all laughed weakly again.

At nine o'clock the younger girls took a lamp and went up to bed. The hall door into the dining room was open when they passed it, the trio inside were in the same positions, the murmur of voices the same. Quite suddenly to Joyce it all seemed right, seemed satisfying somehow. The warm kitchen in order, with the breakfast buckwheats mixed and the stove's red glow dying, dying; the dining room where a mother and father and daughter were talking; the ridiculous square bathroom occupied by a travel-grimed boy throwing towels and soap and hot water about; the two girls on their way to bed, carrying a lamp that sent odd shadows wheeling and moving ahead of them on the narrow stairway.

It would be winter soon. Although the daytime hours were still hot and cloudless the house was cold at night, and leaves were falling everywhere. In the night Joyce heard wind stirring, and the skitter of tossing branches across the porch shingles. It seemed good to be snug in bed, with one's sister safe and close in the neighboring bed, and father and mother, older sister and brother all sleeping under the old farmhouse roof.

## ❧ CHAPTER XVI ❧

"BEN, let's go to the barn dance?" Joyce suggested, at a November breakfast table in the kitchen. The winter day was warm and bright and scented with hot toast and coffee indoors, and sparkling and frosted without. Joyce was sparkling, too, her hair brushed and damp, her checked smock stiff and fresh; she poured coffee into the waiting cups, secured herself a piece of toast, and settled down opposite her brother in obvious high spirits.

William Ballard had finished his breakfast and was melting something tarry and odorous on the stove. Lissy and Dodo were still curled up warmly in their beds upstairs, sound asleep in the late sunrise that was striking in shafts of crystal across the yard. But Ben had been routed out half an hour ago by his father, for Michael was helping in the barns, and he was needed for the town trip this morning, and Sally was leaning against the sink, facing the room, watching the others and occasionally putting in a word. Lastly, Michael had come in, and was seated at the end of the table, enormously enjoying what he said was his second breakfast, but what Joyce suspected was his first as well. In his old leather jacket and worn cords, his boots wet from frost and mire, he breathed of the out-of-doors; the hands of the clock had not yet reached eight, but Michael said that he had been busy for more than two hours. One of the farm horses had been sick and losing weight for several days; both men had been anxious about the valuable big brute, but this morning they reported him as having taken the prescribed doses of medicine from his bucket quite readily, twice in the night, and afterward having begun to pull at his hay, and there was now a general relieved belief that "Jory" would pull through.

Joyce's introduction of the frivolous subject of the barn dance was not therefore out of key. But Ben received it coldly.

"Let's not, and say we did," he answered.

"Michael," the girl asked, "do you ever go to barn dances?"

"I do not." Michael had finished his home-cured bacon and eggs and sat back with a sigh of satisfaction.

"I thought you went down there and hobnobbed with all the men, over elections and things?"

"But that's not going to barn dances."

"I've heard all my life of barn dances. I never realized before what they are," Joyce said, with animation. "Do you know what they are, Mother? It merely means that some-one has built a new barn, and they dance in it before it is used."

"I suppose it's about the biggest place they have," said Sally.

"Come on, Ben. It'd be such fun! Everyone's taking pies and sandwiches and everything."

Michael spoke briefly.

"You don't want to go to a barn dance," he said.

Joyce's dancing eyes were turned upon him.

"Oh, why not?"

"Well, it isn't as much fun as it sounds."

"Well, I wouldn't expect it to be the Junior League,"

Joyce reminded him. "It's just girls and men dancing, isn't it? The girl in the post office was telling me about it."

"I know. But most of the nice ones don't go to it, and a lot of others come in from everywhere—it gets to be rather a riot," Michael said.

"I think it would be fun. I like to see the way they do things!" Joyce persisted stubbornly. In the end she talked Ben into taking her.

"You can always come home in the middle of it if you don't like it," she reminded Michael, when the day came, and Michael at the luncheon table again voiced his doubts about the dance.

"Oh, you may like looking on awhile," Michael conceded. But he seemed dubious.

"Looking on!" Joyce exclaimed. "I shall be the life of the party! I'm going to dress before supper."

Supper at the ranch was at six, but long before that Joyce and Ben were ready to go. The barn dance began with a hearty meal at half-past five, and the dancing would be well under way by seven.

"So that everyone gets home early," Joyce suggested.

"Well—in a way——" Michael said. He would stay at home and play bridge.

Joyce wore Lissy's fur coat over her lemon taffeta; she looked her fresh loveliest as she bundled herself into the car beside her brother.

"The village belle!" she called back to Michael, as they started. Michael did not smile as he watched them go.

The winter day was closing down to dusk; there was a hard cold darkening sky overhead, and the taste of frost in the air. The ranches they passed on the way to the Jellicoes' barn showed the Ballards only grudging gleams of kitchen light; everywhere else was shadow, except when a farmer swinging a lantern moved somewhere among the dark sheds and fences.

But cars were twinkling in radiating lines toward the common destination that was the Jellicoes' new enormous hay barn; their lights fingered the roads and the trees, showed the plain little Jellicoe homestead and the windmill, swept up against the trees and the hills, were dimmed close to the great open doors.

From outside the place seemed but dimly lit, but once inside Joyce found herself in a pleasant bustle that was quite sufficiently lighted; two or three great locomotive lamps were swung overhead below the clean high rafters; there were smaller lanterns everywhere, and a string of Japanese paper lanterns some dozen yards long was looped over the place that had been cleared for dancing in the center of the floor. Apron and ice-cream cone and popcorn and gift booths were all separately and individually lighted.

Off the main enormous space was a wagon barn with four box stalls, and in here Joyce found long tables upon which women were spreading eatables of every variety; the smell of coffee was pleasant in the air. Everyone was ravenous, and everyone was being put off until Mrs. Boggs got the punch ready. Joyce flung herself into the scene with her characteristic friendly energy; the older women liked her at once. A dimpled pink-cheeked plump girl with incredibly golden hair and the engaging name of Bootsy Florence instantly appropriated Ben, and Joyce saw to her great satisfaction that his first silly banter with Bootsy presently changed into something more real, and that he and Bootsy were drinking each other's health enthusiastically.

The punch circulated; Joyce didn't know where the time flew to, but she was eating her first delicious piece of cold fried chicken at eight o'clock, and only a few moments later, dancing, heard the whistle that meant that the prize dances were beginning at half-past nine.

She danced joyously, inexhaustibly, with one tall big farmer after another; with the Sallock boy from the dairy and the Hansen boy who sold tickets at the station. Her face grew flushed and her hair tousled; she went into the improvised dressing room with a group of equally tumbled and breathless girls, and they combed their hair with a frightful old broken yellow comb and powdered their noses from anyone's broken box of tan or pink or white powder.

At any and all times the dancers stopped to eat and drink; new great cocoanut cakes and angel cakes and layer cakes were continually being cut; the plates were mashed and messy with the soft remains of cake; women were washing sticky punch glasses busily; wet towels and spilled dishwater surrounded a saucer into which dimes and quarters occasionally tinkled.

Ham. Turkey. Sausages. Doughnuts. They were lifted out of cardboard boxes and battered old cardboard suitcases that were painted to look like leather; housewives, wearing their best decorous thin silks and with elaborately crimped hair, followed their contributions anxiously to the long tables, to be sure that the custard was not spilled, the salad mushed. Uproariously laughing men were eternally pouring fresh bottles into the punch.

The radio and a loud-speaker supplied the music; the girls and men sang as they danced. Michael, Joyce reflected, had been right about one thing: there were a good many roughs here who did not belong to this neighborhood at all, and their girls were dreadful. The men pressed their faces against the girls' faces as they circled about the wide pine floor that was new and raw and yellow under the lights; as the evening wore on they disappeared couple by couple for long absences; they went out to sit in the cars and kiss and embrace each other. The air was hot in the barn, long drafts of the icy punch were absolutely indispensable; when one stepped out under the cold hard sky and the solemnly wheeling stars the night air felt deliciously fresh and sweet.

Two young men, Bill and Podge, were making the evening entertaining for Joyce. She never had seen either before tonight, but she could call them only Bill and Podge because they hilariously refused to give her other names. Both were big and good-looking and rapid and violent dancers; both admired Joyce openly, and when one was not dancing with her the other waited. Between dances they rushed her about, a strong hand of each under her elbow, and got her sandwiches, cake, or more punch. Her sallies caused them shouts of laughter, and even in the mixed crowd Joyce and her swains attracted some notice, as she was quite aware.

"Still—if you come to a thing like this, you might as well not be a stick!" Joyce told her excited thoughts. She was sure of herself, but somehow it made her a little uneasy to see that Ben and Bootsy were indulging in long disappearances, and that when they did return to dance Ben was almost continually kissing Bootsy's too gold temple, his face wearing meanwhile a look of fatuous adoration and content. However—this was just a country riot—this was an off night. . . .

At midnight Bill and Podge jumped Joyce up to a high seat on the edge of what would some day be a hayrack, and established themselves one on each side of her, their arms holding her steady. All three rested their backs against the wall, and were silent awhile, looking down from their coign of vantage upon the dancers and feasters below. Joyce was amazed to hear that it was so late, but she was tired enough to enjoy sitting still and watching, and made no effort to find Ben and no suggestion of going home.

Some of the revelers had gathered their children from a child's heaven of exploring and tasting and racing about, or awakened them from the group of sleeping babies in a corner, and departed into the dark winter night, with a buzzing of motors and slamming of car doors. The crowd on the floor was thinning, but the eating went on with great

**vigor**, and there were increasing demands for the icy sweet punch. Time went on, Joyce reflected, in the middle of the night with that same celerity it showed in the daytime. They seemed to have done nothing in particular since seven o'clock, but here it was almost one—it was past one, going on toward two, and still somehow she didn't feel like going home; she seemed just to have arrived at the party.

Bill and Podge were silly country yokels, of course, but she had them completely captivated; they would not dance with anyone else, and that was rather fun. Joyce walked about the big space between the two; the few residents of the two towns that she already had known had swelled to several score now, and everyone—the motherly old women who were superintending the supper, and the youngsters skidding and racing on the greased floor—was calling her "Joyce."

"I think I ought to find Ben," she presently said.

"Don't worry, sister, Bootsy has him in hand!" Bill reassured her.

"That's exactly why I think I ought to find him," Joyce answered, and so high were their spirits that they all found this very funny.

They went in search of Ben; he and Bootsy were not easy to find, and were finally run to earth cozily concealed in the back of Bootsy's car, a rug snugly wrapping them both, their heads together, the waning moon glittering in their tired eyes.

Joyce quite suddenly felt cold and tired and disgusted. The whole affair went shoddy; she hated herself and Ben, she hated even innocent Bill and Podge, and she heartily wished that she had never come to the barn dance. The night was cold, her head felt heavy with rich cold food and drink, and Ben would pay no attention to her whatsoever.

"I'll take the car, Ben, and go home alone," she said, trying to speak gayly over a rising tide of anger.

"Take it!" Ben said, his jaw rubbing gently against the cuddled Bootsy's temple. Joyce turned in vexation to her attentive escort; the three walked together toward her own car.

"Someone'll bring him home . . ." she said hesitatingly.

Bill had disappeared; she was standing alone with Podge in the weak cold moonlight outside the Jellicoes' barn. All about the place the quiet hills stood sentinel; the trees of the farmhouse were mere blots in the gloom; the red taillight of a departing motor car crawled like a tiny caterpillar through the dark on some descending length of road.

Podge put his big odorous arms about her; crushed his hard face against hers; his mustache was wet against her mouth.

"How about it, sister?" he said, in a hoarse voice with a chuckle in it. "How about a good—nice—sweet—good-night—kiss!"

One arm held her in a vise; the other was moving down her face and over her neck and shoulder. Joyce, choking and terrified, strained away from him. She could not escape the exploring hand, the wet kisses.

"Oh, stop it!" she panted. The man's breath, heavy with liquor, was hot in her face; his fingers pressed hard against her arms and back.

"Come on, come on, come on!" he said, in leisurely enjoyment of her distress. "You ain't such a baby—you know what it's all about! Give me a kiss!"

"You let me go!" Joyce gasped. She freed both arms to fight him; suddenly she was free.

"That'll be about enough from you, Podge," Michael's voice had said quietly; Joyce heard the impact of his knuckles against the other man's jaw. Podge went down like a log against the frosted stubble of the field; Joyce, guided and hurried by Michael, got into Michael's shabby little open car. He put a blanket about her, and they started for home without a word.

After a long time her breathing quieted, and she said clearly and slowly;

"That was my fault."

Michael made no comment upon this for a few minutes.

"You shouldn't have gone," he said briefly then.

"It was just a—a country party," Joyce presently submitted defensively. "They're all acting like that. I suppose he thought I was—that sort of girl. If the way Bootsy Florence is acting with Ben is any criterion——"

"Yes, I saw them, too. Bootsy's going to tell her mother tomorrow that she's engaged to the Ballard boy."

Joyce experienced a moment of panic. All very funny at the barn dance, but matters wouldn't be quite so droll if these country folk considered tonight's friendliness on the part of herself and Ben as an introduction to the entire family, and began to call on Mother and Lissy! Her cheeks burned in the darkness; she was beginning to feel insufferably ashamed of herself.

"How long were you there, Michael?"

"About an hour."

"Didn't come down until midnight?"

"I came down after you. I thought you might have had about enough."

"Thank you," Joyce said dryly, hating him. "I hope my two friends won't call on me some day this week," she added, trying to turn the matter into a joke.

"They won't," Michael said decidedly. "I know both of them. Bill Harges is a harmless enough fool—he works up on the Rooker place. He was engaged to the Boggs girl, but she broke it off and married a sewing-machine man in San José. But Podge Harris has a wife and a baby—she was the girl in green who was working with the coffee machine. He's got a nerve to try to get away with what he does! His wife knows it, but I suppose she's in love with him!"

The deepest abysses of shame opened to receive Joyce's

spirit. All the long way home she did not speak again because she was unable to speak again.

And when she was warm in bed, with her feet pressed against the cooling hot-water bottle Sally had thoughtfully put there and the blankets piled on top of her, she still could not close her eyes. Hour after hour went by, and Joyce stirred and turned wakefully, reviewing every moment of the whole hateful evening, wishing that she had never gone to the party, wishing that if she had gone she had had the sense to stay with the cake-cutting women, wishing herself dead, and buried a thousand miles deep in the earth!

## CHAPTER XVII

FULLY one third of her white night had been spent in wondering wretchedly how she could ever get up her courage to face Michael the next day, but as it happened her encounter with him took place without any apparent embarrassment on his side and with as little as she could possibly betray on hers. Joyce, not falling asleep until the cold winter light was fingering at her window, slept deep and late, and appeared in the warm bright busy kitchen only when luncheon preparations were under way.

Ben, looking red-eyed and sleepy, was having breakfast at the end of the kitchen table; Sally was busy between stove and sink; William Ballard was sitting awaiting his noontime meal, pleasantly breathless and chilly and weary after the long morning round of barns and fields, and Michael was plucking chickens. An old strip of canvas had been spread under his low chair, he had a sack into which he plunged the fluffy gray-and-white feathers. There would be fried chicken for Sunday's dinner.

Joyce drank her coffee thoughtfully. Once her eyes went to Michael's and she found him looking at her; Joyce's color came up hotly, but they both only smiled faintly, and nothing was said of the previous night's entertainment except what Joyce's mother and father could safely hear. Ben was somewhat noncommittal on the subject, too; late that day he went down to see Bootsy.

Bootsy had telephoned him at about two o'clock; she had been working in the "Dime" since nine, but she sounded fresh and gay. It was Saturday; she would be on duty until six, but then why didn't Ben come get her and they would go out to "Momma's." Momma had won on a raffle and had taken home last night two great roasted turkeys, one of them of course had gone to Gramma Krussinger, but with the other Bootsy and her friends proposed to make merry that evening.

Bootsy Florence, eighteen and beautiful and good, had but one weakness. She was affectionate. She loved Poppa and Momma and her two brothers and her three beautiful married sisters; she loved her little nieces and nephews, she had loved all her teachers, she loved everyone in the "Dime," she loved puppies, kittens, canaries, colts, and calves. When she talked of her love for them she always cried, and she always cried at funerals, weddings, and movies.

Since the Ballards had come to town, and Bootsy had seen Ben, tall and dark and loose-jointed and straight and strong in his unmistakably collegiate way, Bootsy could have put all these loves into the scale at once and would have seen them easily outweighed by what she felt for Ben. When she saw him arrive at the barn dance, fires blazed up in Bootsy, and her senses sang, and the world rocked beneath her pink satin slippers. If she was always beautiful—for the too gold hair and the too blue eyes and the too pink cheeks that Joyce had criticized were unaided by artifice—she was more than ordinarily beautiful when Ben came up for a dance. It had been a flattering surprise to him, the complete surrender of this really exquisite creature to his arms, and later on to his kisses; he had felt quite honestly that night that he was half in love with simple little Bootsy

Florence, and when he went down to get her after store hours on the cold dark afternoon that followed, their meeting was that of lovers; laughing, ecstatic, confident.

Bootsy's mother was a stout plain florid woman who spoke in country fashion; her father was crippled—the old "Cap'n" never left his chair. The house was filled with shells and gift cups, tidies and china frames, souvenirs from county fairs, cushions with fringes, hand-painted smooth slabs of orange wood with "Santa Barbara" lettered on them, little bisque statues, vases, candlesticks, hand-painted ashtrays. Mrs. Florence belonged to a bridge club that had been playing every first and third Tuesday since the days when spades were royals and the fourth hand said "Pray do," and she had averaged a prize a month for thirty years.

The group that had gathered to eat the turkey, and that welcomed Ben enthusiastically to warmth and light and the odor of food, was composed of two young married couples, Walt and Mabel Wiggin and Chess and Dosie Smith, and Bootsy's recently married sister, with her young husband. All these were brides and grooms; there was much kissing and teasing and many joyous references to Dosie not riding this winter and Lily "looking kinder pale," and even Ben —in whom women had taken much interest for several years, Ben who was no novice at love-making—was surprised and a little staggered by the obvious inclusion of Bootsy and himself in this group as another happy young pair.

"You remember Ben, Momma," Bootsy said happily, keeping an arm about Ben as she presented him. "Poppa," she went on, "this is Ben Bullard, and I warn you that you've got to like him!"

The supper was hearty and delicious, and everyone ate, and later admitted to having eaten, much too much. Hot cinnamon buns and cold turkey, squash pies and doughnuts, everybody's favorite pickle, and chocolate topped with whipped cream; the room grew hot and the faces about the board were flushed with heat and food.

Ben easily kept them in roars of laughter. Like all comedians he was at his best with a new audience; everyone loved him instantly, and Bootsy grew prouder and happier every instant. Mrs. Florence began to feel quite comfortable with him—motherly indeed; she sent him to the kitchen for more chocolate, and like everyone else was presently calling him Ben.

Afterward the other eight played two tables of bridge, and Bootsy carried Ben off to the "Den." The den was stuffy with upholstery and rugs, but there was an airtight stove there, two comfortable chairs, an agreeably dimmed lamp— and there was Bootsy, instantly getting into Ben's lap and locking her arms about his neck, and rumpling her gold curls against his shoulder.

Ben never had known so innocently, so gayly affectionate a girl. She was talking home-making already, the little place that they would have, their fireplace, their bright little kitchen where Bootsy would cook Ben's breakfasts, their little car to bring them home to Sunday dinners with Momma and Poppa.

"Momma wants me to stop working as soon as we're married," Bootsy said on a laugh of sheer delight, between two kisses. "But there's time to talk about that. I don't even know your mother yet, do I? But we'll always have to come back here a lot, Ben darling, sweetheart, sweetheart darlingest, because you see I'm the last one, and they were wild when Lily married Floyd at nineteen." And after a long silence when they had both looked at the red eyes of the stove solemnly winking at them, she added in a serious little voice, "Some day I'll have a little baby, Ben, and maybe I'll die. My sister Peaches' chum did when her baby came. And if I do you'll have the baby to comfort you."

Ben sat holding her, loving her, and feeling amused and

superior at the same time, and feeling surprise over all. How had all this come about so swiftly? She was a little darling, of course, but it would be crazy to begin to talk seriously of marriage now; they hardly knew each other —he hadn't a job or a penny—his mother would be wild at the mere thought . . .

But it was sweet to hold her, and kiss her soft little temple against which the baby gold of her hair still clung in baby fashion, and listen to the happy talk that was punctuated by her fierce little eager kisses. Ben went home at eleven o'clock somewhat bewildered, for there had been an unmistakably parental note in the good-nights of both Mrs. Florence and the Cap'n, Bootsy's sister Lily had said shyly to him in parting, "We all agree with Bootsy, Ben!" and Bootsy herself had extracted from him, as a matter of course, a promise to see her as early on Sunday as he could manage it.

"Do you go to church, you bad boy? Then wait for me after church and we'll get the mail and take a walk or something," Bootsy had said, tears on her smiling little face as she had delivered a final shower of hugs and kisses.

Once or twice, driving home under the solemn winter stars, Ben laughed aloud, but it was uncomfortable laughter. After all, she was only a little country girl of eighteen, Bootsy; she didn't matter, and her people didn't matter. It was all sort of silly, but it wouldn't last long. Perhaps it would be as well to taper it off the very next time he saw her; perhaps it might be as well not to go to church and wait for her tomorrow; to let quite a few days go by without making any gesture at all.

But as a matter quite as much of design as of chance he saw her every day for the next ten days. After that, as far as Ben was concerned, the affair faded as rapidly as it had commenced. Ben had felt from the beginning that it must. Bootsy was exactly the affectionate little village belle and

romp and beauty that she had seemed to him when first he
met her, nothing more, and Bootsy's background and people
were—as Ben's honester second thoughts had to put it—
simply and typically "hick." Their interests, their voices,
their opinions, their laughter were equally amazing. "Even
on the stage it'd be overdone," Ben reflected.

But he didn't know what to do about it, for by this time
Bootsy was hinting at announcing the engagement, some
of her more boisterous girl friends could not meet Ben
downtown marketing of a winter morning without coquet-
tish references to his affair with Bootsy, and there was talk
of "showers" of various sorts; a kitchen shower, a garden
shower. Ben uncomfortably mentioned the situation to
Joyce.

Joyce's instant reaction of merriment was sobered by his
own concern.

"Well—but how far did you go, Ben?"

"I've kissed her, of course. Fooling."

"But you're not in love with her?"

"Not any more." It was amazing, even to Ben himself,
how completely he wasn't in love with her any more. When
everything—everything died out of a man's feeling for a
woman it was amazing that he didn't even like her very
much any more. That is, it was amazing how hard it was to
be polite to Bootsy, patient with Bootsy, after the first
fortnight; it was alarming to note how Bootsy's people impressed him. Impressed him as being simple, and a little
common, and uninteresting to an unbelievable degree; one
never said anything to Bootsy's mother or sisters without
first thinking whether or not they could understand it,
without knowing exactly the trim little catch phrase they
would use in reply.

"I'll say," and "Isn't that right?" and "You said it,"
these were their responses to anything and everything; all
of them, the mother included, had a fashion of enunciating

"Oh-oh!" when any little question of sex was involved, with a suspicious, arch little uplilt on the first syllable and a significant, sly little downlilt on the second that Ben thought the acme of bad taste and bad manners.

Early in December he had to go to San Francisco for a week, to be best man at a friend's wedding, and he found the break an infinite relief. Bootsy couldn't telephone him every hour, while he was away, Bootsy couldn't coax him out to take her to movies, or to come to hot noisy rich dinners at Momma's; Bootsy couldn't hang on his neck murmuring in loving reproach, "When's your mother going to ask *me* to come to dinner, lover? I don't mind—I know how things are, you're just getting settled in, and all that. But you see Momma and Poppa think it's kind of queer, and anything that hurts me just makes them furious. I know Joyce and I know Dodo, but when am I going to meet the rest of your folks?"

Bootsy wrote him every day, letters fringed with scalloped kisses. Her loving, untried little heart poured itself out upon the pink scented paper that had a gold "B.F." intertwined in a great embossed monogram. But Ben didn't read the letters; their mere arrival made him uncomfortable; he jumbled them into the pocket of his suitcase and tried to forget them.

On his third day in the city—and how good the city lights and noise and bustle seemed to him, how luxurious the big hotels, how sophisticated and polished his old crowd!—on the third day he met Kate Pollack, who was a newspaper reporter, covering the Lilienkrantz-Merrill wedding. Kate was a slender, straight, well-groomed girl with fine dark eyes and a wide intelligent mouth; she and Ben sat in one of the pews in St. Luke's and murmured, while the rest of the crowd rehearsed for the wedding, and Kate laughed a good deal, and listened to Ben; she did not say much, and what she did say would have been completely unintelligible to Bootsy

Florence, but it was all exactly what Ben was hungry to hear. Books, plays, cities, persons, Kate's talk flickered over them all.

After the rehearsal Ben took her down to the newspaper office; he called there at six o'clock that afternoon, and he and Kate walked to her house; she lived in an apartment on California Street, with her father and brother. The father was a doctor, the brother had known Ben in college; Ben fitted into their group as if he had known them always.

What he felt for Kate was already different from anything Ben had ever felt for any woman in the world before. She was two years older than he, she was infinitely beyond his reach; it made no difference. She inspired him; she thrilled him; she awed him. A slender girl of twenty-three, with white cuffs at her thin wrists, and dark soft curls against her white temples, and life and laughter dancing in her dark eyes, everything she did and said seemed almost unendurably sweet and poignant and significant to Ben. The world was only Kate Pollack from that moment on. After the wedding Ben went back to the ranch dazedly, bewilderedly, trying to readjust life to include the wonderfulness of Kate.

He had not written Bootsy or anyone else the exact hour of his arrival. Lissy and Joyce would be sure to be downtown shopping at about eleven o'clock; Ben took a train that would get him to Merriwell at that time. Bootsy had anticipated his processes of thought; she had run over from the "Dime" where she worked to the station, and was there to meet him, with open arms and blue eyes filled with tears of joy, with incoherence and with delighted and tremulous laughter.

Oh, he had been gone away five years instead of five days, and she had been the lonesomest girl that ever was in the world, she hadn't gone anywhere or done anything because Ben was away! And his sisters' car was parked right outside the post office, Bootsy told him eagerly; if he and she went right over there they could sit in the car and talk, and the girls would be sure not to miss them!

Ben kissed her duly; and they walked over and got into the car, and while she poured out the story of her loneliness and faithfulness Ben sat squared about on the front seat, at the wheel, and smiled at her vaguely and wondered what he could do. What on earth could he *do?* His brief absence, far from cooling Bootsy's ardors, had seemed to crystallize their affair into a definite engagement, with a marriage close ahead.

"And lissen, sweetest darling," said Bootsy. "Momma wants to know when I'm going up to your house for dinner, see? I don't care," she interpolated hastily, her fond blue eyes devouring him, "but Poppa and Momma do. So you go home now—I've got to get back to the store, and you're coming down to supper tonight—Momma's cooking chickens and salt-rising bread and I don't know what all, and you tell her then what night you'll come for me to have dinner with your folks, see? Because—if we're going to be married in February——"

"Oh, and I forgot to tell you that!" she interrupted herself again, in a serious, capable manner. "Momma and I talked it over. Momma's anniversary and my birthday both come on the twentieth of February—well, and my Florence grandfather and grandmother are having their Golden Wedding on the sixteenth of March, that's in Detroit. So Momma and Poppa thought if we were married first, then Chess would drive them to Detroit for the Golden Wedding."

Ben rubbed his thumb slowly across her plump little hand. It was as if he never had seen this blonde, fresh, chattering little creature before. His senses were in complete confusion; he seemed to be two persons at once.

"Look here, Bootsy," he presently said. "We're going pretty fast! Look—I can't get married for ever so long.

My father's lost all his money, you know, and I've not got a penny! I've got to get up to town, and get a job, and see where I stand. We can't talk marriage for a couple of years.

"And I never asked you to marry me, or implied that I wanted you to," he longed for courage to add honestly. "We danced together, and I kissed you, and we talked a lot of nonsense the night I had dinner with your family, but that's the beginning and the end of it. You haven't had much to build all this on. . . . "

He dared not say this. But what he did say staggered Bootsy for a moment, and her exquisite pink cheeks paled a little.

"How d'you mean 'a couple of years,' you bad boy? That's all nonsense!" Bootsy said, recovering color and spirits, and talking on over his murmur of explanation. "There's my grandmother Krussinger's money, you know. It was seventeen thousand dollars when I was only a baby; I don't know what it is now. Peaches' was a lot more, I know, and Lily's was twenty-two thousand. Lily and Floyd bought that place they have and the car and everything. So you see, Mister Scarey, we'll have something to go on. But Ben—you'll have to get a job here. Momma'll never let me move to the city, much less San Francisco! It'd kill her. So now you be a good boy—and come pick me up at the store tonight, and we'll go out home together! I've got to get back, and here come Dodo and Joyce anyway."

Ben's younger sisters arrived in a flurry of welcome and kisses. Their cheeks were red with exercise and cold air; they were full of family ranch chatter. Ben listened abstractedly; he was more worried than he ever had been in his life. What to do—what to do? In whom could he confide? He couldn't—he simply couldn't go down to the hot, noisy, common overdecorated Florence house tonight and eat chicken and dumplings and salt-rising bread and pickles and black currant chowchow and steamed pudding, he couldn't carry on this farce any longer, find himself alone in the "Den" with Bootsy while the others were listening to the radio in the parlor, listen to the girl's talk of engagement showers and plans for meeting his own people!

"No, but Ben, don't you think that's rather ther-*rill*ing?" Joyce was demanding.

"About——?"

"You're not listening! About Lissy, and Archie coming to see her twice, and bringing her candy."

"No, did he?"

"I was just telling you! And Lissy's so gentle and amiable, isn't she, Dodo? And Mother of course is majestic; we're not to tease Lissy, or make any comments on it at all. Isn't it fun? If she'll only," Joyce went on fervently, "if she'll only lead him on, get him to the point of being wild to marry her, and then ther-*row* him down hard . . . "

Ben was not listening. Archie, he was thinking, had somehow managed to slip out of his engagement with Lissy smoothly enough. But no one could ever slip out of anything with Bootsy. The man to whom she found herself engaged would from now on come second with Bootsy; it was being engaged that counted, the excitement and the dinners, the showers and presents and trousseau, the wedding plans. Bootsy would pay but half-hearted attention to any talk of breaking the engagement now; it simply couldn't be done, in the face of Momma's consent and Poppa's approval and the fact that the news had been confided to a score of Bootsy's intimate friends.

Ben looked up at the somber winter hills, he felt the fresh chillness of the country airs on his train-flushed face, and he groaned in spirit. Kate Pollack, with her blue-veined wrists and intelligent wide mouth and plumy soft curves of dark hair, seemed to recede from him. She was not for him. He had wrecked his life.

"Mother's having a turkey dinner to celebrate your coming back, Benjamin my son, my son!" Joyce presently told him.

. . . And Bootsy's mother was cooking chicken and dumplings! Ben smiled a sickly smile, wishing only that a mortal sickness might be laid upon him before supper time arrived.

## CHAPTER XVIII

MRS. BALLARD, complacent and capable, told her two younger daughters that nothing must be said of Archie to Lissy. Lissy, she explained, felt very badly about the whole matter, but she understood Archie's position perfectly, and admired and respected him for the stand he had taken.

"Admired and respected him for jilting her—for ber-*reak*ing the engagement!" Joyce exclaimed, round-eyed.

"I wish you wouldn't put it that way, Joyce, it's so—so humiliating to poor Lissy," Sally reproved her. "Archie is in a very difficult position; his father is far from being a young man, and he is simply doing what he feels to be his duty. I admit it's a pity—it's a great pity—but I believe both of them are acting finely."

"Are they going just to go on being friends, Mother, after all this?"

"No, not at all," Sally said, displeased at Joyce's and Dodo's healthy curiosity. "They are not to see each other again; she explained to Daddy and me last night—I've never known Lissy to be so sweet—that they thought it best not to see each other. But there's a—a perfect understanding, and now I think we needn't discuss it any more."

This closed all general talk on the subject, but Joyce and

Dodo debated it endlessly between themselves. Lissy probably would not marry now; she was going on twenty-six, and whom could she meet down here that was interesting?

"Michael," Joyce suggested once, and they both laughed guiltily. The younger girls had accepted Michael wholeheartedly, but Lissy never forgot for an instant that the young Englishman was one of her father's farmhands.

She bore herself, during this trying time, with a proud sad dignity. Lissy had to have a pose of some sort, Joyce and Dodo decided; her pose of the moment was that of the martyr, and it was obvious that she was enjoying it. Any love affair—even one of Archie's peculiar conditioning—was better than none. Never had Lissy's family known her to be so gentle, so considerate, so adaptable; harmony reigned during the first Christmas holidays at the ranch house.

Ben, too, was strangely amiable and affectionate. He was quiet, and Sally told her husband in an aside that the poor boy was missing his college work and his old associates, but he never complained. Indeed he seemed quite contented to wander off on walks with Joyce or his father; now and then he went down to the village for unexplained evenings, but he always came home early and sober, and Sally felt that she could not complain.

"Who's this Gertrude Florence who telephones Ben?" Sally asked Joyce.

"Bootsy. She's a girl who works in the Dime."

"Is she in love with Ben, do you think?"

"She's the girl he takes to the movies when he goes out nights."

"What kind of a girl is she?"

"Oh, too pretty! Gold, yellow, and blue. She looks like enamel."

"I wish he wouldn't!" Sally said anxiously. "I wish you'd go with him, Joy, when he takes her anywhere."

But Joyce would go to village festivities no more. Her

one scalding experience, at the barn dance, had cured her of any interest in rustic affairs. To have been kissed, grossly and carelessly, by a wet-mustached married express agent, to have had his wife, and any other woman who chanced to be an onlooker, quite aware that he was amusing himself with the youngest Ballard girl—worst of all, to have Michael a witness, Michael the person to extricate Joyce from this predicament—no, it was too shameful a memory ever to be forgotten! Joyce was cured. She stayed at home nights and worked over the tables of auction bridge as if she were studying arithmetic again, and tried to persuade herself that she enjoyed Shakespeare as much as a murder or mystery story.

Dodo sometimes accompanied her brother. Dodo even met all the Florences, and joined them, somewhat flushed and shy and bewildered, at a Saturday supper before the movie. Charley Sallock was there on this occasion, and Dodo reported seriously to Joyce the next day that the Sallocks were lovely people; their grandmother had been French.

And all this time Ben was writhing in Bootsy's net. The best his utmost art could win from Bootsy was but a temporary alleviation. Bootsy had consented to put off the announcement of her engagement until her nineteenth birthday in February, but she was more loving, more possessive than ever. Unless she heard from Ben every day she telephoned to the ranch; in self-protection Ben had to satisfy her with at least a brief note, or a call at the store where she worked. She knew that his ardor had cooled, and he knew that she knew it, but Bootsy was as determined as she was affectionate, and she overlooked his changed feelings with superb unconcern. Ben couldn't break with her—that would be too outrageous, after the way Momma and Poppa and Lily and everyone had treated him; and unless he broke with her, the fine gradations of his feeling wouldn't worry Bootsy.

Ben finally told his father about it. It was the first time

in their two lives that the men had talked together with complete confidence.

They talked up at the barn, Ben lounging against the table in the harness room, his father sitting on an upturned barrel, punching holes in leather straps destined presently to make fastenings on a box stall.

William Ballard's first impression was amusement. The boy had gotten himself involved with a pretty girl in the village, eh? Well, why not, if she was a decent girl, with a good family back of her?

"You'll not want to marry for a while anyway, Ben. She wouldn't want to come here, and you're not fixed up with a job yet."

"Dad, I never was in love with her!" Ben's young face was scarlet, and drawn with distress. "It was just dancing —and of course I kissed her——" he stumbled. "She's awfully pretty, and all that. But the family—her mother and everything, and the house—not a book in it, except Tennyson on the parlor table . . . "

William listened thoughtfully.

"Why'd you ask her?" he presently demanded abruptly.

"I didn't ask her! I give you my word, Dad, I never *thought* of getting married! It was just her—her taking it all for granted—telling them all we were sweethearts——"

The older man was nodding; his narrowed eyes fixed on space.

"Seen someone else you like better, Ben?"

"Oh, my God, yes! Not that I'd ever have a chance with *her*. But she's—she's a gentlewoman, knows things, speaks languages——"

A silence. Then Ben said eagerly:

"But, Dad, long before I met Kate I knew it wasn't any use with Bootsy! Her kissing me—her friends—the whole thing, it bores me so—it bores me so I can't *bear* it—and she knows it, too, only she won't admit it. I've said—I've tried to say that we're both too young, and we've no prospects, but she goes right on talking of linen and china cups! And now it's January," the boy finished miserably, "and her birthday's in February, and she wants to be married then!"

"Well, Ben," William Ballard said slowly, after a long pause, "there's only one thing for you to do. Go down and see her tonight, tell her, right before her mother and father, if you have to, that your feelings have changed—face it. It'll be awful, but it won't hurt you as much as what might come along later would. This sounds more like a romantic little country beauty who has fallen more in love with love than she has with you, she'll get over it. But if you marry and make a mistake—you won't, either one of you."

"Dad," Ben said solemnly, "if it meant running away from home and never coming back, I couldn't marry her. I simply couldn't see it through. I can't even kiss her any more. But this'll mean that I have to get away, and how can I? If you can stake me to even three months in New York——"

They were walking slowly down toward the house. William Ballard spoke decisively:

"No, you'll have to stay here for a while, Ben, for a few months at least. If you go away she'll build against your coming back. If you stay here she'll have to tell her family and friends the truth, that it's over. See her tonight, and then don't see her again."

Ben said nothing as they went into the warm kitchen, but his father noticed that he was unusually serious and silent for the rest of the day. Late in the afternoon they talked together again.

He saw Bootsy that evening. Bootsy was radiant in sky-blue silk, with pearls about her round flawless little throat and perfume heavy upon her gold curls. She met him in animated reproach.

"Oh, you bad boy! If you were coming tonight why didn't you pick me up at the store and come for supper? Where's Dodo? Momma, here's Ben now!" Bootsy sang rather than said.

"I want to talk to you, Bootsy, and then afterward I want to talk to you and Captain Florence, Mrs. Florence," Ben said courageously. His heart was beating unevenly, and his hands were cold. All the time he kept thinking of the moment when he would tell his father about this, up at the barn tomorrow. "She won't die, she won't die of it, they can't kill me," he thought.

But it was all worse than his worst anticipations. Bootsy was incredulous and laughing at first, and then loving and reproachful; she called it a lovers' quarrel; he mustn't be mean to her because she had gone to the Woodmans' Ball with Kane Mason. Kane had been her schoolday sweetheart before ever she had heard of Ben.

Sobered and frightened at last, Bootsy grew only the more resolutely forgiving and affectionate. Her arms were about him, he was to kiss her, and ask her pardon, and not say such silly things!

"I want to tell your father and mother," Ben persisted, trying to free his arms of her. But Bootsy was crying frantically now, and wouldn't let him go. They all l-l-loved him, and this would k-k-kill Poppa! Ben looked at the sprayed chandelier in the parlor that was hung with little suède umbrellas and football pompons, and sighed. If she only wouldn't cry!

But in the end the crying saved him, for Mrs. Florence, not believing her ears, opened the door a crack and peeped in, and Ben called to her.

"Mrs. Florence, I feel terribly about this, but Bootsy and I've been talking——"

Aroused, suspicious, hostile, the mother came in.

"Stay out of this, Momma!" Bootsy commanded, hysterically. But Momma would not stay out of it now. She came in and put her arm about Bootsy protectively, and it was Bootsy who sobbed out the terrible truth.

"Ben's tired of me, Momma! He wants to break our engagement! He says now that he never asked me!"

"She asked you, I suppose?" Mrs. Florence demanded roundly. "Don't you talk any such nonsense as breaking your engagement, to me," she added. "For there isn't a poltroon in the country that's mean enough to hurt a loving child like this!"

"Don't call Ben names, Momma," Bootsy sobbed. "I love him!"

Dad had foreseen all this, Ben reflected; the old man knew a lot. He had said this afternoon that something like this might go on. Ben was conscious of a strange detachment, and again he told himself that they couldn't kill him; he felt himself oddly no more than an outsider, a witness, to this excitement.

"I'm horribly sorry," he said more than once. He said it gently, as both mother and daughter entreated him to come to his senses and tell them that this was all a dreadful joke. Bootsy was flung across her bed, crying wildly, and somehow Lily and Floyd were in the fray, when Ben left at last. Mrs. Florence, roused to fury, flung after him a threat of a horsewhipping; when he found himself alone in the exquisite starry solitude and chill and silence of the night Ben drove about aimlessly for a long while.

Then he went home and joined the bridge players in the kitchen. Sitting down with a book, he nodded to his father; Sally heard them talking, when she was warm in bed, talking late into the night. She couldn't imagine what they were talking about, and nothing that was said the next day gave her any hint. Ben was quieter than ever for a while, and went to the village no more.

## ❧ CHAPTER XIX ❧

Before they had finished discussing Archie's first appearance, he came again. He said that he felt he must have a talk with Lissy's father; he was not satisfied that he had entirely made clear the extraordinary circumstances in which he found himself. His father and his uncle, years before, when Jean had been a very small girl and himself an infant, had agreed upon this family marriage that also involved business considerations,—Uncle James had been a stockholder in the firm of Alexander Ross's Sons for more than twenty years. It was all tremendously complicated—he should have known it—he *had* known it, in a general sort of way, but it was only when he had announced his engagement to Lissy that the full seriousness of the situation occurred to him.

On the occasion of this second visit, Archie found the Ballards about to start off for a Sunday picnic. He came along. He walked behind the others with Lissy, and it was to be noted that Lissy was in extraordinary spirits all day long.

They walked up to Dead Pine Ridge, back of the Cooley ranch. The girls were picturesque in heterogeneous walking wear. Joyce's rich russet mop was subdued by a brimmed old brown felt hat that had lost its band; she wore snug old riding trousers, and a white shirt under a sleeveless dark blue sweater. Everyone carried something; Michael had an army knapsack strapped to his lean broad shoulders; Ben perspired under the weight of the water tin.

Up and up and up went the broken trail, sometimes winding along a ledge under redwoods, sometimes out in the open straggling across slippery dead grass. They stopped, panting, at turns to look back and down at the precipitate heights they had scaled, at the transformed panorama of villages and farms.

In the hot, clear sunshine there was not a breath of air stirring; chipmunks and jays chattered angrily in the woods, lizards whisked away under foot and wherever the grass was tangled, and deep grasshoppers rose whirring. There were no other sounds except their voices, and the crackle of breaking underbrush when the going was bad or the trail lost.

They toiled on; stopped often. All the faces were deeply flushed and wet now; yet still the trail went on, and the Dead Pine continued to cut across a pure blue sky as far away as ever.

But at last a woodland lane dipped to the northwest, encircled a piny mount; they were out among levels of chaparral and manzanita bushes, hardly more than knee high, and broken by bare spaces of hard yellow soil. And just beyond was a deep canyon filled with tall redwoods and the Pine at last. Silent, broken, the party of eight trailed into the welcoming shade; Ben with a groan of amazement set down the water can. There was a spring here and in a deep ferny pool just below it the water lay like a green shadow.

"Wouldn't you think Swede would have told us there was water here!" Michael said.

Everyone sat down abruptly, and there was no sound

but that of straining breath, and the heartening clink of the little white cups against the rocks of the pool. The water was ice-cold, delicious, clear; the men and Joyce and Dodo dipped their arms into it elbow deep, splashed it on their hot faces.

Presently Michael had expert charge of the fire; the coffee pot was filled, it tipped perilously, was straightened again. Joyce began to toast buns; there was cold turkey; there were tomatoes. She handed her mother the first epicurean sandwich. An enthusiastic interval of eating set in. Joyce wished that Paul were there, he so loved that sort of thing!

A new letter from him had been added yesterday to the growing precious collection in her lower bureau drawer. For days after one came she was happy. Life was pleasant enough on the ranch at twenty, with a lover safe in the background to promise rescue some day. However odd Lissy's affair, Joyce's was wholly satisfying.

Winter closed in cold after the springlike Sunday of the picnic. There was never snow, but the roads were deep in mud that froze and thawed and froze and thawed again. The gardens and orchards were stripped bare, except for skeleton trees, frosty evergreens and blackened chrysanthemum plants; chickens took to the warm hay barns; cows came disconsolately home from the hills at three o'clock; the cold sun disappeared before five, and Ben's days were one long struggle with stovewood. The shuddering beginnings and endings of the days made the kitchen the favorite meeting place, and for the discovery of a rusty little stove in a shed and its installation in the bathroom Ben received the encomiums of the entire group.

Michael was now a member of the family and slept in the kitchen bedroom. Lean, long, ginger-colored, laconic, he was on the footing of an affectionately valued friend. Why Lissy didn't transfer her affections to him, Joyce often wondered; but of course Lissy never thought of an itinerant fruit-hand as a possible mate. That he happened to be a gentleman never would occur to Lissy now; his first appearance had placed him once and for all. Then of course Michael was paid no more than something like twenty-five dollars a month; that would be an important point to Liss. Joyce laughed, thinking about it, and told her father she was losing all sense of values.

"Or getting it," William Ballard said.

"Well, or getting it. Because, honestly, Michael seems to me one of the pleasantest persons I ever met."

"He is. The fact that he hasn't any particular ambition to succeed as other men do isn't so serious. Perhaps we Americans make it more important than it is."

"Of course my first impression of him . . . " Joyce mused. "Michael—it seems funny now . . . "

She discussed Lissy's affair with her father. They two often chanced to be alone together; up in the barns or the dairy, pottering about in the sheds and yards. Joyce wore an old leather coat of Ben's, a pull-on leather hat that kept her ears warm. One of the events of the late autumn had been the selection of high laced boots from the tremendous catalog of a Chicago firm. Ben, Dodo, and Joyce often pored over this tome in the winter evenings. The boots had cost seven dollars and ninety cents, and Joyce considered them beautiful. Upon advice from Swede's wife she oiled them at night, stuffed them full of newspapers when they were wet.

Winter evenings went swiftly enough for the bridge players. They had a good fire in the parlor; they were eagerly cutting the pack at ten minutes past seven every night, and stopped, drugged with sleep, at half-past ten. But exactly what to do with the dark hours was a problem that Joyce, Dodo, and Ben had to solve for themselves. They played writing games, nursery card games; they watched each other playing solitaire. Dodo set to work on cross-stitch runners for the bureaus; Joyce read everything she could get out of the local library; there were radio programs worth hearing. Michael and Ben between them had rigged an aërial, and often in the late afternoons Joyce would find her mother lying on the parlor sofa, idle, sleepy, lazy, and openly listening to the "ridiculous vulgar thing" that she never would tolerate in "Ninety-nine." From New York came the great orchestras to flood the little California ranch house with rivers of exquisite sound; from Washington, London, Rome, came the voices of the world; Gracie Allen and Irvin Cobb and Ed Wynn were punctual in their engagements.

When the time came in January for Archie to go to Scotland to keep his promise to his cousin Jean, he was frankly reluctant. He took Lissy's father into his confidence.

"The awkward thing is that I simply don't feel I can go," Archie said simply.

"You don't?" William Ballard asked.

"I cannot," the other man said with firmness. "I—you have no idea how I feel about Felicity. I cannot go on with any—any other arrangement."

"H'm!" Lissy's father said doubtfully. "It is expected of you, of course. That is too bad!"

For they all had come somehow to like Archie in spite of his handsome young pompousness and his stupid management of his affairs of the heart. He was so determined in his helpless way to be a gentleman through it all, and to do his duty by the family and the firm, that first Lissy and then the others forgave him past defections, and came to see that once Archie's loyalty was engaged it was established for life. The awkwardness of the deferred marriage and broken engagement had all come about because Archie never really had included Lissy among his obligations; she was included now, and the situation, infinitely entangled, was a happier one for her than even the first days of her engagement had been. Or if not exactly happier, it was at least more exciting; less certain in one way, more certain in another. Lissy knew that she loved Archie now, loved him with all her heart, and Archie's protestations and Archie's admiration were infinitely more definite than they had been a year ago.

"A year ago!" Joyce said. "Were we all asleep? We seem to have been drifting along in a sort of dream, talking of weddings and servants and trips as if they all came out of books!"

It was finally decided that the only honest thing to do was for Archie to take the trip as planned to Scotland, see his cousin, and have a talk with her. Jean was thirty-five, a sensible nice girl; she would understand. Archie would tell her frankly that his old love for Felicity Ballard had returned, against his will even, and ask her to set him free from his promise, and to use her influence with his uncle to let the business arrangements stand.

Solemnly, tearfully indeed, he and Felicity parted. He would be back in late March, and a year after it had been originally planned their marriage would quietly take place, —this time in the old farmhouse. "For this is my home," Archie said, "and you are all my people. I never have been so happy as I have been on these Sundays; this is the way I like to live, this is the way everyone ought to live!"

Lissy was very pensive for several days after he went away, but she was not unhappy. A grave sort of dignity marked her manner; she fell into musing, listened abstractedly when the others talked, answered them gently.

"We have found each other again," she said. "There will be no more misunderstandings now."

"His uncle," Sally Ballard said, "couldn't be quite so brazen as to call off the business deal just because he loves Lissy! Would he want him to marry Jean, not loving her, pray?"

Lissy played bridge in the evenings now with a certain

shy grace. Her attitude toward all men, Ben, her father, and especially Michael, had gained in charm; she was beloved, she was going to be married soon.

"I wish it could be before May ninth," she said confidentially to Joyce. She and Joyce had more in common than either had with Dodo now; Joyce and Lissy were both engaged to be married.

"Why May ninth? Oh, your birthday? You'll be twenty-six," Joyce said. "What difference does it make?"

"It doesn't, really," Lissy conceded.

She had her lovely trousseau linen; she would need little more.

"I think this little time of trial has developed both their natures," Sally said. "We never knew what a really fine fellow Archie was before, and Lissy has been superb through it all. Well, Dodo," she added philosophically, "what will you and I do, left here alone without the girls?"

Dodo would smile at this sort of thing mysteriously; she was a silent little creature, always happiest when close to one of the others, following Joyce's confident directions, listening to what Lissy or her mother or Ben said. Joyce reasoned with her on the subject of Charley Sallock.

"Don't let yourself get to liking him, Dodo."

"I won't of course!" Dodo answered. "But why not?"

"Why not?" Joyce echoed. "Well, because!"

" 'Because' is no argument," Dodo said quietly.

"Because his family is a regular small-town family," Joyce expatiated it. "His mother has freckled arms and red hair and takes prizes for pickles at county fairs. His father has a feed store, and Marie-Thérèse is going with the Williams boy who delivers milk. You certainly wouldn't want to move over to a ranch in the San Joaquin, and wash milk pans for the rest of your life on a dairy farm!"

"I don't say I would," Dodo said, her small face flushed,

"but it wouldn't be so very different from what we are doing here, would it?"

Joyce regarded her with surprise and alarm.

"Yes, but, Dodo—this is only for a while, with us. We'll not stay here! If Liss marries in June, and later Paul and I step off, we'll—we'll be in very different places. We'll both be in Burlingame, or in San Francisco anyway; this'll all seem like a dream. But if you were wearing eighty-nine-cent bungalow aprons, and driving a muddy Ford into town for bridge prizes and clothespins and jelly glasses——"

"I don't see anything so wrong about bridge prizes and clothespins and jelly glasses!" Dodo said with an unwonted touch of haughtiness, as her sister, impressed by her own eloquence, stopped short. Joyce, stupefied, reflected upon the situation for a few days and then confided in her father.

"Dad, we couldn't have Dodo marry a *yokel* who talks about bog spavin and dances like a tractor!"

"Does he?" William Ballard asked, smiling absently, his eyes far away.

"He's terrible. That is, he's *nice* enough, and he talked to her about riding the range, and grapes, and the bureau his grandmother brought from Woburn, Massachusetts. I mean, there's nothing wer-*rong* about him, but he's—well, impossible. If Liss was married, or I was married, and he turned up as a brother-in-law—I mean it simply wouldn't be funny!" Joyce persisted, distressed. "Mother would lose her mind!" she added, as a final argument.

"You can't tell, when it's a question of your children's marriages," William Ballard said slowly.

"But good heavens, Dad, you can tell when it's just a matter of propinquity, and nobody else being around, and being lonely!"

"Marriage is almost always propinquity, Joyce."

"Mine isn't going to be!" Joyce diverged to say with a laugh. "But, Dad," she reasoned on earnestly, "wouldn't you be afraid that a few years, even a few months, afterward, anyone who married a boy like Charley Sallock would bitterly regret it?"

"Not more than the marriages some of the girls make up Burlingame way," William Ballard said reflectively. "We'll have to let Dodo manage that herself."

"I think she ought to be sent away!" Joyce wanted to say impatiently. But it had recently been made obvious that nobody could go anywhere for a while anyway. For weeks Ben had been mad with impatience to be off, sometimes talking of Alaska, sometimes of Tahiti or of New York, and a quite frank exposition of the family finances always constituted his answer. In the bank were a few hundreds only; each quarter would see four hundred more deposited; that was all the Ballards had. Lissy's wedding would cost something even if the outlay were confined to the "one plain little suit and decent hat" of which Sally spoke so confidently. Both Lissy and her mother were sure nothing wearable could be found nearer than San Francisco, the trip would cost something in gas and oil, and the prospective bride and her mother might have to stay at a hotel for a night or two. No; there could be no mere pleasure trips for a while. "Next year, they tell me, things may clear up a bit," William Ballard said cheerfully to his daughters. To Ben, Joyce once heard him speak more definitely.

"I've put it to you before this, Ben. If you stay here I expect you to help me and make yourself useful to your mother and the girls. I'm not trying to hold you here. It's beginning to be my profound conviction that no man has any right to ask anything or suggest anything to another man of twenty-two, even if it happens to be his son. While you do stay here I'm glad to feed to you and clothe you, of course. When you want to make some change, go ahead!"

Joyce, joining her father and brother as she caught this remark, looked at them fearfully. Was Ben going to be mad? But no, Ben rather seemed to be in affectionate sympathy with his father in these days; they talked a good deal together. Seeing them so, Joyce's heart sang. There was something essentially right in having a man and his father friends.

It was a singing morning, anyway. February sunshine was flooding down on a rain-soaked world, and the first beginnings of spring were breaking Joyce's heart with ecstasy. Grass again, and blue skies; frogs croaking in the cold sweet nights and plum trees great puffballs of white glory. It was too bad to have Dad and Ben out of sympathy at this time of year! Every inch of the ranch was sprouting color and sweetness, adding its note to the devastating beauty of spring. The old lilacs bore plumes of white and purple; lavender and iris formed pools of cool loveliness under the oaks up on the hills; in the canyon forest were brown and cream mission bells, cyclamen, columbine balanced in delicate vermilion bells on feathery foliage and the long ferny branches and white blossoms of Solomon's Seal. Up over the ridges ran the blue of wild lilac like spreading smoke; manzanita and chaparral put on their creamy blooms; even the redwoods spread fresh fans of green, and far below all over the valley floor the fruit blossoms waved in soft airs. Jays laced the air with blue; quail drummed in the woods; every window of the farmhouse was flung open, and the dooryard table was spread three times a day, with birds to do the sweeping away of crumbs, and oak and pear tree shadows lying green upon the checked red cloth.

# ❧ CHAPTER XX ❧

ONE day Joyce and Dodo went with the three men up to clear the source of the spring. It had become buried and choked in the silt and the fallen leaves of winter, and was running awry. They carried spades and brush hooks, and hacked at overgrown branches as they fought their way up the trail. Joyce had insisted on a "casual" lunch being carried. "You'd manage a picnic on the Statue of Liberty," Michael told her.

"Well, why not? I mean, if you went out there about noon, why shouldn't you ber-*ring* a few sandwiches?" the girl demanded.

The job proved to be much longer and more complicated than they had anticipated, and it was with great satisfaction that she presently presented her luncheon to the group: cold biscuit with pink ham showing between the split halves, coffee, applesauce cake. By this time everyone was wet, breathless, thoroughly warmed, happy. Boulders and tough embedded logs had been torn out of the earth; the muddy water, swirling slowly as it came, was forming itself into a clouded pool. Water from the soaked dirt drained back to its course; Michael planted rocks evenly, panted, straightened a stiffened back.

"Oh, Lord, Joyce, that food hits the spot!"

"Well, what did I *tell* you!"

Dodo, leaning toward the little fire, showed her sister a brown small hand for a second; withdrew it. The blood receded from Joyce's heart. On the third finger had been a band of plain gold.

She stared at Dodo, her mouth agape, all the strength gone from arms and legs. But Dodo was looking another way and presently jumped up busily and began to clear away the signs of the simple meal. Joyce followed her into the wood, caught her in a firm grip, faced her about.

"Theodora Ballard!"

"W'at?" Dodo murmured, in a little voice with a giggle in it.

"What on earth did you have on your hand?"

"Nothing!" Dodo bubbled, unashamed.

"You did. Where is it? Dodo, you haven't———"

"Yes, we were! Yesterday!" Dodo breathed triumphantly.

"You and Ch———! You weren't!"

"Sh-h-h! We're going to keep it a secret for a year at least."

Joyce leaned against a tree; her breath failed her.

"You *weren't*, Dodo?"

"We *were*."

"By a justice of the peace?"

"No, you crazy! By Dr. Labaree."

Joyce continued to regard her in dazed noncomprehension.

"Dodo, are you cur-*razy?* Mother will go out of her senses!"

"No, I'm not crazy at all. I'm twenty-three, nearly twenty-four, and I certainly have a right to my own life!"

"But, Dodo, you hardly know him! You've seen him three or four times!"

Dodo's face reddened resentfully.

"I've seen him all winter long, and danced with him, and

I sat with him all through *She Stoops To Conquer*. I don't see how you can say that I hardly know him. All last week he was here in Merriwell when his father was sick, and he and I drove around in his car for whole afternoons. Why, they're people, the Sallocks, like other people!" Dodo, driven out of her usual timid inarticulateness, said roundly. "If you love a person I don't know why dairy cows aren't just as interesting as real estate or architecture!"

"Mother——" Joyce breathed, eyeing her with compressed lips and narrowed eyes, her thoughts ranging wildly over all of the ramifications of this astounding situation.

"Mother won't know for a year; we've decided that."

"Yes, but what are you going to do? Just live along here and not tell anyone?"

"I don't know quite what I'm going to do," Dodo said, showing some first faint traces of nervousness, "but we're not going to tell anyone for a long while anyway. There's no use your staring at me that way, Joyce; people have gotten married before, I hope!"

"Dad'll have it annulled."

Joyce said it thoughtfully, half aloud, speaking more to herself than her sister. The sudden red came up into Dodo's face again.

"He can't; I'm of age," she said quickly. "Come on, let's go back and finish up the spring. Charley won't be back until Sunday, and I'll see him then."

A sudden affectionate compunction shook Joyce's heart. Again she put her arms about her sister, whispered in her ear.

"Darling, I hope it's all going to be happy and right for you!"

Dodo weakened; was weeping. When they went back to the spring both girls wore reddened eyes. But if William Ballard or Michael noticed it, neither made any comment. Presently, lame, weary, wet, they were all swinging down the trail again in the early afternoon light. Joyce's thoughts moved back and forth between plans for a hot bath and a rest before dinner, and the breath-taking change that had come into the family now. Lissy engaged, herself engaged; quiet little Dodo skipping the engagement and stepping straight into the real thing. "A year your granny!" Joyce thought scornfully. "They can't keep it a secret a month!"

At the farmhouse other matters were brewing. Joyce could not imagine what they were, for Lissy and her mother said nothing, and the before-dinner period went on just as usual. But she saw trouble in their set faces and sensed calamity in their carefully held tones.

"William," said Sally Ballard, when they were finishing a custard, "may I speak to you just a moment?"

It was a warm night; the first really warm night they had had; Ben and the girls and Michael sat on under the pear tree and saw the great disk of the April moon rise over the shoulders of the eastern mountains. It hung enormous, red, in a sky of trembling dark blue; a long warm sigh went over the world, and Joyce's cat walked delicately across the young grass and paused to utter a resentful appeal, her round mouth red in her angry whiskered little face. Now and then the girl looked at her younger sister as if she had never seen Dodo before, but Dodo was quite calm and laughed as if nothing untoward had happened. "Married!" Joyce's thoughts said, in awe. "Dodo married!"

After a while Sally's voice was heard at the parlor window:

"Girls, will you come in here a minute?"

Joyce, her heart thundering, arose. Did she know anything of Dodo's marriage, or didn't she? They would question them both, and what line should she take? Pure astonishment, that was best for herself and Dodo, too. "Married!" she would gasp. "Oh, Dodo, you're not! Who said so? I don't believe it!"

Sick with trepidation, trembling, she went into the parlor. But Dodo seemed calm and was humming lightly as they went in. Ben and Michael had already started to walk up to Michael's place; Lissy had gone to bed. The big empty yard was left to moonlight and tree shadows.

The house was stuffy in the humid evening. Sally called again from the sitting room. "Girls, come in here!"

"They know!" Joyce said in a stifled undertone.

"I don't care if they do!" Dodo answered lightly.

Their father and their mother were both in the room; William Ballard was seated in his favorite chair under the lamp; he looked up thoughtfully as they came in. Sally was at one of the dark windows; she spoke over her shoulder.

"Ben go?"

"Yes," Joyce said, almost sick with expectation and fright, "he and Michael had just started when you called."

"What," Sally asked without preamble, "what do you know of Ben and this Gertrude Florence?"

The relief weakened Joyce's knees, and she sat down abruptly in the nearest chair. It wasn't Dodo after all!

"Bootsy?" she asked, widening her eyes.

"I believe she calls herself that."

"She and Ben got pretty far in—pretty far in," William Ballard said mildly. "No harm done, but the boy's tired of it, and the girl isn't."

"Oh, but Dad, how did you know?" Dodo demanded.

"You knew, then?" her father asked shrewdly, by way of answer.

"Well, everyone in town knows how Bootsy feels, "Dodo said simply. Sally gave a sort of groan.

"No harm done," William Ballard repeated. "But the girl was here today, talking to your mother——"

"Bootsy was!" both girls exclaimed together.

"She and her extraordinary mother," Sally contributed

bitterly. "Of course I don't know anything about it—obviously I'm not supposed to know—but evidently the girl had her wedding day picked out! She wanted to know what she'd 'done,' and why Ben was so changed, and who had 'talked him out of it'!"

Joyce laughed cheerfully.

"Trust Bootsy!" she said. "Poor Ben!"

"Poor all of us!" Sally said fervently. "Coming to a Godforsaken place like this—Lissy's life ruined—now Ben's life ruined———"

"What we wanted to say to you girls," William Ballard said mildly, when after a long time there was a pause, "is that Ben is going away for a while, right away. Probably he'll go to Portland. I've an old friend on a newspaper there who may give him a job. And we don't want him teased—don't want too many questions asked———"

Awed, the little sisters agreed. Joyce had enough to think about, as she lay awake that night. Dodo—and Ben —and Dodo again.

"You have to come to the country to have things *happen!*" Joyce thought.

And then suddenly all these things were made unimportant and unreal to Joyce by the reception of a letter from Paul's pretty young stepmother, the blonde stenographer for whose sake his father had gotten a divorce.

"My dear Joyce," Claire von Schwerin wrote, in a somewhat unformed hand, on beautiful writing paper, "Paul is coming home for six days at Easter, flying both ways, and will be with us here on Tuesday. Why don't you come up Monday night, and meet him with us on Tuesday morning at Mills Field? On Wednesday his father is taking us all to Pebble Beach for the golf tournaments, and we will see that you get back safely at some time Monday."

This letter threw Joyce into such raptures as only twenty-one can know. The glory of spring was enhanced a hundred-fold; Joyce felt that her heart could scarcely bear its burden of joy.

It was not only the prospect of the exciting and luxurious visit, the polo and golf, the big cars and the big houses; it was not even the thought of seeing Paul again—handsome, big, carelessly sure of himself, carelessly loving—that brought her pulses to fever height. It was more than that. Paul's people had accepted her; she was Paul's girl. She was the girl who was asked to meet him when he came home after ten months' absence!

## ❧ CHAPTER XXI ❧

CLAIRE VON SCHWERIN met Joyce herself at the Burlingame station on a languid spring afternoon and whirled her away through green leafy lanes and past imposing iron gates to "Joyland," the place they had rented for a summer only, but in which they had been established now for almost a year. Joyce remembered every lovely detail of it and could have danced her way up the wide shallow stairs as she followed Christine, the maid, with her bags.

The guest room where she and Alice Goldthwaite had brushed their hair, and lain talking on their beds, and giggled, and changed their frocks during last year's wonderful visit, was as dainty and inviting as ever, better than ever, with soft airs from the flower-crowded garden swaying the delicate curtains on the window sills, and pink roses in a glass bowl on the table. Oh, beauty was restful, and quietly stepping maids were restful, and to do exactly as you liked and have an army of pleasant and contented folk to do the cleaning was very restful! Joyce got into her third-best frock and went downstairs to find an idle group having cocktails on the terrace. Forgotten touches like canapés, and tiny napkins with roosters embroidered on them, and

209

enamel beauty boxes and cigarette cases, and finely groomed hands, and fine scents and materials and voices were in her life again.

She was content to be quiet, a smiling listener in a big basket chair, with the frills of the old yellow organdy foaming around her yellow slippers, and her eyes glowing in a face actually pale from excitement and happiness. A man she had met before took the chair next to hers, was nice to her.

"Where's Arch Ross now, if you know, Miss Ballard?"

"Well, on his way home from the East as a matter of fact; he's been in Scotland."

"Who has been in Scotland?" somebody else asked.

"Arch Ross. Miss Ballard was just saying that he's on his way home."

"Is that so?" a man said.

"Yes; he should have been here Sunday, I believe," Joyce said. "He was coming down to see us that day, but I believe he was delayed; he had to go to Los Angeles from New York instead of coming straight."

It was not very important, but they were interested, and it made her feel part of the group. After dinner she went to a movie with the King girls, their boy cousin, their brother, and their German Fräulein, and another girl named Margaret Something, and a boy to whom Joyce was introduced but whose name she instantly forgot. It was not a very good movie, but they all sat attentive for two hours, and when they came out the boys suggested sodas. But the governess said much better go home and get some really nice milk and cake, so they all did that. Joyce was faithfully deposited at the Von Schwerin home at eleven, and saw the grown-ups playing bridge passionately in a library some arcades away, and went upstairs without good-nights. She was almost too happy to sleep, and when she did sleep it was to dream that somehow she had missed connections at

Mills Field, she was miles and miles away when the plane came in—or no, she was there, but she was in her nightwear, trying to pretend that faded blue cotton pajamas were correct attire for the meeters of travelers . . .

She awakened with a jump. It was dawn; it was five o'clock. Claire had promised that she should be awakened in plenty of time for the eight-o'clock breakfast; the plane did not arrive until after nine. But for a while she lay wakeful, afraid to go to sleep and miss anything.

"You look adorable!" Claire said, when she went downstairs in trim blue linen, at eight, with a blue hat on the back of her head.

The girls, she had noticed last night, were wearing their hair and their hats in subtly different ways this year; stiff brims and tight curls had not reached Merriwell yet, except in the advertisements of magazines. Joyce thought that perhaps while she was at Pebble Beach she would slip away and have a new hair-do; not that it mattered much, but it would be rather fun to go home wearing the very latest thing.

She could hardly eat her breakfast, and she was silent with sheer emotion as they drove to the field. It was not far; they were early, and saw various big birds come down with a bumping flight, and soar upward again with the sunshine bright on their metal wings. At last the big Eastern plane came in, and circled, and descended, and there was Paul in his brown coat, the first one off, running toward them, wildly delighted to be home again and to see Joyce, natural and eager with his father and stepmother.

"How's the old man treating you, Claire?" Paul said. "You look simply swell; you've had your face lifted!" And to his father he had a confidential aside: "I'll turn over to you the balance, Dad; I don't need it, my allowance is due on Friday. And I want to talk to you about summer work; I may have to take a test over again."

Then he was free to turn all his attention to Joyce, and

she was exquisitely happy driving home in the back seat with him, her hand in his, their eyes finding what was new in each other and what was dear and familiar. Paul asked for each and every member of the family, and Joyce made their histories as amusing and dramatic as she could, and they laughed at everything in the old way.

Paul said "Mammy!" on all occasions now, and somehow the babyish expletive was manly when he said it, and he seemed strangely grown to Joyce, strangely smart, completely charming.

They went around from one house to the other that day, and to the club, and met a great many other girls and young men. And everywhere Joyce was Paul's girl, the girl his mother had asked to come up from the country to meet him. They were going to Pebble Beach tomorrow, and everyone else was, too, and there was talk of dancing there, and of the golf tournament; it was all exciting and delightful beyond words to a girl who had been marooned on a hillside ranch down in the Santa Clara valley for a whole year, and to whose senses delicate glassware, perfect service, the swishing of exquisite frocks and the scent of costly perfumes were in themselves a treat.

That night after dinner Paul asked her suddenly, "Want to go up to the Mark Hopkins and dance?" and after her rapturous assent, went for his car. Everything was easy and ordered for these people because they had money. Paul, handsomer than ever in dinner clothes, slipped into the brown coat; Joyce had the right velvet wrap, she saw to it that comb and lipstick and powder were in her bag; they went off laughing.

So Tuesday ended, one of the perfect days of girlhood, a happy, flattering, perfumed, thrilling day, with the current of her love for him and his for her carrying it too swiftly into the past.

It was the last quite perfect time. For at some point in the next day Joyce began to feel the first wretched fingertip of misgiving on her heart, and although she tried to shake it away, to tell herself it was not there, once entertained she could not lose it again.

They were all going to Pebble Beach at eleven; they were to lunch on the way. There were to be three cars and eight persons in the party: the three Von Schwerins, Joyce, Mrs. Rogers and Consuelo Waite, Mrs. Termini and King Harrington. Joyce did not like Consuelo. It was not mere fear and jealousy, for she had not felt anything of the sort for lovely Alice Goldthwaite last summer, and Alice had been quite openly affectionate with Paul.

Mrs. Rogers was Consuelo's mother and Mrs. Termini was King's mother. They were second wives, as Claire was, resolutely successful and assertive, sure that their changes of mates had been wise; jeweled and overdressed. Claire became quite a different woman in their company; she became noisy and affected, too, and once mentioned her predecessor, Paul's mother, as "that imbecile poor Vic was saddled with for fourteen years!"

As for the younger members of the group, Joyce thought King Harrington a rude, unattractive young man, and Consuelo, who was called "Pidgie," with her dyed hair and affected manners and her chatter of Antibes and Palm Beach, a decidedly disagreeable girl. She hoped that they would not be all together when they got to Pebble Beach, and seized an opportunity to murmur to Paul, "Can't we go alone in your car?"

Paul regarded her with dancing and unsympathetic eyes. "Oh, Pidgie's swell," he said enthusiastically. "You'll like her; she's a sport. She was with these people I knew in New York—her uncle's Senator Waite. Her father sends her five hundred a month; remember how last year I told you she bought a polo pony here for three hundred—bought it just like that! Harry Parsons was jerking it around, he was mad, and she leaned down from the grandstand and said, 'Harry, what's that pony worth?' He was selling his whole string. He said, 'Three hundred,' and she whipped out a checkbook. 'Take my pony to the stable, and don't let anyone ride him again today,' she told the groom. Harry began to laugh; he was folding up the check, and he said, 'I bought him for one-eighty last week.' Well, Hughes was here, you know the malt-chocolate man, and he called out to her, 'Sell him for five hundred, Pidgie?' and she shrugged, and said, 'I'll consider it.' She walked up to sit with Hughes, and he gave her a check—both the Hughes boys were riding last year. But whether it was for five hundred or not I don't know!"

Joyce laughed heartily at this sort of thing; one had to, in this group. They were always telling stories about each other, and they were not very thrilling stories. Or perhaps it was just that she did not find them funny on this unseasonably hot spring day, with this new unwelcome fear gnawing at her heart.

Paul had changed; but then why shouldn't he have changed? The shy awkward boy of a year ago had indeed blossomed out since the days when the simple friendship of the Ballard girls, their home games and family affection had made such a haven for his loneliness and strangeness. Paul had discovered the world now, and the world had found Paul; women liked him, and of course he knew it; he was always laughing, he was in wild spirits.

"Here's where I sit!" Pidgie Waite said definitely, with a little triumphant laugh, when the low-slung red and yellow car had come around to the drive in the hot bright morning sunlight. She sprang, as she spoke, into the front seat, established herself and her smart red and black and white frock comfortably, put on her big dark sun glasses. Paul saw her, of course, knew that she would be his companion on the hundred-mile drive, but made no comment except a grin, and continued to pack suitcases into the box at the back. King and Joyce got into the back seat; the girl heroically determined to make the best of a bad situation. No use surrendering to Pidgie at the first attack.

King was, conversationally, hard going. He was a thin, weak-looking, intellectually inclined young man with a deep beautiful crimp in his thick fair hair. Nothing interested him. Joyce put out all sorts of feelers: aviation, tennis, golf, Germany, politics; it was no use. Presently the chattering couple on the front seat, who were in continual gales of laughter, spoke of some prize fight, and then King leaned forward interestedly, and for some miles he traveled sitting sidewise on the very edge of his seat, with his face close to Pidgie's shoulder and his arm half about her.

During this time Joyce sat back comfortably, studying the scenery—the lovely canyons strewn with great oaks, the already drying golden brown hills where the cows were straying, the flat levels of the strawberry farms on the long road to the sea. Del Monte's rich acres of deep trees came into view, infinitely restful and green in the burning early afternoon; smart cars were twinkling in and out of the shady gateways; a group of polo players cantered by on their springy mounts.

The road rose past the mild creamy walls of the old Mission on Monterey Hill, swept through the old town asleep on the straggling main street that ended with the high barns and complicated odors of the fisheries. To the south the Carmel highway mounted between meadows and under sprawled oaks; they could get the fresh breath of the sea now; they had turned in at the Pebble Beach gates and were winding their way among pines and cypresses toward the lodge that stood in a blaze of flowers and planted garden trees looking out at the blue Pacific.

A few golfers were going the rounds; a few nurses and children were grouped idly in the shade of the oaks, but the lodge seemed deserted. There was polo today, and all the guests had gone to see it. White-clad boys carried Joyce's and Pidgie's bags upstairs through airy halls to a magnificent big room finished in oriental dull gold and lacquer red, with thin tan curtains at the tall windows. The girls had a high balcony over the sea, but at this hot hour it was awash with sunlight, and their bedroom jalousies had been closed, giving a touch of European beauty to the big shaded apartment.

Perfectly appointed bathroom with soft fat towels; deep closets with shoeboxes and padded hangers; a pleasant maid suggesting iced tea and bathing suits and hair-dressing—these were commonplaces to the rowdy Pidgie, whose father sent her five hundred dollars a month, but every fiber of Joyce's being rejoiced in them.

While they unpacked she tried to be friendly and informal with Pidgie. But Pidgie, while not disagreeable, was one of those girls whose minds dwell only upon contact with the male. She was thinking of men as she changed her frock and brushed her dyed golden hair; she had but an abstracted and indifferent attention to bestow on any woman. Even while Joyce was talking, comfortably spread on her bed now, with a handful of magazines, resting and lazy and nibbling at the grapes that were part of a basket of fruit, Pidgie swept suddenly to the telephone and called someone called Budge. They talked for twenty-two minutes, a talk all laughter and ironical murmuring.

"Yes, you did," said Pidgie. "I heard all about that. . . . Who? . . . Oh, for heaven's sake! . . . Who? . . . Oh, Lord. You and who else? . . . He did not. . . . Did he say that? What nerve! . . . Nerts. . . . Is my face red! Go on. . . . Oh, go on, I dare you. . . . Oh, please. Go on. I dare you to! Am I embarrassed?"

This went on for a long time. Joyce turned the pages of her magazine and tried not to think of Paul. If he had

changed a little it was only because he had been twenty-four
and was now twenty-five; he had to grow up, of course. If
he was a little less young and fresh and eager, a little surer
of himself—yes, and of her, too—that was only because they
had been separated for months. He would come back to her,
all the way back. Why, surely it had been in response to
some suggestion from Paul that his stepmother had written
her asking her to meet him!

"I've got to go and see my aunt," Pidgie presently
volunteered. She knitted thoughtful brows. "I wonder if
Paul is doing anything," she mused. Instantly she was at
the telephone again. Paul was just going out to play golf; it
was only three o'clock, he could get in nine holes, anyway.
What course was he playing? Cypress Point? Oh, then
would he be an angel and take Pidgie over to see her aunt,
right near the clubhouse there?

Then there was a halt, and a slight change in Pidgie's
tone.

"She's lying down," she said. Joyce's heart rose with a
leap. Pidgie extended the telephone. "He wants to talk to
you," she explained, as the other girl seized the instrument.

"What do you mean by talking to me with no more clothes
than that on?" Paul demanded.

"Oh, shut up!" Joyce laughed. "I'm extremely lovely. I
have Lissy's dressing gown on; pink, and lace, and blue
ribbons——"

"Want to come over to Cypress Point? I'll only be playing
about an hour. How long would it take you to jump into
something?"

"Two minutes!" Everything was right again for the moment; Pidgie was routed and sulky. Joyce took the front
seat for the little drive along the rocky shore under the
twisted cypresses. But life was on a receding tide just the
same, and no one special big wave could save it. Dinner was
distractingly gay and noisy and broken by dancing; after-

ward there were dog races; there were too many persons
about, there was too much nonsense. In fact there was nothing but nonsense, and bridge, and leaving one's delicious
thick steak when one got up to dance, and coming back to
find it whisked away, and silly unthinking talk that was not
always nice. She grew tired; her head felt very tired in the
unaccustomed whirl of it all, and when Joyce got to bed
that night she felt restless and dissatisfied. However, there
was tomorrow with infinite possibilities, and Friday and
Saturday and Sunday—there was time for adjustment and
improvement.

All the next day there was golf. Joyce had never played
it, but she knew enough of it to trail the players intelligently
and make an occasional apt comment. Luncheon was at the
clubhouse, confused and crowded. Paul was of course among
the fringe of men about Elisa Blandwood. Even bold and
noisy Pidgie could make no headway against Elisa; she was
just one of those girls who had everything and won everyone and did everything, and that was that!

Elisa was naturally fair; there was no artifice by which
those pale taffy curls, that magnolia-petal skin, those sleepy
long eyes could be acquired. She wore white, unrelieved
white-white, no oyster or cream or opal about it; it was as
pure and toneless as fog. She was lazy and slow in movement and rather silent. Elisa did not have to talk. She was
rich, she played magnificent golf; she knew the Eastern and
the English champions and their records; she had a young
English lord in attendance.

"Well, all right, suppose she has and does and did and
is?" Joyce reasoned fiercely in her jealous heart. "There has
to be more than one sort of girl, doesn't there? One man
wouldn't be enough for all these girls, if he were the Prince
of Wales! Girls like that don't always have the happy and
successful lives. What I have to do is just forget her—go
right straight ahead as if she didn't exist!"

The men were trying to persuade Elisa to come to the dog races tonight, and afterward go to Parker's and dance. Elisa had never been to a dog race—she adored dogs, and gave them the short pronunciation that is not "dawg," but rhymes with "fog"—but she never had been to dog races. She had been to hai-alai games in Shanghai and adored them; wasn't there any hai-alai in California? But not dogs; they were so sweet, and it was so mean to race them . . .

In the end she said of course she would go. Joyce had known she would go, and it was Paul who leaped off to secure two good boxes for the dog races that night.

Well, so here Joyce was back in her magnificent room at the lodge again, and it was five o'clock, and the third day of her marvelous visit was ending. It seemed years ago that she had gotten up in such an ecstasy of anticipation and high spirits in the Von Schwerin house to go meet Paul at the flying field, but it was only two days.

Now what to do? Dinner would be at eight; one couldn't lie down from five o'clock until eight. Joyce felt so hot, tired, confused that she would have been delighted to escape from them all for that time, but it would not do to have Pidgie presently dash in and find her sedately settled with a book; it would mean that she was to be pitied, that an effort must be made to amuse her.

Her bathing suit had been neatly dried and was hanging in the bathroom with the blue cap beside it and the white rope shoes neatly set beneath both on the floor. The afternoon was strangely hot and still for a California April. Joyce suddenly decided upon a late dip in the ocean. Sunshine was still streaming over it—the water had been icy cold this morning, and would be colder now, but at least it would be something to do, and something to remember when the merciless heat of July shut down on the ranch.

Bundled into the white woolly coat that Lissy had brought back from Paris years before, her brown slim feet disappearing into the rope slippers, she made her way down across the blazing terrace and the steps that descended to the beach. It was deserted now except for women and children, and the elderly Englishman—at least he was probably forty—who wrote books about bugs and snakes and birds. Monty Lefanu.

Brown, short, square, with very black hair and skin the color of a bay pony, he was plunging riotously about in the surf, shouting with the loud gasps that showed that he was just in. Joyce did her own wincing and gasping, reached for his hard brown hand. They agreed that they would swim together to the float, prearranging definitely that neither was to save the other in a crisis except by cheering words.

"I am capable of der-*rown*ing anyone in a moment of panic," Joyce told him. "I should ther-*row* my arms about your neck and ther-*rottle* you without a second's hesitation!"

"D'you know I'm exactly that way myself? No hero, don't you know? I should probably give you a good one between the eyes and swim off as fast as possible!" the man said, talking exactly like Michael.

They both laughed joyously, liking each other.

"On the other hand," Joyce said, "should *you* get the ker-*ramp,* and predecease me, as lawyers say——"

"Oh, but I say, what a horrible phrase!" Montague Lefanu protested, standing knee deep in the delicious swirl of the clean green water and eyeing her reproachfully. "You're not preparing for anything like that, are you?"

"When I swim to a raft," Joyce said firmly, "I'm prepared for anything." The man's fine gray eyes danced.

"You talk exactly like a little baggage I know in England," he said. "One Mimsey, aged seven."

"Baby talk?" Joyce said, raising dark brows over rounded eyes.

"Oh, no, not baby talk. Mimsey thinks she is ter-*riff*ically ger-*rown* up," he said. Foam rushed about them, they caught at it with their dripping hands.

"My family tells me it's an affectation," Joyce said. "But it really isn't. I do that when I'm interested."

"I'm flattered, Miss—Miss——?"

"Ballard. It's divine when you're once used to it," Joyce said, of a wave that brimmed majestically in waist high and caused her to stagger a little and reach for the brown hard hand again. "Is Mimsey Miss Lefanu?"

"Mimsey's Miss Lefanu, and my only only. We lost a boy three years ago.—Well, come on, shall we try it?"

"Coming back it'll be much easier," Joyce shouted, swimming gallantly along beside him toward the float.

"Getting tired?"

"Oh, no; I could swim to the Farallones tonight! This is the time to swim!"

"This is the time I always do swim," he said, when they were panting and streaming and triumphant on the float.

"Then," Joyce said prettily, pushing wet hair back with both hands, "this is the time I swim, too, from now on!"

"Right!" he said cordially, pleased. They fell into talk of wrecks and drowning. Joyce had found the subject fascinating during the long dark winter and had managed to get into the old bookstores of San José more than once to find old stories of sea disasters and escapes. Monty Lefanu told her he had been thinking of doing a book about them.

They swam back again, with the incoming waves to help them this time, and Joyce found her sun-warmed big robe delightfully comforting, and laughed a dripping good-bye to her companion as she ran up the long steps. Everything was right now, somehow, and to find Paul and some others idling on the terrace with cocktails was only a part of the general satisfactoriness. She knew herself rosy and disheveled and pretty, with the blue cap snatched off and the white crash wrapped about her. She would not have a cocktail, but she stayed to gossip for a few minutes and to eat a thin brown anchovy sandwich.

"What'd you think of Elisa Blandwood?"

"Helen of Troy," Joyce answered readily. She had never been in exactly this situation before, but mother wit inspired the answer, and she felt quite pleased with herself when one of the men said dryly: "But nobody knows it as well as Elisa," and Pidgie struck an entirely wrong note by saying in a bored voice: "She doesn't seem any such ball of fire to me; I mean, she's good-looking in that pale sort of way, and of course she has all that money behind her——"

"Oh, I think she's simply irresistible!" Joyce protested.

And suddenly she felt comfortable and happy, at ease in her wicker chair, not obliged to talk if she did not want to talk, free to stare off over the ocean and smile absent-mindedly at the conversation. Oh, if this feeling would only last!

"Be a sport and get into something and come with me out to the Point. I've got to pick Claire up; she's playing bridge out there," Paul presently suggested, sending her spirits to fever pitch, even though she only moved brown eyes thoughtfully to his, and meditated on his answer before she spoke.

"Will it give us time to dress afterward?"

"Oh, Lord, all the time you want!"

And that was one of the good hours.

"That's the secret," Joyce thought. "When you can't do what you want to do, do something else, and do it hard!"

She came back from the most perfect hour she had had with Paul, an hour that was like old times, to find Pidgie rather disgruntled; her afternoon had not been successful, apparently; she was almost nude, and lying flat, irritably ruffling the pages of a magazine that had bored Joyce in the same situation that same afternoon. She presently spoke bitterly of Elisa.

"I hope you didn't miss the broad English 'a,' for Sir George Hopetree's benefit!" Pidgie said scornfully. "She gives me a great big pain! She used to be Betty Moss when she and I went to Castilleja School!"

"Oh, is she divorced?" Joyce asked hopefully. Somehow one wasn't so jealous of divorced women; they deserved some luck.

"No-o-o! She's only twenty; she's a year older than I am. Her mother was divorced and married an Englishman named Blandwood, and she came home three years ago with 'Elisa Moss-Blandwood' on her cards—oh, yes, and she met the Prince of Wales at a garden party—maybe!" Pidgie grumbled. "I hope he knew it!"

Joyce felt quite light-hearted as she tubbed and brushed and powdered, felt that their common fear and dislike for Elisa was a bond between her and Pidgie.

"I'm borrowing some of your bath salts!"

"Use 'em all! I hate 'em!"

"Oh, delicious bath, and nothing to do for an hour!"

Joyce emerged from the bathroom fresh and cool, with her mahogany hair curled into little wisps and tails from fresh and salt water, and her eyes like stars in a rather pale face.

"This pace kills me!" she said frankly, dropping flat on her bed.

"I loathe the gait they go down here; I don't know how they do it: bridge and roulette and dog races every night, and cocktails before lunch, and golf and polo and tennis. Why they don't all drop dead!" Pidgie muttered. "We're all going over to Del Monte for dinner, then the dog races, and then wind up at Canary Cottage for roulette! I lost nineteen dollars on those damn dogs last night; I *couldn't* pick a winner, and I can't play tonight; Mother says she's broke."

"You want me to lend you twenty dollars," Joyce thought;

"but I haven't got it. . . . I didn't bring any money with me," she said aloud.

"I didn't want to borrow from you, darling," Pidgie said, with a yawn that did not disguise complete untruth.

"I knew you didn't," Joyce answered, with a corresponding air of casualness.

They lay on their beds and discussed not only their position as guests of Claire von Schwerin, but their hostess herself.

"She's having a terrible time holding Victor von Schwerin, and don't you fool yourself!" Pidgie said.

"What makes you think so?"

"Oh, the way she acts; the way they rush around! He's only about fifty-one, you know; he's always on the lookout for something exciting."

"I think that's rather disgusting, don't you, Pidgie?" Joyce asked slowly.

"Oh, I don't know. What did she expect?"

"Well, if I married I wouldn't expect—that," the other girl formulated it hesitatingly. "I mean, what *are* you sure of, if you're not sure of your husband—going on liking you?" she added.

"Why should you want him to, if you got tired of him?" Pidgie asked reasonably.

"But I should think your husband would be sort of the—well, the base you built your life on," Joyce pursued it.

"My mother's husbands aren't! My mother's been married three times—Obermann really didn't count," Pidgie amended it; "they were only married three months. Oh, well, she has a lot of fun!" she finished rather vaguely, after a moment of consideration. "The last time she was married on Lenny Springer's yacht, it was kind of fun! I was there that time."

Joyce made no further comment. She lay thinking. Somehow the atmosphere of this place made her feel unnatural and uneasy; her face felt flushed and dry all the time, and her heart beat hard. Life was like a fierce contest here; one must continually measure one's successes and failures, cutting out somebody here, being cut out oneself there.

During this evening, as far as she was concerned, it was a losing fight. A sense of weariness, of struggle, of despondency grew upon her; she knew it, she fought it with all her strength, but circumstances were too strong for her, and she felt despair and shame and helplessness rising about her like a tide.

## ❧ CHAPTER XXII ❧

ON SATURDAY, Paul and Elisa were drawn to play in a golf foursome with the best of the man players, one Rudy Reiger, and a young woman named Ethel Le Count. Joyce had felt in her soul, from the moment the names went up, that the drawing would result this way. She did not play golf at all; she was relegated to the position of onlooker when the contestants started hilariously at the first tee.

Elisa was lovely in white and dark blue stripes, with a knotted cotton cord of French red on her linen hat. Her long supple body was beautiful in the sweep of her splendid drives; when she walked along between the men, she walked with the free glorious step of a panther. She was flushed, amused, superb in victory—Joyce had known that, too— known that her team would win. "Oh, marvelous partner, good girl!" Paul said, over and over again, as she whipped the white pellet from a bad lie, putted with just the right follow-through for a successful hole.

Paul and Elisa, having easily worsted competitors on Saturday morning, fought a harder battle but won again in the afternoon. That meant that they would play finals on Sunday. There had been talk of a picnic on Sunday, but of course that was all ended now. Nothing else was discussed but the golf. Elisa Blandwood and Paul von Schwerin—imagine, playing in the finals!

Paul wanted to talk of each and every separate shot in the scant moments he and Joyce had together. He was in wild spirits and great looks, the golfing apparel infinitely becoming to him, his waves of wet-brushed fair hair rumpled, his skin burned Indian brown. Everybody wanted to make much of him, and his rôle was the delightful one of success. It was only an amateur tournament, anyway, Joyce had to remind herself constantly; it didn't matter one bit, nobody really cared who won. But oh, if Elisa Blandwood would only do something fatal, break her leg, cheat, make herself ridiculous, how wonderful it would be!

A great weariness came over Joyce as the hours of the hot spring Saturday wore away, and the chill beginnings of the first hard lesson life was to teach her made her soul sick within her. It couldn't be that she wasn't going to marry Paul, that what he had felt for her wasn't the real thing, or that it had changed and wasn't the real thing now, anyway! She wouldn't admit that, she wouldn't accept it—she couldn't. She *couldn't* go back to Merriwell, beaten, heart-broken, infinitely less fortunate even than poor Lissy, whom she had pitied from her own superb youth and sureness so short a time ago.

The conviction, fight it as she would, strengthened and deepened. Paul liked her immensely, found her amusing and companionable, but he was no longer in love. Perhaps he never had been; once such a thing was changed it was hard to remember exactly what it had been. Since his arrival on Tuesday—and this was Saturday!—there had been no love-making between them; no, not even when he had taken her to dinner and to dance in the city. It had been all gay, eager, affectionate, appreciative—not passionate, not tender, not secret. Here at Pebble Beach he had seemed to want the crowd about them. "Let's get the others; let's ask the others," had been his constant enthusiastic suggestion.

Would he take her home to Merriwell tomorrow to make everything right, there in that quiet atmosphere of oaks and hills, home voices and evening lamps? Joyce's despairing heart could not say. Did he feel himself promised to her? She could not tell that, either. His seeing her at all had been arranged by his stepmother; perhaps, had he had his own way, he would have forgotten Joyce entirely.

On the Saturday night after the golf they dined at Del Monte and danced. Elisa could not join them; she was out on the Forces' yacht for dinner; Joyce could be glad of that much respite at least even while she felt a little pang of envy of Elisa's popularity. Paul was sleepy and sunburned and good-natured at dinner; men and women spoke to him of his golf record, and he laughed and flushed boyishly, and said that of course he and Elisa would go down tomorrow like a ton of Coos Bay coal.

"But I was going to drive you home tomorrow, and now, darn it, I'll be playing all day!" he said to Joyce.

"I don't have to go home tomorrow; I can stay until Monday; I don't have to go home ever; ask me to stay until Monday!" her heart screamed. Aloud she said: "Well, being in the finals is *something,* anyway!"

"I can't get over it! Elisa and I were saying at Forces' this afternoon that if she hadn't intentionally hooked that shot on the eight . . ."

They were all talking golf again. Joyce rested an elbow on the table, her chin in her hand, and listened with an expressive face, as if she understood all of it.

"The telephone, Mr. von Schwerin," a waiter said. Paul jumped up. When he came back he was in a great hurry.

"It was Elisa," he explained. Joyce's heart sank like a leaden thing in her breast. "She's got a sun headache, poor kid; she's not so awfully strong," Paul added. "She wants, me to run down and get her; she's going to turn right in. I'll be back in a sec."

He was gone.

"Elisa could throw a couple of bulls single-handed," Pidgie then said. "But how that delicate pose gets 'em! I think I'll go in for tuberculosis."

Paul was gone for a long time. When he came back and slipped into his chair beside Joyce, he was slightly out of breath and excited.

"She's got a sun headache; nothing serious," he confided to Joyce. "Poor little thing; she was all in; I had practically to carry her upstairs. Her aunt's maid was out, so I turned her bed down for her and cut over to Monterey and got her some aspirin. She felt like the devil, keeping me away from you all, but she wasn't able to do anything but collapse. I told her to undress, but she said she might come down after a while and just look on; she won't dance."

"Oh, poor thing," the girls said dutifully. They exchanged cryptic glances. Everything was twisted and queer for Joyce; the sense of having to fight for her friendship with this handsome brown confident boy, the deeper sense of not being able to fight, not knowing the rules. Paul's father, looking smart and sure of himself in evening dress, came over to their table and asked her to dance. While they danced he told her about his tailor in New York, and that he had a better tailor in London. He said that all the world followed the lead of English tailors when it came to men's clothes; sometimes he had to go for four or five fittings on one vest, but it was worth it. He asked Joyce if she was having a nice time and said that she mustn't imagine that old fellows his age didn't know a lovely girl when they saw one.

Joyce laughed; was youthfully receptive to his remarks. He was Paul's father, after all. But she did not like it. And when they finished their dance and got back to the table she could have screamed to have him sit down beside her and continue his flattering personalities. Paul had disappeared.

"I don't know where that son of mine's gone," Victor von Schwerin said. "But I don't think it matters, does it? I think we're having an extremely pleasant time without him. I shouldn't mind one bit cutting out that young man. Now, what are we drinking? It seems to me this is an occasion for wine . . ."

Joyce smiled, answered, lowered her thick lashes, raised them again. Her heart was sick within her, and she knew neither what she was doing nor saying. Everything was a sickening glare of light and noise, with sickening waves of music beating through it, and the squawk of girls' laughter and the clinking of plates for an undertone. Where had Paul gone?

Some of the girls must be having a good time here, but oh, what a horrid time some of the others were having! Life couldn't be handled simply, like the setting of a table or cooking of a dinner; elements came into it that were beyond control; all the joy could suddenly go out of it through no fault of one's own. Joyce could look the situation soberly in the face now; she had thought Paul cared more than he did care; she had thought he would come back from his long absence as unchanged as she was unchanged herself. She had put herself in a false position; she had been carried away by a dream that already seemed to her as vague as a cloud. It was like tearing her living heart out of her body to let it go—no one must guess, no one must know. . . .

Paul did not love her. She knew that he did not love Elisa, either, or anyone. He did not need love, in his superb twenty-sixth year. Playing good golf, tennis, swimming, going out on somebody's catboat and eagerly discussing seamanship, enjoying his meals, liking his clothes, popular wherever he went, the one thing for which Paul had no use and no need was an entanglement with any girl—least of all a girl whose people were doing their own work down on a forlorn California ranch! It was all horribly clear now, only—only she had not seen it before, and here she was in this great hotel ballroom, knowing hardly one of the hundreds who were dancing and dining, out of place, looking her worst in Dodo's blue velvet. . . .

Time went on. Hours, hours, hours. Nobody else asked her to dance, and Paul's dreadful father continued to sit beside her, squared about at the table, murmuring to her.

"I'll tell you something you don't know. I'm going to kiss you before the evening's over, how's that? Yes, sir; I'm going to have a kiss from the prettiest girl in the room . . ."

When he took her out into the hall to show here a photograph of the winning polo team with himself up on a dancing pony, Joyce seized the opportunity to go to the dressing room and look at her haggard unhappy face in the mirror and brush up her coppery hair. She had hoped Pidgie might be in the dressing room and that she could say: "Oh, let's find Paul and go home; I'm dead!" But there was no one there but a pretty little Japanese maid who said, "Powdeh, missy?" and beamed at her with large teeth in a carmined mouth.

When she went out again Victor von Schwerin, animated, handsome, athletic, in middle age, was talking to two elderly women who were evidently quite captivated by his charms. Joyce, wondering desperately if she could not give him the slip, found herself face to face with Monty Lefanu. At the same instant Paul's father saw her and started toward her. She had but a few seconds in which to appeal to the writer.

"Will you save me—will you come in and sit down and talk to me—you'd do me *such* a favor——"

She had time for no more, but he understood, as somehow she had known he would, and he joined her and her host and they walked back to the ballroom together.

"What was the trouble?" the Englishman asked, in a

voice at once amused and sympathetic, when after a few annoyed and puzzled moments the other man made some excuse to leave them. Joyce looked at him with eyes bright with pain and fatigue.

"He was just—he happens to be Paul von Schwerin's father," she said. "I'm—staying with them, so I have to be polite, and I—don't like him."

"I say, that's awkward, isn't it?" the man asked cheerfully.

Joyce's face wore a troubled little frown. She determined not to cry.

"He's—I think he's been drinking a little too much," she said carefully. "He's with a party in a private dining room. I hope he's gone back to them!"

"You're not having a very good time, are you?" Lefanu asked, after a shrewd glance. Joyce raised smiling eyes to answer, found that her lips were trembling and that words would not come.

"I wish you'd talk to me—say anything, about anything," she stammered. "I—I hate all this. I'm afraid I'm going to cry."

"I shall talk like mad!" her companion assured her. "D'you know London? You've never been to London? Strange thing, that fire this morning, you didn't see it in the paper? That very part of London . . ."

She listened feverishly, her eyes fixed on his. Presently she could smile, could talk a little, awkwardly and hesitantly.

"You'll think I'm a hopeless idiot. But I—I rather let myself in for this visit, and I'm—I'm tired maybe. And suddenly it all seemed so—dull."

"Glad to take you home. But it's early. It's only a little after ten."

"Is *that* all it is!" she said, in a dismay that made him laugh. "I thought it was about three."

They walked out to the terrace, past the dancers, and the locked murmuring couples in the shadows, and the dim outlines of palms and flowers, and found Paul in attendance upon Elisa, who was stretched in a long wicker chair. Paul was balanced on the arm of a neighboring chair; one or two other men were on the flags at Elisa's feet. Paul jumped up, and Joyce introduced Monty Lefanu, and Elisa extended a lazily gracious hand to the writer.

"Paul, if you're playing golf at nine tomorrow——" Joyce said in a questioning tone.

"Oh, yes, sure! I've got to get home! I was just going after you. Elisa feels much better; she came down half an hour ago," Paul said, quite unembarrassed.

"There's nobody left in there at the table; they're all dancing or scattered. I suppose the people will understand?" Joyce had a chair now; she waved Monty Lefanu a farewell as he turned and left them. "They'll expect somebody to pay, won't they?"

"Oh, sure they'll understand; they won't let me get away with anything!" Paul laughed. "See the old man?"

"Your father? Yes, he came in and talked to me."

"He thinks you're swell," said Paul.

"He was with some party of men; he just went back to them about fifteen minutes ago."

"Poker. They're playing poker. Dad always comes down and walks around for a while if his luck is bad," Paul said understandingly.

"He said they were playing poker." Joyce hoped that she had not arrived to lay a stone on an animated conversation; they had not seemed to be talking at all when she came up, but there was a pause now that suggested interruption. After a few minutes Paul got up again, and they said good-night to Elisa, who said she thought she would sit on for a while, it was hot upstairs.

They left her with her young English squire in attendance, and Paul took Joyce and Pidgie back to the lodge. There was no opportunity for a word alone with him; he did not attempt to make one. He bade the girls an affectionate, laughing, leisurely good-night, coming up to their room with them, loitering in the doorway, evidently in no hurry.

"He couldn't wait to get back to her, could he?" Pidgie said scornfully, when he was gone. Joyce stood perfectly still for a moment, not breathing; it was in a carefully leveled voice that she said, "Back to Elisa, you mean?"

"Sure," Pidgie answered. "They'll sit on there for two hours. It'll lose 'em the match tomorrow, too—you'll see! Or no," she added, remembering. "You're going home tomorrow, aren't you? You won't see it. They're flying to New York Tuesday morning."

"They?"

"Paul and Elisa. She telephoned her mother late yesterday afternoon in New York and asked if she could stay until Tuesday, and then fly. She was going home tonight; she'd have been on her way if she hadn't made the finals."

Joyce made no comment. She slowly, carefully undressed, shaking her clothes, hanging them in place, brushing her hair. It didn't matter whether she brushed her hair or not; nothing mattered. Nothing mattered except a tall square-shouldered boy with tumbled fair hair, driving from a golf tee, striding after his ball with the sun shining on his brown skin and his white smile and his old white sweater. Big hotels and crowds and cocktails and laughter and rushing about in big cars, what an empty farce it all was, when the one thing that couldn't be—mustn't be—wrong was wholly wrong, when the real things, like love and loneliness and longing, didn't count at all?

"Well," her thoughts ran, as she lay awake in the darkness of the big luxurious room, "suppose he and Elisa lost in the morning, lost because of a stupid shot of hers, not his.

And then suppose he drove me to Merriwell; it's only eighty miles. And suppose on the way he said . . ."

But no, it wouldn't happen that way. He would be playing golf with Elisa; someone else would put Joyce on her train; everyone else would be about when Paul said good-bye. And on Tuesday Paul would fly back to New York and she would be alone again.

The events of the past week wheeled feverishly about brain and mind and soul, as she lay persistently wakeful. Joyce felt as if she never would sleep again. She was brightly, hopelessly wide awake. She could hear faint far-away dance music; on Saturday night at the hotel there was always a dance. Moonlight lay in odd squares and angles in her room; now and then motorcar lights flashed across it; the dancers were loud in laughter and witticisms and fare-wells, down on the dark drive, as party by party they went their ways into the night.

"I'll live through all this because I won't die," Joyce said, half aloud. "Girls do. Bootsy. Bootsy and I. We won't die. I wish I was dead!"

Toward morning she fell asleep. Her last hours at Pebble Beach held a sort of serenity that is won from despair. Nothing could come right now; nothing could happen; no more use for hope or prayer. She and Pidgie slept late. The golf match was well under way when they wandered out to the course. They saw the end of the finals: Elisa and Paul were quite suddenly out; they need not play the last six holes. It was all over. Elisa smiled at photographers, tears in her beautiful eyes. It was all her fault; she was off her game completely this morning. Paul was magnificent and good-natured, and confided to reporters that he had known all along he did not have a "prayer" for the championship.

They all had late lunch together at the golf club, quite jolly and informal, with plenty of nice young men there,

and at quarter to three Paul asked Joyce if she had to go
back to the lodge for her bag.

"No; I put it in Mr. Masters's car this morning, Paul."

"Oh, that's grand; then we don't have to rush. Bill,
Joyce's bag is in your car, isn't it? Do you want to run her
over to the train?"

"Sure," Bill said slowly, after a moment's reflection.

"Then I'm going to say good-bye to everyone at once!"
Joyce said gallantly, when the moment for departure came.
"Good-bye, Miss Blandwood; good-bye, Pidgie. I said
good-bye to your mother after breakfast. Good-bye, everybody! Good-bye, Paul; this has been lots of fun!"

Bill Masters drove her to the train. The ridiculous little
wooden station was only a red-painted shed under the Del
Monte oaks and pines. A hundred or more hosts and guests
and week-enders generally had gathered there to say good-
bye. The train had not yet arrived; she and Bill stood
chatting pleasantly enough, but without inspiration, while
they waited for it. Joyce was in a daze; Paul had simply
waved at her, had whispered laughingly to Elisa again; it
was all completely bewildering and hurting.

Presently a Victorian couple was seen approaching from
the direction of the hotel; the woman with a plumed hat, a
flounced and paneled "pull-back" dress, a little thin silk
parasol with a jointed handle; the man with flowing Piccadilly weepers, striped trousers, gaiters, a full-skirted coat,
and a tall beaver hat.

As the outrageous pair mincingly approached the station,
the man gallantly assisting his companion along the wooden
ties, subdued laughter broke out among the groups awaiting
the train, followed by whispers and murmurs.

"Oh, look at them—it's a movie—look, isn't she delicious!
Look at the ringlets! I haven't seen a dress like that in
thirty years!"

Joyce understood. It was a carefully planned joke. It was

Paul and Elisa, bubbling with laughter under their decorous and dignified surprise at the uproar they created, playing their parts beautifully.

"Why, it's Miss Ballard!" Elisa said, mincingly extending a raised hand. Joyce must laugh, must enter into the nonsense as well as she could, must gasp admiringly, "You idiots! How did you ever—where did you find—why didn't you tell me . . ."

The train came in, and Joyce found a window seat, and still all the crowd and now the travelers in the train, too, had eyes for nothing but the beauty of Elisa, with her chignon and her bangs, her puffs and her pleats, and the absurdity of Paul. Necks were craning and laughter breaking out everywhere. As she had her last look at the green shadowy afternoon peace of Del Monte, Joyce saw Elisa and Paul in the center of the picture, Elisa daintily waving her parasol, Paul bowing with a stiff gesture of the beaver hat he held in his hand.

For a long time she sat at her window, an elbow resting on the sill, her cheek in her hand. The spring landscape slipped by; green fields, orchards already in fine leaf, solemn marches of eucalyptus trees and spreading oaks; she saw none of them. Her eyes were slightly narrowed, her jaw shut. In her face there was a look of pain, of puzzlement, of shame.

At San José she got out, waited in late-afternoon weariness and griminess for a bus; established her bag and herself in it. She thought of the ecstasy of anticipation and triumph and delight with which she had gone through San José a few days earlier, bound for the Von Schwerin home, on her way to meet Paul and have the magic play of youth and moonlight and love begin!

All over. Joyce looked from the bus window; the country was getting familiar now—flat country that had been a river basin countless æons ago, dry country now, crossed and angled with the spokes of a thousand orchards. Farm-houses, each with its guardian oaks and peppers and eu-calyptus, slid by. The bus clumsily stopped, clumsily lumbered on its way again.

In a few moments she would be at home in the familiar kitchen; Dodo's little face would be flushed with stove heat, Felicity slicing bread, her mother, her father with his hair slightly tousled and a surprised look eternally in his gray eyes, would be all interest—they all would be!—in her happy visit; they would singly and collectively question her minutely, nothing would escape them. Only Michael, meeting her at the station and driving her up to the ranch, would understand, would spare her. Or perhaps Dodo or her father would come down with him. . . .

No, it was only Michael who was waiting in the mud-spattered car. His white teeth flashed in his lean brown face, his pleasant English voice was restful and friendly.

"Welcome back! We've been having an awful time without you," he said, taking her bag. "Your sister Dodo has given us the most extraordinary surprise! She was married a week ago to young Sallock, in the town here, and your mother's forbidden her the house. Meanwhile Miss Lissy has gone quietly off to visit her young man's family in San Francisco, and we think *she* may come back with a plain gold ring on her hand! So you see what happens the minute you desert us."

Did he understand already? Was he saving her?

"Oh, no, Mike! And was Mother angry at Dodo?"

"Your mother fainted, and has since repeatedly said that she would never see either daughter or son-in-law again."

Joyce's face was pale and train-grimed; her eyes were set in rings of delicate umber. She looked at her companion blankly.

"Then where's Dodo?"

"Gone off to the San Joaquin ranch with Charlemagne."

"It isn't Charlemagne!"

"It seems it is."

The road began to rise up to the hills; the peaceful country spread about them—orchards, great towering trees above the plain farmhouse roofs, solemn redwoods with the sunset light on their layers of dark green and the living red of their tall shafts. Clean air, scented with grass and turned earth, touched Joyce's hot face. Something of the majestic sincerity, of the simplicity of the everlasting hills reached her troubled spirit as well; she had a moment of surprising, of weary and exhausted peace.

"Then there's nobody home except Mother and Dad?"

"Nobody. And we're glad you're back where you belong!"

There was a silence while they took the south turning at Cooley's corner, and went past Swede's place, and through their own redwoods.

"Yes, I guess I belong here now," Joyce said.

## ✺ CHAPTER XXIII ✺

SHE would be asked no embarrassing questions tonight; there was an atmosphere of death at the farmhouse. William Ballard was struggling with the kitchen fire when Joyce came home; there was no wind and the draft was bad. He seemed almost pathetically pleased to see his daughter. Joyce kissed him with only a distracted question or two, ran upstairs to see her mother.

In Sally Ballard's room dusk and disorder reigned. Sally was lying face up on the bed, staring into the gloom; her eyes were sunken and reddened with crying; there was a handkerchief in her laxly flung hand. The bedcovers were tumbled; books, garments, shoes were scattered about; the air was dank and chill, like the air in a vault.

"Mother!" Joyce exclaimed. Her mother accepted her kiss apathetically, reached out her hand with a hopeless gesture, and began to cry again.

"Did you hear about Dodo?" the older woman demanded in a whisper. "Did you know anything of it beforehand?" she asked.

The last word saved Joyce. She could honestly shake her head. She went into her own room and changed her clothes, came back with her hair brushed and a comfortable old cot-

ton frock on, lighted the lamp and began to set things to
rights.

It was funny to go downstairs and find the kitchen unchanged; the lard and the matches and the tea towels just
where they had been before she went to Burlingame, so
many ages ago.

"How do you find your mother?" William Ballard asked
fearfully.

"How long has she been like that?" Joyce asked by way
of reply.

"Ever since Dodo went; ever since she heard. That was
Friday afternoon. She went down as if she'd been shot,
and she hasn't gotten up since."

"How'd Dodo happen to tell you?"

Her phrasing made him glance at her shrewdly.

"You knew?" he asked.

"She gave me a pretty ster-*rong* hint," Joyce said honestly. "But it was done then, and there was nothing I could
do."

"No; there's nothing any of us can do. He came up here
Friday afternoon, and he and she stood talking out by the
oak. Pretty soon your mother called my attention to them;
Dodo was crying. I went out there then and asked 'em—I
merely asked 'em—if anything was wrong, and she flung herself at me and blurted it out. They'd been married a week.
Your mother heard just that much and she went into—well,"
the man said gravely, shaking his head, "she was very bad.
She wouldn't speak to the boy, and when Dodo came near
her, she screamed. Michael thought they'd better get out,
and Dodo put some things in a bag and they went away."

Joyce turned on the hot-water faucet, tested the water,
filled the kettle without removing her eyes from her father.
A lamp was lighted in the kitchen now, and the stove was
burning cheerfully; she had a sudden sense of being needed,
being adequate.

"What do you think about it, Dad?"

"Why, I—I suppose, if your mother feels as she does, it's a pretty bad business," he said doubtfully. "Dodo should have told us; no question of that. It looks bad, it looks bad, to have a man and a girl steal a march on the family that way."

"Well, but Daddy, she likes him terribly, and she hates fusses," Joyce argued; "it may have been silly, but it seems to me Mother's making too much of it!"

William Ballard's serious face brightened.

"Is he a nice fellow, Joyce?"

"Why, he's an awfully nice fellow, high-school ger-*ad*uate and all that. He's handsome, and his sister told me he'd never been in love before. I never thought Dodo'd *marry* him," Joyce said, "but it seems to me she could have done much worse. He has a big dairy ranch over in the San Joaquin; she may love it there! Mother'll come round to it; there's no real harm done."

"Well, you comfort me, Joycie, you comfort me," her father said, in relief. "I confess that I thought that your mother was taking it a little hard. Poor girl, she blames me more than she does Dodo. She says it's a result of bringing you all to this sort of place."

"I'm going to take her up some toast and tea in the regular old-fashioned way," Joyce said, moving about busily. "Whew! How cold it gets down here in the mountains the minute the sun goes down! I'm going to miss Dodo der-*read*fully," she added, "but it's her life, she's twenty-three, and she's certainly in love with Charley."

"Think she is?" her father asked eagerly.

"Oh, ker-*acked* about him, Dad! I knew that. But I never dreamed she'd actually do it. Don't worry!" Passing him, Joyce stooped and touched a soft flushed cheek to his. "Time cures all wounds!" she said. "We'll drive over and see

Dodo some day, and by degrees Mother'll come to see it
differently."

"You're a wonderful child, Joycie!" William Ballard said.

"Yes, things seem to get normal the minute Joyce gets
home," Michael contributed. He was working with some
sort of hinge or hasp at the table. She made him remove his
rubbish to a chair when the time came to set out the plates
and cups.

"There are only ther-*ree* of us tonight, and I'm dead anyway," she said, on a stifled yawn. "We'll eat out here. You
started potatoes baking, Dad? What else have we? What's
this large bowl of cold peas? Oh, I know what I'll make
. . . "

She found a bowl, a colander, a pestle. In her dark blue
apron, with her rich mahogany hair brushed into a mop of
waves, and her brown hands busy, she was a pleasant sight
in firelight and lamplight.

"We've needed you terribly, Joyce; we've missed you,"
her father said.

Joyce carried a tray upstairs, talked with her mother.
Lissy had gone to stay with the Rosses, had she? Wasn't
that rather a good thing; didn't that look like business at
last?

"I don't know. I'm completely unable to understand
Archie Ross," Sally said pessimistically. But Joyce's father
had told her that her mother had hardly spoken at all since
Friday, except for bursts of despair, and Joyce was corre-
spondingly pleased to have her turn her thoughts to Lissy.

"Oh, they'll be married now!" Joyce said.

Downstairs again the familiar scene was set. Supper
started with hot bowls of pea soup; even the men could give
but an indifferent interest to what followed. Presently they
were all yawning and heavy over the stewed cherries and
the coffee cups; Joyce had to tear herself from her chair to
begin the familiar job of clearing and washing. Michael

brought in wood for the morning; William Ballard expertly wiped plates, inverted pots on the cooling stove to dry.

Afterward there was a brief attempt to play cribbage. It was no use, they were all too tired and sleepy. Joyce and Michael, settling the kitchen for the night, had a few minutes together after her father had gone upstairs.

"Anybody asked you if you had a nice time with the Von Schwerins?" the man asked.

"Everyone too much taken up with Dodo's affairs."

"Well, was it a nice time?"

"Perfect." Joyce shut her heart on the memory of it. It was all over. No use thinking about it.

"And the sweetheart, was he as nice as ever?"

"Paul? Wonderful."

Michael did something knowing to the stove dampers, straightened up to look over his shoulder.

"You're not going to surprise us as Dodo did?"

"No. Want me to call you in the morning?"

"Oh, no; I'll set my alarm. Good-night."

"Good-ni-i-i-ght!" she murmured, on a sleepy moan. She carried her lamp upstairs; went into her mother's room.

"Mother, could you drink a glass of hot milk before you go to sleep?" Joyce asked solicitously. In her heart she said that if her mother did want it, she would die of sheer fatigue going downstairs again.

"Nothing more, dear." Sally was heroic and calm now. William Ballard was undressing in a remote dim corner. "I haven't slept," Joyce's mother said; "perhaps I will tonight. We'll hope so."

"You mustn't feel too badly about this, Mother."

"I don't think you can understand, and I know your father does not understand, how I feel, Joyce," Sally Ballard said readily, in an expressionless voice. "A mother bears her children, gives her life to them in babyhood, watches them develop . . ."

Joyce and her father listened respectfully.

They were destined to listen to a good deal of this as time went on. Spring rushed into summer with Western violence; the arroyos that had run with angry yellow waters all winter long were dry again; all the blossoms were gone; fruit was forming hard and green among the thick orchard leaves; goldenrod and yarrow and tarweed sprang up along the dusty roads, and the sprinklers in Sally's garden whirled and sprayed through the long twilights. The Ballards' supper table came out into the side yard again; the kitchen was darkened at half-past eight in the hot still mornings, only the drip-drip-drip of the faucet in the shining sink disturbing the long hours. At noon there must be a panting session with chops and potatoes and corn for the hungry men, but Joyce had learned to lunch on fruit and salad now and had lost weight, and was the prettier for it.

In the late afternoon of one burning July day she said to her mother: "I saw Dodo today."

Sally's face flushed, and her nostrils moved. She dug her trowel into the ground with a nervous thrust.

"Then you did something you have expressly promised me not to do!" she said, instantly out of breath.

"I know," Joyce said mildly, without apology. "It was when I went down with Michael for the new rake and the mail and the strawberries. Dodo was sitting in Charley's car, outside the post office, and I went over and talked to her."

There was a pause. Sally's back was turned toward her daughter; she was thinning phlox. Presently she said:

"I suppose you'll be packing your bag for a week-end at that delightful country house of theirs soon—a dairy ranch over in the San Joaquin!"

To this Joyce made no direct reply. After a while she submitted simply: "Dodo's my sister." Nothing more was said.

The sight of Dodo in the Sallock car had deprived her of all feeling except one of love for her sister and longing to speak to her. She had fairly run across the baking main street of Merriwell, and the two had been in each other's arms, laughing and crying, before there had been room for thought. Dodo had clung to her as to a floating log in mid-ocean. Their touching cheeks had both been wet. In the empty sunny silence of the town they had sat, clinging to each other on the car seat, pouring out the stored eager confidences of hard weeks.

Dodo had looked pale and sick with heat; there had been a weariness and limpness about her that had alarmed Joyce, but she had reported herself as well and happy.

"It sounds awful over there," she had said, "but it's really lovely, Joyce. There are big trees around the house, and there's always a breeze through the kitchen. I have a puppy —Charley brought it to me—and there's a nice woman on the place, the foreman's wife. Nights, we walk down to the dairy and watch the separator, and we have a radio and everything. Only—" Dodo had faltered in the gallant story, her lips trembling, "of course I miss you all. If we could come up to dinner! I miss Dad so. And being married's not the same as having your sister—I mean, it's nicer and it's not so nice——"

"I don't think Mother can keep this up," Joyce had said. "Give her time. You know how wonderful Mother really is, at heart."

"I know—let's talk of something else," Dodo had said quickly and thickly. They had talked hastily, with shaky laughter, of Lissy. Lissy was a great favorite with all the Rosses now, and stayed there frequently. Sometimes she came home on a Friday or Saturday, but Archie almost always came down on Sunday and carried her off again. They were to be married early in October.

"Mother's got it all written out," Joyce had said. " 'Mr.

and Mrs. William Anderson Ballard announce the marriage of their daughter, Felicity Fellows, which was postponed because of illness in the family of the groom.' "

"Poor Mother! I suppose I broke her heart," Dodo had said. "But she never would have consented to my marrying Charley anyway." And she had gone on to tell Joyce how good her husband was to her; it was Charley who strained the milk and cooked the baby turkeys' food.

"We have about a thousand baby turkeys, but they say there won't be much market for them this year," Dodo had said. "We have some white Plymouths, too, but of course Duke and Lard help Charley with them."

"And are you cooking for all the boys?"

"Well, they help a lot. And Mrs. Sallock came over and helped me put up my fruit and berries. We put up more than four hundred jars last week, and we're going to do corn when the Golden Bantam comes in."

Charley had come out of the bank and had joined them. All very well, Joyce had thought, for Dodo to boast of his goodness and thoughtfulness. But she had been nervous about him just the same, when Joyce's eyes were upon him; she had helped out his sentences with a little shy laugh; had explained that it was so fearfully hot that Charley had just come into town as he was, without coat or tie.

Yet he was a nice fellow, Charley Sallock, serious and clever about his business, devoted to it, and perfect in his manner toward his young wife. Archie was less dignified with Lissy than was Charley with Dodo; Archie sometimes got silly. Joyce had promised her sister a visit, "just as soon as Lissy's back to stay and Mother simmers down a *little*," and Dodo had kissed her good-bye in a very passion of homesick earnestness after Charley had treated them both to double grapejuices at McCann's.

The long vacation was wearing away when the expected letter from Paul came. He was going to England, because his father and everyone thought that it would be a good thing for him to have six months there. Gee, it was kind of tough not to get to California for the summer, but this work would be valuable to him, and they all thought he ought to do it. He had not written since Easter because he'd been working so hard, but listen—

"Listen," Paul's scrawling hand, struggling down the big page, went on. "Here's the thing. Maybe you and I'll get married, and maybe we won't, but look—let's call off the engagement, and then if we do it, we'll jump right into it, see? What do you think?"

She thought as he thought, of course. She wrote him with what dignity she could muster, assuring him that the "slate was clean, and we can write whatever we like there later," and returning to him his grandmother's ring. Joyce did it steadily. There was a great sense of weakness, of blankness, in her soul after it was done, but there was peace, too. She remembered the old days at "Ninety-nine," days she had thought hard and dark then! They seemed bright, cloudlessly happy in retrospect. He had come out to the house in St. Francis Wood every day, he had laughed with them in the kitchen, shouted over games of hearts, he had caught her to him once or twice in quiet corners or behind doors, crushed that fresh hard brown face of his against her own.

The queer cold, bewildered first days at the ranch had been metamorphosed by Paul, too; at least for her. Joyce recalled his noisy and joyous arrival, bringing chops and bakery cakes, the fun they had had the day they cleaned the yard! Those big arms would never take the breath from her body again, those young lips hurt her mouth with kisses; she would not see him, lithe in his white summer wear, against the emerald of Cypress Point's golf greens. That was done.

But life went on, and she moved through it. The Merri-well Little Players gave *Hay Fever* that autumn, and

Joyce played the mother, and ran away—her fellow players assured her generously—with the show. She read *The Taming of the Shrew* and *Resurrection* and *War and Peace* and many lesser volumes; she learned to play good enough bridge to make a foursome with the older members of the family. She and her father worked out cross-word puzzles, and Michael sent to London for paper books of them, explaining that those of the London *Times* were better than any home-grown ones, and they bent over them together. In the shortening days she cooked, swept, went for eggs, skimmed the great pans of milk, fed the three turkeys that were going to provide feasts for winter. The merciless heat went out of the sun; the air took on a crystal thinness and sweetness; prunes were on the ground; grapes were firm and heavy with juice. In the evenings the little stoves snapped and roared; Sally wore a thick sweater when she went out to her garden in the frost-beaded mornings; ice formed in the trough by the barns, where the spillway came from the spring.

Lissy was married in early November. There had been another delay in arrangements, and another postponement, but at last she and Archie were actually wed, and off to Victoria, where the groom was to be manager of a branch of the family business. That part of it was dignified enough, and Lissy looked extremely well in her gray suit, with a gray hat and gray shoes and a gray fur, but the details preceding the affair had been enough to wreck the entire family, Joyce wrote to Dodo. Daddy had given Lissy three hundred dollars and told her that if she needed any more than that he would have to send the bills to Archie; that was the first hitch. Then Mother had wanted the wedding to be at the Fairmont Hotel in San Francisco—everything very simple and only forty or fifty guests—but Dad had instantly said that the expense was out of the question. Then Lissy had said in passionate protest that she would be married at

Georgia's, and Mother had said that in that case she would not be present. A wedding to a man as important as Archie Ross staged in a crazy studio on Russian Hill!

So then—Joyce faithfully reported to Dodo, who was neither asked nor expected at the wedding—"Mother had a perfectly charming letter from Archie's aunt, Mrs. Guthrie, and she asked if the wedding mightn't take place in her house in San Francisco—the old Heckels place in Pacific Avenue. Mother couldn't very well say 'no' to that, so up we all went yesterday; we left here at nine, took a room at the Fairmont, Lissy got dressed, Ben showed up looking adorable, and at noon we all went out to the Guthries'. It was all quite perfect, and everyone praising 'Felicity,' but Dad looked perfectly miserable in town clothes—sort of fat and rustic, somehow, and Mother was like a standing lamp being moved about, just inclining her head here and there, and telling anyone who would listen that 'our country place' was 'so remote.' Poor Mother!

"We saw them, Lissy and Archie I mean, to the boat, and everyone drank their health there, and so off they went. Dear old Lissy, I think she'll be happier than she's ever been!

"But it was too awful, Dodo, to get back to the ranch at about ten, for we stayed in town for an early supper with Ben. He's lovely, and has a job on an afternoon newspaper, and Dad's very much pleased, but it was too awful, getting home, even though Michael had everything warm, and hot chocolate waiting. But it was so co-o-o-ld, and no one in your bed, and Ben's room empty, and Lissy's room empty! Mother collapsed majestically into bed, with her teeth chattering, very gentle and resigned—you know how she does—but she was all right this morning, and Ben's coming down for Thanksgiving, so we're all in great spirits."

On Thanksgiving Day the fattest and largest of the turkeys was roasted; Joyce had decorated the house with great branches of enameled huckleberry and blazing madrone leaves; Ben was coming home for three days; even Sally was cheerful. There was enough fine china left for a handsome display. The candles were yellow today, and on the table Joyce and her mother arranged a center decoration of a scooped pumpkin with grapes and apples pouring from it, plums and golden pears, and one pale creamy squash. With bronzed grapevines to soften the whole, the effect was of dazzling beauty in the plain room. Between the windows chrysanthemums in a jar shone like stars.

Breakfast was late and disorderly, with Joyce making a turkey stuffing at one end of the kitchen table, Sally sipping her coffee at the other, Michael with armfuls of wood tracking in mud, and William Ballard in complete felicity as he manipulated the fresh warm milk, the fresh eggs, the orange-bright persimmons into their destined places. Swede came up with a round, almond-studded cake, labeled "Swedish torte," a Thanksgiving present from Inga; Joyce took her handsomest pie and marked it "American mince pie" and sent it back.

There was no lunch. At three o'clock Ben rushed in, cold and breathless, and there was great laughter and much embracing in the kitchen.

"Oh, this is the way things ought to be!" Joyce thought, giving a last wipe to an irreproachable sink, putting away a last hot clean pan. Her mother sat close to the one son of the family, a hand linked in his arm. William Ballard was opposite Ben, listening with a pleased thoughtful face to the boy's account of the first work he had ever done in his life.

"Eighteen a week, eh?" he mused aloud. "And are you living on that, Ben?"

"You bet your life I'm living on it," Ben said. "A feller and I have a room in Chinatown—up above a restaurant ———"

"Chinatown!" Sally said faintly, closing her eyes.

"But it's swell, Mother. Some Englishwomen run the place and it's swell! Jussertin is on the *Call,* but he's drunk most of the time, and he likes someone to live with him and keep him straightened out. It's all right," Ben finished, pulling Joyce down to kiss her ear as she passed him. "But we eat kind of light. What's cooking, Joy?"

"A rare fowl from Turkey, much prized on festal occasions by the North American natives," Joyce said, kneeling to let a rush of burning air strike her face from the opened oven door, and turning aside as she basted the richly bubbling bird. "With it we have patatas, or potatoes, as some call them, an edible root, the squash or gourd——"

"What is this, a cross-word puzzle?" Ben demanded. "Oh, Lord, Lord, Lord," he added, almost in a shout, "maybe you think it isn't good to get home!"

He did more than say it. Every minute of the happy holiday afternoon proved that he meant it. He and Joyce and Michael walked up to the canyon to see what was choking the water flume; came down again, breathless and starving and muddy, for hot baths; got into evening attire and gathered again in the kitchen to put the last touches to the feast. Joyce tied a great apron over the plain old velvet dress that had made her feel so grown-up at sixteen, five long years ago, and tied other aprons around Ben and Michael. In five hours' slow roasting the turkey had reached complete perfection, the skin breaking in brown crispness at a touch, the fresh cream color touched with pink; the squash was baked, the salad, scented faintly with onion and garlic, glittered in a frosty bowl. Sally lighted the yellow candles; Ben brought out the deep enormous Canton platter. Joyce was everywhere, but if everyone had not been too busy to note what she did, was oftenest to be seen hovering restlessly near the door, as if listening for some sound from the yard.

And at five exactly the yard door opened. Dodo stood there, in her two-years-old winter's blue coat with the beaver collar, her blue hat pulled down over a pale and anxious face that yet wore some sort of a smile.

"Mother——" she faltered, holding out both her hands.

Sally stood perfectly still in the center of the kitchen. Everyone else stood still; William Ballard with a glass water pitcher in his hands, Joyce with a tea cloth clutched tightly in her fingers, her eyes moving swiftly from her mother's to her sister's face. Ben all surprise in the dining-room doorway, Michael only an onlooker over Joyce's shoulder, but tense and nervous and motionless, too.

"So you've come back, young lady?" Sally said slowly.

Joyce's heart shriveled like a closing sea anemone. Dodo's arms fell, and she turned bewilderedly and put her hand blindly out toward her husband, who was close behind her.

"Why don't you come and kiss me, Dodo?" Sally went on, impatiently, in the terrified silence. The tension snapped. Dodo went forward with a sob and a rush; everyone was crying, and Joyce kissed Michael with fervor, and did a sort of dance with him and Ben.

"You're all so *foolish*," said Sally fretfully, kissing Dodo again and again, holding her off to look at her, sending a reproachful glance from wet eyes about the circle. "You dramatize everything so; you're always pretending that I feel this or that, or won't do this or that. It's very tiresome. How do you do, Charles? I suppose you two have had a big Thanksgiving dinner already today, so poor Joyce's turkey will go begging."

"Well, no, we didn't," Charley Sallock answered, almost absently. His concerned eyes were all for Dodo, who had sat down on a kitchen chair, as close as it could be dragged to her father's chair, and who looked pale and exhausted from sheer happiness. "The folks went to my sister Imogen's house today, and took Duke and Lard with them. No, sir, that turkey is going to taste pretty good to me!" he added, slightly reassured by the smile Dodo gave him from eyes brimming with joy and wet with tears, and sitting down beside her.

"It was only twenty-seven pounds; we hope it'll go round!" Joyce said, and everyone laughed. Activities began again.

"Oh, Mother," whispered Dodo, "it's so good to get home! And Ben here, too! And Lissy married! Does she write you?"

"You oughtn't to be driving round in bitter cold weather like this, Dodo; you oughtn't to get so excited, you oughtn't to cry," Sally was murmuring in a sort of monotone. Michael and Ben were setting extra places at the table; Joyce, at the sink, stopped short in the business of washing the roasting pan, and stared first at her sister and then at her father. A great question filled her eyes.

"Yep," William Ballard said with a nod, in an aside. "Looks like new titles all round 'long about March or so."

"Dodo!" Joyce said in a stupefied whisper. "Things— things do happen in the country, Dad," she added, with her own sudden youthful smile. "Remember we all thought that if we came down here nothing would happen?"

"Real things happen," he said.

## CHAPTER XXIV

ONE night when they were alone in the kitchen—she and Michael—they happened to speak of Dodo's choice of a name for her daughter.

"Mary Sallock. I think it's adorable," Joyce said. "Considering the names that our parents, both sides, chose for us, I'm all for Mary! It's pul-*lain*, but it's distinguished."

"The Sallocks are Marie-Thérèse and Charlemagne, and Marmaduke," Michael began, and stopped.

"Duke's Marmaduke, yes, and Lard's Abelard, and there's Imogen. Well, it means reaching for something; it isn't quite Johnny and Mamie and Al and Ida. We have rather fancy names ourselves," she reminded him. "Mother's idea was to express maternal delight. Felicity was going to be Felix if she was a boy, and Dodo, Theodore. Theodore means 'Gift of God.' Benjamin is the child of the heart, and Ben had a girl twin named Gladys, who died when she was about three weeks old. Then I came along and was Joyce."

"I like Mary, and I like John."

"I like Michael for a name," Joyce said thoughtfully. "John is nice, and Jacky," she added, on a burst of enthusiasm, "Jacky himself is simply adorable! Think of

255

Dodo with two babies, and think of us getting round to four years here, Michael? 'Isn't it so strange?' as your British cousin might say."

"Much you know of my British cousin!"

"I know his letters, don't I?"

"I think he'll come out," Michael said thoughtfully.

"Arthur Tallant. Will I like him? Am I apt to fall in love with him?"

"You're what? Twenty-three or so?"

"Don't say twenty-three or so, Michael! 'Or so' means double. 'One or so,' means two, and 'two or so' means four. 'Twenty-three or so' means forty-six!"

"Forty-six would be about right for Arty. He's somewhere in the fifties."

Joyce stared at her companion aghast.

"In the *fif*——! As old as Dad?"

"Older than your father, I should say. But he's a terrifically athletic old chap, tennis and golf and all that. He's brown as a redwood tree, and square, and rather 'ahawhaw!' if you know what I mean."

They had been playing cribbage in the warm orderly kitchen; the board and pegs and cards had been gathered neatly by Joyce, ready to be put away; she and Michael idled on, unwilling to make the effort that must include half setting the table for breakfast, shaking down the fire, mixing buckwheats, turning out the kitchen lamps. The November night was bitterly cold, frost lay icy over the ranch, distant stars shone in a sky of hard ultramarine, branches snapped in the bitter grip of winter. Even inside the farmhouse the halls were like passages through underground vaults, and in the freezing mornings Joyce always wore a heavy coat while she straightened the bedrooms, and sometimes mittens and a cap as well.

But the kitchen was always comfortable, and in peasant fashion the reduced family did much of its living there. To-

night there had been a brief rubber or two of bridge, but
Sally had been tired and had gone up to bed at ten o'clock,
hugging her two hot-water bottles fondly, and William
Ballard had followed her a few minutes later. It was eleven
now. Joyce and Michael had been playing cribbage and
talking.

After his last remark she sat studying him speculatively
for a few minutes. Then she said:

"He sounds like a lord."

"Arty? No, he's not. He's Captain Tallant. He's got a
cousin of thirty or so who may be Lord Thrall some day.
An uncle has about picked him for his heir. But he doesn't
especially want it."

"Doesn't want it? Why not?"

"Oh, we're all rather odd."

"No money to go with the title?"

"Yes, there's money. Two or three places—all that. I
don't know what it's all about. Totty tried in an amateurish
sort of way to get somewhere with his uncle's tenants and
his mines and what not, but it all turned sour, and he gave
it up. Arty'll tell you about it."

"They don't call the cousin 'Totty'?"

"They've always called him that." Michael shuffled the
cards lazily in long clever fingers, and Joyce looked at
him.

"With all these cousins in the peerage, what on earth
were you doing coming down here with that hungry mongrel
of yours, and asking me for food, almost four years ago?"
the girl demanded suddenly in a suspicious voice.

"I told you. I had hurt my foot; I didn't think I could
get down as far as Swede's. I was feeling very rotten,
with no car and no telephone and no—well, no grease," he
said, unashamed.

"I remember the ger-*rease* talk. You ought to have been
ashamed of yourself, Michael," Joyce said, with a touch of

severity. "You had my heart all but ber-*roken*. And here your cousin has a cousin who's a lord! I thought you were the most pitiful object I ever had seen!"

"I probably was. I'd been living on cornmeal and apples—delightful diet when you have a bit of bacon or some cream along with them," he said. "But I remember feeling quite dizzy as I walked across your yard."

"You poor simpleton," Joyce mused affectionately. "I wish we could see ourselves as we were that afternoon," she went on. "You were a skeleton. How much more do you weigh now?"

"Seventeen—eighteen pounds when I last tried it. Probably a stone by this time."

"And I'm down pounds and pounds from what I was then!" the girl exulted. "I mean naturally, comfortably down," she went on. "I must have been a perfect roly-poly!"

"I don't know, it seems to me you were rather nice. You gave me chicken legs and pork chops and chocolate custard."

"You remember it all." Joyce smiled at him across the table, the fine brown checks of her gown exactly the color of her eyes. Lamplight shone softly on her thinner, older face; there were firm positions of the jaw that showed more clearly than they had four years ago; there were definite expressions in her thoughtful glance; cadences in her voice that were new.

"Of course I remember it all," the man said, still lazily shifting the cards. He glanced up, glanced down again.

Joyce's thoughts went off at a tangent.

"Is your cousin Arthur married?"

"Wife died during the war. She was having a baby, and they couldn't get a doctor."

"And you never married, Michael?"

"Never."

He answered naturally enough, but she saw the color come up to the tips of his ears, and felt for some reason she could not understand a sudden flush in her own cheeks. She laughed.

"In spite of the gypsy your grandmother picked for you?"

"Not a real gypsy, you know; just a girl who was sort of wild. She was the darnedest girl I ever saw!"

"Did she marry?"

"I don't know. I only saw her once."

"But you were in love with someone else?"

"Probably. I've forgotten."

"Do you know that you would make some girl a marvelous husband, Michael?"

He looked up; spoke with a visible effort:

"No, I don't know that. I'm afraid in any case the nice girl is down on her luck. I shan't ask her."

A little disheveled, a little tired, and with her liquid brown eyes all the softer for it, her elbows on the table, her firm chin in her hands, Joyce said teasingly:

"On the general principle that if you can't have what you want, you won't have anything?"

It was said carelessly, lightly, as if half to herself. The man looked up quickly, an odd expression coming suddenly into narrowed eyes. The color that had receded from his lean brown cheeks came up again. He got to his feet, pushed in his chair.

"Exactly," he said briefly. "I say, it's after twelve. Suppose we turn in?"

Joyce was scarlet with consternation. She crossed the kitchen and stood beside him, detaining him with a quick hand on his arm.

"Michael, what a fool I am! I don't know why I said that. I could bite my tongue out; I don't know what I was thinking of! Please—pul-*ease* don't think me quite such an idiot——"

He held her gently, a hand on each shoulder, looked down at her from his height.

"Why, you'd be an idiot if you *didn't* know, Joyce," he said mildly, in a thoughtful voice. "I've known you knew for a year now. But there's always been Paul. And I didn't want to make you uncomfortable, and perhaps have to go away."

He shook her lightly to and fro. Her stricken eyes did not move from his.

"For a little while after he went to England I hoped that the Paul dynasty was over; then he came back, and the letters commenced again. I think he loves you. I don't think he knew it in that first year or two; it sounds more as if he did now. I'm not in the picture at all."

"I'm horribly sorry I said that stupid thing!" the girl murmured, her cheeks scarlet. "You've done so much for me; you've been so wonderful when I was heartbroken and impatient and—and dumb about everything. You've let me talk to you when I couldn't talk to anyone else. I'd—I'm ker-*rying,* but I don't know why!" she said, smiling with brimming eyes. "I'd say you were like a ber-*rother* to me, Michael, only you're nearer than Ben ever was. And if ever I've made you unhappy I'm sorrier than I know how to say. You—you——" She stopped, out of words, flushed and confused. "You know that, don't you?" she stammered in conclusion.

"It would be very hard for any man to have been here as I've been all these years and not love you, Joyce," Michael said. "You were an adorable child when you came; you're a woman now. I've seen you cooking, playing with your kitten, raking the yard, scolding, happy, crying, comforting them all when you needed comfort so badly yourself! I've seen you in old sweaters on picnics, and drying your hair, and dressed as Lady Teazle——

"But I've never seen you when you weren't the most wonderful woman God ever made," he added in a silence. "You know how poor I am; you know exactly what life would be up in the lumber shack. I've never offered it to you, and I never will! I'm going to stay on here after you go away, and work out things with your father; you'll come back for visits, and so will Dodo and Lissy and Ben, and pretty soon I'll be Uncle Mike to the crowd."

"You know that what you have has had nothing to do with it, Michael," the girl said in a voice she held low and steady. "I was in love with Paul when I came here. When I thought he didn't care for me it didn't make any difference; I loved him just as much. I used to take his picture in those awful times and hold it tight against my heart, and try to send a message to him, wherever he was: 'Paul, I need you, my dear; I love you!'"

"I knew you did, I knew you did!" Michael said. "And when he started writing again—when was it, almost a year ago?" he began.

"September first, last year," the girl supplied.

"Last September—when he started again, it was to me you came with the first letter," Michael said.

"Oh, what a day that was!" Joyce said, remembering.

"And this June he will be home again?"

"Well, perhaps later than that. His stepfather died, and he's been helping his mother get her estate. I told you that. But they say it will be all settled in June or July. Then he comes out here."

"To stay?"

"To per-*act*ise law. He'll be in his father's firm."

"And then I suppose we'll have some news?"

The brown eyes met his honestly.

"I don't exactly know," she said hesitantly. "He writes as if we—sort of—belonged to each other, but he doesn't *say*."

The man looked down at her gravely for a minute without speaking.

"Then we'll just have to wait for midsummer," he finally said. "And suppose that even then it isn't right, Joyce?"

"I don't know," she said.

There was the click of a latch behind them, and they both turned to see William Ballard in his pajamas, with his hair tumbled, standing looking at them bewilderedly.

"I'm glad you're up, Joycie," he said. "Your mother isn't well. She's got a pain in her side. I'm going to dress and get a doctor, and you go up to her."

"Chest, too?" Michael asked quickly.

"No; she didn't say so. It seems more under her arm. She put her hand here."

"I'll get Nubbins," the younger man said. "I'm dressed. We ought to have a fire, hot water, I should think."

Joyce had run upstairs. It was the first step in a long Calvary for them all.

## CHAPTER XXV

AFTER a while the short cold days and the long bitter nights began to blend together, and it was all like a dream. Lamplight made strange angles on the walls when Joyce was going up and down the steep kitchen stairs. Sally's droning voice rang through the house in the quiet, winter-bound afternoons, rang through Joyce's brief troubled dreams at night. There were always trays to carry up and down, to clear, to set again. There was no hour of darkness or of daylight in which Joyce must not stumble up, shaken and wild with fright, to fly to the sickroom again.

William Ballard, silent and anxious, did what he could. The kitchen fire was always burning; Swede's oldest boy, towheaded and muddy-booted, brought in the eggs and the milk. Essie Millar came to nurse. Essie was as strong as a horse and almost as big, and she took the heaviest of the burden, but Joyce was never free.

"Jo-o-oy-ce!" her mother would cry desolately, and Joyce would force her tired feet up the stairs again.

On many a bright day Dodo would drive the fifty miles between her new home and her old, bringing the delicious Jacky, standing crying quietly with her father in the halls.

Ben took to coming home week-ends. Finally Lissy came. The six Ballards were together for the last time.

Despite the warning weeks of illness the end seemed stunningly sudden. Joyce felt dazed and broken when it was over. When Lissy and Ben and Dodo had gone away, the house was empty, seemed echoing with voices and memories that were gone forever.

"And we thought things were so bad when we came down here almost four years ago, Dad," she reminded him, in a sort of sad amusement, on a sweet January day when they two and Ben and Michael had taken their lunch up to the Ridge. "But we were all together then; we had each other!"

Her father shook his head. He was strangely quiet; he wandered about the place like a person in a dream. When he did talk, it was of his wife, and of the days when their babies had been small, and they two had had happily, lovingly, to share all their problems. That Sally had been unreasonable, difficult, unhelpful in all the crises of the last few years, that she had clung to the social standards of her girlhood in a fast-changing world, fretting herself and her husband and children to attain the impossible, was all forgotten now. They only remembered now her fierce loyalties, her quick impatient cleverness in kitchen and garden ways, the vibrant energy that spread about her like a visible thing and made life always exciting.

It was very real grief that was felt by all Sally Ballard's children. Dodo, in her busy farmhouse, wiped tears away as she gave Jacky his rubber ball, lifted tiny Mary to her young breast. Lissy, far north in Victoria, was magnificent in crape, declining dinner invitations "because of the recent death of my dear mother." Ben was gentle with Joyce and his father, talked with them, tried to interest them in his own interesting work.

But nothing brought emphatic, loyal, ambitious Sally back. The eager, interested voice, the partiality that interpreted all her children's gifts into genius, their acts into wisdom and goodness, was silenced. The shriveled chrysanthemums were sending up green shoots from between winter's slimy blackened stalks, but the square-tipped blunt little hands in old gloves would nervously, swiftly manipulate them no longer.

Joyce had hours, days, of carrying a sober heart. She wanted her mother back; she wanted to fix trays again, to spring out of bed again crying, "Coming, darling!" before her eyes were fairly open, to stumble exhausted through bitter-cold halls and enter again the strange unforgettable atmosphere of the sickroom, with its odors of blankets and antiseptics and wood smoke and fresh lilac water. Every other thought was something that would "interest Mother"; meals were still planned with Sally's likings in mind; the weeks went by, and the shadow did not lift. Even when the early Western spring was bringing February's grass and wild flowers to the hills she sometimes started up wildly in the night, her heart thundering, her throat thick, her mother's plaintive cry of "Joy-cie!" sounding in her ears.

But she was busy. Hard times were upon Merriwell, and the women of the town were doing what they could to lessen the strain. There had been a meeting in the schoolhouse on a cold November night. Joyce and Michael had gone, had sat in the small uncomfortable schoolroom seats twisting about to study seriously the honest, troubled faces of the men who had wheat, who had dried apricots and prunes, packed tomatoes and peaches, potatoes, milk, cheese —who had everything for which there was no market, and for which there would be no market that winter.

And fringing the hot, overlighted room Joyce and Michael had seen other men and women—silent these, except for the eloquence of their anxiously knotted hands and the fear in their eyes. No sales meant no jobs, and the new chain stores were not like the comfortable little old family groceries that would trust a family through a hard winter. The spruce clever clerks in the "cut-rates" were not empowered to establish credits. Even the milk man was ousted, for milk was two cents cheaper when one bought it in a self-service shop and carried it home, and the old morning whistle that said the milk had been delivered was a thing of the past.

They had all talked: the mayor, the president of the Farmers' Union, the head of the now-closed packing plant. There was no money, and where there was no money there were no sales, and where there was no business there were no jobs. The Alhambra Market, the pride of the town, was closing except for the feed counter and the coffee stall; McCann's candy store had failed; Brown's had turned off nineteen men.

Quite toward the end, and in defiance of Michael's clutching hand that would have dragged her down, Joyce Ballard from the old La Perdita ranch up on the hill had gotten bashfully to her feet. She was the new vice-president of the Women's Club. The president, Mrs. Hal Tafts, had been unable to come tonight.

Her voice becoming almost audible as she proceeded, Miss Ballard had said that the women of the club and the Parents-Teachers Association and all of the relief societies wanted to make a proposition to the meeting and would like an immediate action.

"Most of us have more food than we can use," Joyce had said, trembling and smiling in an ecstasy of earnestness and nervousness. "What we would like to do is take the market, the Alhambra—it's right in the center of town—and have any of you who have spare supplies ber-*ring* them there. I mean apples and eggs and milk—and flour, too, from the mill, Mr. Jorgensen, if you will. We women want to give the children of the lower grades their lunches, and a good tea after school. Mrs. Tafts," Joyce had gone on,

speaking quite loudly and authoritatively now, in a dead
silence, "says she'll see that food isn't wasted, and they have
good soups and ber-*read*—and cookies," Joyce had added
thoughtfully, and for some reason everyone had laughed at
her tone. "We're not begging for these things," she had
hastened to say. "We per-*ropose* to issue receipts for them,
against the town. When better times come, town bonds will
pay everyone for everything. And meanwhile all the children'll be fed, and that'll take *some* of the anxiety off their
parents, and if we have any food over and can afford it,
we'll feed a few others. Mr. Curran," she had added, with
a friendly glance for the village editor, "says we can have
space in the *News* to ask for what we want. Anyway, I'm
coming down with potatoes and milk tomorrow—lots of us
are—and we'll get started."

Michael had attempted to reason with her on the way
home. But Joyce had said serenely that it would do no
harm to try the experiment; it would make the less fortunate of the villagers feel that something was being done, at
least; something quite different from the grand ideas of
government help and changed state laws.

"The place is running over with food," Joyce had said,
"and it's much better to eat it than destroy it."

"But, Joyce, the whole matter goes so much deeper than
that. It's an agricultural problem; it's nation-wide. You
can't solve it by feeding a few children. These people are
faced with ruin; they may lose their farms; there's no
market for their crops. Can't you understand that it's not
just California—not America, even? It's everywhere!"

It had been no use. Joyce had persisted that food was for
everyone the only real consideration. "They all have homes
and blankets, and goodness knows that the orchards give
us all the firewood we need," she said.

And so the experiment had started, and Michael had
watched it with an impatient kindly scorn that had turned

to surprise, and a surprise that was sometimes almost awe.

The women had gone steadily forward; the miracle had leaped ahead of them; they could not keep pace with it. Great loaves had been baked, great soups and stews had simmered on their big stove, jam had been spread on acres of bread, rivers of cocoa had been poured into cups.

To the outward eye it had been sufficiently unsensational; just a barn of a market with empty tiled stalls and neglected counters suddenly possessed by resolute women in kitchen aprons. There had been whiners, beggars; there had been plenty of puzzlement and hesitation; plenty of problems to solve every day. The black-eyed children of Latin parents had had to be taught not to throw dregs of soup and chocolate on the floor; the almond-eyed children of the Orient had had to be taught to use spoons.

Stout Mrs. Tafts and slender eager Joyce and all the others agreed a hundred times that the whole thing was a failure; it was a lot of work for nothing, and if things continued to go badly with the nation, Communism would get in, and no effort to settle the lesser problems of the depression would be of any avail anyway.

But they continued to feed the children of Merriwell, and incidentally some of the children's mothers and fathers. The after-school collation turned itself into an early dinner; the parents who came to get their girls and boys began to form a habit of accepting a cup of cocoa, more chowder, another sandwich, another cooky. The food poured in, and Mary Sparks wrote cash receipts for some of it on blue slips that said, "Incorporated Town of Merriwell." But for much more of it no receipts had to be written. Girandola, the great chocolate king, drove down from San Francisco to see what was going on, and sent the women of Merriwell all the chocolate they could serve; from Watsonville came Mayor Porter with sacks of flour and great tins of lard; from Hollister, Gilroy, Morgan Hill, San José, the women drove in with food for the Merriwell experiment.

There was unemployment in Merriwell that first terrible winter of the California depression that followed the Eastern collapse; there was anxiety, change, there were mortgages and depreciations. But there was no hunger, and there was a great deal for everyone to do.

After her mother's death, Joyce went downtown oftener than her promised two days a week. Michael would drive down to pick her up after the four-o'clock tea to find her tired, flushed, sometimes laughing at the general absurdities of the situation, sometimes indignant at imposition or malingering. The market would be swarming with women and children; country wives, in mud-splashed little cars, would have honey or quilts to exchange; Joyce would be jerked this way and that, her apron spattered with soup and butter, her hair roughened. Driving up the hill in the sober winter twilight she might be quiet, her shoulder against Michael's shoulder, but if he asked her she always said that she was happy, she was not tired.

She and he and William Ballard had their supper together, usually in the kitchen. The girl's young face glowed as she turned it from one man to another, but she laughed rarely in these days, and was more silent than she had been. When Ben came down, or Charley and Dodo shared the meal, things were more formal. Otherwise it was a diminished group that enjoyed a game of cribbage in the ordered kitchen and put the lights out at nine o'clock.

On the days when she was not on duty in the village Joyce got into the habit of following the men about the farm. The earth was stripped now, and the solemn encircling hills seemed shrunken and low. Cool airs blew over the barns and the sheds and fences; in the shade the turned earth and the woodpiles wore a fine frosting of ice all day long. Voices echoed a long way in these days. When Dodo brought her year-old Jacky to the farmhouse his imperious little orders sounded loudly in the quiet old rooms. Dodo's Mary was still too small to be carried about much over the cold winter roads.

Only now and then Michael saw Joyce falter; she might lean against him suddenly, breathless and white. Once she said in a whisper, "I wish I could see my mother!"

Sometimes when she was alone she spoke to her mother. "I wish we hadn't laughed at you that day, Mother darling!"

She did not break often. Her life had fallen into quiet, into sometimes serious grooves now, but they were the grooves of her own choosing, and she was safe. Home was infinitely safe. No one would hurt her feelings here; there was no strain of artificiality, of competition. One had one's work to do, and it was engrossing; for one's leisure there were a thousand occupations that had nothing in common with what the Burlingame crowd was doing. Joyce worked cross-word puzzles, and cross-stitched smocks; she experimented with cookery; she carried Dodo's boy back from the milk ranch for a visit with Gram and Aunt Joy. There was always Shakespeare, always walks, always the radio. It was all restful, safe; it was Joyce Ballard living the way she wanted to live, eating what she wanted to eat, doing what she wanted to do.

"I see what you get out of it, Dad," she told him. "Why don't all men, when they get to be fifty, come back to gardens and barns and hens and cows?"

"Afraid of their children," William Ballard might reply, after thought. He and Michael adored her and did their best to spoil her. They never returned from San Francisco or San José without bringing her a little present; a cake of fragrant soap, a penknife for her puzzle pencils, a pair of fine silk stockings. In the evenings, when she sat flushed and lovely between them, with her stiff white collar framing her lean, fine young face, and her mahogany mop a little

tumbled from the excitements of dinner-getting, the two
men would watch her as she talked, lose the sense of her
words for the sheer pleasure of watching the red mouth
enunciate them.

Occasionally she saw Bootsy, in the "Dime." Bootsy was
going with a newcomer in town, the handsome young man
who managed the Piggly-Wiggly, and was very cool to
Joyce. Bootsy looked older and soberer, too. She never asked
for Ben.

Now and then Paul wrote to Joyce. There was never anything but nonsense in the letters, but the sight of his hand-
writing always made her heart leap. She would keep the
letters unanswered as long as she could force her courage to
do so; after ten days, two weeks, she would write him in
the same flippant vein; she would save ridiculous anecdotes,
work out fantastic phrases to make her replies amusing. It
was a sorry business; she loved Paul, she didn't want to
write to him in this fashion, but he had set the pace and
she could only follow. Neither Michael nor her father ever
heard her speak of Paul, but deep in Joyce's heart lived the
undying thought of him; he was never long absent from her
mind.

She wondered—wondered—wondered how they would
close the gap of this parting or if ever they would see each
other again. She would not go to meet him this time; she
would never again enter that hot crowded hurried world of
his to be confused and hurt. It wasn't her world. It wasn't
the world of girls who had kitchen work to do, who fed
baby chickens and watched the tiny radishes and lettuces
come up in the chill sweet spring sunshine. It wasn't a place
for a daughter mourning her mother. "He must still like
me, or he wouldn't write to me," Joyce would muse, ending
her long thoughts of him impatiently. "But there may be a
dozen other girls in his life now. I'd never know it if there
were!"

# ❧ CHAPTER XXVI ❧

ARTHUR TALLANT came out from England, and Michael went up to San Francisco and spent two days with him, bringing him down to the farmhouse on a March afternoon when spring was just tiptoeing into view. The willows all along the creek were green, the first fruit blossoms were out, and yellow mustard had washed like a wave over the grain fields. Sally's flowers, the lilacs and the banksia roses, began to bud. Everything looked its best, and Joyce looked her loveliest, too, as she welcomed the English visitor.

She and her father and the two men scrambled up the long hill to Michael's cabin after luncheon. Grass was beginning to spurt up green and fresh in the sheltered places; on the hills there was a delicate film of green over the burned brown grass of last year. Larks were whirling up; the creek rushed noisily in a yellow-brown swirl. "Arty" liked the cabin immensely; it had been much improved in the years since the Ballards had come to the neighborhood; it had a porch now, and a shower, and Joyce and Michael and Ben had constructed a sort of arbor with a grill in it, where she sometimes broiled chops or cooked Spanish macaroni.

"Why shouldn't we batch it here for a bit?" Arty asked enthusiastically.

"Why shouldn't you stay in our spare room?" Joyce said. It was settled that the English cousin should stay for a fortnight anyway, and that he and Michael should divide their time between the farmhouse and the cabin. They all walked home down the hill in great harmony of spirits. There was a delicious dying sweetness in the warm spring afternoon. In a few weeks, Joyce thought, it would be time to move the table into the yard again; there would be soft sunset light all over the hills and orchards while they ate their supper.

Arty was really a sort of "ahaw-haw" person, as Michael had said, but he was friendly and jolly and nice, too. He liked Joyce instantly, and she liked him. He was middle-aged, florid, not too clever; he had none of Michael's subtle and sardonic wit, but he was kind, and an enthusiast about everything Californian. The Ballards adopted him at once.

He had been as one of them for about ten days, and still showed no signs of departing, when late one afternoon Joyce came out from the kitchen to see the spokes of a smart car flashing under the oaks, to see it sweep about the drive and come to a halt within a few feet of her. A man, a tall man in a brown coat, jumped out. The green sweet world went slowly in circles about her. *Paul!*

Their outstretched hands met; their eyes met; she was in his arms; they were both laughing. But when they drew apart, still linked by their hands, Joyce's eyes were wet.

"You're wonderful!" Paul said.

"It's so good——" she said, rushing her words a little lest sudden tears of joy interrupt them——"it's so good to see you again!"

"Claire said she wrote you I was coming."

"She did, and she was sweet about it; she wanted me to

come up, as I did two years ago. But I couldn't! But, Paul, you weren't to arrive until today."

"And I didn't, darling!"

"You didn't arrive *today!*"

"This morning at ten. Claire met me and we went into town and had lunch with Dad. At two I was on my way. This is the car a fellow and I brought across the continent. Some car!"

"This is—let's see, Tuesday. When did you start?"

"Last Wednesday, in the early morning. Yes, sir; we drove through Columbus Circle at five o'clock. And we didn't rush it, either."

"It doesn't seem possible!" There was a bench under the oak; she had drawn him to it; they were both seated. A lull came in their eager talk, and they looked at each other. Paul said that Claire looked fine and his father looked fine, and asked for Joyce's father. His face flushed a little and he added:

"You've had it rough. I'm so sorry. I—you had my letter?"

"You sent me a lovely letter." Joyce's face wrinkled; she bit her lower lip. "It's made a tremendous change here," she went on, not very steadily, clinging the while to Paul's big comforting hand, her misted smiling eyes on his. "That was why I couldn't go to Claire and wait for you; Dad's so much alone. He's—you'll see; he's so much quieter than he was, and he seems a little—ber-*roken*. They—they did love each other," Joyce finished, her voice breaking.

"Poor kid!" Paul said. There was another silence. "And Dodo's married," he stated rather than asked.

"Oh, yes; and with two babies! Jacky and Mary. Mary's getting so adorable!"

"And Lissy?"

"Yes, and she and Archie have great expectations, too. It seems so sad," Joyce said. "Mother loved babies so, and she'd have ther-*ree* grandchildren already. But they do help Dad," she added, "I mean Dodo's babies do. He likes Charley, too."

"Isn't Charley kind of a local yokel?"

"Oh, no. Or, well, yes, he *is*," Joyce answered honestly. "But he's terribly good to Dodo, and he's—I mean, he's the kind of a farmer who reads books about chicken diseases and takes a bath every day—a modern farmer. They all are that way now. No more chewing ster-*raws* and smelling of stables. And he loves to talk politics with Dad; I mean Charley does. To me," she went on, with a dimple showing in her cheek, "to me he's much more restful than a man like Lissy's Archie, who's always wondering if the claret is warmed, and how you pronounce 'Eschscholtzia,' and what his friends think of him! Archie's grandfather was Peveril of the Peak, or Walter Scott was in love with his aunt, or something, and he does rather de-*well* on it sometimes, if you know what I mean," Joyce finished with a little smiling sigh.

Paul regarded her with great satisfaction.

"Gosh, you're thin!"

"Well, I am a little thin now, but it's all right. I eat like a hired man, and I sleep ten hours a night. But I've been awfully busy, there's something to do every minute, you know. We have this Woman's Civic Relief going like mad in the village, and I'm in that, and then there's always a lot to do here."

"You're doing it all now, I suppose?"

"Oh, no; I have Isabelle Dunker to help in the kitchen. She's marvelous. She can't make salads or desserts very well, but she simply whirls through work. The place is always like a pin. Only I can't leave Dad long. He comes down sometimes and helps me in the village."

"What is it? Soup kitchen?"

"Soup nothing! We feed two hundred and twelve school

children every day, and about a hundred mothers and fathers every afternoon, and whatever tramps come along. But we only give tramps three days' food, and then we pack them a lunch and send them on their way."

"Bums?" Paul said good-naturedly.

"Not all of them; not half of them. Lots of them are old. They go the rounds of San José and Mountain View and Palo Alto, and then come back again."

"Don't you make 'em work for it?"

"Oh, sometimes. We make them split wood, or hoe weeds, or mend the roads. But there isn't any work. We're having a depression," Joyce reminded him.

"You'd know darned well the world was having a depression if you could see Berlin and London—whoops!" Paul said. He scowled. "What good do you do feeding a few kids and women here? You don't touch the *causes;* you don't change conditions!" he said.

"No, I don't suppose you do," Joyce conceded, somewhat discouraged. Suddenly the feverish scenes in the Alhambra Market seemed to her a waste of time. Sticky children rushing about, throwing good bread and jam on the floor, idle dirty women whining and explaining, serious-faced farmers taking blue "town certificates" in return for hams and cracked wheat. "Still, if they're hungry . . ." she offered doubtfully.

"But it's developed, Paul," she presently went on. "We have a clothes bureau, and two shoemakers half-soling their shoes, and the doctor comes in every day. It does—it *does* lessen human misery in the world, just by a little. And the people who sign things, who feel that it's just a big community exchange—an emergency like in a fire or earthquake—they do feel happier than if they were worrying and sker-*rimp*ing in their own cold houses!"

He was not listening; he was eyeing her smilingly.

"So you manage to fill up your time?"

"Oh, Paul, I never *have* any time!"

"Where's Michael?"

"Oh, he's here. We couldn't live without Michael. He's fixed that old cabin in the canyon—it's quite cute! There's a grill up there, and we often have Sunday lunch there. And his cousin's here. Arthur Tallant—Captain Arthur Tallant of the Royal Somethings."

"What, living up there with him?"

"Living here, really. He's terribly nice, and we have a ber-*ridge* game again."

"What a little sport you are!" Paul said, watching her. She tightened her fingers in his.

"You're home," she said simply. "For how long this time?"

"For keeps. How does that sound?"

"Heavenly."

"I finished two weeks ago. I had to go up and see my aunt in Boston, and pick Tony up. It took us about a week to get started."

"And now what?"

"Dad thinks I can loaf for a couple of months, and go into the firm about the first of August." Paul's voice lowered, he drew nearer to the girl and put his arm about her. "And if, in about six weeks, you and I should step off . . ." he began. His voice thickened with feeling, he spoke gruffly. "How about it, Joyce?" he said. "I lost you once through being a fool. What a *damn* fool I was! But I'll never let you go again."

"You didn't lose me," she said, trembling, her brown eyes close to his.

"I know, but I acted like a skunk the time we were down there at Del Monte—let you go home on the train, didn't write for months——"

"It didn't matter. I didn't really belong in that group. I couldn't compete with Elisa," Joyce said, with a smile for the remembered miseries of that visit. "What's become of her, anyway?"

"I don't know. I never saw her after that. Pidgie's going to be married to Sam Trotter; he's about thirty-eight and fat, and he's been the pet bachelor for emergency calls for twenty years, but they tell me they're cracked about each other."

"It's like a world I dreamed about," Joyce said.

"Well, it's your world now. Shall we tell your father today, Joy? This is March. Why not early in May? That would give us all June and July for a honeymoon; we could take the car and go up to Banff and fool around—go down to Santa Barbara. My mother's rolling in dough now; she's going to come out and take a place in Santa Barbara. She's divorced again, or rather, it never was a marriage—this third one."

"Oh, horrible for her!" Joyce exclaimed. "What did he do,—desert her?"

"Oh, no; she was the one that found it out. You see, her second husband—the man she only lived two months with— died last December," Paul explained amusedly, "and he had a tremendous lot of money. So Mother had a lawyer fix it that her divorce from him never was legal, and she left Pete cold in Paris, and came over here and started a claim on Louie Crowder's money. And she got it, too. So now she's fat," he ended simply. "She'll be here in ten days, and she wants me to drive her down to Santa Barbara to look for a place. And why not you, too? We could have a peach of a time!"

"Oh, but I couldn't leave Dad!"

"Why, but look here, you're going to leave him for good, aren't you?"

"Yes, I know." Her face was flushed with exquisite color. He thought he had never seen her so lovely as she was this afternoon in the fresh soft March greenery, under the oak.

"But—we've planned if I did," she explained, "that Dodo and Charley shall live here with Dad, and Isabelle Dunker will stay on after she has her baby. It can be right here with Dodo's babies——"

"Good heavens, a city feller got hold of Isabelle, did he?"

"Oh, no," Joyce said, a little shocked and quite serious. "Nothing like that. She's a widow, and she was starving— actually starving, when she came to the Alhambra Market. She was just—trembling, and when I gave her a cup of coffee her hand shook so she could hardly hold it. That's the sort of thing we do all the time, even if it isn't so impressive," she diverged. "She was widowed last August, and the baby is coming in six weeks, and she hadn't a cent or a friend. They'd just come here from Kansas when he was killed. So she came up here, and we all just *love* her!"

"Michael and Isabelle might console each other," Paul suggested.

"Oh, no; she's not Michael's type. Michael's, after all, a gentleman!"

"Who told you so? Michael?" Paul asked, laughing. Joyce turned to him a reproachful face.

"But you know it, Paul!"

"Well, of course I know it, idiot! How sensitive you are!"

"Michael," Joyce said, mollified, "Michael's cousin is cousin to Lord Thrall, so I suppose Michael is, too. At all events Michael's cousin is cousin to a lord."

"Yep, and a lot of 'em are bums, if you ask me! His cousin evidently didn't care enough about either of 'em to keep 'em in England. Well, anyway, I'm sorry for Michael," Paul said.

"Why sorry for him?"

"Because, of course, he's in love with you. If he isn't, he simply isn't bright," Paul said, laughing. Joyce's color rose; she tipped her head on one side and seemed to be considering.

"I know he likes me," she submitted with an air of doubt.

"Well, so do I!" Paul said, suddenly abandoning Michael. "Let's talk about us!"

"Let's talk about us," she agreed. "I've not seen you for so long, I've not heard your voice for so long that it all seems like a dream! Do you know how long it really is?"

"It's years," he said soberly, tightening his hold of her.

"More than two. It was the spring Dodo was married— oh, dear, it's been a long time!"

"We'll tell 'em here, and tell Dodo tomorrow. How far away does Dodo live?"

"The milk ranch is about fifty miles. But she's here in Merriwell now with Charley's family. They're having terribly hard times on account of milk and butter being so terribly overproduced. Oh, they're all *right*," Joyce said, somewhat uncertainly. "But they've gotten rid of lots of their cows, and they are sort of—well, shortening sail."

"Say, listen, how long has this depression been your favorite topic?" Paul asked, with a grin. "As far as you're concerned, it's over. We tell the folks tonight; how's that? Then you and Dodo talk over the date, and how you want it. I don't care; I don't suppose we want a big fuss, do we?"

"Oh, no!" the girl agreed eagerly. In her heart she said, "Oh, Mother, Mother, Mother!"

"Well, we'll be married somewhere. If my mother has a place in Santa Barbara she'd like it there—or Claire would let us use her town apartment; that doesn't matter. Then Mr. and Mrs. Paul von Schwerin get into their car—and away! Does that sound good to you?"

"It sounds too much happiness. We talked of it four years ago, Paul, before we ever came here; do you remember? Lissy was engaged to Archie then, and he had just decided to go to Scotland, and Mother was so wild at the idea of our coming to the country. Poor Mother, she said no one would want to marry us!"

"Well, after June—let's say the fifteenth, that's my birthday—let's hope nobody does want to marry you, anyway, because you'll be married to me! Listen, Joy—here's about money: we'll get piles of presents, of course, chairs and clocks and things, and silver, and Mother'll give us a big check. So that'll start us off with a bang. Then I'll have about four hundred a month from some bonds, and the firm will pay me something to start with—a hundred anyway—and we'll spend all our week-ends with Dad and Claire to save money, and because it'll mean a lot of fun—there's always something going on at the club. We can do it on that, can't we?"

"We'll be rich," the girl said, thinking of Dodo and of some of the families she knew in the village.

"We'll be rottenly poor!" Paul altered it. "But Mother'll come through; she's got all kinds now."

"It's like a dream—your being home again!" Joyce sighed from sheer happiness, leaned her shoulder against him, and felt his arm about her. Somehow she didn't want to talk about the money.

The long soft shadows of the spring afternoon lengthened, and spears of light came through the redwoods. Joyce was suddenly on her feet. Paul would stay for dinner, and she must make it festive. She took him into the kitchen, introduced him to the cook.

"Isabelle, this is Mr. von Schwerin; you've heard me speak of him. Paul, Mrs. Dunker."

"Gee, you wouldn't know this kitchen!" Paul ejaculated, looking about. Joyce laughed in satisfaction.

"No, would you?" she said. "We painted it, and got a linoleum, and made the curtains; it isn't such a bad room, even if it is a bad shape."

Paul sat in his old place at the table and watched, and the two women set harmoniously to work together, Joyce tying a practical big gingham apron over her gown. She and Isabelle consulted over bowls; murmured over bread box and cake tin. Isabelle was a strong, sad-eyed girl with black hair and a round young face. She moved slowly; once Joyce reproved her sharply for climbing on a chair to reach a high shelf.

The last sunlight slanted in through the western windows; was gone. With night a chill was coming down upon the world; the young leaves outside the window stirred restlessly in a spring wind. But the fire burned steadily in the stove, the kettle hummed, and the cat lay warm and sleepy on the woodbox ledge.

"I got both stoves lighted in the good rooms, Joyce," Isabelle said in her low hoarse tones.

"We'll need fires tonight."

"Like me to git the spare room het?"

"No; Mr. von Schwerin is going home after dinner."

William Ballard came in with a round wooden pail filled with eggs. He welcomed the newcomer cordially, but with a sudden shadow in his eyes.

"Feels like winter out," William Ballard said.

"I was telling Joyce I wouldn't know this room. 'Member what it looked like when you first came over here?"

"It was a bleak-looking place! But we've grown—we've grown fond of it, Joyce and I." Quite suddenly Joyce's heart ached fiercely for her father. Oh, it was sad, it was fundamentally sad, when children grew up and went away from their parents! She went over to him, and put her arm around his neck, and laid her flushed cheek against his cold one.

"Did you get freezing up at the barns?"

"It was cold out. But it's fine here."

By this time it was pitch black outside, and the dinner-table candles were lighted and the meal ready. Michael and Arty came in just before dinner. The old road that circled below Swede's to the summit had been opened again, and they had driven down in Michael's ramshackle little car. Paul was introduced to the strange Englishman, and dinner was served. Joyce looked about the circle of the men with great satisfaction; it was romantic to have a sweetheart as wholly charming as Paul turn up in this adoring and eager mood, and it was gratifying, too, to have Paul see that her isolation—her exile—had not turned out too badly: pink candles burning, Isabelle bringing in the fried chicken and new asparagus, three men about the board keeping the conversation moving. Not so bad a result, considering the despairing outlook of four years ago!

Joyce thought that she had never been so happy in her life. This was one of the hours that repaid a woman for waiting and hoping and enduring. The candlelight shone in her brown eyes and touched her cheeks with a soft glow; she liked the look of the stiff white cuff at her wrist, the feeling of the broad white collar on her shoulders; she liked the sound of her own voice tonight. There was a certain easiness, a certain security in the quietness of home, the affectionate familiar voices of the men, the crackle of fires in the stoves, and the soft high breezy sighing of the spring night outside.

She went into the kitchen after dinner and helped Isabelle; Michael went about with lamps, put platters away; it was all highly informal and usual. Paul came out from the parlor and talked to her as she polished the hot clean glasses and set the washed-and-dried plates in the china closet.

"Listen, do you have to do this?"

"Certainly I do. Why not?"

Paul glanced cautiously at Isabelle's back.

"Why doesn't she?"

"Oh, Lord, it would take her until ten o'clock! Salad plates and all those glasses!" It was part of tonight's charm that she felt so comfortably sure of Paul, need not consider him, fit her moods to his in the old anxious way. Something in his manner told her that she was in no danger now of losing him again, and it was a happy feeling. Her look went to her father, to Arty, to Michael; in her brown eyes there welled and shone a light none of the men ever had seen there before. There was a sort of radiance about her tonight, a sort of demure joyousness.

"It's good to see you so happy, Joyce," Michael said to her late in the evening, when Paul had long been gone.

If there was a questioning note in his voice she did not hear it. Straightening the parlor, putting away cards and emptying ashtrays into the stove, she paused to answer smilingly:

"It's good to be happy!"

"You're going up to visit his people?"

"His father and stepmother, yes. He comes back for me on Friday. And later we may drive down to Santa Barbara to see his mother."

"Definite plans?"

The girl flushed and laughed.

"Well, per-*etty* definite. For autumn some time, I imagine."

"What he said at dinner—about Canada, you remember? —made me think it might be sooner."

"I know. He said June. In fact, he said May. But this is March; that's *too* soon! I've been thinking about him," Joyce said seriously, with a little upward jerk of her head that indicated the direction her father had just taken on his way up to bed. "I don't want to—shock him with too much change," she said. "I'd rather wait and see how things go with Dodo and Charley here. And then there's Isabelle's baby."

"Isabelle's baby? I *say!*" Michael laughed, under his breath.

"I know it sounds silly to let a—a cook's baby affect your

wedding plans, but I wouldn't feel comfortable if everything wasn't finished off here. As far as the Alhambra Market goes," Joyce said, "I don't believe we'll need that sort of relief next winter; even if we do, it's working as smooth as butter. But, I don't know," she added, standing close to Michael now, looking up at him with a half-troubled and half-amused smile; "I knew Paul was coming back, of course, and I knew he'd want me—at least, I hoped he would!" the girl interrupted herself, confused and laughing. "But now that it's happened, it seems too much like—ber-*reak*ing things up, like leaving—leaving more than I'd gain —I don't mean that of course—because when you love a person——"

Michael was looking down at her, his lean intelligent face very thoughtful.

"It'll all seem much more natural to you after you've seen him a bit," he said simply, after a pause. Joyce, whose eyes had been fixed expectantly upon his face, gave a sigh of relief.

"Oh, I think it *will!*" she said fervently. And then, with a sudden complete change of manner, "I'm so sorry I didn't know the two cul-*lubs* were good, Michael!"

"It was quite all right; we got the rubber," Michael reminded her, just before their brief good-nights. He had lighted a candle in a green glass stick that had started life at the "Dime"; Joyce took the lamp. Its light turned her ruffled soft mahogany hair to an aureole as she smiled at him from the stairway.

## CHAPTER XXVII

"Dad," she said suddenly, out of a long silence. Her father looked up.

They were in the parlor; it was night; Arty and Michael and Ben had gone off to bed. William Ballard had had some little anxiety about a new-born heifer calf that had been installed upon some old sacks in the closed end of the wood-shed, and had left Joyce and Isabelle in consultation in the kitchen to go out to see it. There were to be buckwheats and new sausages for breakfast, as tomorrow was going to be a hard day for the men; they were going to clear the southern-most acres of brush and scrub, to let the sunlight in on the upper orchard. Joyce and Isabelle had talked about break-fast, and about the baby that was due in another month, and had fallen into other idle lines of women's talk until William had returned. Then, in the parlor, father and daughter had somehow been drawn into a conversation, too. William had taken his chair and his pipe, Joyce had balanced herself on the arm of the chair opposite his, as if ready for departure at any moment, yet lingering on and on while the clock ticked and the ashes fell, and the furniture in distant parts of the house gave forth odd late-evening creaks and snaps. The room was lighted only by one lamp; its corners were filled with mellow shapes and shadows.

"Dad," Joyce said, "before you—before anyone marries anyone, how can they—she—be sure?"

Her father gave her a thoughtful look.

"You mean of being happy, Joy?"

"Well, not exactly that. That sounds so—flat somehow, as if one had to be amused with dances and songs! No. I mean of one's own heart," Joyce formulated it slowly. "I mean—to be sure it's all right, to be sure it's the most you could feel for anyone, ever."

"I think you *know* that, Joyce. There's a sort of buoyancy, of exhilaration, that carries you along. You're impatient. You can't wait to belong to each other, to have yourselves in a little world inside the world, and no one else in at all. You don't really know what that happiness is," the man added, half to himself, "but you think you do! Now with you, darling," he added. "You and Paul. You've tested your affection with years of absence, letters, joys and sorrows. You have all that to assure you—to prove to you that you needn't be afraid of any change."

He fell silent. Joyce looked at him a moment, with her head tipped like a bird's head to one side, looked at the stove's glowing eye, looked back at her father again.

"Suppose you are afraid you *won't* change?" she said in an undertone, her cheeks very red, her eyes bravely meeting her father's eyes.

For a minute he regarded her gravely, without speaking.

"Is it so, Joyce?" he asked then. "Does that mean that you have changed toward Paul?"

"No, I don't think I have! I think I like him even better than I ever did; certainly he's nicer!" the girl answered with a perplexed little shred of vexed laughter. "I mean, if ever there was anything years ago, that I—sort of—wished was different in Paul, it really is changed," she explained it.

"He's working hard, and he's more sensible, and he feels about the way his friends act just as I do—of course, he *does* the things they do—but he's quite different from Claire and all of them——"

"What things do they do, for example?" William Ballard asked, as she floundered into silence.

"Oh, well, you know when I was with them last weekend?" Joyce began slowly, went on in a rush. "I got there Friday for dinner," she said, "and we were all going over to the Friedmanns'—there was hardly time to dress—and we all had cocktails downstairs. A lot of people came in for them, and we were about an hour late for dinner, but so was everyone else, so that didn't matter. At the Friedmanns' there were more cocktails, and then the silly stuff began about your husband and my wife and what was Yvonne Porter doing up in your room and all that sort of thing—they never get tired of it! Then we had part of the dinner—soup and fish and chicken—and we six rushed away, Bobby and Barbara Friedmann and a boy and Olivette Shepard, and we went to the Barrows' for Elizabeth's dance, and it was a terrible flop.

"She's a débutante, you know, but she couldn't come out last fall because her father was killed and she was ther-*rown* from a horse and hurt her back. But anyway she's all right, and they had this dance in a perfectly magnificent house; they had the Misses Worn decorate, and they say the decorations cost thousands. But Elizabeth looked horrible, and everything was cold and slow somehow, and the boys began to take the girls down to Rotty's for der-*rinks*. Elizabeth's grandmother would only let them have punch, and a lot of people didn't come, and it was terrible. So about one o'clock Ratsy Taylor asked us all to go over to her place and we could turn on the radio and dance. Lots of the boys were drunk then, and everything was awful; nobody said goodbye to the Barrows, and we all went, and the boys made up twenty dollars and waked up the Taylors' butler and asked him to get them drinks."

"Ha!" William Ballard commented simply, watching her.

"And Paul and I didn't go home until after ther-*ree,* and everyone by that time was simply—bul-*lot*to," Joyce said impressively. "And even Paul had had much too much. *That* wasn't any fun!"

"No," her father agreed slowly, "that wasn't any fun. Then what?"

"Oh, then everyone slept late, and we all had breakfast in our rooms, and at about one we all went to watch the polo. Paul played; his father says he will take care of the ponies if Paul will keep it up. And then it all began again, cocktails from five on until after seven, and everything so— so frivolous, somehow, and so ker-*razy,* and so—so talky. I get so mad at myself for talking so much, but they all do. They make fun of everyone; they are most of them divorced and—and everything!" Joyce finished with a sudden flatness in her tone and was silent a moment. "I want Paul and me to be different," she presently added. "I'd like to do things, now and then, and wear clothes like that. You never saw so many beautiful women or such beautiful cul-*lothes.* But— well, when he drove me down here on Sunday somehow it seemed——" Joyce stopped to laugh. "Of course it *was* getting home!" she said. "I was going to say that it seemed like getting home. I mean, I wanted to hear about Dodo and Isabelle and the heifer and you and Ben and everything, and I felt I'd missed something!"

"I think that's perhaps because you and Paul haven't seen each other for so long, Joy," her father said after a moment. "You'll grow together in a few weeks; the strangeness will wear off. I wouldn't take it too seriously now, it seems to me. I'd visit there, and have him visit here; he's only been home ten days, after all. In any case you've decided not to announce your engagement until just before the marriage, so that you've time to think it over."

"But, Dad," the girl persisted, "that's the ter-*rouble!* Or well, no, there's no ter-*rouble*," she corrected herself hastily. "But that's the—the thing. I *do* love Paul. I've never liked anyone else half so well and I never will. He's got the most marvelous disposition—he's *always* laughing, and he's generous—I mean, he hates me to stop and give ter-*ramps* money, on the road," she amended it, after a moment's thought, "but he's generous in the way he *thinks!* And this last week-end, in his white polo outfit, when the match was over, he came and jumped over the barrier into the grandstand, and came up to me with his cap and his mallet in his hand—looking so *won*derful——"

She paused, musing, and presently added: "No, it's not Paul. It's just—the way they live, the way they talk. It makes my skin feel dry. I think I'm like you, Dad. I don't want to be doing things all the time.

"That's not it exactly, either. If they all say, 'Let's go down to Santa Barbara next week-end!' or 'Let's go to a movie!' or 'Let's go up to the Mark Hop and dance,' I want to go. Or if Paul says: 'We're all having dinner with Pidgie tonight,' I'm delighted; I think, 'What fun we have!'

"But then when we get started," Joyce presently recommenced as her father did not speak, "it's always the same thing. Jammed in with a boy you don't like in your lap and someone's arm about you, ignoring red lights and watching out for cops, and cocktails and heat and too much food——

"You see, all that makes me unhappy, Dad. I can't help it. I like a good time, and I can be exter-*rav*agant, too, about a hat or a party. But to do it all the time—it makes me nervous!"

She stopped on an appealing note and looked at him expectantly. She was still half standing, half leaning against the broad low chair arm opposite him.

"It's one of those things you have to think out for yourself, Joy," her father said slowly, looking away from her.

"I know. And I know Paul and I will be married in the fall," she answered confidently. "Only—now, for instance, his father and Claire are lending us their apartment until January," she added. "At least Paul said that his father was keen to have us get married before they start around the world and would be glad to have us in it. It's a beautiful place—I think they pay seven hundred for it. They'd leave three servants in it, and Paul says we'll have cocktail parties two or three times a week and have the crowd drop in whenever it likes. And he says his mother'll come up for a visit, and *that* seems to me queer; she's been married to two men since she was his father's wife. I sound prudish," Joyce finished, with a shamed little flush, "but it's just that I want to start right."

"You're right. That isn't a very good start, Joycie," her father presently said somewhat hesitantly. "But if you love each other, and the first excitement of it all wears off, and you find some little place down Burlingame way, you'll work it out! You could always be here at home in two hours, you know, if you wanted to see the babies and Dodo——"

"And Dad! Yes, I know," she finished it for him smilingly. She went over and kissed him on the forehead and picked up her lamp. "I guess all the rushing and excitement tires me, that's all," she said. "I ought to be thanking God for being so lucky! It's a nice feeling, too, that you don't want to leave home. We all," she ended, at the foot of the stairs now, carrying her lamp, "we all like to be home these days, Dad. Ben never misses a week-end, and Dodo cried with joy when you asked her and Charley to live here if I went away. It must be wonderful to be able to ask them here, and have them so happy to come."

"It *is* wonderful," William Ballard said simply. He followed Joyce upstairs. Within ten minutes through the thin farmhouse walls she heard the steady sound of his sleeping breath, coming and going, coming and going.

But Joyce did not sleep for a long time. Instead, when she had undressed, she rolled herself in a thick new blanket and went to the window sill, and knelt there, with the cold soft air pouring over her, and her eyes fixed dreamily on the outlines of the sleeping hills, and the shadows that were redwoods and barns and fences, and the wash of milky moonlight over the dark world.

The skies were powdered thick with stars; the moon was setting. Joyce could study the Milky Way like a lowered scarf that touched the rounded tops of the oaks. In the orchard blossoms were in pallid beauty; the soft sigh of a spring breeze brought down all the good woodland smells of growing things, and in the dead silence of the night the creek's rushing music could be heard, the far-away cry of a coyote, the woodeny hoot of an owl.

"Oh, it is too beautiful!" the girl whispered. "I wish I knew why I'm so afraid to let it all go!"

## ❧ CHAPTER XXVIII ❧

Joyce lay in her bed, stretched straight and slim beneath the fine linen sheet, her hands locked on the pillow under her head, her eyes fixed upon the ceiling. The clock had struck ten on a hot July morning. There was no hurry, nobody would be stirring in the household of Emylie Bent-Crowder for another hour at least.

Emylie Bent-Crowder was Paul's mother. She had begun life as Emily Bent, she had legally worn three different names since, and had picked Crowder from among them for momentary use as being perhaps the prettiest. She was forty-eight, dashing, undaunted; just now she was extremely rich, and had taken the Knight place at Santa Barbara for the summer.

It was in one of the beautiful guest rooms of the Knight place that Joyce was lying. She had been a guest of Paul's mother for six exciting, amusing, astonishing days; tomorrow would be the last of them. Tomorrow Paul would take her home, and a month later the quiet announcement of their quiet wedding would be made. It was to be in San Francisco, after all; somehow Joyce did not want it to be at the ranch. She would miss her mother too much at home.

Lissy would come down from Victoria; her father and Dodo would go in to the city a day or two earlier and stay at a hotel; the wedding would be in their own sitting room. Paul's stepmother, Claire, didn't like the idea; Paul's mother, Emylie, wasn't even coming north for so entirely informal an affair; but it would suit Paul and Joyce best that way, and they were the ones to be considered, after all.

The date was set for mid-August. "And this," Joyce thought, lying in bed, staring at the ceiling, "this is already July——!"

It was a beautiful room in which she lay, part of a beautiful house. The Knights had built the place just before the crash and had not spared expense. In the twenty or more different apartments there were such beauties of furniture and drapery as Joyce had never imagined. Dim old Spanish canvases hung on the cleverly distempered plaster walls; dim old rugs sprawled on the flagged floors; candles burned at twilight in twisted old iron holders from Toledo. Through lowered shutters the blazing California sunlight sent even blocks of bars across wide shadowy spaces; there were polished steps up and down between room and room; there were many patios, green cool spaces of palms and peppers where lazy fountains spurted and splashed idly and striped awnings cut across a turquoise-blue sky. Flowers glowed everywhere, indoors and out. Joyce's room had a grilled balcony above an enclosed court on the eastern side, and on the west windows that looked straight out over the sea.

"Jimble Place," as Jim and Belle Knight had ingeniously named their home, was set in three acres of garden, close to the sea. Between it and the highway lay the garages and the riding stable; between it and the ocean were only descending terraces set with jars of flowers, shaded by great trees that framed endless and exquisite vistas in every direction.

Here Emylie held court, her son the chief among her adorers. Everyone who was prominent at all in Santa Barbara drove down to see her; the richest man in this part of the world, bloated, garrulous, half mad, was a constant visitor; movie stars came; everyone came. Drinks were served at half-past six in the morning as a finish to a big night, and served again at eight o'clock as a "pick-me-up" before an early breakfast. Dance music went on incessantly; bridge tables were always waiting; maids went about filling boxes with cigarettes and taking away ashes and dirty glasses and rumpled napkins.

Meals came at any time. At eleven, at two, at nine in the evening Emylie might say to some attendant: "Oh, by the way, we'll all lunch here—in about twenty minutes? You'd better count us!"

The servants never counted; there was no counting this shifting crowd that moved so indifferently to and fro. They set the tables for eighteen, twenty, with glasses and damask and flowers, and if only six sat down there was no harm done. Everywhere there were delicious platters of cold chicken, bubbling icy glasses of champagne, hot buttered finger rolls, crisped Spanishy-looking preparations of ravioli or enchiladas or spaghetti in brown earthenware pots, plates of delicate sandwiches, laced with color and rosettes and garnishings. Everyone was hospitable, and many of the men talked food with tremendous enthusiasm, waiting for duck season, remembering a tapioca dish in Java, praising the *crêpes suzette* at Foyou's in Paris.

Into all this, armed with the two new linens and the organdy, Joyce had plunged fearfully, six amazing days earlier. She had known that her clothes were not quite right; she had been anxiously conscious that she was the stranger among them all.

But it had all turned out to be quite simple and delightful. Everyone was having too good a time to notice her much at first, and before the third day had ended, the attentions Paul von Schwerin was paying her had established her once and for all. Paul was in high favor with this group, ringleader in plans and escapades; Paul's girl could not but be important.

They rode sometimes before breakfast, when it was not too warm, a dozen of them cantering along the green roads near the sea; they played tennis and golf; they ate ravenously, and went into Santa Barbara for movies, giggling all through them, and some mornings and often late in the afternoon they swam. With meals interspersed between all these diversions, and some little sleep at odd moments, the time raced by. Everything was laughter and fun, compliments, nonsense, movement. A sense of popularity that was absolutely intoxicating after years of exile made the sun seem brighter to Joyce than it ever had seemed before, the sea bluer, the magic of moonlight and the scent of flowers' sweetness almost unbearably sweet.

There were quiet families living in the neighborhood of Santa Barbara, old residents whose families sat down to three regular meals a day and discussed the price of a new gown or a card party with interest. But these were not in the circle to which Joyce had been welcomed. It was a narrow circle; its extravagancies flourished on the staid older stock like a brilliantly colored parasite on the branches of an old oak. For a few feverish months big hotels were crowded, beaches strewn with gay umbrellas and bathing suits, dancing floors filled all night long, and smart cars glittering in the shade of every clump of great trees. Then suddenly the season was over and the visitors gone, and Santa Barbara settled down to normal living again.

July was the height of the season, and Joyce's visit happened to be made in an unusually brilliant one. There were yachts in the harbor; shining little planes swooped the blue waters of the bay like great birds; press photographers from

San Francisco and Los Angeles were busy in hotel lobbies. "The Baron" was going riding; "Sir Ashley Tothers and Lady Tothers" were playing bridge with Constance Beverly and Ogden Porter of Hollywood; the Russian Countess had lost her bracelet again.

A continual sense of gala, of sunshine on white sails, warm sand under wet bodies, fresh frocks and greensward, dancing ponies and flying golf balls permeated the whole scene. The moon shone milk white on the gently breathing ocean; the stars were warm and close; the strains of the "Blue Danube" and the "Kiss Waltz" and the "Merry Widow" were continually, faintly throbbing through the perfumed summer air.

Paul's mother and Joyce were of exactly the same figure. Joyce found herself the embarrassed, happy recipient of many a beautiful frock: a French linen with dark red and blue stripes, a flowery silky organdy that billowed about her dancing feet enchantingly, a loose soft mustard-yellow coat, broad hats, transparent evening wraps, a bathing suit from the Rue de la Paix that had a cape and a cap to match it. Emylie Bent-Crowder was going to New York in September to "go dotty," as she herself expressed it, among the shops and *coutouriers*. She quickly tired of her clothes anyway, and Joyce's round-eyed delight in them pleased her. It was her mood at the moment to win the heart of Paul's girl, and to a great extent she succeeded.

Joyce did not like the careless talk or the swearing; she knew Emylie drank too many cocktails, and she did not understand—or rather she feared that she understood only too well—the position of Count Kyryl Orsitzski in the house. Quite simply and with a vociferous regard for his own comfort and disregard for everything else, "Kyryl" occupied the handsomest guest suite. Nobody explained him; nobody especially liked him; he simply was there. He was about thirty-five, bearded, black, penniless. Joyce gathered that if he had not been the actual Tsar of all the Russias, he at least had been one of the nearest relatives and friends of the late Tsar, and an important person in old Russia.

Also Emylie's history was against her. She had two living husbands, not counting the last mate, whose union to her she had herself caused to be proved illegal. Emylie wanted money, position, excitement, and nothing else. In her almost half-century of living she had attained these things in many forms and ways.

But it was impossible not to like her. She made life gay. She wanted everyone to be happy. She shrieked with joy at any good joke, screamed and laughed like a parrakeet over the bridge table, was affected, noisy, generous, vital all at once. And she really liked Joyce.

"You have a good effect on Paul," she told the girl. "I've always adored him and never gotten on with him. But you're a one-man girl; you'll straighten him out."

It was no thought of Emylie as a mother-in-law that was making Joyce serious on the last morning but one of her stay as she lay in bed with her hands locked under her head and stared at the ceiling. It was no thought of Paul's father, handsome Victor von Schwerin, or of Claire, who were up in their cabin on the Rogue River. It was no criticism of this wonderful visit. Throughout it, she had felt herself just what every visiting girl longs to be: lovely, popular, adequate; she had felt that everything, herself included, was just right.

No; it was something much more serious than that. Joyce had come quite simply and definitely to the realization that she did not love Paul.

For a day or two she had been shrinking away from the fear of it; she had been in a continual state of balancing the full wretchedness of it against its utter incredibility. She *must* love Paul. She *did* love Paul. Any other idea was completely absurd! But it had grown stronger in being denied; it had crept in upon her with an increasing conviction. She knew it now. She did not love Paul as a sweetheart should, as a wife should love her man. She could not marry him.

All very well to tell herself, as she did a hundred times a day, that this was girl nonsense, this was just the natural fear that came to every girl before the complete surrender. It would not work. The self-knowledge that had come to her was not nonsense; it was a moral, a mental, a physical thing far stronger than she was herself. She knew now that it would be easier to marry some man she had never seen, some unknown suitor out of the great unknown world, than to promise to be the wife of Paul von Schwerin.

Joyce felt dazed and cold and sick at the discovery, but it was there, like losing an arm or getting the measles. Everything was changed; one could not do anything about it; it was simply that way.

The feeling of strangeness and doubt had come to her when she and Paul had been alone on the first night of her week-long visit. Before that it had all been perfect; their drive from the ranch, their luncheon together, their arrival in Santa Barbara for a fresh salty swim, for dressing in cool white for a big dinner at the hotel, for dancing, laughter, new faces, new friends.

But afterward, in the moon-drenched patio of the Knights' beautiful Spanish villa, he had suddenly been the lover, and Joyce had begun to suspect even then that her utter lack of response to his kisses, her odd feeling of detachment and reluctance in his arms had been more than a girl's shy withdrawal from the unfamiliar thrill of the man's eager domination. She had not been able to respond to it; she had felt embarrassed, confused, her cheeks burning red in the cool night shadows, her responses to his whispered incoherent words half protestant, half amused. She had slipped away quickly, pleading fatigue after the long day's drive.

It had been so ever since. The daytime hours had been swift and enchanted; the inevitable time of love-making, late at night, had continued to perplex and trouble her. And from this beginning the whole relationship between them had changed. Joyce had come to see that in no way could she feel what she must feel if she and Paul were really to be man and wife within a few weeks' time.

He was handsome, amusing, tremendously popular and admired; he did everything well; he leaped into the swimming contest, the tennis tournament, the golf matches; he could fly a plane, shoot straight, he danced magnificently. When the movie troupe came to Santa Barbara to do *Summer Madness,* Paul had a little part in the picture, and danced a tango with Magda Morrill herself.

Splendid in white flannels and evening mess jacket, riding his polo ponies hard, keeping tennis balls flying in the sunshiny air, scowling over a golf drive, Paul was the darling of all hearts this year in Santa Barbara, as popular with the men as the women. And he was openly, eagerly the slave of Joyce Ballard; he made no secret of it. They were going to be married; it wasn't announced, but everyone knew it. When Paul and Joyce were alone he wanted to talk of the "fun" they would have. They would have his father's apartment in San Francisco for five months and then they would find some smaller place, and every summer come down to Mother for a couple of months . . .

It had all gone dead in her ears. It did not mean anything. She could not look for an apartment, open wedding presents, order new cards, accept all the hospitalities that would be involved in her marriage to Paul von Schwerin because it was all dead. Lifeless. She liked him enormously, indeed she really loved him; he was the only man who ever had kissed her, to whom she had talked on terms of affectionate intimacy.

All that meant nothing. All this beauty and pleasure and

excitement were only distractions that kept her from thinking, as she did think in every quiet moment: "I can't do it. I've got to tell him! Oh, what on earth will I do!

"And if I think this *here*," Joyce reflected, "here where half the girls in the place are madly in love with him, and where they stop dancing to watch him dance, how much more I'll think it when I get home and can see the whole thing quietly! *Home!*" she said in her heart, over a sharp pang of longing for it. Before her eyes quiet pictures of it rose: her father coming down from the barns with the milk on a frosty clear winter morning, the quiet ripple of the little flume that ran from the spring to the dooryard and that always sounded sweet and cool under the oaks on a still summer afternoon.

"Today," she thought, "the grasshoppers will be jumping ahead of Michael when he goes up through the meadow, and Isabelle will have the baby's basket out on the north porch with a mosquito netting over it. She'll have put big peaches on the ice. Dad will have come in early and gone to sleep in the hammock. They'll have supper, outside, with everything getting cool, and the mountains looking as if you could stick your finger through them . . . "

She would be there tomorrow. But there was a bad hour to get through with Paul today. He would not believe her. He would laugh at her. No girl in her senses could refuse Paul von Schwerin just now, when all the world was at his feet and his newly enriched mother was showering him with gifts.

Joyce sighed. Slowly she got up, began the refreshing processes of dressing. They were all to meet at the club for lunch at one. Paul was playing golf this morning; the girls were all sleeping late. Joyce stepped into a perfumed bath in a tiled bathroom that might have been once a chapel in the Escurial. She made herself charming in thin blue organdy; the wide hat that went on her coppery head was of the same blue, with cunningly chosen scarlet ribbons dangling down her back.

For a long time she sat at the dressing table looking thoughtfully at herself. Brown eyes with copper in them; firm smooth skin burned to an even creamy tan; wide mouth with red lips closed over big teeth. Against the low forehead the blue hat pressed strands of red-brown silk; the rounded throat descended to the young breasts that rose firmly under the delicate organdy.

A French maid came in. Madame Bent-Crowder and the Count were ready when Mademoiselle was ready. Mademoiselle was *ravissante* in the blue robe. Mademoiselle smiled her appreciation of the compliment and went out to face what she must face.

It all came about sooner than she expected. At the club were the Jimmy Hollidays, motoring up from Los Angeles. The Hollidays were old friends of all the Ballards, and they were delighted to see Joyce, and to hear all the news—of Dodo's babies and Lissy's life in Canada, and of Ben. Quite suddenly, on an impulse, Joyce asked them to take her with them when they started northward at three o'clock. And immediately afterward she drew Paul aside for a private talk.

They took two deep chairs at a deserted end of the club veranda. A few hundred feet away the sea rippled and shone in the hot afternoon sun, but a breeze flapped the awnings, and gently rotating electric fans made the clubhouse cool.

"Paul, this is the hardest thing I ever said to anyone in my life," Joyce began courageously. "I'm so sorry to say it! I know you'll make it as easy for me as you can. I'm going home with Jim and Anita tonight because—it's just simply this: I don't want to get married—I don't want to be engaged—not to anyone——"

A halt. His laughing incredulous eyes gradually lost their

amused look; he saw that this was serious, and his face grew serious.

"What's the matter, Joyce?" he asked in his quick kind voice.

"Nothing. That's the trouble. I mean that's what makes it seem so completely idiotic in me to change."

"You haven't changed."

"I have, Paul. You know there's a feeling that makes you want to marry a person," the girl floundered on uneasily, "and a feeling that makes it impossible. I—it's hard to explain, when I like you so—love you, really—but it wouldn't be honest not to say that I can't go on!"

Paul considered this a moment, looking at her attentively.

"What have I done, Joyce?"

"Oh, Paul, you haven't done anything!"

"Too much of Sid's punch night before last?"

"That was *nothing*. They all do that! No, it's just——"

"Oh, I wish this was over, I wish this was over!" Joyce said in her soul, "it's just that I don't want to marry anyone," she explained feebly.

"No; tell me the truth, darling; what's it all about? You know I'll do anything—change anything. Is it Mother?"

"Your mother's been simply an angel to me; she's been only too kind. No; it's something in me. I'm a fool, I know it, but it just doesn't seem as if I could get married next month!"

Paul was watching her attentively. He smiled.

"All girls feel that," he offered.

"Yes; I know. And it may be, some time, years from now—— But I just want it understood that we're not engaged," Joyce said. "Now while there's time—while we're just fer-*riends*——"

The man looked up in the pause, looked away again.

"We're a lot more than friends, Joyce," he said slowly.

"Yes, I know we are!" she admitted tonelessly.

"I've never loved any other woman except you, and I never will," Paul said. "What's happened? What have I done? I don't understand."

"Nothing's happened. It's nothing you've done—ter-*ruly*. I've never liked anyone else either. But I can't leave my father—Dodo. I mean, I belong at home. It was different years ago; I didn't feel that way then. But now—now I want to be free—I mean I don't want to get married. I think," Joyce said, tears coming to her eyes—"I think Mother's death made me feel older—not so sure of myself."

"Your mother's death had nothing to do with it, and you know it," Paul said quietly, as she hesitated. And for a full minute neither spoke.

"You can't think how terribly hard it is for me to say this," Joyce said then. She got to her feet. The talk was over. "I'm going home with the Hollidays; I'll leave a note for your mother," she added.

"I'll drive you home to Merriwell, of course," Paul said.

"Please—pul-*lease*——" the girl began, a hand on his arm.

"You mean you really don't want me to?" He was more puzzled than alarmed; he was infinitely gentle.

"Please not."

"Then I'll at least take you to our place now, and help you pack."

He would do it. He hardly spoke on the way; his eyes were always on the road ahead. But Joyce talked feverishly in explanation, in apology. You loved a person that way or you didn't; you might adore him in other ways, but unless you felt completely sure—absolutely sure—of yourself, you might only make yourself and him miserable. Paul had been just an angel to her; he had carried her over the hardest years of her life, and if he and she had been married four years ago it might have worked out all right; they would have had the New York and English experiences together then, they would have grown together. But now all Joyce Ballard wanted was the ranch and the garden and theatricals in the village, and her father, and Lissy's and Ben's and Dodo's lives to share and problems to solve.

Paul was very silent when they reached Jimble Place. He came upstairs with her to her bedroom quite simply and sat watching her while she packed. Joyce went to and fro, shaking frocks, smoothing folded garments, rolling cream jars neatly in tissue paper, talking irregularly, hesitantly, and stopping to look at him as she talked.

"I've been lying awake thinking about it; I've been despising myself. I feel such a fool, Paul!" she pleaded.

"You'll straighten out when you get home; you're not used to the pace here," he said slowly, after a while.

"It isn't that."

"It must be that, Joyce. Why, after all these years, you couldn't—I don't believe you *could* throw me down!"

"But it *isn't* throwing you down! It's the hardest thing I've ever done, but it isn't anything like that—like a quarrel or a change of feeling! It's just—just knowing that you and I aren't—aren't *right*—that I can't go on, not feeling more than I do."

The beautiful bedroom was filled with tempered afternoon light; the jalousies were down, and strips of shade and brightness lay softly over the coolness and daintiness and delicate color of the place. Through the orange-and-blue awning on Joyce's high balcony bars of pearly gray and faint brick color fell upon the tiles; below it the fountain pulsed regularly, a jet of water, a sinking of the jet, a spurt upwards again.

All about them the spread roofs and empty patios of the house were very still. Doves crooned somewhere out of sight; their dreamy notes and the lazy splashing of the water seemed to accentuate the silences that were broken only by the two troubled young voices in the bedroom.

"A girl has to feel—thrilled, sure of herself, Paul."

"Oh, but you do, Joyce, of course you do! You're tired now; we've been going too hard a pace. But this is our *lives!* Why, we were going to hunt houses and cruise around Chinatown looking for things. Don't talk as if we could end it all with just one talk, like this!"

"I'm not. I don't mean to. I mean, as far as friendship and *liking* you and loving to have you come down to the ranch, as far as all that goes——" Joyce paused, hoping that he would meet her halfway. The man, frowning slightly, looking into space through narrowed lids, was silent.

"Suppose you were trying to end it all, Paul, what would you say?"

"That's not what you're trying to do—end it all! That's nonsense! Besides, I never could try to. I've loved you ever since I met you at Marie Louise Towers's."

The girl snapped a bag shut; straightened herself, regarding him thoughtfully. She was remembering, and not with resentment, not with anything more than a sort of wonder, that earlier visit when she had been with Paul's father and stepmother at Pebble Beach. She remembered her sense of hurt and shame, her desperate attempts to establish herself in the charmed circle where Paul and Elisa Blandwood had reigned supreme, her appeal to the kindly Englishman, Monty Lefanu, who had rescued her from open tears at the Del Monte dance. She remembered that Paul had been too happily engaged to drive her home and that she had left on the afternoon train, her heart bursting with humiliation and despair and the misery of love set aside, and that Elisa and Paul, in exquisitely amusing fancy dress, had come along the tracks to wave her a Victorian farewell.

But all this was long ago, back in those years when one burned one's hand on saucepan handles and threw away the bacon fat, back in those years when Mother, eager, ambitious, loyal, had been the center of the home group, when Lissy had been alternately proudly silent and angrily critical of Archie, when Dodo and Joyce had lain awake talking in the hot summer nights, wondering if any man would ever want them in marriage. Joyce felt today a hundred, a thousand, years older than the girl of those days; she could feel achingly sorry for Paul now, as he had been too young, too happy, too occupied to feel sorry for her then.

"Well, listen, we'll not talk about it any more," he said finally, when the honking of the Hollidays' car sounded in the road and it was time for Joyce to go. "We'll not talk of this any more. I'll be down to see you Saturday, and everything'll seem very different then. Just one thing, Joyce: there isn't anyone else?"

"Good heavens, no!" she said, wide-eyed. "I'm not *thinking* of marriage. I'm happy as I am. I want to get married some day, of course—and naturally I'd think of you when I did," she diverged, close beside him as they crossed the largest patio and went through a grilled gate to follow the flagged path across the lawn. "But for a while I want to just stay along with Dad—I like that way of living."

They joined the Hollidays; bags were stowed; Joyce got in with Jim and Anita on the wide front seat with only a parting brief kiss from Paul.

"Good-bye, dear," Paul said. "I'll be down for lunch Saturday."

"Isn't he a darling!" Anita said. "I think he's the stunningest thing I ever saw."

"He's as nice as he's good-looking," Joyce said.

"Serious?" Anita asked, delighted.

"We've been fer-*riends* for years; we saw each other this year for the first time since he went East to law school," Joyce answered soberly. "We like each other very much."

## CHAPTER XXIX

AT NINE the next morning she went into the Merriwell post office and spoke to Marie-Thérèse Sallock.

"Ma'tress, want to run me up the hill? The friends who were bringing me up from Santa Barbara got into engine trouble last night and we had to stay at King City. I took the bus the rest of the way."

"For heaven's sake—this weather!" Marie-Thérèse said interestedly, through the grill that said "Registry Window." "Wait a minute!" she added, untying her alpaca apron. She came around to the front. "Uncle Harry, keep an eye on my desk, will you?" she called. She grasped one of Joyce's bags. "Lissen, I've been bustin' to see you; j'eer about Sarah Planter?" she began. They were not silent for one minute of the run up the hill.

But Joyce was not talking so hard but that she was drinking it all in: the orchards simmering in early-morning heat, the blue-aproned fruit cutters gathering in the long sheds by the packing plant, Swede's horses at the bars in the shade of the big sycamore with their necks laid against each other. The scent of tarweed and ripening fruit and pine resin was in the air. When at last she was at the kitchen doorstep with her bags about her, and Marie-Thérèse had gone, there was not a sound to be heard on the ranch except that of jays squawking in the orchard, and the ripple of water running quietly through the little flume from the spring.

The day was hot, still and blue, with a flawless sky arched above it. The eastern mountains might have been made of gauze; they rose only a shade deeper in tone than the sky. Chickens were gathered in the shade of an oak, fluffing and drowsing, their little white-skin lids half lowered over their beady eyes.

It was delicious to go up to her own airy bedroom among the pear-tree leaves and change to comfortable cotton home wear and low old buckskin shoes, to splash her hot face and comb back her wet hair, to find great peaches dripping in the cooler and to sally forth in search of company while she stripped the silky thin skin from the fruit and bent herself double to take great plunging bites of it.

She washed her sticky fingers in the trough, where the cold water brimmed over mossy edges and wet the slippery ground, and dried them on her handkerchief. Then on to the great open doors of the hay barns, empty except for scratching chickens, and to the airy, orderly stable, where Molly looked at her reproachfully from the box stall.

"I know, Molly, I know," Joyce said aloud, her voice echoing oddly in the sweet quiet place. "But what did you do last time? You had your colt 'way up in the draw, and stepped on it and killed it. You've got to be good!"

She wandered on. Faint chattering noises began to make themselves heard, far up in the orchard, and Joyce spoke out in sudden comprehension:

"Of course! They're cutting peaches! No wonder no one was in sight!"

Her face was flushed now and her forehead damp. The relentless heat of mid-morning beat down. The men who were working at the ladders under the peach trees were dressed only in jeans and canvas shoes.

Further up was the cutting shed—just a long roof over a table where a score of women and girls and children were seated with knives and pans, peeling peaches as fast as their sticky fingers could fly. In spite of the roof and the tall trees above the roof, glints of sunshine came in on them and touched the rich color of the fruit and the faded tones of the women's open-necked, short-sleeved cottons. Yellowjackets buzzed about them. Boxes of heaped limp wet peels were carried away by children, but they piled up on the wooden flooring, too, and stuck in dark brown curls and strips to the workers' bare arms. The air was motionless and hot and scented with peach. In the low shed everything was motion and murmur: "Peaches!" the women called authoritatively, and attendant men started fresh-filled boxes of the still sun-warmed fruit down the tracks that ran the length of the table. For each finished box the worker received a little disk which she slipped into her pocket or into a discolored, fruit-soaked little gingham bag she carried for the purpose. At the end of the day these disks were redeemed at the rate of ten cents each, and some of the women could peel forty boxs of peaches in a day.

Joyce saw her father, with his shirt widely open at the collar and a straw hat on the back of his head, and went up to kiss him, greeting everyone on all sides as she went. Many of these cutters came regularly to the ranch when the cherries began in May and stayed until the last of the prunes were in in October; they were old friends.

"Father, where did you get this hoosier effect on your head? Who do you think you are?"

"Joyce—well, welcome home!" William Ballard said. He was in his glory in this hot weather, with the peach crop pouring like a rising tide about him, and these absorbed busy men and women chattering and working under the loose shingles of the shed.

"Missed me?"

"Missed you! We've all been lost!"

She loved to hear it. There were blackened sticky knives in a little box up at one end of the table. She took one to the water faucet and washed it in the dishpan that was standing there on an inverted fruit box. Isabelle was there, busy with lemons, sugar, a big clean aluminum saucepan.

"Where's Tommy?"

"Asleep right here in his basket. It's no hotter here than anywhere. Joyce, it seems real good to see you back." The women's hot wet faces touched for a kiss.

"What are you doing?"

"Why, we're givin' 'em sandwiches and iced tea up here this week, and they're workin' right through until four-thirty. Fruit's spoiling so fast we've had night shifts since Monday," Isabelle explained. "Last night some of 'em were workin' until 'most eleven. Swede's asked 'em all down to his place tonight; he's goin' to barbecue a sheep and have dancin' on that old platform of Cooley's."

"Dancing! This weather!"

"Well, it got real cool last night."

"Where's Michael?"

"He had to go into San José for sulphur. Two of them sacks they thought was sulphur turned out to be lime."

Joyce was drawing back the carefully draped mosquito net that sheltered Isabelle's seven-weeks-old son. Sprawled on a clean bit of thin linen, he lay nude except for a loin cloth; perspiration stood out under his fuzz of dark hair, but he was sleeping peacefully enough.

"You beauty!" the girl said, lightly touching the small curled petal of a hand. "Here, I'm going to get to work!" she added, finding a place at the table, calling familiarly for her first boxful of fruit. The ragged skins dripped in her hands; the mellow great firm half-globes of the peaches spun into the open crates. The woman opposite her, Greg Finn's wife, had stopped in her work to nurse a great fat rolling baby whose curious eyes went all about the scene as he lunched. Water formed on the mother's face in great drops and fell to the child's little face; she wiped it away with a tip of her peach-blackened apron.

"Hear about Sarah Planter, Joyce?"

"Yes. What's the matter with that girl? Crazy?"

Heat. Scent of peaches and flicker of changing sunlight. Voices of children. At noon the children had the fat thick corned-beef sandwiches first; then the paper plates began to come down the table. Joyce was ravenous. She took great bites of the bread and meat and mustard, and drank two tin mugs—three—of the tea in which ice was clinking. The ranchers were supposed to supply the pickers and cutters with lunch, but most of them did it with raw materials. It was a new idea to put it all ready to eat into their hands, and they liked it. Isabelle mixed the tea in great vats; it was served with a tin dipper. Somebody started a wet towel on the rounds, and the women wiped their hot faces and buttery fingers on it before starting in again on the peaches.

The hot afternoon hours flew by. It was four o'clock when Joyce and her father walked down to the house. She had not yet seen Michael. She had not been over to the sulphur house that was on Swede's southern property line, and that was shared by all the four neighboring ranches; Michael was usually there.

In the quiet of the farmhouse she started dinner preparations. Presently all the grime and stickiness and weariness of the day was washed away in a luxurious bath, and Joyce, fresh again, could descend the stairs in a thin old organdy to set the supper table for four out under the oak. The world was cooling now; there was a delicious sense of relaxing and resting everywhere. Chickens were going to bed. From the barns a line of cows was lazily starting away across the hill. The clank of the runaway Whitty's bell came pleasantly down through the orchard. Birds were going to bed, too, flashing and fussing in the low bushes. Sleepy murmurs came from the honeysuckle mats over the porch where there were nests.

Joyce went into the kitchen on some errand; Isabelle had carried the baby up to bed, but the room was not empty. Michael was there, taking a drink at the sink's tap.

A tall lean man in cool tan; his teeth very white against the burned brown of his skin as he turned about and smiled at her. One brown hand was in the running water, waiting for it to cool; he waved a glass in the other hand when he saw Joyce.

"Well, hel-*lo!* I thought it was to be tomorrow."

The room went slowly about in enchanted circles. The late afternoon light slanting into the orderly shaded kitchen was the light of Paradise. Joyce's heart mounted, sang, took flight into unknown ethereal regions.

"Michael," she said. His voice was ringing in her ears like bells; it was all right, everything was all right. It had been Michael all the time, of course; there was nobody else in the world, nobody else mattered. Joyce put her hand out to a chair back and steadied herself.

"Have a good time?"

"I—yes. Oh, yes; wonderful!" She was still unable to breathe normally, and her voice fluttered. "I—I—you were in San José all day, weren't you?" she stammered.

"I got back to the sulphur house about two. I didn't know you were home." He was talking as naturally, as easily as if the world had not turned upside down! "Swede happened to mention that you were up at the cutting shed," he added, enjoying his drink. "But when I went up there you'd gone.

So I went home to change and get Arty and I'm just here.
How was everything?"

"Wonderful." Joyce was trembling; she had difficulty in
controlling her voice. It was so astonishing that he didn't
feel it, see it, too! "Oh, Michael, Michael, Michael darling!"
her heart said. "It's been Michael all the time. That's why
Paul and Santa Barbara and everything seemed so dead;
he wasn't there. If *he*'d walked in, if I could have danced
with *him*——"

But at the thought of dancing with him her senses seemed
to go into a sort of swoon, and she felt suffocated. She had
never danced with him!

They went out to the yard, and he helped her distribute
the knives and forks and glasses from the basket. They
talked meanwhile, Joyce not in the least conscious of what
she said. What she did know was that he was close to her
and that his hand sometimes almost touched her own.

Shadows in the dooryard under the oak; long last
streamers of dying light coming over the hill; her upstairs
windows opened into the pear tree; Isabelle coming out
with a plate of fruit—figs, peaches, apricots, plums,
nectarines. It was all perfect; it was all home, and he was
there. She was talking to Michael, listening to Michael's
voice again.

"Paul here for dinner?"

"I beg your pardon?"

"Where's Paul? Didn't he drive you home?"

"Well, no. No. I came with the Hollidays; they were coming up, anyway. We had to stay last night in King City."

"Hot?"

"Frying."

"When do we see Lochinvar?"

"I beg pardon?"

"Joyce, what's the matter with you tonight? Going to
sleep?"

"No; and I do beg your pardon! But I was thinking of something else. Did you miss me, Michael?"

"All of us. Sickeningly! It's two places, Joyce; one with you and one without you. Your father was wandering around here yesterday like a lost soul. He said: 'I walk all over the place and never meet a girl!' "

"Oh, the darling!" Joyce said.

"Sunday, Ben brought his girl down. Kate Pollack."

"Like her?"

"Oh, she's a grand girl! A little older than Ben, Dodo said; she looks as if there was no nonsense about her! Ben," Michael said, dragging the name out and glancing sidewise at his companion with a little quizzical smile, "Ben paid me back four dollars he borrowed from me two months ago."

"Ben," Joyce said significantly, "is waking up. Remember how wild he used to be because Dad wouldn't borrow money and send him to New York and all the rest of it? Remember that he used to leave home about once a month, never to return?"

"Your father certainly took it on the chin in those days."

"From Mother, too, and Lissy, and even Dodo and I weren't very much good! But now Dad," Joyce ended thoughtfully, "is the happiest man of his age I ever knew."

"And your mother was happy, too," Michael said. "And Ben," he added, amused again, "is in the circulation department of the paper, and running a bunch of newsboys; he's going to bring them all down here next week for a picnic, and now he's got Kate to keep an eye on him. She's going to keep on with her job and move right into that Chinatown apartment; she's got it all figured out. You'd hardly know Ben. He's grown up ten years in ten weeks."

"I thought so the last time I saw him. Dad says he's learned values. But Ben says all he's learned is what it is to be broke and hungry, fired and dirty, shabby and—something else—cold, I believe."

"Maybe those are values, Joy."

"Maybe they are."

A pause. Then Michael asked cheerfully:

"When does Paul come again?"

"Saturday, I believe."

"Well," Michael said, "if you believe it, I'll believe it, too!"

Arty came out. William Ballard, tired, hungry, at peace with the world, took his seat at the head of the table. Joyce carried out the biscuits and honey and blackberries; Isabelle put a smoking dish before the master of the ranch; Michael had cold artichokes on a platter. There was still strong daylight, but the shadows were gone; the world of mountains and orchards and solemn rising redwoods stood transfixed in a strange clear radiance; only in the west was there color— burning apricot under a steel-gray bank of ocean fog.

The air was still warm, but cooling. A new moon rose tremblingly against the clear ultramarine of the eastern sky. From far off came faint sounds of laughter, the rhythm without the harmony of music. Swede's guests were already enjoying themselves.

The four at the table sat on late, sat on after the last of the daylight was gone, and the glimmer of frail starlight and the tips of the men's cigarettes were the only guides through the thick soft early dark. Joyce sat squared about, her chair drawn so close to her father's that her shoulder was almost against his shoulder. They two faced the other two, Michael rather silent tonight, William Ballard and Arty intermittently animated on the subject of strikes and unions, Russia, Italy and Germany, wars, peace, and the dole.

High above their head the tops of the poplars and the pear-tree branches moved softly in a warm summer wind. Joyce looked at the vague pale patches of lighter gloom in the gloom that was Michael's face and his hands, his white shirt, his tan coat, and thoughts more solemn, more exquisitely content than any she had ever known swept about her like rising deep waters. It was good to be herself, a woman sitting here with these men, her hand in her father's hand; the soft shadows all about her hiding home—home with its garden and barns, its trees and porches, its books and fires, its familiar turns of stairway, its chairs and pots and pans. Life was moving in a steady current through these homely rooms and over this rambling hillside ranch, and it had found her; she was a part of it now. In a few days, or weeks, or months, she would put her hand into the hand of the man she loved, and they would climb together to the little cabin at the top of the canyon.

Nothing else mattered. It was only important that he should be hers and she his. Poverty wouldn't matter. It would be only a joke between the two of them, so rich in love and books and talk and dreams. Michael might masquerade for a few years more as a California fruit picker if he liked; she knew him better than that; she knew that he could find himself an important place in the big world outside when he chose; the definite voice, the clear mind, the quick apprehension would some day reach a higher level than this. Soon or late, it didn't matter. There would be Dad and Dodo and Dodo's babies and long sweet winter walks and idle summer evenings like this one to fill the interval.

"Asleep, Joyce?" Michael's voice said.

"No; just too happy to talk."

"Bridge?" William Ballard suggested half-heartedly, on the voice of a yawn.

"No, it's too hot! Let's just sit out here and talk, and all turn in early."

So they talked for a while longer, and gradually the talk sank into silences, and Joyce's head rested against her father's shoulder. It was with an effort that at nine o'clock they all tore themselves from their chairs, parted in an agony of sleepy words, the guests to start their little car up the hill, the Ballards to stumble into the warm darkness of the house and find their way upstairs to bed.

# ❧ CHAPTER XXX ❧

It was two full weeks later before Joyce talked to her father about it.

"I lay the blame on you, Bill," she said. Now and then she called him Bill, and she knew he liked it. After all, no one used a man's short name after his wife died. It must make him feel old, she thought, not to have Mother's appealing "Will" sound in his ears ever again. So sometimes she called him Bill.

"I lay the blame on you. You brought us here; we had to stay; we all changed—anyway, I changed. I can't live in the city ever again. It just doesn't seem real to me. I've told Paul so."

Her father glanced at her more in expectation than alarm.

"You'll live in Burlingame or San Mateo, then?"

"No, darling, that isn't country. Everyone lives just as much as possible like the city people there. You don't get your own eggs there, or bring in wood, or mix mash for calves."

"Yes, but Joyce, Paul in his profession couldn't very well live in a place like this."

"No; and that's why I'm not going to marry Paul, Dad."

William Ballard looked steadily at his daughter.

"I hardly think you mean that," he said presently.

"I do. I've been all this time, since I got back from Santa Barbara, convincing him of it."

"Why, he was here today!" the man said, perplexedly.

"I know he was. But he's not coming any more."

"Joycie, you don't mean that?"

"But I do, Dad. I told him in Santa Barbara that I couldn't. I told him it just didn't—ring true. I couldn't go in for all that ber-*ridge* and dressing and cocktail parties, and I'm not ster-*rong* enough to cut my own way clear of it."

"Joyce, you haven't broken your engagement!"

"To fer-*linders*."

A pause.

"Was that fair to him?"

"No," Joyce answered frankly. "But what else could I do?"

"But he is exceptionally free from all that sort of thing, dear. Paul—we've said it a hundred times, and in the very beginning I know your mother thought so—Paul has never been contaminated by that empty life."

"I know, Dad. And yet his idea always is one of big cars and champagne and polo ponies——"

"But there's no harm in those things in themselves!" the man said, troubled, as she paused. "Paul is fine. He'd never give them undue importance. For a few years he might like a good deal of gayety and excitement; it wouldn't last. You'd both settle down to home-making; your sisters both have children; there'd be children to hold him steady. Don't move too fast, Joyce."

"At first I told him that I only wanted to put off our marriage," Joyce said. "I couldn't bear to leave you and Dodo and everything here; but it wasn't that. It was that every time he kissed me, every time I thought of house-hunting, getting a ter-*rous*seau, being called 'Mrs. von Schwerin,' I just felt cold, unutterably bored. When I tell you that Molly's colt—to say nothing of Isabelle's Tommy—meant infinitely more to me than anything he could say or do, you'll get some idea of it! Down there at Santa Barbara I was so homesick I thought I would die."

"There isn't anyone else, Joycie?" her father asked, after thought.

"Well, that's just it," the girl answered ingenuously. "You see, there *is*."

"Oho?" His gray eyebrows went up.

"Yes. I didn't know it. But there is. There was, all the time!"

"You didn't *know* it? Who did, if you didn't?"

"Well, nobody, I guess."

"Anyone I know?"

Joyce moved her head slightly in the direction of the southwest canyon. Her father's eyes widened.

"Ha!" he said, struck. There was a pause.

"Michael," Joyce said simply. Her father sighed heavily, shook his head.

"You're pretty sure?"

"Pos-i-tive!" She made it three words.

"Joycie . . . " he said slowly, in a troubled tone.

They had been having breakfast together in the kitchen. Now she came over to him and sat close to him, her chair squared about, her elbow on the table.

"Why not, Daddy?" she asked.

"No reason, dear, no reason at all! He's a good deal older than you are, Joyce. And he's poor."

"Eleven years; that's nothing!"

"He's told you? He's asked you?"

"No, because I think he thinks of me as belonging to Paul. But when I came back from Santa Barbara two weeks ago I knew I didn't belong to Paul. Only then I thought

I just wanted to be fer-*ree,* to be here with you and Dodo and the cats and the dogs. . . .

"The minute I saw Michael I knew better. I knew what all the ter-*rou*ble had been. I'd been growing away from Paul all these years, and toward Michael. But of course I had to wait until it was all straightened out with Paul. He came Sunday, and then yesterday, and now it's *over.*"

"And you think Michael loves you?"

The brown eyes, with a coppery glint of laughter in them, came up to meet his.

"If I don't, you do," Joyce said simply.

"Yes, I suppose I do. Your mother'd say it wasn't a very brilliant marriage for you, Joyce. He's a gentleman; I'm very fond of him. But for a while anyway you'll not have any of the things girls want—clothes and entertaining and silver."

"I'm not a girl, Dad. I'm past twenty-four. I know what I want. It's Michael. That two-room cabin up there, with the sun rising right in the front yard, and the whole valley for our view, will be all the heaven I'll ever need. Just to potter round with him, into the dairy and the barns, and to watch him mending the pumps or the cars, is my life. I don't dare think what travel or success or having a baby like Jacky would add to it; it's too much joy for one woman as it is!"

"You're just in time, then, Joyce," her father said. "Michael goes tomorrow."

"Goes?" Her hand went to her heart, and her color faded. "Goes where?"

"He's going to England with Arty."

"Who said so?"

"It's been arranged for a week—since that Sunday Paul was here, as a matter of fact. Arty has to go, and Michael suddenly has decided to go, too. He was going to say good-bye this afternoon and go in with Arty to stay at a hotel in the city tonight."

"Oh, Daddy, *no!*"

"It makes me feel very badly; it makes me feel quite lost, and thinking of you as getting married in a few weeks made it worse," William Ballard said. Joyce was not listening; her brows were knitted and her full lower lip bitten.

"He can't go to England!" she said.

"I don't know that he intends to stay there. He talked as if he'd always want to come back sometimes to California. But they have their passage on a Panama liner."

"Dad, why didn't you tell me!"

"Well, for one thing, Dodo was afraid that if I told you Michael was going, you'd be unwilling to get married and leave me. And then Michael wanted it kept quiet."

A determined look came into Joyce's narrowed eyes that were staring into space.

"All right, Bill," she said, jumping to her feet. "Lend me a hand with these dishes. I'm going up to Michael's. We'll see about this business!"

An hour later, comfortably busy with the morning papers in a basket chair out on the side-yard grass, he saw her crossing the yard, lithe and tall in her old linen riding clothes. She rode back to wave him good-bye, reining in to keep Molly from stepping on the zinnias.

"Tell Isabelle I'll probably bring Michael and Arty back to lunch. Ask her to hard-boil about a dozen eggs and soak the lettuce, and I'll do the chickens. We'll have to be late, anyway, if we're going to wait for Ben."

Molly's satin flanks moved nervously. Joyce settled in the saddle and turned the horse's head toward the hill.

The still sweet Sunday was hot, but up past the barns the dirt road turned into deep shady woods, and Joyce rode slowly, enjoying the summer silence under the great redwoods, the scents of pine resin and dry bay. When sunlight broke through the thick levels of the feathery branches it lay like gold on the forest floor, and columns of gnats spun in it giddily. Molly switched her tail, the muscles of her strong legs moved visibly as the grade mounted. Presently they were out in the chaparral and manzanita bushes; the clump of hilltop oaks and the little brown cabin were in sight. Michael perhaps heard a clink of the horse's hoof on a stone, for he came forward as Joyce rode up, and she caught at his hand to dismount. A tall lean brown man, smiling. Her heart beat fast.

"Hello, Michael! Alone?"

"Yep. Arty went down to send a telegram. I thought he'd stop in at your place."

"He didn't. Swede's Otto brought Dad the papers. Michael," Joyce said, without further preamble, but trembling inside, "what's this about your going away?"

"Father tell you?"

"About an hour ago. What's the idea?"

"Oh, restless, I guess. It'll be a wonderful time for the canal trip; we go right through to Hamburg. Arty wanted company, and I've been in one place a long time now!"

"You come back?"

"Some day, surely. I've had the happiest years of my life in this little shanty." He looked away as he said it toward the valley that was dreaming below in the sunshine, the spokes of the fruit trees that covered the level floor, the rising towers of the eucalyptus and oak trees over the low-roofed homesteads.

"I love it," Joyce said, her eyes following his. There was a pause in which she could not seem to speak. Her throat was dry.

"Where's Paul this morning?"

"Oh, he went home last night."

"Paul did?"

"Yes, quite late. He and his mother," Joyce added, with elaborate carelessness, "are leaving Thursday for New York; they're going around the world—they and the Count."

"You too, of course?"

"Oh, no!"

A silence. Michael, who had taken out his penknife, very attentively cut a small chip from his gnarled walking stick.

"You're not?" he asked.

"No."

"Quarrel?"

"Nothing like that. It's just that—I've called it all off," Joyce said simply. The penknife closed with a snap; Michael looked up.

"Your engagement?"

"I didn't want to go on with it."

"He'll be back for you?"

"No. It's over. He's gone," Joyce said. "I couldn't tell you before, I didn't even tell Dad until today, but it's been all wer-*rong*. We didn't—or at least *I* didn't feel for him what you have to feel for the person you marry. I've been thinking all these years that I did; it sort of carried me through to think that I did. Otherwise I believe I would have run away in those first days, and gone on the stage or something. It's all worked out so queerly—our hating it so, and then coming to love it. I'm not trying to edify you, Michael," she paused to say apologetically.

"You're not edifying me!" Michael said hastily, and they both laughed nervously.

"I'm not trying to edify you, but I've come to love this way of living. It's real to me, and the other way isn't real."

They were sitting in the green shady brightness of the grape arbor at the table where breakfast disorder still was spread. In the hot mid-morning there was no sound from the meadows or the woods.

"It's only fair to tell you," Michael said, "that you've

made it all real to me, too. I left England—I ran away from whatever responsibilities I had there, they weren't much at the time—because I didn't think I could do anything about cold and hunger, unemployment and poverty and slums and all the rest of it. You taught me that I was mistaken, Joyce, you and your everlasting cups of cocoa and your peanut-butter sandwiches. That's why I'm going home. There's always something anyone can do. Anyone can lessen suffering, and maybe the big way to solve poverty will come out of the little ways. You remember what you said one day last winter? Down in the Market, I mean, when you were pretty tired, and that queer woman was trying to make you buy her poetry, and the children were all so noisy?"

Her bright eyes were fixed on him.

"I don't remember."

"You said something like this: 'Only one ministry in the world ever really helped, and that ministry worked like this!'"

"Did I? I was probably quoting someone. I'd forgotten it, anyway."

A silence. The fragrant beauty of the cloudless noon-time seemed to deepen and rise about them and engulf them in sweetness.

"Joyce, I'll be coming back," Michael said.

"You say so now. But when Piccadilly gets its deadly grip on you, you'll weaken."

"I may not go," Michael said suddenly, almost in a tone of resentment, as if arguing with himself.

"We'll be horribly alone."

"I——" Michael hesitated, repeated his former phrase in a vague, puzzled tone. "I might—Arty has to go. I might follow him," he said.

"You'll miss everything here—Melissa," Joyce said, of the cow, "and Groggy and the chickens and everything. You'll not have figs and muscat grapes in England; look at them! Just ready to pick! You'll never have my quail aspic or play anagrams there."

"I shan't stay long, of course."

A silence. Michael cleared his throat.

"When do you see Paul again?"

"They go Thursday. I shan't see him at all, again."

"And you mean when he comes back—you mean that when he comes back you'll not have any—any understanding with him, that he'll not feel he still has a claim?"

"None whatsoever. That's *over.*"

Again there was a brief pause. Then the man said, somewhat confusedly:

"It would make a great difference, of course. What I mean to say is, my coming back. I'd much rather wait a bit and say this to you later——"

She had never seen an expression like this on the brown lean face, or in the hazel eyes. He was flushed. His hand, suddenly touching hers as it lay on the table, was trembling.

"You see, my dear, there's something I'd say to you if I thought you'd forgive me—you'd not feel I was just adding to what's disturbing you so just now, making more trouble for you——"

Riding up the hill, Joyce had imagined, and with a wildly beating heart, that he might say something like this. She had imagined herself saying to him at this point: "Michael, why don't you ask me to marry you?"

But no memory of this came to her now; her throat felt thick and dry, and her voice failed her. Everything seemed to be wavering and quivering in the sunshine, and a dreadful feeling that she was going to cry made her eyes prick.

"Michael——" she whispered.

"But you see it's not true," the man said lightly.

"What's not true?" There were tears on Joyce's lashes, but she was smiling. Their eyes never moved from each other.

"It's not—I'm not letting myself think—I mean, I like you so horribly," he began.

"Why not?" Joyce said trembling, in the pause.

"Because I can't believe that, my dear."

"It's ter-*rue* though," she said stubbornly.

"Perhaps we're not thinking of the same thing," he said.

"But of course we *are*."

"Joyce," he said, "I can't believe that. You seemed further away from me even last night than you've ever been."

"Paul was there. I had to have one more talk with Paul. But I knew then——"

"Knew what?" he said, as she stopped, smiling at him.

"That it was you."

"Oh, no, Joyce!" he whispered. And she saw his hard thin brown fingers pressed tight against his eyes.

"It has been—always. Or if not always, for a long time. Only I didn't know it until I got back from Santa Barbara. Knew how terribly, how horribly fond of you I've come to be," Joyce said simply.

"Of course you know that I've loved you from the very beginning," Michael said. They sat staring at each other, hands locked now, their eyes wide with the wonder of it. Suddenly they both laughed, and Michael said reverently, "Oh, Joyce," as if magic lay in the two words.

"It's you," she said. "It's you and the top of this hill, and Sunday lunches with Dad and Dodo. And d'you know what that spells, Michael? Just heaven."

"Not you for me, Joyce?" he said.

"If you want me!"

"*If* I want you! My dear, my darling, when haven't I wanted you, all these years! In the kitchen," Michael said in an undertone, as if he spoke to himself, "playing cribbage late at night, in the orchard—everywhere—when haven't I wanted you!"

The brown eyes opposite his own were dancing with triumph, but Joyce's lashes were wet.

"That's what I came up the hill in all this heat to tell you!" she whispered. And as Michael got to his feet, she got to her own; he put his arms about her, tipped her head back and kissed her on the mouth.

After a while they were sitting close together with his arm about her, looking down across the shoulders of the low, oak-studded hills to the orchard-carpeted floor of the valley, and the burned brown meadows, and the clumps of high trees that meant homesteads. And Joyce knew that nowhere in that peaceful world or in the bigger world beyond it or in any world anywhere was there ecstasy, was there joy, was there deep content like that that filled her own heart and sent her soul soaring into uncharted heights of sheer bliss. Michael's definiteness, his fine voice on fine words, his brownness and leanness and kindness and understanding were intoxicating enough in mere friendship. Now when he was shaken and trembling with a joy and an amazement as keen as her own she felt that she had never even glimpsed what lay before them.

"We'll be poor," she said. "But who cares? I mean, what would we use money for if we had it? You can't do more than eat the freshest milk and eggs and fruit in the world, and read the books you love and be with the people. We'll run the Alhambra Market every winter——"

"We might have to go to England some day," he suggested after a while. "You mightn't like it."

"We'll go; we can go third class, you know. We'll be the Micawbers, with our sprightly children amusing the steerage. No, I'd like to go to England because it's your country," Joyce said dreamily. "I'd like to see if conditions there are so much harder than they are here. I'd like to go to Limehouse."

"It mightn't be London. It might be mines, you know——

further north. That's where I was, up near the mines. Some of it was—very bad," Michael said musingly, as if half to himself. "But somehow it'll all seem different with you there, Joyce. You'll ask for two-and-six worth of soup bones and begin to butter bread, and I'll—it'll all seem different."

"We'll be right in it, and we'll understand how they feel. And if things got too bad, we could always come back here for a while and get our breath."

"I wish," the man said—"I wish there was some way of telling you what you've put into my life, Joyce. I wish there was some way of getting over to you the change it's made. I—well, I didn't want to live, and now I do. I didn't think there was any break for anyone, and now I see that each of us can make a break for *someone,* and that if all of us did, why, the world's problem would be solved."

"Then you've gone a long way further than I have, Michael," the girl said. "But I do feel this," she presently added. "I *do* feel that it's safer—it's *securer,* somehow— being poor. It's not fer-*right*ening—not that I call it being poor to have your own ranch on the top of a California hill and everything you want! As Dad says," Joyce went on dreamily, "what we have here we *have.* It's not much— that is, rich people wouldn't call it much—but it's ours!"

"Joyce," the man said, "I can't believe that it's all going to be like this. It's turned my whole world topsy-turvy. You gave me no hint that things were going that way between you and Paul. I thought I was off to England tonight, and that before I got there you'd be married. What's your father say?"

"Dad? He was a little jarred," Joyce explained, "but in the end he said that he loved you like a son already."

"And we just go down the hill now for Sunday dinner, and tomorrow's to be like any other day?"

"Exactly. Isabelle hanging out all the towels and stockings, and you bringing in firewood."

"Do we tell them tonight?"

"We don't have to be in any hurry to tell them. But of course they'll guess."

"We'll tell them," he decided. And then, as the chugging of a laboring motor sounded through the Sunday stillness, he added: "That's Arty. The old boy'll be pleased! He's taken me through some pretty black times up here, when you and Paul were wandering around under the oaks, and I didn't know what to do with myself."

Arty, in the battered Ford, drove up to the house. He took his handkerchief out and wiped his ruddy face, got out of the car, loaded his arms with newspapers and packages.

"There was a lot of stuff for us down there at the express office," he said. "Your suitcase is here. Lucky thing I arsked!"

"Arthur, old boy," Michael said, "you can't sail for Panama tomorrow. You've got to wait for my wedding!"

Arty took in the scene, looked at their two faces, let his bundles fall.

"I say!" he said. And then, "Where's Von Schwerin?"

"Going around the world with his mother," Joyce explained, laughing joyfully, returning with both her hands the handshake Arty extended with both his own.

"Totty, I'm no end glad of this!" the older man said.

"I knew you would be," Michael said.

" 'Totty'? Do you call Michael 'Totty,' too?" Joyce asked, diverted.

"Call Michael 'Totty'? We've always called him that," Arty said. "She wasn't to know that, was she?" he asked rather apprehensively, with a glance for Michael.

"But I thought 'Totty' was the cousin who was going to inherit the money, and who didn't know what to do with it, and whose uncle——" Joyce turned bewildered eyes from one man to the other. "There *is* a 'Totty'?" she demanded in dawning suspicion.

"Yes, but I'm he," Michael answered. He tightened his arm about her shoulders; her amazed eyes moved to his face. "I told her about myself in the very beginning," he said. "I wanted her reaction to it. Only I said it was a cousin. She told me what a coward and fool this 'Totty' must be, and she was right!"

"But then you're—you're not——"

"Certainly he's Thrall, if that's what you mean," Arty said. "Our uncle died last spring."

"You're—but then you're rich, Michael?" Joyce said, piecing it together, speaking slowly.

"I wasn't when I first talked to you, dear. I hadn't a penny. That was all honest enough. I was honestly trying to see if it could be done."

"And we had no idea where he was; we thought he was in India somewhere, Siam perhaps," Arty supplied.

"You weren't writing home, Michael?"

"There was no one to write to. My uncle didn't like me; he thought I was crazy. My grandmother had died, and my sister and the two brothers were killed in Flanders in the beginning of 1915; there wasn't anyone except Arty here, and he was out in Mukden."

"You found him, though, Arty! But *how?*" the girl asked.

"Through you. You talked to a great pal of mine, Monty Lefanu, over here at Monterey. And when I got home I met Monty at the club in London, and I told him Michael had gone off his bean a little, and was wandering round the world somewhere, and he said, 'He couldn't be in California, could he? Anyway there's an Englishman there who sounds rather like him, calls himself "Michael Tallant."' I came out at once; I knew it was! And when I got here the news was here that Uncle Arthur had dropped off in his sleep. Ever since I've been trying to talk the old boy into going home and doing his duty."

"And we'll be rich," Joyce said slowly.

"Only until you can scatter it all right and left, dear," Michael said. "Arty tells me there've been strikes up in the mines; the minute we get there we'll have to settle things, adjust things. It's a small thing, as mines go, but I leave it to you to solve it in some way that'll work for the big mines, too. Your work's cut out for you, Lady Thrall."

"Lady Thrall," she repeated. And then suddenly, "Oh, Michael, wouldn't Mother be pleased! Oh, *isn't* it too bad she doesn't know! She'd *love* so to write it out—to have the papers have it!"

"You *would* think of that, Joyce," Michael said, with a glance for the other man. "We'll go to England before the winter," he said. "And you'll see London, and meet—meet whoever's left. We'll have supper at the Savoy after the show, and we'll drive to Oxford, and I'll show you things. And then we'll go north and see what it's all about, and what we can do."

"But Michael—I don't want to sound like little Lord Fauntleroy," Joyce said. "But if you have money, and if you care, you can do *anything!*"

"Money does nothing," he said.

"Money does *everything*," Joyce contradicted him firmly.

"You'll have to show me. I know this: it'll buy you a fur coat in Bond Street," he said, "and maybe a hat."

"I'll love them!"

"But when it comes to lifting poverty and dirt and drink and slums," Michael began, "they're like a great shadow hanging over life."

"They aren't if you're *doing* something about them!"

"D'you know you two are the most ext'rodin'ry pair I ever saw or heard?" Arty demanded at this point. "Just engaged to be married, everything roses and bells and all that

—don't you know?—and you can't speak of anything but slums and poverty and mines. It's years and years since Evelyn and I——"

Joyce's laugh interrupted him.

"We are crazy," she said; "we're not sane. But you see it's because we're so—so horribly happy, Arty.—And by the way, you're both expected for dinner. And it's broilers, Michael, so you had better saddle up and ride down with me. I said I'd be right back. Ther-*all*, eh?" she added, trying the sound of it on her own ear. "Lady Ther-*all!* Lissy'll be pleased. And Charley Sallock's mother will die of joy, her son married to the sister of Lady Ther-*all!*"

"I'll go up to the corral and get Smoky Joe, and Arty can drive himself down when he feels like it," Michael said.

"I'll go up with you and help you," Joyce offered.

They went along the little trail together and into the deep sweet shade of the redwoods.

"D'you know I've never even kissed you, little Lady Thrall?" Michael asked her. "Not really, that is," he added thoughtfully, and Joyce laughed.

THE END